C. M.

The Prince of Kashna: A West Indian Story

C. M.

The Prince of Kashna: A West Indian Story

ISBN/EAN: 9783337165802

Printed in Europe, USA, Canada, Australia, Japan

Cover: Foto ©Andreas Hilbeck / pixelio.de

More available books at **www.hansebooks.com**

THE

PRINCE OF KASHNA:

A WEST INDIAN STORY.

BY

THE AUTHOR OF "IN THE TROPICS."

WITH

AN EDITORIAL INTRODUCTION BY

RICHARD B. KIMBALL,

AUTHOR OF "ST. LEGER," "WAS HE SUCCESSFUL?" "UNDERCURRENTS, "STUDENT LIFE," ETC.

NEW YORK:

CARLETON, PUBLISHER, 413 BROADWAY.

MDCCCLXVI.

PREFATORY INTRODUCTION.

BY THE AUTHOR OF "ST. LEGER."

In the spring of 1863, I received from Santo Domingo City, by the hands of an esteemed friend, a manuscript, which, on perusal, impressed me as every way so remarkable that I decided on its publication in book form. Giving it only the revision which the writer's absence made necessary, I prepared a volume for the press, and it was published under the title of "IN THE TROPICS." The public not only indorsed my judgment of the work, but began soon to manifest a personal interest in the "young settler's" destiny. I was applied to, from all parts of the country, for information respecting him; one letter, indeed, reaching me from the Sandwich Islands. It was at this time that the fierce war broke out between the Dominicans and Spain which has just resulted in the new birth of the Dominican

Republic. During that strife, our friend was forced to quit the island, and take refuge in Jamaica. For nearly a year I heard nothing from him ; when, early last summer, I received a large package, together with the following brief note :

"KEITH HALL, JAMAICA, *May* 31, 1865.

"DEAR MR. KIMBALL:—You are already acquainted with the cruel manner in which the Spanish soldiery desolated the dear homestead which you have already so kindly introduced to the American public, and of my forced departure from it, for a temporary refuge in the Island of Jamaica. While there, I heard a great deal about an intelligent and educated Mahometan slave, the son of an African king, who was equally remarkable for his moral worth and mental ability, and who, even in the fettered life of the plantation, had won many friends and a good English education. On pursuing my inquiries, I had the good fortune to obtain his journal, and other memoranda of his early life, and from them

I have arranged what might fairly be termed an "Autobiography," but which, with this explanation, I have concluded to call a West Indian Story. Dare I ask you to take the same trouble for the Prince of Kashna which you so disinterestedly volunteered in favor of the simple narrative of Life in Santo Domingo? I place the matter absolutely in your hands; and, whatever may be your decision, I shall remain, as ever,

"Your obliged friend,   C. M."

This short letter, instead of satisfying my curiosity respecting the "Prince," served only to stimulate it. I wished to learn more or know less about his majesty. A vague suspicion that he might be an imaginary personage haunted me—a suspicion which I now confess was an unworthy one. Still I thought best, before communicating with the public, to confer with my correspondent; and, in reply to my particular inquiries, I was assured that the Prince of Kashna was really no fictitious character. I was told that, in

Jamaica, as late as 1828, travelers still recalled the Mahometan slave, Sidi Mahmadee. He was at that period free in all but in name, and was, to a certain extent, actually treated as an equal by the neighboring planters. My correspondent further informed me that, when in Jamaica, he took up his residence at Keith Hall, a romantic old West Indian chateau, dedicated in days of yore to pleasure and pleasure-seekers, but now an almost deserted, though by no means desolate, spot, where the orange and banana still flourish, and the pimento grows. This fine estate had been the residence of some of the highest officials of Jamaica; and among the books and papers scattered around the chambers of the Hall, our friend encountered some extracts from the journal of "Sidi," printed in an old periodical of 1848. He was so much attracted by these that he instituted a searching inquiry into the subject, until at length the journal itself, together with other memoranda, was brought to light from the escritoire of the secretary of a former governor of the island. From these documents the present volume was actually compiled.

Having thus satisfied myself as to the authenticity of the work, it seemed but fair that the public should be equally favored. I have only to add that, beyond cutting out some portions which deal rather too freely with certain social relations and family secrets, the editor has literally found nothing to do in the preparation of the work.

GLEN PARK, *November*, 1865.

P. S.—Since the above was written, I have received intelligence that the " young settler " has returned to his quiet *Estancia* near Palenque, and is now actively employed, repairing his walks, restoring his gardens, pruning his lime and orange groves, while preparing to resume the pleasant labors which were so unhappily interrupted. I hope, therefore, soon to give a further account of his achievements in developing the resources of his adopted home.

CONTENTS.

Contents.

KING ABDALLA, THE WHITE STRANGER.

CHAPTER I.

AFRICAN ROYALTY.

My father, Abdalla ben Abu,' was king of Kashna, and, with it, of a large surrounding territory, which we, its children, call Houssa, though I now know that it is not exactly the district so marked on the maps of Africa of those days.

My father, King Abdalla, was not strictly a negro, as, though black, or nearly so, in complexion, his hair was not woolly, nor his features of the flattened type so prevalent among the black races of Africa. I inherited these peculiarities, and conclude from them that my family was, more or less purely, of the Desert stock.

I have no very clear ideas as to the relations

of the different tribes of blacks that inhabited my
native town of Kashna, but I know that its population was divided in faith between Mahometans
and Fetish worshippers, and that my father was
a follower of the Prophet, and even claimed to
be his descendant, although there were many Obiah
men—priests of the Fetish—among his chief captains.

I have no certain recollection of my father,
as I was only five years old when he was killed
in repulsing an enemy from Kashna. There rises
grandly in the chambers of memory a tall chief-
tain on horseback, in the midst of many other
blacks, and it seems to me this · chief was my
father.   He had a large turban on his head, in
which shone some glittering ornaments, and three
long ostrich-feathers fell over it toward his shoulder.   He wore, too, a white tunic with a broad
border of bright colors.   As he mounted, some
one handed him a long spear, but who that person was, or how dressed, has left no trace on my
memory.

This may have been a dream, I know not ;
or, it may be—as I loved to imagine in my early
days of slavery—that, on the last busy, dreadful

morning of his life, my father stopped in this way
to give some orders at the "Women's Court,"
and his person and appearance thus left a permanent impression on me, though all the other circumstances were soon effaced.

My mother was, I think, a slave captured from
a neighboring tribe with which ours was, almost
every dry season, at war—for no other reason,
that I ever heard, than that each wanted to get
plenty of horses, cattle, and slaves from the other.
She was born free, but captured, with many others,
from a country far to the north of Houssa, and
had been sold to, or captured over again, by
the tribe from whom my father won her in battle, with several other slaves of her own tongue.
She was a Mahometan, like my father, but she
was not so black. She had been taught in her
father's house many things which the common
negro women looked upon with admiration, as
white ladies would regard the accomplishments
of those more highly educated than themselves.
She became my father's wife and ranked with the
other two women who held that station, though
she had brought him no portion, being, as my
people say, "the slave of his spear." He had

plenty of other wives, but, among them all, only
these three had each a house and servants of her
own, and these were also addressed by the title
of Lella. My mother knew many verses of the
Koran, taught her by her father, Sidi Mahmadee,
whose name she conferred on me; and, besides the
Koran, she could chant from memory a great
number of songs about her country. It may have
been this gift which obtained her so much respect
and affection from the king, my father, of which
I was told many things as I was growing up,
though, of course, I remember nothing of them:
still certain points have much impressed me. She
was not a negress; she could repeat verses from
the Koran, she had been taught to recite long
stories in Arabic, and was brought far from the
north. When it was too late to verify these
facts, I began to put them together, and weave
out an opinion that my mother was an Arab herself, and that from her I inherited my passion
for poetry; and I was about five years old, and
her only child, when the first terrible blow fell
upon me. The events of that fatal day left on
my soul a wild sense of pain and terror, which I
believe haunted my dreams for years.

The hostile tribe of which I have spoken made a sudden march upon our town. The attack commenced about daybreak, and they set fire to the houses on the side by which they entered. The blazing houses, the frantic, flying women, the men shouting, fighting, bleeding, falling, the red glare lighting up the court round which the houses of my mother and the other wives of the king were built, the blood, the shrieks, the rushing, whirling horror of that hour are still before me like a frightful dream. I remember, too, my mother snatching me up and urging me to ascend a high, thick-foliaged tree in the fruit-grove at the back of the king's council-hall. At a near tree another woman was trying to render the same office to another child. It was, perhaps, younger or less active than myself, for twice it fell back to the ground, and, before it could rise, some wild horsemen burst in with fearful shouts, and pierced them both with their long spears. Then some of our own Kashna horsemen rode in upon them, and, after a furious din, all seemed to me to vanish together. Some groaning wretches, who lay around writhing in pools of blood, were all that I could see as I gazed down in an agony of terror through the leaves. Presently a boy some years older, descended from another tree near mine, in which he had taken refuge, and stole away. I recollect nothing more of that dreadful morning until I was again at my mother's side. She lay on a mat, bathed in blood from a wound given her by the retreating enemy. The king had hastily collected his horse-guards and driven back the invaders. His people had rallied at his appearance and made a stand in the market-place, where the great bulk of the enemy had collected with their booty and prisoners, thinking the place entirely theirs. My father rescued his own "Children of Kashna," and made prisoners of the enemy collected in the market-place. He made prisoners of more than three hundred men with their arms and horses, besides the scattering ones taken by the men of Kashna, who, according to our customs, remained the slaves and private property of the captors. When this work at the market-place was nearly over, there arose a loud and sudden cry for "The king! the king!" in the direction of his own house, which was on the edge of the town on the side opposite to that burned by the enemy. My father rode there in answer to that cry. He

found a party of horsemen, which, for some reason I never understood, had separated from the
main body of the enemy, and was slaughtering
right and left. Their object seemed to be to take
and 'sack the "Women's Court" of the king's
house. Abdalla rushed upon them, and they fled
before him beyond the town. He followed them
until, being joined by more of their friends who
had escaped from the fight in the market-place,
the invaders turned and gave battle. The fatal
javelin of destiny thrown from the hand of their
chief, entered the king's side, and wounded him
mortally, just as he raised his arm to transfix the
nearest foe with his lance.

Abdalla had saved Kashna, but he lost his own
life. He was brought back a corpse, and buried
like a brave chief in the middle of his own hall
of council. The joyful shouts of the rescued people informed my bleeding mother that Kashna
was saved from the enemy. Soon after, the wild
death-chant, sounding over the whole town, and
repeated from door to door by the inhabitants,
warned her that the king, her husband, had fallen
in battle. She hastily sent to call an old Bushreen, named Hadji Ali, to receive the gift of me,

her only child, from her dying hands. It was a wise and tender thought in my loving mother, and I have often reflected in my riper years, that she must have been a superior woman, not only in her instruction, admitted by all as high above that of the black women around her, but in an infinitely finer and clearer moral tone.

I remember the last scene with my dying mother. She lay, scarcely able to speak, in the arms of a weeping slave, a woman from her own country, who had been given to her by Abdalla on that account. She uttered a few words with difficulty, in her native tongue, to this woman and to the Bushreen, Hadji Ali, who was kneeling on the other side of the mat, with his prayer-beads in his hands. Blood was on the door-posts, on the dresses of the women, on that of the old man, on mine, on every thing. It lay in pools in the court, and seemed to crowd against and sear my burning eyeballs. My mother kissed me fondly, as Fatma, her favorite slave, held me gently to her lips and breast. She charged me to obey the Bushreen in all things, to love him as a son, to kiss his hand and call him grandfather. I was taken to him by Fatma, and by her direction kneeled before him to kiss his hand and call him my grandfather. In reply to my salutation, he put his arms round me and called Alla to witness that I should be "the child of his soul, the treasure of his house." I threw my arms round his neck, and, as Fatma often told me, I fainted on his bosom, in the last agony of suffering and excitement, protracted beyond my childish strength.

This is the last that I can recall of the events of that trying time. My mother's face, calm, and to my eyes sweetly beautiful, as she lay in the repose of death, is more like a touching picture tenderly remembered, than an actual bodily presence. After this there are three or four years nearly blank in my memory.

My father's brother, Taleb ben Abu, succeeded him to the rule of Houssa. All that I ever saw of him was when he came to Kashna to collect his tribute of slaves and horses to complete a cafila, which he was preparing to send to the coast. I was then about eleven years old, and he made me a present of a horse of no great value, and an old slave worth still less. He tried to enhance the merits of these poor gifts,

by telling me the old horse was of some wonderful breed, and the old man was of my mother's
country, and that he had been a slave in the
house of the king, her father. I was old enough
to think my uncle's gifts were too mean for an
acknowledged nephew, but, to my present regret,
I was not old enough to profit by the chance
thus offered me to learn something about my mother's country and kindred. The old man, who
was in every way useless, asked for his freedom,
and permission to go to another place where he
had children living, and it was granted most will-
ingly by Hadji Ali. Almost as soon as my uncle
Taleb ben Abu departed from Kashna with his
tribute of slaves, the old man he gave me left
also, and we saw him no more. At that time I
also heard Fatma and Hadji Ali say to each other,
that had my father only lived till then, I would
be a richer and a grander prince than my uncle.
They rejoiced greatly over the verses of the Koran which I had repeated to my uncle. My own
pride and vanity was also amazingly puffed up
when I was able to read the Koran to him in
the presence of all his officers. He had a handsome copy of that sacred book, brought, they

said, from Mecca itself, and bought at the price of ten camels. It was taken reverently out of its many infoldings, and held up on a kind of tray while I was reading it.

Another circumstance assisted to swell my pride. Nobody but myself, no man or woman in Kashna, at least, was permitted to sit down while speaking to the king. I was allowed the honor of calling him Lord Father, and encouraged to visit him every morning and evening while he remained in our town. Fatma declared —and I believe it may be so—that it was the next thing to proclaiming me as his son and heir. He had no children of his own, and my father was the only full brother he ever had— that is, brother both by father and mother. My adopted father said it was all owing to the fine education he had given me. "Your old grandfather (he always called himself by that title) has given you his eyes and his heart. He would give his life to make his Sidi Mahmadee a great prince. Your uncle the king cannot read the Koran—may his wisdom increase—but when I brought him my tribute, I said there was one of his blood who was able to read the Koran

and write charms of power out of its chosen
verses—strong spells for the safety of his person
and the confusion of his enemies."

"It is true, my father," said I, and I am
conscious that I said it in grateful affection.
"The king sent for me to read the Koran, but
it was only when I recited the prayer for the increase of his greatness, which you had prepared
for me, that he embraced me and called me his
son before all his chiefs."

Learning is such a rare possession, among
even the Mahometan blacks, that one who can
read the Koran, and especially a boy like me, is
considered something superior to the common
kind. The effect of this display of my learning
was continued on me through life. It filled me
with the desire—the fever, I might say—to acquire learning. The reading of the Koran was
but a mechanical repetition of what my kind
teacher and an excellent memory had piled up
in my head, but I was proud of it beyond all
bounds, and, from that time to this, I may say
it has been a ruling desire with me to improve
in knowledge.

The affectionate Hadji Ali and my mother's

slave Fatma—now mine as my mother's heir—
fully shared in the pride of my success, and the
people about us began to give me the title of
king's son, all of which must have greatly in-
flated my self-conceit, since I remember it so
well.

This bright summer ended, however, in dark
clouds. My indulgent guardian had a large field
outside of the town, in which, at certain seasons,
he kept many slaves at work, and I was often
sent to it, both on foot and on horseback, with
messages to the laborers, or to have them bring
home corn and grass, but never, that I can recollect, was I set at any regular work. Coming
back from the field, one day, in company with a
slave of our house named Mattoo, who was a
great coward—besides being a great fool—he
startled me very suddenly by setting up a frightful yell and throwing himself on the ground,
where he rolled and writhed as if in the ago-
nies of death. I hurried off my horse to inquire what ailed him. He only answered by renewed contortions and a fresh outbreak of groans.
It was near the town, and the road was full of
people. They began to collect round Mattoo, and

2

I heard a woman exclaim, "The white man has cast a *spell* on him." I raised my head in surprise, and looked straight into the blue eyes of a white man. I was almost struck dumb with fear and wonder. He sat on his horse, which he had brought close up to us, to learn the cause of these terrible outcries, and gazed at us as calmly as if he had no concern in causing them. He was dressed as any man of substance in Houssa might be on a journey. He wore a sort of umbrella hat over a turban, and a loose robe confined at the waist with a goatskin belt. All this was much of the style and make of what I had often seen on Hadji Ali, but it was his white face, and his blue eyes, and his beard so red and straight, that shocked me with their unnatural appearance. I had *heard* of white men, but never *saw* one before. Houssa is rich in wild tales of their magic arts, by which poor blacks are insnared and devoured in the white man's land. They have the honor to be regarded as sorcerers and cannibals in my country, but even the negroes have so many of the habits and ideas of a high civilization, that those offenses are less vile in their eyes than poverty.

I saw the white sorcerer sit calmly on his horse, attended by two Houssa men leading baggage beasts and mildly inquiring for the Kashna market-place, and my fright abated. He did not speak in the Houssa tongue, but in the language of my mother's country, which I had learned to speak of my mother and Fatma, which few in Kashna besides Hádji Ali and those of his house could understand. I recovered myself so far as to salute the stranger in respectful terms, and offer to conduct him into the town. I ordered Mattoo, with a great parade of authority, to banish his cowardly fears, and keep the people from crowding too close upon the "Lord Magician." It was the grandest title I could think of, and it served better, perhaps, than any other to define his position honorably in Kashna. His interpreter brought orders from my uncle the king to the captain of Kashna to take care of the stranger and convey him safely, with all his goods, to some place in the direction of the Great River, when they were to have some important business together, though what it was I never thought of inquiring.

The captain of Kashna was a round, laughing,

talking, kindly negro, as I remember very well, but he was horribly at a loss what to do with this distinguished visitor, and begged hard of Hadji Ali to take him into his house. It was one of the best in town, large and well kept—of that I have a lively recollection—but my guardian was not in good health, and he positively refused to receive him. Hadji Ali was a man of too much consequence to be forced out of his way, and so, to my own great personal disappointment, the "white sorcerer" was lodged elsewhere.

The people crowded upon him to stare and beg, but few or none offered him any kindness. I was even reproached for my too respectful conduct toward him, when I waited upon him into the town. Many of the women predicted that a *spell* was upon me, and that death or some other great misfortune would "overcome my strength." My adopted father, however, defended me. He said: "The stranger who comes in peace to your door is sacred. The Koran forbids that he shall be robbed or insulted." That kind, just, generous old man was always inculcating, by deeds as well as words, charity and humanity. He daily reproved the inhumanity to beasts and slaves, which is the common sin of the poor and ignorant in Houssa as well as in Christendom.

This stranger only stayed two or three days at Kashna, but while he was there he made us a visit, and gave me a small round looking-glass, such as the richest youths of Houssa were proud to wear as medals, when they were able to buy them of the traders, who brought them up from the coast. He talked with Hadji Ali about his pilgrimage to Mecca, from which he derived the name or title of Hadji, which signifies one who has made the sacred pilgrimage. They had both seen wonderful things, and I longed to travel as far and know as much of those distant countries as they did. The "White Lord," as my adopted father and the captain of Kashna called him, left us some medicines to bring back the lost appetite and strength of Hadji Ali, and he soon recovered his usual health. Other people in Kashna received medicines also—though not half as many as had begged for them—yet among those who received and those who were refused them, almost all the Mahometans, in fact, blamed my poor godfather for using the gifts of the white sorcerer. The people of Houssa are not all Mahometans—per-

haps the larger portion worship their Fetish idols
and practice Obiah—but this class had nothing to
say against medicines, charms, sorcery, or the
devil-worship imputed to the whites; it was all in
their own line of faith. The Mahometans had
been taught that idols and sorcery were forbidden things, and a white man and his medicines
were, they said, too much like magic to be proper
and wholesome for a priest and pilgrim of the
true faith. The Hadji felt this popular censure
so severely that he resolved to abandon Kashna
without delày. There was also something, which
I never fully understood, that he feared from my
uncle on my account, and, having decided to depart from Kashna, he pressed his arrangements as
rapidly—though, also, as privately—as he could
manage them, for a change of residence.

CHAPTER II.

THE FATAL JOURNEY.

ON the death of my father, Abdalla, his brother Taleb—who was then a tributary chief on the confines of Houssa—came to Kashna with five hundred horsemen, and took possession of every thing belonging to his predecessor, even to his surviving wives. They were both young men. I—being then only five years old—was the oldest son of Abdalla. This must have been the customary course, since I never heard it spoken against by my friends. Neither custom nor common sense would permit a child to succeed to the chieftainship of such a barbarous country; and when my mother's private property, consisting of some slaves, a few horses, and a flock of sheep, were handed over to the guardian she had appointed for me, my uncle was probably considered to have done his whole duty by his orphan nephew. He never lived at Kashna, and

I am told only made that one visit there of which I have spoken, after the time in which he came into power. He had his residence at three days' distance, in a region famous for fine horses and a great abundance of sheep and goats. Hadji Ali took the entire charge of me from the day and hour of my mother's death. He was a tender and careful parent to me, and kindly with everybody. In his character of a priest who could read the Koran, and a pilgrim who had kissed the sacred stone of Mecca, he was much respected, and had made many converts. He had a school in which all who chose to come were instructed to read and recite verses from the inspired book of Mahomet, but none was so closely and continually taught as myself. I was apt in tracing the Arabic figures, and in this I particularly pleased him. "O son of my heart," he would exclaim, "you are born to be a king; and when that happy day arrives, you will bless the name of old Hadji Ali for giving you all this learning." Yet he often talked fondly of his native village near the sea. He said but for the love he bore me he would go there to end his days, as he had enough to support him in case

the rest of his life. Still he continued to re-
side at Kashna, engaged in many schemes of
trade. In one case, if not more, he was concerned in a kafila bound to Morocco. He dealt
largely in horses and slaves, as every one who
can does in Africa. I remember that one of the
reproaches cast against the white magician after
he left Kashna was that he would not buy any
slaves. He was an unprofitable visitor, as well
as a suspicious one, in the eyes of the whole
town, but the good old Bushreen never had a
word against him to the last. His richer scholars
began to fall off about this time, and even the
poor men, who used to pay for their instruction
—and for the beautiful verses from the Koran,
which they were so happy to have him paint
over their doors in blue letters—by working for
him in the field, began to fall off too, and talk,
like their betters, of the scandal of a true believer using the cures and charms of a white
magician. They asked him whether his medicines had not given him a longing for hog-flesh,
and some even hinted that a faithful follower
of the Prophet, like my uncle, might have something better to do than putting a king's son un-

2*

der the charm of one who had looked so close
into the homes of the evil spirits that his beard
was scorched by their fires.   The white stranger
had a reddish beard, and the color was thus accounted for in Kashna.   The Hadji finally lost
all heart, and told his neighbors that he was no
longer able to work his land.   He therefore sold
it for a hundred slaves, to make a venture in a
kafila then preparing to start for the coast.   My
impression is that houses and lands are generally computed by slave-values throughout the interior of Africa.   There was an immensity of
palaver and trafficking before the bargain was
completed, for it was no small transaction for
Kashna, but it was settled at last, to my intense
delight.

I had now passed six years—the most easy,
cheerful, and abundant period of my life, with my
kind godfather.   The Mahometans have that sacred form of relation as well as Christians, and
observe its obligations quite as scrupulously—at
least mine did.

Young as I was at this time, Hadji Ali bestowed upon me a surprising share of confidence.
He told me that he should not sell his house at

all, though it was one of the best in the town,
"as it would open all the mouths in Kashna."
He left it in charge of Fatma, with a gift of her
freedom, and particularly recommended to her care
the old horse so magnificently presented to me
by my uncle, the king. It was making my slave
the gift of the house as well as her freedom, but
he did not choose to let her know that exactly,
though he had confided to me his intention never
to return to Houssa. He had before asked me
whether I would not rather go to my uncle than
accompany him to the coast. I replied, with all
the warmth of sincerity, that I would run away
and fly to him if he left me behind. He embraced me, with tears in his eyes, and answered
that nothing remained then to do but finish our
preparations with as little display as possible, and
join the caravan at the last moment.

It was known in Kashna that Hadji Ali was
going toward the coast with the kafila, in which
he had so large an interest, and arrangements were
made accordingly, but it was given out and generally believed that I would make but one day's
journey to a walled town belonging to my uncle,
and there remain with a friend of the Bushreen,

to see a great fair. The king was expected to attend this fair, and it was reported that he had ordered Hadji Ali to bring me there, and deliver me into the charge of one of his captains, in order that I might begin my military training as became a king's son. We joined the kafila so far as to keep it constantly in full view, before it had made two miles of the journey. What a noisy confusion of men and animals it was, and how I revelled in the tumult and action of the day! At night we camped under the walls of a large town, and there we were informed that the king had detected and punished with terrible severity some conspiracy against his life, and that, among others, the captain of his guards—the man to whom I was ordered to be delivered—had been put to death. No one appeared to claim me, for my uncle had other things more important than me to occupy him just then. The fair was not to open in a week, in which time we should be in the territory of another prince, and I out of my uncle's reach; so Hadji Ali and I went on our way rejoicing. Why he was so anxious to slip me away with him I never exactly knew, but he was such a true and affectionate friend, and so calm

and considerate in forming his opinions, that I
was sure he had good reasons for his distrust
of my uncle. I knew that he expected me to
return to Houssa and reign there when I should
be a strong and learned man, but said he would
be too old to go back with me, at least all the
way, he would add, but he never should cease to
pray for my advancement to my father's place.

We had traveled with that caravan, about
ten days, as nearly as I can judge, when my
kind godfather was taken sick. He held out a
day or two, until we reached a large walled
town called Medinet, when he grew so much
worse that he was obliged to leave the kafila.
He exchanged many of his slaves for ivory, and
sent others on with the chief of the caravan,
besides keeping about twenty men and women
with us, as well as most of our horses and other
animals.

We hired a very comfortable house in Medinet, and a piece of ground not far from the
gate, which the Bushreen set his slaves to culti-
vate directly, as he did not know how long we
might remain here—besides, we had the camels
and the oxen to feed. Hadji Ali had plenty of

money and goods, and we used to buy grass and
corn at first; · but it was not many months before we had raised some of our own. The weakness of the old man continued longer than he
expected, and, the rainy season coming on, we
sold the beasts of burden, and Hadji made up
his mind to remain where we were—at any rate,
till after the water should have abated. As he
could not bear to be idle, he opened school again
at Medinet, and got a great many scholars of
both sexes. He was the gentlest and most amiable creature that ever lived to instruct children
—such patience and perseverance I never saw
surpassed; his happiness consisted in teaching, in
beholding the improvement of his pupils, and in
their merry and joyful society. He was as fond
of romping and playing as any of the boys and
girls, and had always some winning way of engaging the minds of even the most stupid to
attend to his lessons.

The rainy season was over at last. The waters
had subsided, and Hadji Ali, being again in tol-
erable health, determined to take the first opportunity of continuing his journey to his native
home. I do not mention the name of the place,

for, as I never reached it, I am not positive
what it was. It was my destiny to be torn away
from the old man upon the route.

At the close of the rains we joined a smaller,
and a much more disorderly kafila than the one
in which, almost a year before, we had left Kashna. Hadji Ali from that time always said *we*,
in speaking of our arrangements, and he often
reminded me that I was his heir, and that if
any thing happened to him on the journey, I
must claim, as my right, all the property he
left. "You will need all I can leave you, Sidi
Mahmadee," he used to say affectionately. "You
cannot return to your own country without plenty of presents for the king and the head men;
remember that." While we were at Medinet, the
chief merchants of our Kashna party returned
from the coast—or wherever our slaves had been
sold—and accounted for them entirely to Hadji
Ali's satisfaction. They brought him what I now
know were coarse European prints, but of very
showy patterns, together with some powder and
several muskets. He bought a fine-looking pair
of horseman's pistols and a gay saddle-cloth of a
merchant, who declared that he had given three

fine slaves and an elephant's tooth for them to the captain of a great ship on the coast. There was still more chaffer over that purchase than we had over the sale of the land at Kashna, and this time I watched the proceedings with an even keener interest, for my kind godfather publicly avowed that these articles were for me, and bought with my own slaves. After the business was concluded, he had a great supper prepared at our house for all the Houssa merchants, and then, to my unbounded discontent, those great horse-pistols and that fine horse-housing was, with much ceremony, delivered to them, as a present from me to my uncle the king. The cunning Bushreen made a flourishing speech about his and my desire to prepare myself to be of service to him. The father of Kashna, he said, had placed this beloved child of his own blood under his, the Bushreen's, charge, to be instructed in the true faith, and we were now at Medinet learning wisdom; but after the rainy season, which was now near, had passed, we would strive to obtain other presents still more worthy a great king, and take them to him in his own city. The loss of these grand things afflicted me sorely for a time, but my godfather consoled me, after a while, by the present of a light gun, and plenty of liberty to shoot wild-fowl with it for the rest of our stay at Medinet.

He also made me comprehend somewhat of his motives in sending back such a valuable present to Houssa, and I still think, as I thought then, that he was one of the best and wisest men in my native Africa. Every one at Medinet loved and respected him, and when we departed with the caravan, I am sure we were loaded with more presents for our use on the journey, than any one of their own citizens. It was during our residence there that I first began to think with real appreciation of the old man's fond and faithful cares, and to lay to heart his religious precepts. He often said that the spirit of my mother should never reproach him for neglecting the child she had committed to his care.

Whatever Mahometans in general may say about the souls of women, Hadji Ali taught me to believe that the spirit of my mother constantly watched over me. While we were getting ready for the kafila, I one day rode my horse very hard, and then, from boyish forgetfulness,

left him standing in the court all night without
food and water. My godfather reproved me with
more mildness than I deserved, and I have not
yet forgotten the pain it caused me when he
said, with solemn sincerity, "Your good angel is
angered at such cruelty, and your mother covers
her face with shame for you. Her spirit can suf-
fer no pain except what the child of her bosom
causes her by his sins." These were lessons I
could never *unlearn*, and when, in after days, my
Christian teachers attacked them, all their efforts
to make me forget only branded them deeper in
my heart.

At length all was ready, and we were well
started on our road with the kafila. We were
finely mounted, and had three house-slaves with
us—two men and a woman—that we had brought
from Kashna for personal servants, besides the
slaves for sale and those in charge of our loaded
beasts. We traveled, of course, very slowly, for
we had to comply with the pace of the kafila.
The country around us was beautiful; and, so
directly after the rains, it was fresh and ver-
dant. We were entering a more hilly and heavily
timbered country than we had seen this side of

Medinet, and we often lost sight of the caravan,
as it wound itself, like a. long snake, into the
narrow wooded turns of the steep hills, but never
for more than an hour or so at the longest. It
was a careless habit, that cost me long years of
bondage; what it cost my dear old father I never
could learn.

In passing a defile in the Kong mountains,
for some occasion or other, we were in the rear
of the kafila, which was to have encamped, if I
remember right, at the outlet of it. The old man
had seated himself on a rock, and our two horses
were fastened together by the bridles. The slaves
were in advance with the rest of the kafila, and I
had clambered up the side of a precipice to gather
some blue flowers which grew out of the face of the
rock. I sang and shouted in the mere excess of
boyish spirits; and, being so high upon the precipice, I thought I might venture to the summit.
Unhappy venture! I had no sooner reached that,
than a stout man, who had been lying there,
crouched like a lion among the bushes, sprang
upon me, threw me down, out of breath as I
was with my exertion, and, before I could cry
out, stuffed my mouth so full of grass that I was

nearly strangled. I believe I fainted away, for, on coming to myself, I found my hands and feet tied, and I could discover, by the glimmering of the sun through the trees which surrounded us, that it was getting very late in the day. I immediately began to supplicate the ruffian who had thus seized me, to restore me to my father, Hadji Ali, who I told him was rich, and would give him two slaves for me in a moment, or goods to the amount of two slaves, or three slaves, or any thing he could ask, so he would but restore me. Alas! I pleaded in vain; he either understood me not, or affected not to understand me, and answered in a language which was new to me. He kept me in the bushes till dark, and then took me away from the course we had been pursuing, and led me to the north, and then to the west. It is of no use now to describe the sufferings I endured in mind and body. I was all but broken-hearted, and yet I believe I grieved more, if possible, for the loss which I knew that Hadji Ali had sustained, than for my own individual wretchedness. I had been ever of a religious turn of mind, and I really thought I should in some way be restored to my beloved guardian.

To be thus carried off into slavery was too horrible to be accepted as a fixed fact.

We traveled all night through woods, amid the howlings of lions and hyenas, and in the morning fell in with two ivory hunters, who had an ass loaded with elephants' teeth, and were marching, like my new master, to the westward; I was exchanged for this beast and his load. The robber who had made prize of me returned by the course we had come, and my new-masters conducted me toward the Foulah country. I was marched from town to town, and passed through at least six pair of hands in the course of the four or five months that elapsed, before I found myself on the sea-shore. There I was sold to a man who had much to do with the large slave-dealers in the supply of provisions, I am inclined to think, for he owned himself few or no slaves. He spoke Houssa, and told me he should bring me up to his own business—whatever that was— and promised me plenty to eat. After a long stretch he sent me back into the yard to get some supper, repeating that he liked my looks, and that my last master said I was such a good boy that he never had to tie or beat me. That

was true of him, at any rate, and, thanking him
with my best Kashna obeisance, I went back to
ask some food of a woman who was bending
over her cookery under a rear shed. I touched
her shoulder, and, as she turned, respectfully
opened the way by saying that our master had
sent me to assist her and get something to eat.
She answered by springing to her feet, and calling out, "The king's son! the king's son!" The
master ran to the door, on hearing these words,
and asked what it meant. I threw myself at his
feet, told my story, and begged him to return
me to Hadji Ali. The young woman told him
who I was, that she had known me in Kashna,
and that my uncle had given to me the robe and
sash, only allowed to a king's son, together with
the customary horse and slave for my own service, and much more that I cannot remember.
"Is there any one here who will buy him, Tatee?"
he inquired very seriously. The girl said, any
merchant from Kashna would give a strong man,
or two strong men, for me, to take me back to
my rich godfather, who would return three slaves
and any amount of presents, to any one who
would "bring back to him the joy of his eyes."

My new master searched the market, but no merchant of Kashna could be found, nor was any one anxious to buy me when it was discovered that Hadji Ali had left Kashna with me, and was no one knew where. So this momentary gleam of hope faded away, and left me in deeper despondency than ever. Tatee tried to cheer me, by predicting that Hadji would search for me all along the coast, until he found and redeemed me. Alas! neither of us had any idea of the vast extent of the slave-coast of Africa. But even had there been a reasonable foundation for such a hope, we were doomed to be cut off from its faintest shadow by a new misfortune.

I had been about three days with my last negro master, when, as we sat comforting each other with projects for getting back to Kashna, Tatee was called away, and, to my surprise and uneasiness, she did not return in all the afternoon. I at last ventured to make inquiries, and was horror-struck to hear that she had been sent to the barracoon, or slave-pen, to be confined until she should be shipped with the rest of the live cargo on board a slave-ship in the offing. The barracoon was not far from my master's house, and I flew to see her, without waiting for my master's permission. Poor Tatee shed tears with me. My master had exchanged her for me, but she did not know she was thus disposed of until she was brought to the slave-pen, to be "put on the string" with a number of other girls, among whom were several from Houssa. She advised me to try hard for my liberty, and hinted that those of our tongue would all attempt something together, and then would help me to escape, if I would join them.

Tatee was a brave girl, and she contrived, on the very same night, to get herself loosed from the chain in which she was bound with a great many others, and then hurried to my master's to help liberate me. She tempted me to run away. I was alone, the only slave of the person who had obtained a claim upon me, and I slept in the same hut with him—he lying at the door. Had I been a few years older, or had I then known that I, too, was marked for the slave-ship, I might have been more desperate and resolute. It was necessary to kill my tyrant, as he lay across the doorway, and, not daring to do this, he surprised me in the very moment of my stepping over him,

the girl holding out her arms, as it were, to receive me after I should have passed this bar-
rier to my liberty. I was armed, too, but I
had not the heart to shed his blood, even when
he seized me by the leg, and threw me down.
I returned him his own dagger directly, which
I had taken from him in his sleep, and begged
of him, as a favor, that he would plunge it into
my heart. But that was a sacrifice which he
had no notion of making. He did not punish
me for my mad attempt; on the contrary, he
was grateful to me for his life, and declared that
if he could afford it, he would have made me
free. He even shed tears when he had secured
me, and said I was a good boy, a kind-hearted
boy, and he wished he had not given the girl
for me, that it went against his heart to ship
me off, after I had renounced my liberty rather
than kill him. Then he bemoaned Tatee, and
wanted to make the exchange back again, little
thinking it was this poor thing who had set
me upon the attempt. Finding her project had
failed, she returned at once to her companions,
and gave up, for the moment, her plans for de-
camping. She formed other schemes for escap-

3

ing, and assured me, with tears in her eyes, that
she would get both of us back to our country,
if I would only be resolute and assist her. But
alas! the schemes of poor Tatee were all in vain.

When the slave-ship was ready to sail my
fate was decided, and I was finally handed over
to a white man for I know not what—scarlet
cloth and rum, I think. This white man took
me on board a ship, with a great many more
slaves, three hundred at least, men, women, boys,
and girls; and if I had any consolation in this
misery, it was that poor Tatee was in the same
ship with me. Yet for some time I scarcely saw
any thing of her, the men being confined in one
part of the vessel, and the females in another.

No pen can over-paint the horrors of a slave
in a full-freighted slave-ship. Crowded to suffo-
cation, sea-sick, manacled, leaving behind him all
that he knows of hope and delight, his native
land and his friends, with no prospect but that
of captivity in a strange country—except, indeed,
that many of us thought we were going to be
eaten by the whites—I only wonder how the
poor slave lives through the voyage. Many of
our cargo died under the complicated sufferings

of which it consists — disease, stench, filth, dirt,
bad diet, confinement, and low spirits. Some died
of despair, and three, as I can well remember,
threw themselves overboard, when it came to
their turn to be allowed the fresh air on the
deck. But I was young, and hoped on instinct-
ively. The captain of the ship took a liking to
me when he found I had been rich and free in
my own country, as I could prove by my country marks on my breast, as well as by the tes-
timony of Tatee and three or four others on
board, who knew Hadji Ali very well; at least
they knew he was a priest and a merchant in
Kashna, and they remembered that he had adopted the son of the late king. I presume the quiet,
respectful manners taught me by my good old
godfather — may his ashes have rest! — disposed
our captain to mercy. He allowed me the lib-
erity of the deck and exempted me from man-
acles. These were privileges only enjoyed by a
few of the most orderly women, and Tatee was
among them. I was so grateful that I thanked
the captain with tears of joy when he beckoned
to Tatee to come and sit under the awning with
me. She, like myself, loved to talk of the place

we came from in Houssa, and we spoke the
same language, which was very different from
that spoken by many others of the slaves, some
of whom came from Senegal and Gambia, and
were Mandingoes. The captain was very kind to
Tatee, for my sake, I believe. He gave her something to wear and a necklace of glass beads;
but the conduct of the officers on board the ship
toward some of the women slaves was very far
from decent; and what was worse, the girls themselves seemed careless of decency.

The most impressive event of this terrible
voyage was a battle with a French privateer.
Our ship was well armed, having twelve guns,
and she had a large crew of white men. The
captain set all sail, but the Frenchman set all his
canvas, and came sweeping down upon us with
a three-colored flag flying at his mizen-peak. The
ship, however, was cleared for action, and the
rest of the slaves on deck at the time were ordered below. I was young, but I was, or rather
had been, indifferent about life, since I had lost
my liberty, and I felt, I cannot describe what
it was, a reckless idea of throwing myself in the
way of any change. I remained on deck, took

my station beside a water-cask that stood at the
foot of the main-mast, and waited to see what
these white men would do to one another. The
Frenchman had the wind of us, and came up
rapidly with us, firing his bow-chasers at our
stern three or four times, without doing any
great mischief. The shot flew over us, except
one, which went through the main-sail. The fire
was returned from our stern guns, and the captain himself took a musket, which he carried
while he gave his orders. We had a netting to
prevent the enemy from boarding; and the sailors' hammocks were stowed at the bottom of it,
so as to afford a bulwark for the men to fire
from. There was a young gentleman on board,
and he too came on deck with arms in his hands.
He beckoned to me to come and stand beside
him, giving me also a musket. I knew well
how to use it. The privateer was, by this time,
so near that her bowsprit almost came over our
taffrail, and some of the Frenchmen were crowding forward to board us, upon which our captain himself putting down the helm, our ship
ran up into the wind, and the enemy fell about
fifty or sixty yards to leeward. At this moment

she opened her fire from four or five guns, which,
to my ears, made an imposing battle-thunder.
The shot from one of them went through the
water-cask against which I had leaned before the
young gentleman called me away. We returned
the fire from our larboard guns, and the Frenchman put down his helm in like manner, and
passed under our stern, giving us a volley of
musketry at the moment of passing, for his deck
was crowded with men. One of their bullets
struck the young gentleman in the throat, as he
was in the act of firing his own musket. He fell
first against me, and then reeled toward the
captain, who caught him in his arms, although
he was nearly knocked down by his weight.
The youth was killed; the captain laid him gently on the deck, and immediately discharged his
own musket into the privateer, calling out at the
same time to his crew to animate them: he fired
a pistol also, which he had in a belt, at a man
who had lifted his head above the privateer's
bulwarks. He then bade me follow him into his
cabin, where, with the assistance of five or six
other men, we fired two carronades, which were
there, loaded with grape-shot. They were either

eighteen or twenty-four pounders. He pointed
them accurately, and they did most dreadful execution, as we learned afterward. When we
returned to the deck, the privateer was sheering
off, and we soon lost sight of her. The captain was in great distress for his friend; and
I felt much, that such a kind, nice young gentleman should have come to this sudden end.
For my own part, I was at first indifferent about
my life—but after firing the carronades, and hearing the shrieks, I began to be alarmed, and was
quite glad to see the Frenchman sheer off. My
master spoke highly of me, and said I was a
brave fellow. I did not tell him that I was a
coward—perhaps I was not—but I did not like
fighting, of that I am convinced. We sailed directly to Carlisle Bay, in Barbadoes, to repair our
damages, and, while we were there, a ship came
in with part of the crew of the privateer. They
had been put on board of a prize, which the
privateer had made the day after our fight, and
had been retaken by an English schooner. They
gave a dreadful account of the mischief they and
their ship had sustained. The first of the carronades killed eleven men, the second nine. We

staid but three days at Barbadoes, and then sailed for Kingston, in Jamaica, where we arrived in the month of March, 1806.

CHAPTER III.

IN JAMAICA.

As soon as we had cast our anchor in the harbor, several persons came on board the ship to look at the human cargo, and perhaps select slaves. The ship had been well cleaned and scrubbed in Carlisle Bay, though not before it wanted such cleaning, for it was dreadful even to me to go among the slaves below.

They had shaved our heads, and given us all a thorough purification, so that, when we came upon deck, we did not look so miserable as might have been expected. Most of the men were still chained, notwithstanding, two or three together, by the legs. The women had each a cotton handkerchief given them for the sake of decency, and so had the men; but the boys were all exhibited naked to those persons who examined us. Some of the slaves had all along entertained a notion that they were to be eaten upon their arrival, and when they saw the white men come upon deck, and handle them

3*

all over, their fears became more active, and many
trembled with fright. This examination, notwithstanding the white men laughed with them, and,
to my mind, seemed good-natured, filled many of
them with feelings of horror. Among the visitors
on board there was one old man, with a large white
hat, and spectacles on his nose, who fixed upon six
girls, who came all from Houssa, and said he should
buy them. They were a part of thirteen who came
from the same country, all girls, and they had several boys and four men of their company, all speaking the same language, and generally known to one
another before we sailed. These wished, naturally
enough, to be purchased by the same old man—a
wish in which I did not exactly share, however, for
his face did not please me at all. But every other
thought was swallowed up in the dread of being
separated from Tatee. She was like a mother to
me, and the choice of any particular master, or
even the recollection that a life of slavery was before both of us, scarcely entered my young mind:
it was absorbed with the fear of losing her. The
old man passed by Tatee, to my instant relief, and
said he wanted no more than the six girls he had
selected. They were all young and good-looking,

and I own I was shocked and altogether disgusted
to see a white man handle my country-women as
he did, a Kafir, a Christian! I had then hardly got
rid of that prejudice against the white men which
had so much affected the health and happiness of
Hadji Ali, and perhaps had indirectly brought
about the catastrophe to which I owed my present
situation. This old buckra turned them round
and round, to see that they were sound of body,
and his eyes twinkled through his spectacles like
stars in a mist over his bargain. But I shall say
no more of him, except that he bought the girls
and one boy. This lad was brother to one of them,
and whom the merchant on shore compelled him
to take, or he would not have let him become the
purchaser of the boy's sister. They were landed
at dusk in the evening, and I have seen no more of
them to this day.

The next morning, the great body of slaves
were sent on shore and lodged in a large place,
where many people came to see the fresh cargo of
slaves, and choose those that they wanted to buy
from among us. Meanwhile we were allowed to
amuse ourselves, as we had done on board ship,
with African plays and games. We were well fed,

and everybody seemed kind to us. They looked
kindly and spoke good-naturedly, even while they
were examining us limb by limb. The whole cargo
was quickly disposed of, and it was my lot to be
sold to a planter from Westmoreland, who bought
Tatee. Tatee, and four or five others from Houssa,
were kept together in one lot—or rather bought together—with some more men from other parts of
Africa, by this Westmoreland gentleman. The
captain was in looking at us, when that gentleman
came in to select a lot of hands for his cane-fields.
I saw by the captain's manner that he recommended the Houssa party to his notice. These, one
after another, were examined, stepped aside, and
given to understand this was their master. When
Tatee was accepted she crossed her arms, and, with
a pleased and thankful air, bowed low before him
in the fashion of our country. The gentleman
smiled pleasantly, and my eyes followed him with
anxious looks, imploring to be taken also. The captain turned his eyes on me, and, I am sure, said
something in my favor, but the gentleman only
shook his head, and my heart sank within me. He
did not want to buy children, and I was but about
twelve years of age. Moved by my silent tears,

Tatee ventured to kneel at his feet and ask him to buy me too. ⸱ He thought a while, and then he did so instantly. Without any more words, he pointed me to go to the place where the rest of his purchases were gathering into a knot by themselves, and, taking my hand, he put it into Tatee's, saying, as I was told by our interpreter: "There, Quasheba, as he is not your brother, I suppose he is your sweetheart." Tatee was four or five years older than I was, and sensible and steady beyond her years. She had, too, a prompt and cheerful manner, and was, in all ways, a smart, active, willing girl. We found a kind master in Mr. Davis, and he found in us servants worth all the money we cost him.

The captain of the ship came to see me the day after, and gave me a pistole. He gave another to Tatee, shook hands with us, and wished us all well, saying, at the same time, that our master was a rich man, and very humane to his slaves. I was furnished with a coarse linen frock and a black hat, as were all the other males. The women had short dresses given them, and handkerchiefs to wear on their heads. We were in all twenty, six of the party girls; and we had three negroes from the plantation in Westmoreland to take care of us, and conduct us there. Two of these negroes had mules, the other was on foot, and they had all three cutlasses. We walked the first day two and two, that is to say, the men did, handcuffed to one another. The women and I were at large. In the evening the buckra, our new master, met us, and gave us in charge to the overseer of an estate on the road, where we were put into their hospital to sleep, having first of all plenty to eat, and some rum and water to drink.

The interpreter gave us a long lecture before we left Kingston, on the folly of running away, and the impossibility of escaping, even if we attempted it. We were told that no ships went back to Africa, except by first going to England—that nobody dared to take us off the island, and that if we ran into the woods, we should starve, even if the free maroons (to whom a reward was paid for every negro they brought in) did not catch us. On the other hand, we were told that we should be well fed and clothed, have houses of our own, and lands for ourselves, and only be made to work for our master nine hours a day out of twenty-four.

I, for one, had no thought of running away.

After being so many weeks at sea, the sight of the
green earth was too sweet and pleasant. We had
been sold and resold—most of my companions had
been slaves in their own country, and hunger and
hard work were no novelty to them. Beside, where
could we run to ?—in a strange land, without friends,
or arms, or tools! Another negro from the estate
where we passed the night could speak in our
tongue, and he encouraged us greatly by his accounts of the country. The second day only half
the slaves were handcuffed at a time. After that
we all walked at large, and I believe none of us
once contemplated running away. We were about
a week on the journey, always well taken care
of, and we walked with comparatively light hearts,
after what we had suffered in Africa upon our
march to the sea. For my part, I thought the
worst was over. Everybody spoke to .and looked
kindly on us. The slaves on the estates through
which we passed seemed well fed, happy, and cheerful. They talked to us, some of them in our native
languages, and they had ever something good-
natured to say. There was one thing which troubled me, however, and that was the sound of a.
whip cracking, which I heard now and then, as

we passed a gang of negroes at work; and we
saw once a man, who was laid on his face on the
ground, while a driver flogged him with a long
lash fastened to a little stick.   He flogged the
man very hard, and blood followed every stroke.
This man called out to us, in a rage, "to see what
we should come to," and the driver, at the direction of a white man, who was standing by, added,
that we certainly should come to it, if we turned
out to be thieves and liars like him.   I had seen
and heard plenty of cruelty in Africa before that,
but it always sickened me then as it did now in
Jamaica.

At last we arrived at my master's estate, and
to my eyes all about it seemed grand and pleasant.
Busy, bright faces of our own color greeted us on
every side, and we were as well received by everybody as if we had come home from a journey to
friends and relations.   All the negroes crowded
round us, and spoke kindly to us, and asked after
their acquaintances in different parts of Africa.   I
mean, of course, those who, like ourselves, had
crossed the water.   Many of our fellow-slaves
were creoles; indeed, the greater number by far
were natives, and spoke none of our languages.

We were distributed among the most trusted servants, who seemed to contend, before our master and his overseer, to have the keeping of us, promising to do this and that for us, to adopt us for their children, and teach us all we should have to do. I was consigned to the care of Pompey, an African, about forty years of age, who was my master's head waiting-man. He had been brought, like myself, from Africa (Bambarra), at a very tender age, and though he had two wives he had no son, one of them having only a daughter, and the other no child alive.

Pompey treated me very well. I had to work in his grounds for him, besides doing light work on the plantation, such as weeding the cane-pieces and Guinea-grass, driving mules, and other jobs, which were no hardship. I lived well, Pompey always supplying me with plantains, or cocoas, or yams, which his wife Myrtilla cooked for me, with salt fish, and sometimes fresh fish, and we had very often fowls and pork, and rum and water enough. Then I was not required to do any night work. I had plenty of sleep, and every evening, after the day's work, the rest of the new negroes, and sometimes myself, would get together and dance and sing, and sometimes tell stories of our own country. On Saturday nights all the negroes on the estate used to have a dance, with goombays and other musical instruments. My master always spoke kindly to me when he came into the field where I was at work, and his wife was universally beloved by everybody, white and black.

My mistress seldom saw or spoke to me, but it was the desire and dream of my life to be taken into the great house and live in her own personal service. Could Tatee and I but enter that paradise, I thought I should be perfectly happy. Tatee was not so ambitious for this honor, but told me to be careful to obey my master, and be always ready to oblige my fellow-servants, and it would come to pass for me at least, if not for her; but my own wish and hope was that both might be called under the immediate orders of my master and mistress.

The day after I arrived upon the estate, my master offered me a new name, as I suppose he did not like Mahmadee. I knew but little English yet, though I could understand what he meant. He said we were the second lot he had bought, and we were all to be called by names beginning

with a B. There was Bradwell and Belton, Bob,
Bogle, and several other B's, Bonaparte and Bacchus. He mentioned Bacchus last, so I repeated
the name, and Bacchus I was put down in the
slave-book, a native of Kashna, in Houssa, aged
twelve or thirteen years. Tatee was called Beauty,
but at the request of my mistress, who had heard,
no doubt, of my poor shipmate's regard for me,
she was called Ariadne as well. For my part,
Bacchus was as good to me as any other name,
especially as I was to live among persons who
were of another religion, though it seemed to me
as if they had no religion at all. I never saw anybody pray for months after I was settled on the
estate. Of course I did not know what was going
on in the Great House, as I never went beyond
the kitchen or hall door; I only know that among
the negroes, and at the overseer's house, I never
saw a single being go on his knees, nor did any
of that set go to the church, which was not above
three miles off. There were other Mahometans
beside myself on the estate, but they never said
any of the five prayers those of our faith ought to
repeat daily. They told me they would soon get
flogged up again if they were to fall down upon

their faces to pray, instead of minding their work, and that all the rest of the negroes on the estate would laugh at them. One of these said it was of no use for a slave to pray. If God had put his eye upon a black man to make him a slave, he could not shake off his *spell* till he died, although he should pray ten times a day. However, I did not find the condition of a slave so intolerable as I had expected, and this absence of religion was at first a relief to me, rather than a subject of complaint, for Hadji Ali, with all his kindness, used to be very rigid, and made his scholars always attend most punctually to the prayers and to the fasts enjoined by our religion. Perhaps he was a little too fond of preaching to us, that we should go to hell for this and that, and, more than all, for the least want of faith. Here I heard nothing about faith, or hell, or fire, or the evil spirit, except when people were angry and swore. The men and women lived as they liked, after they had done their work, and seemed not to be accountable to anybody for their conduct, so long as they were peaceable, and did not rob one another, or their master.

Yet I often thought of the spirit of my mother, and sometimes dreamed of her and often of Kashna.

The deep impression of the old Bushreen's constant precepts and example clung to me with singular tenacity. My will had nothing to do with my faith, neither was there any thing in the habits of those most directly before my eyes to change it. If the white people had been true, strict Christians, I think I should have felt a respect for their religion; but their carelessness on this matter, and their profligate habits, made me feel doubly averse to giving up the true faith for one like theirs. My mind was always running on my own neglect of duty, and calling up before me the image of my old teacher, until I began to see him in my dreams. One of these dreams was repeated more than once, and with such distinctness that for years it had upon my mind all the force of a solemn reality. I had been employed all the day in some light duties about the Great House, and lay down to sleep in a cross passage that opened into the kitchen. I felt happy at being called in to serve the family, and dropped asleep in a free and hopeful spirit. Suddenly, and, strange to say, with a consciousness that it was in a dream, my beloved Hadji Ali stood before me, as I had often seen him in the mosque at Kashna, in a long white robe, with the Koran in his

right hand, and a string of beads in his left. He
looked long and affectionately on me, and sighed
deeply. He spoke not a word, yet I could see tears
stealing down his withered cheeks, and he raised
his arms above his head, and lowered them over
mine, as if to implore a blessing on me. Good and
kind old man! or blessed spirit! for I dreamed that
he perhaps was dead, and this his ghost come to
reprove my irreligion: "Never, never," said I,
"shall my heart forsake the true faith, or cease to
cherish the memory of your affectionate instruction.
No, my father, I am yours forever." When I
awaked, I felt relieved, and I resolved to perform
the ceremonies of my religion, though by stealth,
for I felt that the spirit of Hadji Ali had his eye
upon me, and I was but too proud to merit his protection.

I used, accordingly, to repeat the prayers I had
been taught in my infancy, and when the appointed
times arrived, I sometimes ran into the bush to
kneel down, or if I was alone in any apartment of
the house, or stables, I kneeled down devoutly on
the floor, and prayed for peace. I even prayed out
loud, and, what strikes me as curious, I would often
add something in English, but my Arabic was

never extensive, and my native tongue was becoming less familiar to me than the language of our masters.

This dream, or vision, had another effect on me. I was smitten with an anxiety not to forget the verses from the Koran, which my beloved instructor had taught me with such patient affection, and, with bits of chalk, or even charcoal, I was continually inscribing them on the walls of the negro cottages. The owners thought them charms against Obiah magic and the evil eye, and were not only much pleased to have them, but were careful to keep the secret among themselves.

The overseer surprised me at my devotions one day, and ridiculed me without mercy. He mentioned it and my writing "African charms," as he styled them, to my master and mistress. My master paid no attention to it, for by this time I had won my way into his good-will by my earnest and evident desire to do his pleasure in all things. No one, not even the overseer, *reproached* me, but one day my mistress took me kindly to task, and asked me if I did not know that Mahomet was a cheat and an impostor. Alas! mortified and confused, I had little or nothing to say, because I had no means

of speaking my ideas in a language which she could
comprehend. There was an expression of pity upon
her features as she smiled, but it was not a sneering
pity. "Go to the Bay," continued she; "Pompey
shall go with you on Sundays, and you may be of
the religion as we are. I assure you, Bacchus, we
do not mean to go to perdition. We hope to be
saved through the merits of our Redeemer." When
she dismissed me, she said, "You had better talk
to Mr. Wodenlone, the Moravian missionary. He
preaches upon the next estate once or twice a week,
and your master will allow you to go and hear
him." "Thank you, mistress," said I, in return,
"but I could not understand him." "Indeed," replied she, "you could, he preaches in the negro language, and we mean to let him come and preach
at Orange Grove." As I found there were other
slaves who went to hear Mr. Wodenlone, I joined
them on the next occasion—out of curiosity, I confess, to hear a white man speak in my own language. I found that it was not my own language,
when I came to hear it. I could understand a
word here and there, and sometimes make out a
sentence, but, for the generality of his palaver, I
was as much in the dark as before I went to be en-

lightened. I could understand that he said Jesus Christ died for us, that he was a good man, a great man, and that he would come at the last day to judge us. But this preacher did not pronounce his words right, and though his speech was, perhaps, in a negro language, it was very different from that spoken in Houssa. The next Sunday, Pompey took me to church at the Bay, where an English parson preached for a long while about the three Gods and one God—the Trinity, which, to my understanding then, was idolatry, having been always taught to consider such doctrines very wicked. I attended the church repeatedly, at the recommendation of the overseer, and might have derived more advantage from it, but that he used to jeer me at my return, and ask if the buckra parson had routed the Turkish devil out of me, as he chose to call the Prophet. I did not laugh at his wit, nor was I converted. He was a good, just man, though very sharp with the negroes—that is, he made them work, but he was good-tempered. He used to ask me, too, if Mahomet had not provided good dinners, and *lots of pretty girls* for his disciples, in the next world. He said he knew the Turks called the Christians dogs, but he contended

4

that the Turks themselves were brute beasts; and
that a religion which allowed a man four or five
wives was only fit for pigs. Pigs! I could have
answered him that some of his buckra countrymen,
as I already saw on several estates, *practiced* the
faith of Mahomet, if they did not believe or preach
it.   It grieved me to think my mistress, to whom
I looked up with so much reverence, should despise
me for my religion.   The biting ridicule of the overseer was daily repeated by one of the drivers, an
African of a mean and savage temper, who spoke
Houssa very well, and far better English than most
of the Creole blacks; and to add to these mortifi-
cations, I had of late been scarcely called into the
Great House for any purpose whatever.   Tatee
sometimes tried to console me, but she had made
a match with the cooper of the estate, and had the
less time to waste on me.   That fall was to me a
most restless and discontented period, and it turned
me more and more, and with deeper regret, to the
remembrance of Hadji Ali, who still used to visit
me in my dreams and urge me to confine myself to
him and the true faith.   There were two or three
of my shipmates who harbored notions of decamp-
ing, which they had communicated to me in confi-

dence, and I was silly enough to listen to their suggestions, and relate, in turn, the dreams with which I had been so long visited.' The poor fellows believed them the direct interposition of God, and I believed them correct in thinking so; yet they were Kafirs themselves. No followers of the Prophet were included in our secret but myself, and I was forbidden to make a confidante of Tatee, who had by this time (it was the month of November) become settled and contented in her own cabin with her husband, the cooper, and, as my comrades rightly guessed, would not be likely to approve of such a reckless scheme. It was harder work to engage me not to tell our plan to Tatee, than to enlist me in its dangers. I sought to obtain her opinion indirectly, by asking her if she would quit her situation, in case she could return to her own country, but I soon saw she had no favor for any such idea. She was as affectionate to me as ever, notwithstanding she was the cooper's wife, but she had long ceased to give me any hopes of escaping from slavery. Under these circumstances, I kept my own counsel, or rather, the counsel of my companions, but never was a more silly conspiracy planned or executed. One of my com-

panions had a faith, he said, that if we could get
to the end of the island, we should find a ship to
take us back to Africâ. Another believed there
was land all the way to the first place we had
come to (Barbadoes), and doubted very much if it
was not all land to Africa, the buckras having
put us in a ship, and brought us by water, just
to confuse us, and make us think it impossible to
get back again. They had seen a returned slave
in their own country, who had come back from
England, and they even contemplated getting to
this last-mentioned place, in order to be sent (as
they had heard they should be) to the English
settlement of Sierra Leone.

We determined to defer our escape until the
Christmas holidays, that we might have more
chance of not being missed, till we should have
got three or four days' journey toward the rising
sun. In the mean time, we kept as smooth faces
as we could, consoling ourselves, for the present
evils of our condition, with the prospect of better
fortunes in our own country. This was not so
unreasonable a hope on my part as on that of my
comrades, two of whom had been slaves in Houssa
—slaves by captivity in war, not slaves by birth—

and the other a slave from his infancy. There was a chance that they might all be reclaimed as slaves, even in case we succeeded in getting back to Africa; but I was free, and had a right to expect my long-promised inheritance, even if Hadji Ali should be dead. If he lived, and I could find him, my condition would be equal to my most sanguine wishes, though I confess I despaired of our enterprise. I knew too well we were on an island, with the ocean all around us. My hopes were not very high, and perhaps my courage was not of the firmest, but my mates were madly bent upon it, and I was carried away by their foolish urgings.

"We will not leave you behind," said they all. "Hadji Ali will lead us through to the end." "Only trust to me," said one. "Trust in God," said another Kafir, who promised in the same breath to steal a stocking full of dollars and pistareens, which the negro watchman, who had charge of him, kept in a chest under his head. "If we are to have luck, we must have no violence," said I, in return—"no fighting or murdering. God made us all free alike at our birth, and we have a right to run away if we can. If we are caught, we shall get flogged, and perhaps trans-

ported, and we must bear it as well as we can."
Once I made sure we were found out or betrayed,
for the overseer sent for Bryan, Belton, and Brad,
of our party, before the month of November was
out, and had them branded with our master's ini-
tials on the breast and the shoulder. This was
done with a silver brand, heated in the flame of
one of the lamps in the boiling-house; and if it
did not cause any very great pain, it was a sad
presage of what we had to expect, in case of being found out by the Maroons, to whom it would
serve as a proof of our condition. A few days
healed the wounds of the blister caused by the
burning; but we had not recovered entirely from
the alarm caused by this incident, even when
Christmas was on us, and the hour and the moment of our departure had arrived. I kept secretly invoking the spirit of Hadji Ali to direct me,
for my confidence was not strong in our safe out-
come; but when such stout, stubborn men as Bryan and Belton were shaken at the final step, a boy
of thirteen may be excused for feeling some
tremors.

CHAPTER IV.

IN THE WOODS.

IT was a dark night, the eve of Christmas, when I left the abode of Pompey and Myrtilla, and met my companions, four in number, at a negro-house upon the next estate. We had been so secret that the owner of the house where we met had not the least suspicion of the business we had in hand. One of them had seen an Obeah-man a day or two before, and consulted him whether he should have luck in what he meant to do at Christmas. The Obeah-man bid him beware of Friday, and he would succeed. Now, Friday is our Mahometan sabbath, and the Kafir, knowing this, suspected I was alluded to in the Obeah-man's injunction; so that we had scarce commenced our march before he told me of his suspicions, and made me swear, after his own fashion, that I would not betray him and the rest of my companions. I was very indignant at this, and for a while was more than half resolved to turn

back and leave them; but I found I was no more
my own master, and some hints they threw out implied that it was on this point that the superstition
of the Obeah hunter hinged. He feared my turning
back, and had I finally decided on so doing, they
would have put me out of the way. My companions were named Bogle—cut down to 'Bo—Bryan,
Belton, and Bradwell, all names commencing with
a B, on the same principle as my own plantation-
name of Bacchus. Bryan had stolen the dollars
which he had seen in the possession of the negro
who had the care of him; and Belton had abstract-
ed a rifle gun, with powder and balls, from the
overseer's house. We had, besides, a couple of
machets among us, and each of us had a small
woven basket—called in Jamaica by its African
name of *bancra*—filled with plantains and salt fish,
which we hoped would last till we could either kill
a wild hog or fall in with some person disposed to
give us food for love or money. The rifle was a
stupid encumbrance, for with it we could not hit
any one of the pigeons we continually met, whereas
a fowling-piece would have supplied all our wants.
As a weapon of offense or defense, one rifle could
do us little good, and might involve us in a great

deal of mischief. But it was quite as sensible as any other part of our rash arrangements.

Thus equipped, we left our rendezvous with great resolution and struck for the sea. We started at about nine o'clock at night, and traveled till morning, by the high-road, uninterrupted, except by one gentleman on horseback, who came cantering along in the dark; and, though we got into the bushes to avoid him, he espied us, and called to us to know who and what we were. Bryan said it was the doctor of the estate, and wanted to rob him; but I swore that I would call out and warn him if the thing was attempted, let the consequence be what it would; and the other three, luckily for our future safety, were of my opinion. The doctor called out to us a dozen times in vain, and then proceeded on his way.

As soon as the dawn appeared I prostrated myself on the ground, and begged the blessing of God upon our expedition, resolving, now that I was at liberty to do it, to be regular and punctual in my devotions. We left the high-road and the sea, and struck into the woods, through which we had often to cut a passage with our machets, the bushes were so terribly thick and tangled. We walked till

4*

noon, having stopped a little while in a small grassy dell by a spring to eat some of our provisions; but we were, by this time, too fatigued to continue our march. We crept into a thicket and lay down to sleep for several hours, as I guessed, for the sun was sinking into the sea when we resumed our journey. We had been undisturbed in our sleep, and took a good meal before we started, which considerably lightened the load of our wallets.

We marched the whole of this second night, as we had done during the last, not hesitating to take the high-road as soon as it was starlight, and again we met with no creature after nine or ten o'clock. We heard the negroes on many estates, as we passed along, drumming and singing, laughing and dancing, in Christmas glee, but we dared not approach them. About midnight we saw a church, or a meeting-house of some kind, near enough to hear the preacher tell his congregation that the souls of all the indecent, filthy, beastly, dancing, drunken negroes, who were thus profaning the nativity of the blessed Redeemer, would burn in an unquenchable fire for thousands of millions of ages. However, *we* runaways were neither dancing nor drinking, so we consoled ourselves by thinking we did not incur this curse.

The stimulus of our expedition kept up our spirits, and we journeyed gayly on again toward the rising sun, though where we had got to by morning none of us could tell. We were on lofty land, in the midst of an apparently interminable forest, without a river or any other water than what we collected from the wild pines—a parasite as common as the trees it grows on in the woods, but the dew it collects in its heart is often rather bitter and unpalatable. We had struck into the woods at daylight, but we did not stop till about ten o'clock, when we made a fire by means of the rifle, and roasted some plantains which we stole from the negro-grounds of an estate as we passed along in the night. We were now quite in a wilderness, and, as we thought, almost out of reach of mankind for the present, for we could hear no sound, except the chirping of the crickets. There was no wind; not enough to wave the trees, which were very high; and though we had listened at times, since sunrise, we had not once heard the crowing of a cock, nor a plantation shell-blow. I felt as if I were free again, and, though dreadfully

fatigued with so long and wearisome a march, I
could scarcely sleep from the delightful excitement.
I experienced at the thoughts of liberty.   Alas!
this pleasant dream was dissipated with my first
sound sleep in the forest.   I happened to awake the
first, and to my unutterable dismay missed our rifle,
which was between Belton and myself when we laid
down.   Had one of the dreaded Maroons—one of
• that *forest police* of which we had heard such tales
of their bringing back runaways—stolen upon us,
and taken it in our sleep?   Or, had some fugitive
slave, like ourselves, stumbled upon us, and thus
mocked our want of care?   Were we in the power
of those dreaded Maroons, who were, but too surely,
strong enough to recapture us, or was this the work
of a chance thief?   All this flashed like hot light-
ning through my mind, as I hastily roused my comrades and signified our loss.   They stared at each
other and all around them in speechless alarm.
The daring thief had cut away the thong by which
Belton carried his powder-horn across his breast,
and stolen that too.   When we came to look for the
bancras, the remnant of our provisions, and the
baskets in which we carried them, were gone also.
It was a bitter shock.   One machet only remained

to us, and the stocking-full of dollars, with which
we knew not, however, when or how to get to market. This would have been a prize too, and a pretty good one, but that Bryan, who considered himself the proprietor, actually lay upon it, and so concealed it in his sleep. The worst consequence of
this business which we had to apprehend, was the
probability of our being discovered and betrayed.
Yet we were inclined to hope that those who had
robbed us could not be Maroons, or they would
have alarmed us. One man, indeed, a Maroon or a
fugitive negro, might have done all; but a party,
even a couple of Maroons, after having secured our
fire-arms, might have taken us prisoners, or put us
to death for resisting, a practice at which, as I had
been told, Maroons are not apt to hesitate long.
What could we do in our helplessness? I was
young, and I trust I shall be excused when I own
that, in spite of my devout feelings, my heart failed
me, and I even wished to return to my master; but
my comrades scouted the idea, and taunted me with
cowardice. They were four grown men, and they
had a stocking-full of money. If they could have
spoken even enough of the negro English, we might
have furnished ourselves again with all we had lost,

but our speech was, as yet, very imperfect, and we
had *no paper* (as the negroes say), no passport of
any sort to show, in case of being stopped and in-
terrogated, as we most probably should be by the
first white person who might meet us. We had no
choice but to go on. Those who had robbed us
would know too well where to seek us again, if indeed Maroon eyes and hands had been about us,
and anywhere else was better than this place. Belton said, with set teeth, and with a look that
made my blood run cold, that we must overtake the
thief and cure him of stealing. Yet I was as ready
as the most savage of them to fight desperately for
my liberty, if we were attacked; it was only Belton's short, ferocious mutterings about his catching
somebody to cut in little bits and eating them all
up, which startled me for an instant. By the time
the hurried consultation was over, I had buried all
my fears in the excitement of a forward movement.

Fortunately for us, we had made a meal before
we resigned ourselves to repose, and though we
could have drank a gallon or two of water among
us, we feared no hunger before night. Bryan set
actively about hunting for the traces of the robber
or robbers. He possessed considerable talents for

such a work, and was not long in deciding that only one man had ventured up to us, even if there had been others at hand, and this person had retreated from us eastward, by the very course which we meant to pursue. We followed upon his track with all the expedition we could use, intent on overtaking him, as much for the purpose of preventing his betraying us, as for the sake of our goods which he had stolen. We struck upon his trail directly, though he had dived under thickets which, at first view, seemed impenetrable to us. He had also doubled upon his path repeatedly, and had tried every scheme to divert us from the road he had taken. We were five to one, and though he often baffled us, we must have gained so considerably on him as to distress him, for he had thrown away one of the bancras, which we found in his path. Soon we came upon another bancras, and then a third, but all the little baskets—already made lighter by our last meal—were now empty. They proved that Bryan was true on the trail, and that was the greatest want we then felt. Presently we opened into foot-paths, very faint, indeed, but showing that these wild forest thickets had human inhabitants of some kind. That these inhabitants

were hog-hunting and slave-catching Maroons we
hardly dared to doubt, and, without stopping to
reckon what might follow after that, Bryan and
Belton more eagerly declared we must find the
thief and *finish* him. As we advanced the country
became more rocky and broken, and the paths more
intricate. In reverting to this affair, in after years,
I have often wondered that there was not sense
enough among the whole of us—ignorant negroes
though we were—to know we were marching into
the very den of danger. We had but one present
aim, and that was to prevent the robber from doing
us more mischief, and so, with one heart, we fiercely pressed along upon his track. We traveled
miles before we came to a sudden halt. In a curious little grotto we found the ashes of a recent fire,
about it the remains of a wild pig, and beside it
the last of our missing bancras. The thief had
paused here to eat our cold roasted plantains. The
crumbs of the feast were scattered about. He had
not stopped to make the fire—that was an older
affair—but he had taken his ease in eating our
provisions. We could trace where he had lolled
against the bushes, and that so lately that they
had not fairly resumed their places when we drop-

ped into the dell. It was a large natural vault,
very spacious and lofty, open to the day by an
immense arch, and inclosed in front by a huge wall
of rough piled rocks, partly constructed by human
hands. It was a vast hall, given by the bountiful
God, a ready dwelling for his poor, wandering
children. There was such a grand air of strength,
seclusion, and independence in this rocky fastness,
that it inspired me with a confused proposal that
we should remain in it, and try to make an alliance
with those who frequented the hold. Bryan started in anger from his investigation of the "signs,"
and threw at me a heavy stick he had in his hand,
calling me "dog and fool," for the mere suggestion.
Brad, who was a good-natured giant, capable of
any thing but long sullens and hard thinking, took
my part, and for a moment there was a division
in our sage counsels.

"Mahmadee may stay if he likes," said Bryan
savagely, "and you may stay with him, but I will
not stop till I have finished that thief." So saying,
he strode on without even looking back, and Belton
and Bo followed close after him, as if afraid to lose
sight of their leader. Brad and I stood and gazed
at each other a minute or two in uncertainty, and

then, without a word, he started after our comrades, and I attended his steps. I cannot explain,
even to myself, the cause of the sudden and complete revulsion of sentiment, but from that hour I
abandoned all hope of final escape, and heartily
regretted that I had suffered myself to be led into
this runaway scrape. It was not that Bryan had
thrown his staff at me. It did not touch me—was
not intended to reach me, probably—and I had
not the slightest feeling of resentment. Indeed, I
am not of a vindictive temper at any time, and I
was used to rough play on the plantation; but a
sense of his and our incapacity settled heavily upon
me. My heart had not been in it from the beginning, but these men had put it to me as a kind
of treason, when I had now and then made my
feeble protests against carrying out the plan. Long
afterward I learned that I was dragged—literally
dragged—into it from a superstitious idea that my
Arabic prayers and verses from the Koran were
potent spells, which in some wonderful manner
would facilitate their escape. In brief, Brad, who
was a Houssa man, was convinced himself, and
was able to convince the rest, that I would be a
lucky companion, and therefore the wiseacres en-

cumbered themselves with a half-unwilling boy of thirteen.

Brad and I plodded along in the rear of our comrades in perfect silence, neither speaking to them or we to each other, fully occupied with our thoughts and the difficulties of our rough and stony way. I said something, at last, of the burning thirst, which the water in the wild pines seemed rather to inflame than quench.

"It is hard for you, Sidi Mahmadee," Brad answered in Houssee; "very hard for a boy who had every thing he wished in his own country, and plenty of slaves to wait upon him; but have courage, prince, we will soon get back to our own country again."

"Never, Brad," I exclaimed, in despondent anguish; "none of us will ever see Houssa again."

"Never! king's son? Are we not on the road there now?"

The athletic man stopped and cowered on his staff before me, with an air and aspect of utter, overwhelming dismay, that it is impossible to describe. I replied that we were, truly, on an island, as the white people had always told us, and that we were too poor and ignorant to find our way off of it. Why this conviction had never come to me so strongly before I am sure I cannot understand, but the sickening certainty of my fate was then branded upon my soul as clearly, and as ineffaceably, as my master's mark was before me on the breast and right shoulder of poor, terror-stricken Brad. The rest of the party were hidden from us by a sharp turn in the narrow wood-path, and we had a few minutes to recover ourselves and come to a kind of understanding respecting our position. It was then rather understood than said, that I was not to be the first to bring up this subject to our other comrades, and that the obligation to take all chances with them was as strong upon us as ever. Beyond that we did not go, and could not see our way. There was an intimation, or only a suspicion, perhaps, that I would be sacrificed without mercy if I should hint at misfortune, when I had expressly been brought along for *good luck*.

We had scarcely rejoined the other three when I caught, in the distance, the welcome sound of rushing water. For an instant—but one single instant—Bryan said it was only the breeze coming over the tree-tops; in the next, with a joyful step, he was leading us in its direction. He tore through the thorny paths and over steep rocks in a frenzy of delight, as the musical waters sounded nearer and nearer, as if wooing our parched lips to their caresses. A parting through the trees revealed to us the spray of a waterfall, and above it hung, like a banner of promise, its lovely colors fairly defined in the light of the descending sun, a small rainbow. Forgetting all prudence, we broke into noisy exclamations of delight as we hurried to the margin of the stream. It rushed foaming and tumbling through a succession of steep and broken rocks, forming, alternately, dashing cascades and clear, silent pools. Into one of these still and shaded basins we plunged eagerly, to cool our feverish bodies and slake our burning thirst. How we reveled in that bath! I was the last to leave it, and tore myself away with regret, when Bryan, after a hurried indulgence, reminded us that we must not lose sight of our chase. "Yes," said Belton, as he resumed his only garment—thrown off to enjoy his plunge without hinderance—"Yes, after dark we can do nothing in these thick woods; and now we must give up the thief, since we left his track to come to water." Bryan thought we

might go back to it, but Brad, who had never
before launched an opinion of his own manufacture
since we had started, proposed that we should " let
him go, with a curse from Mahmadee, *a good strong
curse*, from the Koran, and after that look out for
our own road out of trouble." Brad was not a
Mahometan, and cared little for the doctrines of the
Koran or the precepts of the Prophet, but he had a
devout faith in the efficacy of the curses, especially
when forcibly delivered by one who could read
them from the text. While Brad was setting forth
this luminous idea of overwhelming the absent
thief with curses, and then taking up our own eastward course without further regard to him, Belton
had fixed his eyes on an immense cotton-tree, which
towered from the top of the bank, and seemed to
overlook a wide space. He proposed to ascend this
king of the forest, to obtain a survey of the adja-
cent country, and report to us below how the land
should lie to the eastward; and whether we were
near smoke, settlements, and plantations. We
helped him up, and watched every inch of his
progress, as he clung to the high and perpendicular
shaft, almost afraid, sometimes, that he was too fatigued to keep his hold in such a situation. Our

eyes followed him anxiously till he was almost lost
among the high branches. But what was our surprise to see him stop suddenly, as if scared at sight
of something, and to hear him call to some one
above him in the forks of the tree! We then saw
the crouching figure of a man, who had chosen this
extraordinary place as a place of concealment.
"Hi! you dam rascal! where for me rifle gun?"
cried Belton. The negro did not understand him,
or would not. Belton repeated his hail as he made
his way up to him, and, bracing his feet and knees
in the forks, boldly closed in with him. He managed someway to clutch the individual whom he
had treed so very unexpectedly, and threatened to
strangle him, or toss him down, if he did not instantly deliver up the stolen property. But the
negro was a match for him, and it seemed as if
Belton were just as likely to come down headlong
as the other. Bryan hastened up to his assistance,
and Bo and myself begged them all to come down,
which, on a kind of truce, they finally did; the
stranger declaring his innocence, and putting an
oath to every yard of his descent, that he "nebba,
nebba see de rifle nor bancras. Him 'clare to him
God, nebba tief nutting since him lilly baby, and

tief him mudder milk." He landed, like his pursuers, out of breath, and Bryan instantly put the remaining cutlass to his throat, swearing, half in his own tongue, and half in negro English, that the last moment of his life was come, and that the johncrows should pick out his *yeye* before noon next day. He was so enraged that he even began to chop at him, and had already given him an ugly cut on the head, when I interfered, and told the negro that if he would deliver up the goods he should be spared. But nothing was further from Cudjoe's mind, notwithstanding the knock he had received, than to confess the robbery. He swore he was a poor runaway from an estate in Vere, and had been hidden in the tree all day. Belton called him a liar, and insisted that he only pretended to be a runaway. Bryan, finding he could make no impression on his fears, was now bent on putting him to death, either to prevent his telling upon us, or because he had already shed his blood. Again I interposed, and so did Brad, who seconded every thing I advanced. Still we were at a loss what to do. We did not wish the negro's death, yet our situation was critical; however, I asked, though scarcely expecting the answer I received, whether

Cudjoe, for that was his name, could find us where-withal to satisfy our hunger. He promptly said he could, and would, and did, in fact, lead us through a sort of labyrinth among the woods to a lone hut, which he said did not belong to him, although a dog came out as we approached, and fawned upon him. We were, of course, upon our guard, for fear of a surprise, and kept entreating him for the rifle, or for some fire-arms, as we walked along, and after we were in the hut, but it was all in vain.

5

CHAPTER V.

RECAPTURED.

CUDJOE, as even I—inexperienced boy that I was—plainly understood, did not lead us directly to his house, which was scarcely one hundred yards from the tree in which we caught him roosting. He wound about in the thicket-paths four or five times that distance—Bryan and Belton growling to each other that they would kill him if he tried to deceive us—before we brought up at his little hut. On the side we came it was edged in the border of the thick wood-lands, but on going round to the door in front, to our surprise and consternation, we looked suddenly down upon extensive sugar-cane fields in the plain below. This hut had been built for a watchman, and Cudjoe said, perhaps truly, that he belonged to the plantation, and kept guard there against the depredations of runaway negroes. He expressed, however, the greatest horror of the Maroons, who, he said, were all about in the woods, and must have " teifed de gun and de bancras."

Belton persisted in accusing him of the theft, and of having climbed the tree to watch us when he heard us in the water, but Cudjoe swore and re-swore that he was a paragon of honesty. So far from robbing poor runaways—which we did not pretend to deny we were—he vowed he would hide us from the Maroon slave-hunters and share with us the last morsel of his provisions. As the seal of his sincerity, he brought forth some rum, and we all drank of it with infinite relish. We poor negro Mahometans are not very exact about drinking wine, and besides that, it was not wine, but strong new rum, that I tippled with old Cudjoe. We soon discovered in one corner of the hut a well-filled basket of yams, which we did not long delay from the fire we found still reeking on the floor of the hut when we entered.

Our intention of viewing the country from the top of the cotton-tree had been defeated by the incident I have related, and we had experienced so much fatigue that we gave up all idea of traveling this night. Cudjoe, having tied up his dog, offered, if we wished it, to conduct us through the bush to

an estate's provision-ground, where he said there
was an old sore-foot watchman, whom he would
well-drunk, and that we might help ourselves to as
many yams and plantains as we could carry.

It was very clear that this vagabond lived by
thieving, at any rate. To trust him was impossible,
but we were not inclined to go further that night.
He might intend to betray us, but we were not yet
in want of *victuals*—as we call ground-provisions.
We only longed for the restitution of our stolen
goods—rather forgetting that they were stolen first
by ourselves. After we had dispatched the yams,
Belton said he was determined to search the hut,
and as by this time the evening had begun to
darken around us, he took a fire-stick and some
dry trash, and made a blaze, by which he searched
the outside of the thatch. Cudjoe affected to help
him, and, having found nothing, they re-entered the
hut to search inside. In the zeal of his assistance,
Cudjoe awkwardly knocked down our very powder-horn from under some trash crammed under
the roof. We all started, for we had seen the falling
horn plain enough to be sure of it, but, before we
could seize it, we were scattered right and left by
a blinding explosion. Cudjoe was nearest to it,

and made a hasty effort to catch it up; but it had fallen among the coals of the fire, and before he could recover it, some grains of the powder must have escaped, for the whole took the blaze and exploded between his hands—burning his face most horribly, besides singeing all of us, and setting the thatch on fire. All ended in the swift destruction of the pile of dry *megasse* (the trash of sugar-canes) of which this temporary dwelling had been built.

"Tief and liar," exclaimed Belton, scarcely recovered from the dazzling blaze caused by the explosion—"you don't tief the gun? No mo (only) you steal the powder, and it blow you to jumby. The gun no use now the powder gone, but you *shan't not* tief no more." With this he gave him a thrust with the machet, which must have injured him severely, though it did not kill him, for he managed to stagger away, leaving us confounded and half-blinded by the blaze of the powder, first of all, and worse still by the glare of the burning trash.

This illumination was not likely to be beneficial to us, as it was calculated to call the attention of any neighbors, and to subject us to the risk of detection and apprehension. We did not attempt to follow Cudjoe. We dived into the jungle, and, by a tolerably clear but tortuous path, pursued our course for several miles, until we came to a river. This stream I have since fancied was the Agua Alta, somewhere near Annotto Bay. We had crossed its bed several times in our course, for the night was clear, and the moon bright enough to guide us on our way. Our great anxiety was to reach some point at which we might take some steps toward finding out where we were, and to what point we wished to steer. Both of these were rather important subjects to us, and on both of them we, in our wisdom, were equally in the dark.

Our course had led us along the verge of a large plantation—perhaps more than one—after we left Cudjoe's blazing hut. We kept in the path, but ever holding ourselves ready to take to the bush at the first sight or sound of human beings. We hoped these paths would lead us to a road or settlement, and enable us to watch for a chance of safely communicating with some straggling negro. We had learned a grain of caution, and began to look out for some lone hut, where we might ask questions without much risk of being recaptured.

We had followed the winding path from Cud-joe's, near the fields and pastures of which I have spoken, a mile or more, when we descried a hut close to the road, snugly inclosed in a penguin hedge. It was placed at an elevated corner of an extensive cane-field, evidently for the occupation of a watchman, who could from his door command the whole range of cane-fields. We listened a moment outside to a fearful snoring, and, hearing nothing else, I was directed to enter and report on the state of the premises. I found no one but the old watchman himself, who was so drunk that he was as helpless as a fallen tree or a dead pig. He had provided against accidents, and had made his fire so as not to endanger his dwelling; but he had not reserved sense enough to keep his feet out of it. One of his toes had touched a coal, and it was already so scorched that it had filled the hut with the stench of burned flesh.

He was making a disgusting noise—between a piggish moan, a hog grunt, and a human snore, but he did not make a move to help himself, or even show the least return to consciousness, when I snatched his foot from the fire with a force that whirled him round on his center, and loudly called to my comrades to come in and take possession. Brad helped me to bind up the poor old creature's foot in fresh plantain-leaves, and then—by way of doctor's fee, let us say—he filled a baucra with a lot of roasted yams, which this exemplary watchman had put to the fire, and drank himself to sleep before they were ready to eat. Close beside him stood a bottle half full of rum, which was quickly finished—the rum I mean—by his friendly visitors. As we were looking round in search of any chance eatables worthy of our attention, I thought I heard a voice outside. I raised my hand to warn my companions, and, before they or I could well collect our ideas, a voice, which we took to be Cudjoe's, addressed us from the outside, and predicted misfortune to us. The hollow and melancholy tone in which the oracle was delivered to us, set Belton's teeth chattering, and Bryan, staring out of the hut, declared he could see Cudjoe's *duppy* (ghost) leaning on a bamboo stick a few yards off, and applying his left hand to his wounded side. I also looked out and saw a figure to a certainty, whether of flesh and blood, or a spirit, I could not determine. It raised the stick in a threatening manner, and again bid us prepare for trouble, reproaching

us for eating his yams and then *killing* him. We
slunk into the back of the hut, too much disconcerted to even dream of following this visitant and
make sure whether it was man or duppy. After a
short and perplexed stare at each other, we all huddled out in a close mass, and took the road at a
pace that indicated a general and extreme desire
to put a considerable space between us and that
hut at the very quickest.

Two or three hours' steady walking in the cool
night air brought us, as I before stated, to the bed
of the Agua Alta—or, Wag Watar, as the negroes
will always have it. Here we rested a while, and at
daybreak we entered another lone hut, and found
another drunken man and his not altogether sober
wife. I say *we* entered, but, in truth, I was sent in
alone, both on account of my speaking better English than any of the rest of the party, and because
my youth would be likely to ward off suspicion. I
was directed to say that I had been sent on an
errand, and been lost all night in the woods. The
woman was cross, but she gave me the directions
we needed to find the best course to Buff Bay. I
had heard some talk between my master and the
overseer about ships at that place, and we had

5*

mixed up all our foolish plans and superstitions
into a common knot, to the effect that from some
place toward sunrise we must make our escape
back to Africa. Buff Bay and Port Antomo were
both toward sunrise—that much we had found out
before—and now I learned that we were within a
day's easy march of Buff Bay, the nearest of these
two points. Bryan, meanwhile, thought the conference rather long, and cut me off in the midst of
my polite thanks to the woman, by putting his
head in the door and roughly demanding some
bananas. A fine large bunch hung in tempting
view, and he was determined to have them. I
urged and entreated him to desist, but Belton came
up and joined him in taking the fruit. I was exceedingly vexed, and told them both, after we were
out of sight of the hut, that it would bring us bad
luck, and that we would have all the country up
and after us at this rate. They only laughed at
me, but Brad and Bo took sides with me, and told
the others that we three would leave them and go
our own way, if they were not more careful.

We were walking along, still rather out of
humor, when, in climbing a hill—always through
lonely by-paths—the woods suddenly broke away

as we reached the summit, and the wide, blue sea, and a long chain of settlements, was all at once unfolded to our view. We hastily retreated into the bush and went into council. As had now become the usual course, I was to be sent, but not till later in the day, to spy out the land and buy provisions. We passed another hut, but saw no one stirring about it, though there was a bunch of ripe bananas hanging almost over the door. Bryan and the rest helped themselves without hesitation, and threw the stripped stalk back into the hut, as a hint to the inmate to keep better guard in future.

The Christmas holidays were even a better season for our purpose than we had the sense to conceive. It is a week of drunken license with the negroes, of general feasting with the whites; and, with care and coolness, three or four active runaways might make their way from one end of the island to the other; but, unfortunately for us, we had nowhere a place of refuge wherein to hide, nor the wit to win our freedom.

Hitherto the weather had been in our favor, but now two days of almost constant rain set in, and we suffered much from hunger and the chilling wet. At the close of one of those dreary days, as we

were coiled under the wet bushes, Belton seized
my arm, and, absolutely trembling with terror,
gasped out, "*Duppy!* Cudjoe's duppy!" I could
see, as I lay, a figure moving slowly along the path
near which we were concealed, but to my eye it
was larger than Cudjoe, and I would have followed
the figure, but we heard the sound of a horse's feet
at a distance, as if cantering up toward us; so we
drew back in the bush again, and, after the horseman had passed on, we looked in vain for the duppy.   But, though I somehow felt assured it was a
living man, and no ghost, the others were certain
that it was the troubled spirit of the person whose
food we had taken and then killed, and that his
appearance presaged misfortune.   This idea did not
make our bed on the wet ground, with no blanket
but the chilling drizzle, any the more sweet and
refreshing, but the night wore away without any
fresh alarm.   The sun rose clear, however, and
with my bancra and some small silver out of the
stocking, I made my way toward a few detached
houses we had noted near the mouth of the river,
to try whether, for love or money, we might find
something to eat.   While on this expedition I witnessed a sight which would be incredible anywhere

but in Jamaica. I had succeeded in buying some
sweet potatoes and dried fish at a little negro shop,
where the old woman who kept it asked no trouble-
some questions, and was returning highly elated
with my prize, when, on coming close to the river,
I observed that the waters were rising, and I also
caught an increased roar of the current of water, a
kind of subdued thunder, far up the stream, which
I did hear when I first passed it. My comrades
were on the other side of the stream, in the woods
beyond the cane-fields, and I eagerly watched an
opportunity to cross it unobserved. Seeing some
persons with a wain (the long heavy wagon of Jamaica), apparently going across to a cane-piece for
canes, as the mill of an adjoining estate was at work,
I hid myself until it should have moved a little way
from the river. But while the cattle were taking
here their morning draught, the river suddenly
came down in a rushing torrent, and carried all
away, except the negroes, who fled in clamorous
fright. Eight oxen and the wain were tumbled
over one another, and carried into the sea.

I was welcomed by my companions as one
may expect to be who brings hungry men wherewith to satisfy their ravenous wants. We had

not tasted food, except the bananas we had stolen from the unoccupied hut, for two days. The rain, and the repeated view of habitations, which we wished to avoid, had kept us in continued check and discomfort, and this return of sunshine, and with the prospect of a full meal, was wonderfully cheering. A retired place was selected, and if only a fire could have been had to cook our potatoes, we would have enjoyed it like a royal banquet. As it was, we joyfully gathered round our repast of hard codfish and sweet potatoes, and were attacking it with the keen relish of famine, when, to our unspeakable dismay, a tall negro, with a musket in his hand and a pig on his shoulder, stepped out of the bush and stood mockingly before us. He surveyed us an instant in silence, but with an insolent composure that warned us, on the instant, that he was a Maroon, one of that terrible forest police, whom every slave learns to think of with horror. Bryan, who feared nothing but ghosts, sprang to his feet and seized our only weapon, the cutlass, but, as he did so, three other tall fellows presented themselves, and then the first comer demanded, in negro English, our "paper for trabel."

Bryan glared fiercely at him, but made no reply. I heard poor Brad muttering how the duppy told us there was black trouble for us. The Maroon repeated his demand in a more peremptory voice, and then Belton took up the word in a tone intended to be at once independent and conciliatory. " 'Spose we lose de paper? Dat no hurt you. You keep on mind you hog, like good fella. Don't trouble we." But the Maroons laid hold of him, and that too with all the confidence of free men and agents of the law. "You are runaways," said one of the hunters; "where do you come from?" Belton gave some lame story of our being a party of free men bound for a dance at the Bay. "Oh, dance you want," the Maroon said, jeeringly; "you get plenty of dance by'm-by, presently. Floggee dance. Oh yes, floggee make much dance, plenty." Bryan answered this speech with a furious slash with the cutlass, which, fortunately for all of us, fell short, and he was leveled with the butt of a musket before he could repeat the rash attempt. Although we were foolish enough to make some further resistance, we were forced to yield without doing any harm. We were all roughly handled. Belton was knocked down, and his hands and Bryan's sharply bound together before either of them fairly recovered their senses. The Maroons amused themselves with scoffs and insults at our story of being free men, as they tied us all together, in a string, with a *Mahoe* rope, and drove us before them to the Bay, where they delivered us over to the keeper of the workhouse as captured runaways. There we were accommodated with the bilboes—each being made fast by one leg—and left for the night to our own meditations.

CHAPTER VI.

RETURN TO ORANGE GROVE.

SORROWING, supperless, and in bonds, I yet, by one of those seeming inconsistencies of life, slept soon and slept sweetly, that first night of my return to slavery. I dreamed, too, of my still dearly-remembered Hadji Ali and of my mother. What was singular, and had never occurred to me before, they appeared to be *white*—not of the ghostly pallor of death, but with fair complexions and flowing hair, like living and handsome persons of the purest white race. I was unable to recall what they said, or even the incidents of the dream, but I thought they came to console me, and I was consoled.

The keeper, a stout, bustling sort of a man, passed us all through a sharp course of cross-questioning the first thing in the morning. We had all agreed upon our story, and we steadily persisted in saying that we were free, but our jailer only laughed at us. He was a humorous, good-natured fellow, and laughed pleasantly as he—as in duty bound—examined our bodies, marks, and features, measured our heights, and noted our brands in a book.

The Maroons wished us good-bye, and told us to beware of them in future. After they left, the work-house man again tried to prevail on us to tell who we were, and to what estate we belonged, but he got nothing from us, except the stocking with the dollars. Out of that the Maroons would have helped themselves, but that we told our keeper how many there were, much to the annoyance of the black man-hunters, whom we were glad to disappoint.

Our provisions were served twice a day, in one large dish, out of which we all helped ourselves, in true African style. The crabbed old darkey who brought this kettleful of food to us, and remained till we finished the contents, had with him some fine basket-plaiting, at which he worked while we were eating. I had seen these neat basket-pouches made in Africa. Medinet is famous for this kind of manufacture, where the rich have fine praying-mats of this fabric to kneel on in the

mosque. I had learned to weave them while at
that place with my adopted father, and—as I now
recalled with tears in my heart—I had then taken
great pride in forming a very nice traveling-pouch
for each of us. I had mine over my shoulder the
very day I was captured, and I felt that whole
scene over again. The sight of this man sitting
in the corner, busy at this half-forgotten work,
following so closely on my last night's dream of
my kind and lost protector, brought back the
whole bitterness of my lot. I bent down my head,
and, for the first time since I had landed in Jamaica,
I gave way to an unrestrained flow of tears. Bryan and Belton began to taunt me with my weakness, calling me a girl-baby, and I know not what,
in Houssa; but the old man ordered them to let
me alone, and added, that he knew a youth like
me never would have "got in this black mud if
they had not led me into it." This random shot
struck home, and silenced them. For my own
part, this interference in my favor so soothed and
consoled me that I felt anxious to do something
to show my gratitude.

"My father," said I, addressing him in the po-
litest form of Houssa, "my good father, I know

how to weave Medinet work, and, if you will allow me, I will help you while I am here."

My offer was instantly accepted, and the material put in my hands to make—or rather finish, for it was half done—a neat shoulder-pouch. A gentleman came in while I was at work. Bryan was extended on the floor, with his face downward, the rest looking on in moody silence. This buckra had come to see if two runaways of his own—a father and son—were not among the captives. I fancied I read a kind pity in his eye, as it rested intently on me. He shook his head and turned away. He recognized none of us, but as he was passing Bryan he shoved him with his foot, and ordered him to get up and show his face. Instead of obeying in the respectful manner required by his situation, Bryan only flung himself over on his back, and looked up in the face of the strange gentleman, with a glare of sullen defiance. I raised my eyes from Bryan's face to that of the buckra in alarm and supplication, for it really seemed to me that the man was under a *spell*. If I had known how to frame such an appeal, I would have entreated for mercy to a miserable creature who was not in his right mind. The gentleman rested his foot for an instant on the upturned breast of the staring savage, and scanned the marks left by the silver branding-iron. Then, with one parting glance of careless scorn at the prostrate form, he said to the keeper of the workhouse, who attended him: "This lot has been advertised. I know where to write to their master, and shall do so this evening."

Making a step toward me, he tossed me a piece of silver, saying: "I hope your master will not be hard on *you*, my poor boy. This brute has enticed you into the scrape." How quick and keen he had been in discovering the real ringleader of our flight, for, in truth, Bryan it was who had started, urged forward, and commanded our ill-fated expedition. Two persons had already expressed an opinion that I had been led away by the older ones, and, though one of these was but a poor negro, the sympathy was inexpressibly cheering. It gave me hope and strength. The next morning—the second of our confinement—I set about my basket-weaving as early as possible; but first I repeated the five prayers and several verses of the Koran, to which my comrades listened with devout attention. I was never ridiculed for my religion by a negro. I then implored them to confess to the keeper who we belonged to, and ask to be sent back to our master. They would not hear of doing so, believing that the buckra had only pretended to know where we came from, in order to frighten us into telling the truth. He certainly did not mention our master's name, yet, all the same, I felt sure that he did know all about us, and, being equally sure that there was no hope of escape, I contended that the sooner we gave up the better would be our chance for an easy pardon.

In the course of the next day, Brad gave me a private hint that he for one was ready to follow my advice, and Bo was not much behind in doing the same, each without the knowledge of the other. So matters stood, and I was industriously plying my work, when, about the third day of our imprisonment, the Custos of the parish was announced. He asked a number of questions to which Belton, who had become our chief spokesman, told the old concerted tissue of foolish lies, which the rest confirmed as usual. He said little to me, but I followed every word and motion with eager looks. I was stupid enough to imagine that he resembled Hadji Ali, and must, of course, be a kind, just, and wise man. It need not be said that the resem-

blance between this fair, noble-featured white gentleman and an African negro, was an absurd freak
of my excited imagination, but it seemed a real fact
to me, and I began to expect some special kindness
from him, the moment he opened his lips. I received it, too. Black Ben, the under-keeper and
basket-maker, had told my whole history, even to
my being a king's son, to the warden, and he represented me in such a way to the Custos, that among
them I was relieved from the chain that bound me
to my comrades and allowed the freedom of the
yard.

On the second visit of the Custos I made use of
this liberty, which enabled me to speak to him out
of sight of the rest, to beg him to intercede for us,
promising not only to tell the whole truth, but that
we would, one and all, be the best and most dutiful
of servants in future, if our master would overlook
our past foolishness. He said he would do what he
could for us, and then I told him truly and without
reserve every thing he desired to know. I explained that it was not from ill treatment that we
ran away, for our master was not hard, though the
drivers were pretty sharp on the field-hands, but
because we were heart-sick to get back to our own

country. I did not accuse the others of coaxing,
and almost forcing, me to join them, as I might
have done with some truth, for I did not wish to
prejudice my comrades. My whole mind was bent
on softening the punishment that it was too clear
was hanging over all our heads. My efforts and
entreaties were not fruitless, for the old gentleman
not only said he would write in our favor, but he
actually did write such a kind and earnest letter
to my master as effectually helped to smooth my
path for many a long after year.

When the Custos had departed, I handed to
black Ben the money which the other buckra had
thrown to me, and begged him to buy some bread
and rum for a sly treat at night. My object was
to conciliate my comrades and prepare them for the
news I had for them. When I made my confession
to the Custos, he assured me that he already knew
my master's name and residence, and that a letter
was already on its way to him informing him of
our apprehension. We might, therefore, expect to
be sent for in the course of a few days, and would
do as well to stop silly assertions that we were all
free native negroes. Ben refused to take the
money. " You better keep your ' white music ' (a

Houssa name for silver trinkets), and lay one piece on top of another to buy yourself, as I did myself." The possibility of buying my liberty had never before crossed my mind, but then I seized upon that dim and distant hope, and carried it to my comrades as a very possible and comforting prospect. It did not help much to break to them the intelligence that we were really found out, and would soon be on the march back to the plantation. They were in despair, and nothing seemed to relieve them so much as my standing up with them to "curse" our captors. Each of them put his right hand on my breast or shoulder to *strengthen the spell*—as I cursed. Then I "cursed" the Maroons for an hour, in tolerably bad but very energetic Arabic. Nothing could be more ridiculous than the incoherent torrent of disjointed and meaningless texts and adjurations that I poured out on the heads of our captors, but we all believed those fellows would be terribly the worse for it. I certainly ought to have felt considerably relieved after discharging such a load of frothy nonsense.

I mentioned confidentially to black Ben what we had done, when he inquired, next morning, what we were palavering about so late at night. He

was dreadfully shocked, and begged me to take
back the curses. I refused to entertain the idea.
He offered to bribe me with the bottle of rum I
had wanted him to buy. I was inexorable. He
finally limited himself to a petition in favor of one
of the Maroons, who was a friend and relation of his
own. Ben had been kind and friendly to me, and
I relented in behalf of his friend. We secretly retired to his own room, and, both of us kneeling
there, with my hands firmly clasped in his, I fervently repeated the five daily prayers in a certain way, declaring that it was done in the name
of the said Maroon, to save him from being given
over to the curses due his sins. This done, we rose
and went out doors in the perfect and serene conviction of the efficacy of our highly meritorious action. Ben was profuse in his admiration and gratitude. He presented me with the pouch I was
about finishing, and another small one for a purse,
in which he put a new English sixpence for *luck*,
and as a sign of that future pile of "white music"
which was to achieve my liberty.

Such was our superstitious weakness, and equally weak would it be to record it, did it not serve
to explain that any instruction, even such narrow

teachings as my African godfather had to bestow, carries in it some germ of power.

On the eleventh day of our stay at the work-house, my friend Pompey arrived from the plantation. The Custos then wrote another letter, for one had already been sent by mail, asking mercy for all of us, but most particularly craving a full forgiveness for me. I happened to hear that kind letter read years afterward. The good gentleman was then laid in his final rest, but my heart blessed his memory forever.

Pompey had with him another negro, named George, a resolute and powerful fellow, but not remarkably quick-witted. Still, between them they were a quite sufficient guard for our party in their fetters.

Some free negroes were about the work-house door to see us start, and they showed their unworthy natures by shouting and laughing at us as we marched out chained together. Ben had reported that I was born free, and the son of a king in my own country, and for this they were hardest of all on me, snapping their fingers to remind me of the whip, and wishing my "black kingship a pleasant walk back to the *white* king's trash-house."

I was glad to see the Custos ride up, for the sound of his horse's feet silenced the scoffers. He gave a few injunctions to Pompey and George about looking well to us on the road, and was particularly kind to me. He gave me a dollar at parting, and exacted a promise from Pompey that he would not ill-use me, and that he would signify to my master, by word of mouth, as well as by delivering the letter, that he begged I might be forgiven, as I was but young, and had been free in my own country.

Pompey kept the promise he made to the old Custos. He quizzed me now and then for running away, but he never abused me, and I was even allowed to walk alone, while my comrades were handcuffed two and two together. We went in this order through St. Mary's and St. Ann's, in our way back to Westmoreland. We were regularly indulged at night with a sleep in the hospital of some plantation, and as regularly with each a leg in the stocks. We traveled slowly, for we were worn down with toil and disappointment, and it was a week before we came in sight of the plantation where we had met to take our start on the night of our running away.

This evidence that we were, in very deed, so

near the dreaded scene of renewed slavery, threw
two of my companions into a sort of frenzied despair. Belton, who had hitherto behaved with
manly composure, burst out into loud lamenta-
tions; and then Bryan, with an equally noisy outbreak of execrations, threw himself on the ground,
and refused to proceed another step. Pompey
talked to him, reasoned with him, threatened to
tie him to the mule's tail, and finally beat him
with his riding-whip. This last argument prevailed. He got up, foaming with rage, and walked
fiercely and hastily forward, dragging after him
the negro to whom he was handcuffed. We had
still two or three miles to go before we reached
the plantation, and this distance afforded an ac-
cidental opportunity for another vain and silly
effort for our freedom. George was so tired with
the journey that he tumbled asleep off his mule.
Bryan, snatching his cutlass from the scabbard,
made a cut at him, by which he nearly severed
his nose from his face. Bryan was mad, actually
mad, and foamed at the mouth—but force mastered
him, and at night he found himself in the stocks
at Savannah-la-Mar work-house. All the others
were taken directly to the plantation hospital;

and as we filed slowly past our master, he had a
serious, but not over-harsh, word for every one
of them but me. He scanned me with a close,
but rather mild expression, as he held out his
hand for the letter Pompey brought from the Custos. He read it with a smile, and patiently heard
Pompey's long story through. When it was done,
he sent to call Tatee to the house. She came,
poor soul, and burst into tears at the sight of me,
so woeful and desponding must have been my appearance.

"Ah, Mahmadee," said she, in our Houssa
tongue, "you forsook Tatee—you tried to get
back to Kashna, and left me a slave in Jamaica."

"Forgive me, little mother," I said, humbly;
"I am now sensible that a more foolish attempt
was never made. Tell old master I know I was
a fool. I was born a king's son, and it is hard to
be a slave, but I will be true to him for the
future."

My mistress spoke kindly to me, and *for* me
to her husband, who merely said, gently, in response to her intercession, "Bacchus, I am not angry—I am sorry; but keep heart, my boy, I will
try to lighten your load."

Tatee was impressed with the impossibility of my bettering my condition by running away; and, besides that, she felt a sort of obligation to encourage me in the ways of obedience, on account of our master having bought me, at her request, that we might remain together, though he did not care to have me on his own account. When I was expected back, she incited her husband, the cooper, who was a favorite with his master, to make interest for me, by setting forth my honesty and superior aptitude for service in the Great House. The letter from the liberal and kind-hearted Custos tended to the same point, and the upshot of the matter was, that Pompey was ordered to take me in training for a family servant.

Behold the power of kindness. One blow of the whip, when I was brought back, humbled and heart-sick, but truly disposed to repay a ready forgiveness with the most faithful obedience, would have destroyed my good intentions. I repeat, that one blow of the whip, at the crisis of my return to Orange Grove, would have changed an honest, willing boy into the crafty, deceitful time-server which slavery makes of most of my race.

The mild tones of my master, the gentle consideration of my mistress, who ordered Pompey to take me to the kitchen and see that the servants treated me well, the tearful welcome of poor Tatee, and the winning words of a lovely child, melted me into grateful affection, and molded me into a really attached and almost contented slave.

CHAPTER VII.

MASTER HENRY.

POMPEY conducted me into the kitchen when I was dismissed to his care, and had something to eat produced forthwith. While we were partaking of it a beautiful child, with lovely flowing hair, bounded in, and, putting both of its small white hands on my great swarthy paw, demanded my name.

"Mahmadee, my beautiful young master," I answered.

"His name is Bacchus, Massa Henry," said Pompey.

"Which is it?" the child asked, shaking back his curls and gazing in my face.

"Mahmadee was my name when I was free and in my own country, but since I am a slave I am called Bacchus," I answered, in such English as I could muster.

6*

"Mahmadee is a pretty name. I shall call you Mahmadee," said the charming boy, still leaning with his hands upon me. "Don't you like to be called Mahmadee?"

"I love it better than any other name, because it is my own," I replied; and bending over, with a sudden impulse, I imprinted a fervent kiss on each of those little milk-white hands.

"Why, Mahmadee, you have straight hair," the child exclaimed, in accents of surprise, as my bent head caught his eye.

"It is because my father was a king and a descendant of the Prophet," I explained, in grave sincerity, for so Hadji Ali, Fatma, and others, had taught me to believe, in Kashna.

"Oh, I have story-books about a fairy king. You shall read them. Was your father a fairy king?" warmly inquired Master Henry.

I did not know what a fairy king was. I had never heard the name before, so I replied that I could not tell, but that my father was king of Kashna.

"Well, you shall read all about it in my story-books, Mahmadee. I will give you one to-morrow."

"I wish I could read your books, my young master, but I have never learned how."

"Well, you shall learn; but come now and take me to walk," said the child, with pretty willfulness, starting off to the door.

Pompey directed me to do as Master Henry desired, and, only too glad to follow this captivating vision, I caught up my hat and went whither he pleased. We met Tatee not far from the door, and she briefly informed me that it was a little visitor whom the young ladies had lately brought with them from Montigo Bay, and made the pet and the life of the house.

I felt the fatigue of the late trip, and with any other companion than this gay young prattler, who led me a bewildering chase all round the lawn and up and down the garden, I would have been glad of the release afforded me by the dinner-bell, when it called him away, but I parted with him reluctantly. I did not expect to have the pleasure of attending him so intimately again, and kissed his hands over and over in a sort of leave-taking, as one of the women appeared to repeat the summons to dinner.

The family dined about the time their slaves

had their supper; and after Master Henry vanished into the house I loitered toward the hospital, not quite assured whether or no I was to be locked up at night with my fellow-runaways. There was nothing of the kind to fear. My pardon was free and absolute; and, so far from being hindered, I was encouraged by Pompey to visit and talk with them in the evening, when they returned from their work to their sleeping quarters. They escaped almost as well as myself. They were locked up in the hospital at night for a month, and after that all three were allowed to take wives and settle down in their old places. They all soon became as able and contented hands as there were on the estate.

Bryan was kept at hard labor in chains at Savannah-la-Mar about the same length of time, as much for his violent assault on George as for his leading part in the runaway scrape. But George was forgiving, and the overseer stood his friend, for he was, in fact, an active, serviceable fellow. One fine Saturday evening, when all the other Africans were singing and dancing before the cooper's cabin, who should step into the ring but George and Bryan, as fine and friendly together as a pair of turtle-doves. In the Easter holidays Bryan chose a young sister of George's for his wife, and they had their provision-lots together. When I finally left the plantation, Bryan and George were both drivers, that is, each of them had a working-gang of field-hands under his direction.

As my old comrades subsided into steady field-hands and I into a trusted house-servant, the distance widened between us, and, with our new occupations, we all thought and talked less of our native land.

Meanwhile we saw no more of Cudjoe's *duppy*, and it remained a doubt with us whether we had been deceived, or whether it was really his ghost, which had threatened and forewarned us of our disgrace. The circumstance of his appearance preyed a long while on my mind, and we all thought our discomfiture a judgment on us for shedding the blood of one who had entertained us with food, though evidently a thief and a rogue, who had first robbed, and then would probably have betrayed us to the Maroons, had we given him an opportunity.

But I love best to speak of Master Henry. The morning after our return to the plantation, Pompey roused me to feed the poultry, and help him groom the carriage-horses. This he told me would be my regular duty every morning, and it suited me exactly, for I am naturally fond of animals. I was in the midst of a small army of fowls, ducks, and turkeys, and was stooping down to search into the ailment of a lame chicken, when Master Henry came behind and sprang upon my back: clasping his arms about my neck, he bade me play horse for him. Pleased to feel his arms about me, I humored his playful caprice, and went curveting to the house, he digging his little naked feet into my side, in imitation of spurring, and I pretending to shy and leap, and both of us laughing in high glee. I held my head so low, that I did not see my mistress and almost ran against her, as I went to deposit my burden on the back piazza. I started back in confusion, and, scarcely knowing what I did, I made my apology and reverence in the best style of Houssa. The lady only smiled in her own gentle way, and said, "Master Henry has fallen in love with you, Mahmadee, and you must pay particular attention to him." She then led the laughing child into the house to be dressed, for he had run out in his night-clothes on hearing my voice and the flutter of the poultry on the lawn.

I went back to my work brim-full of contentment. I was to attend to this charming Master Henry, "who had fallen in love with me" (heaven knows it was fervently reciprocated), and my mistress called me by my own name of Mahmadee. I fancy a vain young officer, newly promoted, must have some such sentiments of vastly increased self-importance as I did when I flourished about the carriage-horses that forenoon. It was a step—a vast step—forward for me, but yesterday a returned runaway, to be chosen for the particular attendant of that darling boy. He was my pride and joy, and he became winningly attached to me. He would be out betimes in the morning, aiding—or, we both fancied he did, which was the same thing—to feed the poultry. When he had gone through his morning lessons, I would have done with the horses, and be quite ready to take him before me on one of them, for a ride round the park.

I was quite at home in the cavalry department, as my old bushreen master had been a sort of horse-dealer in Africa, and I took a pride in presenting my Christian massa with his horses in the cleanest

and handsomest condition. So far from stealing
their corn, as was a common practice among negro servants, I felt rather an inclination to steal the
corn to give them. But there was no need of that,
for my master was a liberal provider; and the old
planter, seeing that I kept his beasts in beautiful
condition, allowed me to take out Master Henry
as often as we pleased, which was nearly every
morning, after his French lesson was over.

It was a month or two before either of the
young ladies noticed me particularly, and when
they did, it was owing to Master Henry's playful
pranks. After the horses were attended to, it
was my duty to have on a clean frock, and wait
in the hall, attend the bell, and be at hand if
wanted for a message. Above all, it was my
welcome duty to keep a vigilant eye on the restless little Master Henry. Lighter work, kinder
treatment, and a better will to deserve it, was
never the lot of a slave. Little Henry was pleased
to amuse himself teaching me to read. The young
ladies had enjoyed the advantage of a French
teacher; and believing that the younger it is acquired the better, they insisted on their pet repeating over to one of them a short lesson every

day, until it was committed to memory. I was frequently present at these lessons, and invariably had them by heart before Henry had half mastered them. For practice, and to conceal what they chose to say to each other from vulgar ears, they used the French language between themselves almost continually. I thus picked up a large, but rather promiscuous, assortment of French words, which I would parade off in the kitchen, to the unbounded envy and admiration of the other servants, and often without the smallest idea of their meaning. Nevertheless, I did learn my letters, and that rapidly. Henry had teased his cousins to get him a new slate, that he might be able to give me his old one; and we used to set in the cool piazza and "play writing," while the rest of the family were taking their noon siesta. We often made English and Arabic letters by the hour. I was intensely anxious to acquire *learning*. It almost seemed to me that I should grow white in acquiring the white man's knowledge. The young ladies had ruled lines on Henry's slate with a nail, and used to write a word or two between them every day, as a copy—more for his amusement than for serious practice. Yet we both "played writing" with such a will, that our progress became a subject of comment and surprise in my own desire to learn, I persuaded Master Henry to "play reading and writing" with me nearly every noontide.

The Great House, as the planter's own mansion is universally styled in Jamaica, to distinguish it from the village of other buildings belonging to the estate, was very spacious, with ample room for a large family, but it was all of one story only. It had wide piazzas, and deep wings for baths and bed-chambers, with sashed doors opening upon a green secluded space, ornamented with choice flowers. Among them a great variety of roses, which were never out of bloom the year round. This January I particularly remember how their fragrance filled the air when I played horse to Master Henry, and brought him through this place to the rear door of the hall. Having now become familiar with this side of the Great House, I was often employed a short time in the early morning pulling up and carrying away the weeds. One morning, about sunrise, I had filled a basket in this way, and was stooping to carry it off, when down over head, neck, and shoulders, came a heavy dash of cold water, closely followed by a triumphant laugh from Master Henry. I put both hands before my face and pretended to sob, eying, through my fingers, the young rogue the while, who stood at the window, balancing on the ledge the pitcher which he had just emptied over me. Observing that I continued to sob more bitterly, instead of echoing his merry laugh, his beautiful face clouded with regret, and I saw him leave the window, in order to come through the door and console me. I darted for the basket, intending to run round the corner of the wing and give him a nice chase to catch me. As my hand touched the basket, I saw something shining behind it, on the freshly weeded ground, which I caught up as I fled. Henry soon overtook me, of course, and then we examined my prize.

"It is a guinea, Mahmadee," said Henry, at last. "It is a gold guinea, but it is older than old Nancy." Nancy was a cross, decrepit old black nurse, the terror of all the picaninnies, and such a dried-up mummy, that Henry thought the world and she must have been babies together. Rachel, a bright young mulatto, and the petted maid of Miss Lucy, joined us while we were handling and depreciating the gold piece, and she advised me to hide it and say nothing about it. "Massa Henry will never tell of his Mahmadee, and we can buy plenty of lovely things with a gold guinea," she said, coaxingly.

"No, I will take it to the mistress," said I, stoutly; for, young negro and ignorant boy as I was, I had no instinct for stealing. A feeling that revolted from making my sweet young Master Henry a partner in any sly trick was, perhaps, an additional motive. Besides that, in our retired situation, where there was nothing to buy, and every necessary freely provided, I had not learned the value of money. Any way, I felt no special temptation to keep it, and therefore there was no special merit in my dispatching the flattened and battered coin forthwith to the Great House, by the hands of little Harry. He came flying back to say, "Uncle Davis wants to see you directly, Mahmadee." I followed him, with some trepidation, into the parlor, where I found both the young ladies standing by their father, and all of them in quite a state of excitement over the guinea.

It was not a guinea, after all, but an ancient and very rare Italian coin, worth, as Miss Lucy remarked with great animation, "a purseful of new guineas to those who understood its scarcity and value." I believe its scarcity is the main part of its value, for there was no beauty to admire in it. It had been missing a long time, under peculiar circumstances. Miss Lucy had been exhibiting it one day to a young lady friend, and laid it down with her handkerchief on the dressing-table, and left it there. That much she remembered; and when she was summoned to lunch, shortly after, she recollected it, and sent Rachel to bring it to her. Rachel brought the handkerchief, but could not find the money. Search was vainly made for the lost treasure—it was nowhere to be found. Mr. Davis suspected Rachel of having secreted it, and Rachel's young mistress suspected the other servants generally, but would listen to no imputation on her maid, and so the matter slipped by, until I had the extreme good fortune to find it. I have a right to say extreme good fortune, for it was a lucky finding for me. My master had called me in to reward me liberally for restoring the much-valued curiosity, and he now put it to my own choice, whether it should be a handsome Sunday suit, or what else. Money he was not disposed to pût in my hands; but money's worth, to the value of a gold guinea, I should have, in any shape, at my own selection. I was so overcome with this sudden weight of riches, that I could do nothing but stammer out thanks upon thanks. I could not recollect a single wish at the critical moment when it might be had for the asking. Miss Lucy came to my aid.

"Take time to think about it, Mahmadee," she said, pleasantly. "Consider well what you would like best, and when you have made up your mind, let me know."

"I can tell you, Cousin Lucy," broke in Master Henry. "Mahmadee wants copy-books and an ink-stand. He told me so last night."

The child had touched the true spring, though I had failed to hit it. I now caught at it eagerly.

"If master pleases, I would like to write letters."

"But you cannot read yet. You don't even know your alphabet, I fancy," Mr. Davis good-humoredly replied; "unless it be such letters as you scrawl upon your slate."

"Yes, indeed, papa, Mahmadee begins to spell short words, and even tries to read. You ought

to hear him at his lessons with Cousin Henry,' rejoined Miss Lucy, archly smiling at the thought.

"Yes, Uncle Davis, Mahmadee is a very attentive scholar," chimed in little Henry, in the words
so often applied to himself, without, perhaps, so
exactly deserving the praise.

"So be it, then. Mahmadee (since you are all
so bent on keeping to the boy's Mahometan name)
shall be taught reading and writing. We will
make him a scribe and a Christian, but never a
Pharisee, I hope;" and with these words he ended
the conference.

Rachel was very glad I had not taken her advice to keep the gold piece for *us*—which, being
interpreted into English, meant for the purchase of
finery for herself—since it was such a precious concern to her young mistress. She had probably
flirted it out of the window herself in taking up
Miss Lucy's handkerchief; for, as she was a giddy
creature, and declared she had never seen it in her
life before—to notice it—she had no cause to be on
her guard. The only wonder is, that it was never
searched for on the outside—for the dressing-table
stood close beside the window—instead of rushing

so hastily to the conclusion that it *must* be stolen by some one or other of the negro servants.

It was a small affair to others, but not so to me, for I was immediately sent to an evening-school kept for free blacks, about a mile down the road, by a famous mulatto teacher and preacher. Famous, I beg to be understood, among the negroes, and not unacceptable to the planters round about him for his useful Sunday lectures to their slaves. He was a curious genius, with a nose and upper face in amusing caricature of a likeness of William Pitt, which hung, in company with King George the Third, in the Orange Grove dining-room.

This brown genius had a decided knack for teaching, and I caught with avidity at the opportunity of acquiring knowledge, for I had often thought that if I had been a scholar, I could have imposed on all my masters and jailers, tyrants, and oppressors. I would have forged a *pass*, and so put off the illiterate Maroons, whose very memory I abhorred. I was determined to render myself capable of over-reaching, on any future occasion, these bloodhounds! They had acquired their freedom by the means we had attempted, and then se-

cured their vile grog-money supply, by waging war
on all who should follow their example.

What with the evening-school and the opportunities I enjoyed with Master Henry, who would
have me along when he was at his own lessons, I
learned to read very speedily. I had been a tolerably apt scholar in Africa, and although I had never
seen an Arabic character, except those I traced myself, since I left my country, the early, constant,
and careful cultivation my mind had received from
the faithful Hadji Ali, had prepared me to learn
with facility. I have also, from my youth upward,
been blessed with a retentive memory. My mulatto master loved to load me with lessons to learn
by heart. He invariably took them from the Bible,
and I *fagged* through a great many chapters of it,
but I preferred story books—Robinson Crusoe, Pe-
ter Wilkins, the Arabian Nights, and Fairy Tales.
I found a translation of the Koran in my master's
library, and I read that from time to time, but I
confess, with some shame, I thought it very prosy,
and very inferior, in general, to the Old Testament,
but, all the same, I secretly plumed myself on my
constancy to the true faith, and seldom missed saying my five prayers in Arabic, in the course of the

7

day or night. I considered this a sacred obligation, •
and entertained a vague fear that the reproving
spirit of Hadji Ali would appear to me if I neglected it.

My mistress did not urge me any more to become a Christian, neither did the young ladies lay
any stress upon it, though they interested themselves most kindly in my general improvement.
Miss Lucy did not disdain to set me copies, and
even made me a present of a blank-book, and
showed me how to keep a journal as she had been
taught to do by her own instructors, in order to form
correct habits of spelling and composition. Miss
Emma, the youngest sister, wrote me out a multi-
plication-table, which I learned in two days. I had
a particular turn for calculation, which some of the
learned Christians in England assured me, in after
years, was the consequence of my brain's configura-
tion. I became an adept in arithmetic, and I wrote,
in a twelvemonth, a very creditable hand, so that
my master employed me as a scribe, and made me
also keep the house accounts.

I had, by this time, learned to read with fluency,
though I had rather too closely imitated the twang
of my pig-nosed preceptor, whose assistant I became

on Sundays, in the profound science of the alphabet. I had also the task of teaching his scholars, free children of color, to sing psalms, but I had the help of an old guitar, given to me by Miss Lucy for this purpose, and which she kindly taught me to tune. This instrument introduced me to the violin, on which, in after years, I acquired considerable power. I even studied thorough bass, and found out the art of tuning piano-fortes, as well as playing on them, after a fashion, in succeeding years.

During these pursuits, my tutor never ceased dinging into my ears his arguments about my conversion, yet I must frankly declare that every repetition of them drove me farther from the haven to which he would have urged me. He was proud of heart, and mean of understanding, a narrow-minded bigot, and, as I unfortunately discovered, not too pure of life. I could not bring myself to believe in the lectures of a man, who, if not a set hypocrite, was, at least, a contemptibly weak sinner.

Long before I had reached this point of my life, a heavy misfortune had fallen upon me. A misfortune that dressed my master's family in deepest mourning. Henry, the gay darling whose merry, loving ways was the delight of all hearts, was sud-

denly taken from us. It was not long after the
Easter holidays, a period of revelry, next to the
Christmas week, for the whites, and a time for frolic
and feasting among the slaves, when some friends
of the family came to Orange Grove, and persuaded
the young ladies to return with them for a week's
visit, and take little Harry along. My mistress almost insisted that her "young chatter-box," as she
fondly called him, should remain with her, as the
house would be too lonesome, if all the children went
away at once. Henry had heard of the proposed
trip, however, and wanted to have a carriage-ride
with his cousins, so he pouted up his rosy lips, and
coaxed and kissed a consent out of his "dear, sweet
Aunty Davis," and was gayly carried off by the rest
of them. I was so used to him and his lively, laughing little ways, that I felt as if the whole plantation
and all the people in it drove away in that carriage.
It left me more spare time to study, but I felt so
lost without him, that I could not settle myself con-
tentedly to any thing like a lesson, though I at·
tended the evening school as usual.

To pass away the time more lightly, and to have
a little present ready to welcome his return, I employed myself in weaving a Medinet pouch, similar

to the one I had been helped to by Ben of the work-house, but of a size suitable for Henry's childish figure. My mistress, seeing me working at it so zealously every odd minute, inquired at last who it was for, and, when I told her, she smiled and said, "I guessed as much," and then added, pleasantly, "The carriage is to go for them to Cross Roads Lodge on Saturday, in time to be home to dinner, and you may ride over on the box with the coachman."

"If mistress would allow me to ride the pony, Master Henry would be pleased to have it part of the way," I ventured to suggest, for Henry had become quite a little horseman under my tuition, and loved nothing better than a ride on this gentle-paced animal, who was rightly named Easy. Mrs. Davis readily consented, and Easy and I were at Cross Roads Lodge an hour before the appointed time. It was a place rarely occupied by its owners, who lived at a larger and more convenient mansion several miles further on; but it had been arranged that they were to spend a few weeks at the Lodge, and from thence interchange a round of festivities with Orange Grove and the neighboring plantations.

In the excess of my blind love I felt a pang of disappointment that the lively darling, who at home would hardly stay a whole hour away from me by day or night, had so forgotten me in a single week, that, instead of bounding out to meet me, as I had fondly promised myself he would the moment the carriage drew up, he neither made his appearance nor sent for me to come to him. Miss Lucy leaned from the window and asked if all were well at home, and then retired without adding a word. After a while a servant of the house said, from the door, "Master Henry wants his own boy Mahmadee." I flew up the stairs, but as I stepped into the parlor, I saw Henry reclining on the arm of a sofa with a pillow under his head. A pale, slender gentleman was leaning over him, and Miss Lucy was sitting beside him holding his hand. He withdrew it and held it out to me.

"I want to go home to Aunty Davis, Mahmadee. I am sick." He spoke in his natural tone, almost, but his face was very red and his beautiful eyes were heavy.

"The carriage is at the door," I said, looking at Miss Lucy for orders. She glanced from little Henry to the tall gentleman.

"You will attend your young mistresses in their carriage, and I will take Master Henry home in mine," said the gentleman, without waiting for her answer.

"I want Mahmadee to go with me," said little Henry, sitting upright, in his sweet, earnest way. "Can't Mahmadee come with me, Cousin Lucy? Can't he, Uncle Holgrave?"

"Certainly, my dear boy, if you wish it. You will allow Mahmadee a place by your man, Mr. Holgrave?" turning to the gentleman, who bowed assent.

Little Henry entreated to go at once. He rose from the sofa and made a step or two, but staggered, and I caught him in my arms.

"My head aches, Mahmadee," he murmured, and dropped it on my shoulder.

I bore him to the carriage, and supported him in my arms all the way home. It was a sad arrival to Mrs. Davis, who loved him so well, and was unprepared to meet him in a burning fever. I carried him to his bed, and was never far from it until he left it for the last time. The dear boy was spared much suffering, though the fever was so rapid that in one short week he was laid in his holy

rest in the family grave-yard.   Every thing that
love and care, wealth and skill could do, was done
for that darling child.   He wandered a little sometimes, but he, knew me always, and knew me to
the last.   He departed just as the sun was setting
on the seventh day.   Only a few minutes before he
said, with a sweet, a heavenly smile,

"Don't cry for me, dear Aunty Davis.   Mah—
ma—dee—"   The name melted softly from his
parted lips, and with it his innocent spirit rose to
heaven.

I had suppressed my grief to wait upon him
while there was life and hope, and even after his
spirit had left the form, while his beautiful face lay
calm and uncovered, my pent-up grief was still,
though my heart was bursting.   But when he was
laid in that deep bed, and the black earth was
filled over my loving angel, I lost all self-control.
I cared not for person or place.   I thought—I
could think—only of this: "I shall never, never see
my sweet, my good, my kind little Henry again."
I was really insane, I think, the night after the
funeral, for I stole out to his fresh grave and cried
myself asleep upon it.   The plantation-bell awoke
me at six in the morning.   I arose and dragged my

heavy heart and aching limbs to the stable, for a slave must not neglect his duties because his heart is breaking. Ned, Mr. Holgrave's own servant, reached there as soon as I did. He had orders from his master to relieve me that morning from my stable-work. I went back to the grave-yard and gave way to a fresh burst of tears. Some one touched me gently, and said, mildly, "Will you assist me to plant a white rose at little Henry's feet?" It was Mr. Holgrave. We selected and planted the white rose and a fragrant jessamine, with many other flowers, about that sacred bit of earth. I wept as I worked, but the labor of love consoled me. I went the next morning to water the plants, and, while thus engaged, I was told that I was to go home with Mr. Holgrave, and his man Ned was to remain at Orange Grove. Ned was to take charge of the stables, and I was to fill his place by going to Savannah-la-Mar, for a month or two, as Mr. Holgrave's personal attendant. It was at first much the same to me whether I went or stayed, but in a few days I became truly grateful for the change of place.

7*

CHAPTER VIII.

NEW SCENES.

MR. HOLGRAVE was little Henry's guardian, and he was worthy of such a precious trust. I reverenced him, and my service with him made another distinct era in my life. He was an educated Hadji Ali. I write it with reverential love, with profound respect, with all due regard to his high position as a white gentleman in universal esteem. Still, I deem my dear old tutor one in a thousand among even the chosen of the good, and I cannot feel that I am wanting to the memory of the just, excellent, and observing Mr. Holgrave, in saying that my African benefactor was, in his own country and condition, eminent for the same virtues that distinguished the Jamaica gentleman. They both loved to do charitable deeds, both were faithful students, both had inveterate habits of domestic independence, they were both apart from and above the level of the people around them, and, above all,

both—each in his own degree—were true friends
to me. Even the situation of their dwellings had
a kind of resemblance, only that ours in Africa, the
house of a rich priest, and an extensive slave-trader,
had no equal in Kashna, except the king's house in
the day of Abdalla, my father; while that of Mr.
Holgrave was poor and inconvenient for a gentleman of his standing. His books and his personal
quiet were Mr. Holgrave's luxuries, and those he
enjoyed completely, if any man ever did.

He lived in a small wooden house, near Savannah-la-Mar, built upon stone buttresses, with some
cocoa-nut trees in front, and a garden behind. It
was never lonely, and, among others, we had abundance of visitors of color. My master had some
skill in medicine, which, perhaps, was one great
attraction; but the pleasure of his company and
conversation was the chief inducement, I believe,
for he was a most especial favorite with these simple people. They frequently brought him presents
of fruit, and would come with their baskets at other
times, as if to offer their vegetables for sale, but
they rarely left without begging "a lilly drop of
medicine." He put in plenty of sugar with wine or
spirits, in which the peel of the bitter orange had

been steeped (a simple and unrivaled tonic by the way), and other things which could do no harm, and might do good.   He kept bottles of these preparations on hand for distribution.   I had to measure out doses from these bottles almost every day, and soon became interested in their preparation.   I observed Mr. Holgrave and his very clever, but marvelously ugly black cook, were exceedingly careful to follow the recipes, and that inspired me with faith.   Mrs. Bates (we black slaves pique ourselves on our politeness, and always address each other by suitable titles), Mrs. Bates then, the Congo cook, knew these pet recipes practically by heart, and was astonished beyond measure, when I came out one day to assist her, paper in hand, and read off—as only a conceited puppy could read—the directions from Mr. Holgrave's written notes.

"Hi! you brack niggar—read doctor larnin?" she exclaimed.   "Whar you come from?   You born so?"

In place of enlightening cook as to whether I was born a reader, I went, with increased magnificence, into some such important matter as "strain the water and keep the vessel closely covered," and wound up grandly by expressing a patronizing con-

fidence in the superior efficacy of the prescriptions.
I declared them so excellent, that I should write
out copies for my own use. The old woman was
completely subdued.

"Mr. Mahmadee" (hitherto, being but a mere
boy, she had disdained to Mister me), "oh, Mr.
Mahmadee, make a paper for L Much pain here,"
laying her hand on her chest. "Give I paper for
cure him."

I was trying to impress upon her the folly and
inefficacy of this negro superstition of applying the
paper outside, when, in the loftiest flight of ex-
patiation, I happened to turn toward the door,
and there, to my confusion, I saw, scarce two feet
out of it, Mr. Holgrave. In his usual attitude,
with one hand in his coat breast, he stood with
an air of composed attention; and not even when
I collapsed, in silent confusion, did he wither me
with so much as a smile of contempt.

"I am not sure but the prescription might do
cook some good, *since she desires it so much*," he
said gravely, and, without a moment's hesitation,
entering on the subject at the point where the discovery of his presence had killed it, like a bird shot
on the wing. "She might try it written on clean,

thick paper, *well oiled, and laid between folds of old flannel* before it is applied to the chest." I was too abashed to reply. "Take care to rub the flesh well · night and morning, cook," he added, turning his serious face toward the old woman, who stood bobbing at him a succession of grateful courtesies at every other word. "I trust the faith, the liniment, and the friction will help do her good, Mahmadee, and the paper can do her no harm," said Mr. Holgrave, as he walked back to his arm-chair in the piazza.

I copied some Latin formula or other, in a large, straggling hand—I could do no better then—and cooky applied it as directed, with the most brilliant results. She considered her cure but little short of miraculous. She did not stay cured, however; and about the time Mr. Holgrave and I went back to Orange Grove, she had added some Obeah charm to our Latin prescription, and thought their united forces were "killin' de pains fast." · I had begged him to favor me with something in Latin to copy for the cook. I thought it would be · more impressive—from being more unintelligible—and also less likely to lose its magic powers by the chance possibility of reaching profane eyes. Mr.

Holgrave furnished me with paper to stitch into a kind of book, and I nearly filled it up with useful selections, which he singled out for me.

But, to my taste, his gift of gifts was a book of ballads. It was an old edition of songs and ballads of the Robin Hood and Chevy Chace order. That book taught me to find a meaning in the words I read. I learned Chevy Chace almost before I slept. A ballad of Robin Hood, in which he dilates on the charms of the wild wood, Mr. Holgrave taught me to declaim in character, for the amusement of his friends. Fancy a *black* Robin Hood, declaring, "in kirtle green, with bended bow," that "England's king was less the lord of his forest dales and antlered deer, than the bold outlaw and his merry men." Yet, had it occurred to us—which I think it never did—Jamaica even then possessed a startling parallel to the merry men of Sherwood, in the lawless and defiant Maroons, who so long held the forest hills of the island, in spite of the most strenuous efforts of many successive governors. Was this black Robin Hood, with his wild boast, and woodland garb, one of Mr. Holgrave's keen, though quiet, ironies? It only now occurs to me that it is very possible it *had* an arrow in it.

At all events, it was a serious and downright fact that Mr. Holgrave took great pleasure in my improvement. He never spoke of my faith; he did not read the Bible with me, nor explain it; he always referred me to Mr. Wodenlone, and told me to open my ears to his words on Sundays, and open my mouth and thank God, every night of my life, for my youth, health, and opportunities. However, Mr. Holgrave talked to me freely on all other subjects. He showed me how the world was round, and that the stars might be worlds. He also taught me the use of maps, and explained to me many of the discoveries which have been made in the mysteries of nature. I felt the most excessive gratitude to Mr. Holgrave, and to my master and his family also, for the instructions I had received from them. I forgot to dream of my liberty, nor did any of these good people ever even mention the subject to me. I did my work as usual, waited at table, and attended to the horses. I also kept a journal of all occurrences of any moment, as Miss Lucy had recommended me to do, though I never could revert to the first five pages without a swelling heart, for they were taken up almost entirely with what

"Master Henry said," and what "Master Henry and I" did with our slates and the horses.

I have that old journal to this day, and it is only since I began these feeble recollections, that, having turned to it to seek some dates I needed, I noted the mile-stones of my progressive steps. Then I saw tho pale traces of the tear-marks where I had kissed the scrawls that darling boy made, by way, as he said, of helping me "write journal." It was, perhaps, the very last time his little hand held pen or pencil. I had barely reached the point of proficiency which induced Miss Lucy to propose my keeping a kind of journal, and this was the book she gave me for the purpose a little before they went on that fatal, fatal visit.

Mr. Holgrave directed me—as a point of my regular duty—to write down on a slate every evening the occupations of the day, and copy it at noon in my journal.

"I beg pardon, sir," I said to him one day, when he called for the book, and found nothing had been recorded for nearly a week, "I am sorry to appear so lazy, but there has been nothing to write about."

"Nonsense, Mahmadee! You go to market,

you exercise the horses every day, and you do a great deal in the way of medical prescriptions. Use your eyes, my boy, and you will see enough every day to fill a book. I only insist on four or five lines, but those must be regularly served up—neat and clean, mind you—every day, while you are with me. See that you do not disappoint me."

By this kind discipline I was instructed, and meanwhile I was led, by constant occupation, to overcome my disposition to brood over the loss of little Henry. Oh how I dreaded the time when I should have to leave Mr. Holgrave!

There were two circumstances connected with this visit to Savannah-la-Mar which in themselves would have been sufficient to render it of lasting interest. The first dated from the night of our arrival at the margin of the sea. We reached the house of an old college friend of Mr. Holgrave's about dark, and there we supped and stayed all night. I cannot say *slept*, for sleeping was out of the question. Mr. Holgrave had remained up chatting with his friend rather later than was usual with him, and he had not much more than put out his candle, and I, drowsily, stretched my limbs for repose, when the most horrible clatter startled me.

I listened in breathless suspense. ' It sounded to me
as if ten thousand work-house prisoners were striking off their fetters by pounding them with stones,
as I saw Bryan vainly attempt with his, after our
capture by the Maroons. Then hurried voices were
heard, as if the guards had discovered the purpose,
and were interfering to prevent it. The din was
bewildering, and I ventured to speak to Mr. Holgrave through the open door, and ask him what
the noise meant. He replied by telling me to strike
a light. The flint and steel lay on the table near
him, and as I stepped toward it I perceived him,
half dressed, standing upright on his bed. Just
then lights flashed up through the window on his
face, and I turned my anxious · looks to him for
succor. The clattering din continued, increased,
came nearer, but there was no change in his calm,
grave face. I believe nothing could drive that man
into a show of fear any more than a show of violent
temper. How I managed to strike a light, Heaven
only knows, for I scarcely moved my eyes from Mr.
Holgrave's, and they were as steadily fixed on mine.
Neither was a light necessary in that bed-room, for
the red glare of torches from the outside illuminated
it in every corner with wavering flashes, as if keep-

ing time with the frightful, never-ceasing din. Yet
I did, somehow, get a candle alight, and held it,
with an unsteady hand, I fear, toward Mr. Holgrave.

"Set it on the washstand, Mahmadee," said he,
speaking in the calmest manner, and for the first
time since the clamor began. "If they get in here,
you had better take to the dressing-table."

"Who are they, sir?—the Maroons?"

"The Maroons?" And he almost smiled. "No,
my poor Mahmadee. The Maroons would hardly
venture to take this place by storm, as the crabs
are doing."

"The *crabs*, sir?" I felt slightly reassured by
that calm tone and half smile, but not quite, for the
confusion outside had, if any thing, become more
bewildering.

"Certainly, all this fuss is about crabs, and
nothing but crabs. Have you never heard of the
black crabs of Jamaica? They are a great luxury;
one of the choicest of the gifts of Nature to men
who live for eating. You shall have a surfeit of
them to-morrow, I can promise you that," said Mr.
Holgrave, sitting down on the bed.

"I hope, sir, I shall find them more agreeable

after they are cooked than I do now," I answered, very cheerfully. My courage had come home again upon this explanation. The clamor, though equally loud and continued, did not strike upon the ear with such a terrible jar when I understood that it was only made by innocent, eatable crabs, and the people who were catching them. The irruption had burst suddenly upon that locality in the form of a compact mass of crabs, a black but moving carpet, rising and spreading back from the beach over every thing in its path for a mile. We were in a one-story house, and our chamber looked toward the sea. They have been known to climb a house-wall in solid phalanx, search a path through and over the apartments in their direct line, and drive the inmates to take refuge on the highest pieces of furniture until they had passed. The only harm they do, is to pinch somewhat sharply any thing that is caught within their claws.

Mr. Holgrave heard the invading army clattering among the out-buildings, and thought they might get into the house, but he said he was principally interested in noting my unqualified bewilderment.

"But," said he, finally, "you are no coward,

Mahmadee. It is a blessing to have steady nerves, and I wish you joy of yours."

I was not so sure of my courage; but I thanked him for his kind opinion, and asked permission to go out and have a share in the stir of the night. It was readily granted, and I was soon in the midst of it. The road was lit up with scores, nay, hundreds of torches, in the hands of the "crabbers." Women and children, as well as men, were swarming, with bags and baskets, along the outskirts of the steady column, gathering up the stragglers. But the main body moved on, in unbroken compactness, neither hastening nor slackening its course, nothing impeding its progress, nothing diverting myriads from their line. When I went out they were moving in a close black sheet over a long, temporary shed in the corner of the yard, and the low-roofed stable adjoining it, and thence straight along to the end of the back piazza, and, beyond it, into the road again. I had left the house by a side door, and was at once on the fretted and broken edge of this wonderful legion; and, mingling with the excited crowd of hunters, I followed the current up-stream for half a mile, and had not yet reached the sea, nor come to the end of the column.

I came upon something else, however, that startled the crabs entirely out of sight. I had left behind almost the last of a set of mean hovels, that looked as if they were ashamed of themselves, and had straggled away from the town, to get out of the sight of decent people. Passing them, I was picking my way along in search of where the crabs started from the sea, and was thinking of nothing else in the world, when a kind of groan, close in front of me, caused me to lift my eyes from the ground. Plainly before me, perfectly visible in the flickering glare of the not distant torches, a *duppy* —Cudjoe's duppy—was staring me into stone. I was dumb with consternation, but I felt that my senses were not disordered. I knew that it was Cudjoe. He stood leaning on his staff, just as I saw him when he appeared to us runaways at the hut of the drunken watchman, threatening us with the misfortunes that had but too surely overtaken us. He slowly extended his hand, as if about to renew the curse. I threw up both of mine in an agony of deprecation, and recoiled a step in silent dismay.

"What, you no shake hands? Him mighty high for nigga slave, but all same to Cudjoe."

"Is that you yourself, Cudjoe?" I exclaimed, in a revulsion of feeling impossible to describe, when, with the first rough, but hearty and natural, tones of his voice, came the sure faith that it was no ghost, but a living presence of flesh and blood.

Crab-hunting had lost its charms for that night. I only cared to hear what had brought Cudjoe so far from his hut, and how he came to dog our steps that night. The explanation was simple enough, as such marvels generally are when we obtain the clew. The old rascal was a Maroon scout himself, and owned he would have led us into the net the first night after we met him, and so saved us "de trubel to walkee, walkee, tree day, an' do nuffin," but that our obstinate refusal to be guided by him, and the explosion of the powder-horn, had spoiled his game. He went by a short "cross-cut" over the hill to the other hut, not to intercept us, for he was, in fact, surprised to meet us there, but to get something for his hurts, but he could not keep from "cursing" us when we came so conveniently before him. He owned that he put the other Maroons on the track, but, to his loud indignation, the men who captured us refused to share the reward with him. It was to claim some portion of this and some other blood-

money, that he had now taken this long trip. Mr.
Holgrave extracted all this out of the old Maroon in
about ten minutes the next morning, while he was
sipping his chocolate, and, to my inexpressible delight, he assured him that all the money that ever
would be paid on our account had already been
handed over to our Maroon captors. The next
night, the old fellow was out again with the crabbers, and the next night after that, as well. I met
him on both; for from dawn to dark, for three
nights, did the teeming legions swarm up from the
sea, and as regularly lose themselves out of view
when the sun was up. The old sinner caught and
feasted on their delicious flesh, until, with plenty of
that, and the liberal aid of sundry bottles of new
rum, Cudjoe became consoled, and departed in peace
to his own rural shades. The case might have been
slightly different had he accepted mý pressing invitation to visit at Orange Grove the friends he had
entertained up among the cascades of the Agua
Alta.

I made another acquaintance at that time, which
I was fully as much delighted to retain as I was to
lose sight of Cudjoe and his *duppy*—and that is putting a strong case in the way of defining the extent

8

. of my satisfaction. Among the persons of color
who came to see Mr. Holgrave, was a rich quadroon, who lived two or three miles in the country,
on a handsome place of her own. Even the white
ladies of that aristocratic little Savannah-la-Mar esteemed Madam Felix for her charitable character
and amiable manners. She came from St. Domingo
with her husband, an English merchant, long a resi-
dent at Port au Prince, but who was forced to leave
the country during its sanguinary war of races.
He bought this estate and some other property
about there, in which he was much guided and assisted by the judicious advice of Mr. Holgrave, but
he did not live long to enjoy his new home. His
death left Madam Felix a rich widow, with all the
right and title to the property in - the amplest legal
form, but with a drop of gall superadded to her
cup of loneliness. Being tainted, though but in a
minor degree, with the blood of the outcast African, and having been married by a Catholic priest,
the rank of wife and widow was denied her by the
ladies of pure, unmixed European descent, and she
submitted with singular patience to her enforced
position. She received, with polite hospitality, the
visits of a few persons of her own country, who had

taken refuge in Jamaica, but rarely made any herself. Mr. Holgrave was a marked exception to this
rule. He visited her rarely, while she called on him
about once a week. But then he was her solicitor,
and, of course, she had to consult him frequently.
She made her visits in the most correct style, having always with her her maid Victorine, and sometimes a bewitching little romp, whom she called
her ward, and treated like an adopted daughter,
and who bore the very suitable name of Aimée.
This spoiled child was a dark quadroon; a shade
lighter than Victorine, but not so fair as Madam
Felix. This trio never spoke any thing but French
with each other, or with Mr. Holgrave, so that, at
first, their visits did not promise me much pleasure.
Madam Felix spoke very little English, and laugh-
ingly declared she had no use for the language, for
every creature she had ever seen in her life, that
was worth speaking to at all, understood French.

She was a liberal and indulgent mistress, and a
most devoted friend. I saw she admired Mr. Holgrave, and liked me because I was a favorite with
him, and still more, perhaps, because she noticed
my assiduity to serve him in the way it best pleased
him to be served—that I was vigilant to meet every

wish, and, as he often said, was quick and quiet about my duties.

"You ought to live with Mr. Holgrave always. He loves you and you love him. You must not leave him," she said to me one day, when some of Mr. Holgrave's numerous patients had called him out of the parlor.

I replied, from the bottom of my heart, that I wished, above all things, to remain with him.

"*C'est bien*. We'll manage it. I will write to Mr. Davis, your master, and you must beg of your mistress to favor our little plot, for the *cher philosophe* needs an honest, attentive, affectionate boy like you in his sick-turns."

Here we were interrupted by the return of Mr. Holgrave, and Madam Felix took her leave. On her next visit, which was the farewell one, for we were packing up for Orange Grove, Madam Felix made me the handsome present of a fancy suit, in which to recite Robin Hood in character. At the same time she slipped in the letter to my master, with an injunction not to mention it to any other person, not even Mr. H., until my purchase should be an accomplished fact. Victorine was as gracious as her mistress in her parting words, rather more so, for she bade me " make haste and grow up, for she was only waiting for that, to marry me."

I replied that it was an engagement; but when I attempted to snatch a kiss in ratification of the bargain, she boxed my ears, and said that all the *kinks* had been boxed and pulled out of my hair for my impertinence to the girls.

Aimée, Madam Felix's lively little ward, brought her parting present also, in the shape of a package of her own French story-books, to which she added a handsome new prayer-book in the same language. This she very earnestly enjoined me to read, for she said she wanted to meet me in heaven when she went there with her dear Aunt Felix. I had made some start in reading French, and these books were a help and a consolation in many a weary evening at Orange Grove. As to the Book of Prayer, I to this day guard it as a peculiar treasure, though I do not follow its forms.

CHAPTER IX.

THE MISSIONARY.

WE returned to Orange Grove on a pleasant Saturday afternoon. Tatee had come down this road to meet us, though she could only courtesy to the passing carriage and wave a smiling welcome to me. The affectionate creature knew I could not quit Mr. Holgrave and the horses, but she felt it would be kind, or, as she worded it, "mo lucky," if the first thing I met on my return should be a friendly face, with an intimation that all was well. Rachel was with the young ladies and their mamma, on the front piazza, when we drove up. They had all hastened out to receive their dear Cousin Holgrave, whose superior qualities they were themselves so well fitted to appreciate. While the ladies were exchanging greetings and family news with him, Rachel was turning my silly young head with her flattering praises. I spoke "*buckra* for true"— that is, used the language of a white gentleman—

and had, she assured me, "ways 'cisely like Massa
Holgrave." Heaven knows I watched and aped
every word and motion of my honored patron; and
to be told by a disinterested observer that I was
precisely like him in language and manners, fairly
intoxicated me with delight. I paid back Rachel,
partly in kind, by asserting that *she* was the very
image of Belle Bessie, the prettiest colored girl in
Savannah-la-Mar.

This was a quadroon, whose proper name was
Bessie Bell, which the white gentlemen had changed
to Belle Bessie. She had about the size and figure
of Rachel, who was a tall, comely, well-built damsel
of fifteen, but their faces were not much alike, for
Rachel had the negro cast of features, while Belle
Bessie, as I noticed on an after-acquaintance, had
a finely-cut profile of Grecian regularity. However,
Rachel was handsome enough to please me wonderfully, while she was pretending to compare me with
Mr. Holgrave. Besides the return compliments, I
repaid her absurd flatteries with a nice bandanna
handkerchief—a tribute of gratitude from the cook
for my paper cure, and which I had treasured up for
Tatee. I never wore those things myself, affecting
to find them too warm under my hat, but, in truth

—since I am at my confessions—from a vain desire
not to hide my straight hair. When I recollect
what a clod of untempered self-conceit I was in
those days, I wonder how it was that my fellow-
servants did not beat it out of me, with sneers and
sharp knocks, instead of continually lavishing upon
me so much unmerited kindness.

Rachel, in particular—comely, coquettish Rachel
—was enough to spoil twenty young fools with her
insinuating attentions. She forgot, in the midst of
our mutual flatteries, to tell me, when I first arrived
with Mr. Holgrave, that my old shipmate and faithful friend Brad was in the hospital with a broken
arm, and that my master and the doctor were there
with him, when the carriage drove up; which accounted for Mr. Davis not being with the ladies, to
receive his valued friend. When he came in he related the circumstances to Mr. Holgrave before he
sat down. It seems a neighboring gentleman had
been taken insane very suddenly, and making his
way over to the Orange Grove sugar-works, he
frightened every negro out of it with his violent
language, and the energetic use of a great stick
which he wielded right and left.

The overseer, in spite of the astonishment such

an apparition was calculated to produce, had comprehended the difficulty, and directed the frightened negroes to go for their master, and bring back with them a blanket or two. Meanwhile the madman launched himself upon the book-keeper—the only other white man present—and drove him out after the flying blacks. None of the negroes remained to defend the overseer, who was so placed as to be cut off from escape by either door. The lunatic flew at him, and would have ended his days in that dark corner of the boiling-house, had not Brad, at that critical moment, rushed in and thrown himself upon the raving assailant. He caught the upraised stick on his left arm, and the limb fell shattered to his side; but the powerful and resolute black wrested away the stick with his right hand, while, with head and knee, he bore the foaming maniac to the ground. The overseer came promptly to his aid, and, with the blankets brought for the purpose, the lunatic, still raging in impotent fury, was securely lashed in an extemporized strait-jacket. His friends had followed him so closely, that this scene was hardly over, when a carriage and servants were on the spot to convey him home.

All this had taken place in the two hours imme-
8*

diately preceding our arrival; and Tatee, who had gone from her own cabin down the road to meet me, knew nothing of Brad's misfortune, when she informed me, by her smiling nod, that there was nothing amiss among our friends.

Perhaps Brad's accident ought not to be called a misfortune. It was, in fact, a blessing, though it came with a veil over its face. He was such a quiet and capable hand with animals, that he had charge of a cart all through the late sugar-making season, and his mule-team had been noticed with particular satisfaction by his master as well as the overseer. He happened to be passing the "works" when the sight of half a dozen negroes rushing out of the boiling-house in a tumult of fright, and the loud voice of the overseer, called him to the rescue. At the cost of a broken arm to himself, he saved the life of one man whose good-will had already been of benefit to him, and won the confidence of another— his master—who had the heart as well as the power to release him from many of the hardest of his slave burdens.

I embraced the occasion to state to Mr. Holgrave that Brad had been brought up in Africa by a man who owned a large number of animals, and was a

noted horse-trainer, and he could very well fill the
place then held by Ned, his own servant, in the stables. Mr. Holgrave said little or nothing to me in
reply, but our master had a talk with Brad about
the care of horses, and in a week he was walking
about with his arm in a sling, the head-groom at
Orange Grove, and the proudest "nigga"—except
myself, for, in the article of self-conceit, no one could
exceed *me* at that time—inside of the Island of Jamaica.

The presence of Mr. Holgrave filled the Great
House with that sort of placid enjoyment which
seemed to follow him like his shadow—I ought
rather to say, the reflected light of his own good-
ness—wherever he carried himself. Never did I
know another person, who, without being at all
mirthful in his own moods, had such a gift for ban-
ishing sadness from others. He had such a fund of
accomplishments, was such a mine of entertaining
knowledge, was gifted with such a happy art of
finding something to engage the interest of himself
and every one about him, that dullness and the sullens could not live in the same house with him. His
company was universally sought by all the gentle-
folks far and wide, but he was very sparing of it

with most people. His delicate health did not permit him to partake of the sumptuous hospitalities for which Jamaica is so famous, and he made no long visits, anywhere except to my master's family, with now and then one of a day or two, to an old college-mate and brother free-mason, the eccentric Mr. Martineau. This gentleman had a reputation as wide as the island for his vast reading, his biting wit, his odd habits, and his reckless courage. I had heard Madam Felix talking to Mr. Holgrave about his peculiarities, but, as it was in French, I could only understand that she was laughing at *ce cher Martineau*, and that her more *cher philosophe* was defending him against her good-natured criticisms.

I was highly interested, therefore, when I heard my master say, as they were all at coffee after dinner, that Mr. Martineau would pass a day or two with them at the close of the week.

"I hope he won't take it into that death's-head of his to bury any of us alive," said Miss Emma.

"Take care, Em, what you say about your cousin Holgrave's bosom friend," said her father, holding up his teaspoon with a mock air of censure.

"Cousin Holgrave *can't* love that cross-grained old horror," replied Miss Emma, no whit abashed.

"I have heard you say, papa, that he respects no one on earth but Philip Holgrave, and has no pity for any thing that has feelings except his own pet slaves."

Mr. Holgrave asked Miss Emma if she would not have a little more sugar in her coffee, instead of replying to her remark; but Miss Lucy observed gaily, as she rose from the table, "I have made up my mind to fall in love with this redoubtable Monsieur Martineau. His appreciation of our cousin proves that he is a man of sense, and his kindness to his slaves speaks well for his heart. I shall come out with my best airs and graces to make a conquest, and you, Cousin Holgrave, must help me by keeping Emma from playing the rival."

Mr. Martineau came in due season, but not before I had, one way and another, picked up a very curious account of his life, character, and circumstances. I really wondered how such a thin, bloodless creature should have the strength to sit a horse, when he rode up to the door; but he dismounted nimbly enough, and made his salutations with the air of a gentleman altogether at his ease. His reception was polite, though not so warm and cordial as might be given to some other visitors. Still, he was the friend of Mr. Holgrave, who was the dearest friend of my master and the cousin of my mistress, and no pains were spared to make his stay agreeable.

I came near dropping the plate I was handing him at dinner, when he remarked "that I seemed to be, in every way, the boy I had been represented, and he hoped to take me back with him."

"I have not yet decided to part with him," was my master's reply, and there the subject dropped for the moment. I was horror-struck. The idea of being sold to any one except Mr. Holgrave, had not crossed my mind. Yet it was too plain that, in some way, my transfer to Mr. Martineau had been agitated. I thought that dinner would never end, although, in fact, the gentlemen did not sit very long over their wine. I scanned their looks, and I weighed all I had learned of Mr. Martineau, as I waited upon them, but I could not reconcile my mind to be sent away from the pleasant, portly master of Orange Grove, to serve that grim stranger, who was, at that time, under forty years of age, but he appeared fifty. He was a member of the Assembly for an adjoining parish, and had passed the greater part of his life in Jamaica. He had the reputation of having been an admirer of the ladies, but it seemed to me impossible that he ever could have been admired by them. His father had sent him to Europe for his education, and he had graduated at the same college with Mr. Holgrave; and after that they had spent a year or two together in France and Italy. He was much attached to Mr. Holgrave, and, as I heard afterward, had rendered him important services in their early life.

At last the gentlemen separated, and I was alone with Mr. Holgrave in his bed-chamber. I asked him anxiously whether my master thought of selling me to Mr. Martineau.

"He will never do so while you remain a good boy. You may be assured of that, Mahmadee," was his prompt reply. "Unless, indeed, you should wish a new master, and asked him to sell you."

"Oh, I shall never wish it—unless I can go to you, sir."

"That, I fear, is out of the question, Mahmadee."

"Oh, sir, please don't say so! I hope it will come to pass."

Madam Felix's letter to my master, which I had delivered into his own hand, but of which I had heard nothing more, now strongly occurred to me, but as I had been so strictly charged not to speak of it until questioned by my master, I kept silence.

"Mr. Martineau is the warm friend of Madam Felix, probably the most sincere and devoted friend she has in the world," observed Mr. Holgrave, after a short pause.

I caught a ray of daylight, and looked up in breathless expectation, as he added, slowly, "It would make a difference, perhaps, if you knew that Mr. Martineau was acting for her, and not for himself."

"Oh, yes, sir, a great difference," was my eager reply.

"It would make no difference with me, Mahmadee. None in the world," said Mr. Holgrave, gravely.

"Oh, sir! oh, Mr. Holgrave," I began.

"We will drop the subject for to-night, Mahmadee," said Mr. Holgrave, in his quiet, decided way; and I had no choice but to obey him and retire, but not to sleep. I considered myself free, now that the subject had been fairly broached, to solicit the kind intercession of my gentle mistress.

I have not said a great deal about Mrs. Davis, because she was one of those still, calm, amiable ladies, of whom one has little to record. You live among their kind ways and good works, as in the soft summer air, in unthinking content. It is only when the storms arise to trouble us that we feel the beauty of the calm, and pray for its return. So now my best hope was to remain with my mistress, in the secure peace of Orange Grove, since Mr. Holgrave appeared not to favor Madam Felix in her plan of giving me to him. Nevertheless, I still trusted to have a slight chance of pleading my case with him, when I went in to take his early cup of chocolate and attend to his morning toilet; but while I was waiting to hear his bell, the door opened, and, to my dismay, his own man Ned walked out, closely followed by Mr. Holgrave himself, ready shaved and dressed to join the ladies at coffee. My heart stood still. I felt that it must be all over with me, since I had been thus thrust away from him, and Ned called back to his regular place.

Rachel's voice, summoning me to assist in waiting on the coffee-table, forced me from my anxious broodings, and we went together into the breakfast-parlor. There the circle were amusing themselves at my expense—no, that is not exactly just. Mr. Martineau was drawing a witty comparison between the Mahometans, who made a reasonably good use of an absurd faith, and the Christians, who made the most absurd use of a good religion. My mistress was observing that I was a thorough Mahometan, though unusual pains had been taken to bring me into the light of Christianity.

"Let loose upon him the Reverend Buckly. Set the missionary upon him, madam. He will run him down in a week," said Mr. Martineau, turning upon me his pale, solemn face, and glittering eyes.

"You mention Mr. Buckly as if he were a bloodhound, or a Maroon at the very least," Miss Lucy remarked, with a slightly reproving smile.

"You have expressed it perfectly, Miss Davis," and the pale, ugly face turned on its long neck toward her. "He is, spiritually speaking, a bloodhound on the tracks of the unregenerate; an evangelical Maroon in chase of unbelieving runaways. The description could not be more accurate." And then those terrible eyes traveled back and settled on mine.

"Pardon me, Mr. Martineau," replied Miss Lucy, still smiling, "this description of Mr. Buckly—if it is a description—is yours, not mine. I have never seen the gentleman."

"I have no doubt it is near enough the mark," said Mr. Davis, setting down his coffee-cup. "Half these missionaries are but wolves in sheep's clothing. I would as soon see the boy a decent Mahometan, as such a Christian as they will make of him."

"My dear!" began Mrs. Davis, in a tone of mild remonstrance, when Pompey entered to announce—

"*The Reverend Mr. Buckly.*"

"Speak of the devil, and so forth—eh, Holgrave?" said Mr. Martineau, as the gentleman in question—the missionary, of course, not the black one—entered the room.

He was a short, compact, coarse-featured man, with thin, reddish hair, and eyebrows to match; by no means handsome or elegant, nor was he, on the other hand, decidedly ill-looking. He had at that time a clear, rosy complexion, and full, red lips, inclined to a pleasant smile. He looked so much fresher and kindlier than Mr. Martineau, that, seen side by side, the missionary was a perfect beauty compared to the planter.

A Jamaica gentleman makes it a point of honor to treat every one who seeks the shelter of his

roof with attentive politeness—that is, every white
person of tolerably decent appearance—and the missionary was immediately set at ease, both in body
and business. He was making "a tour of religious
observation," he so explained it, preaching to the
blacks on the several estates, where the planters
did not object, and organizing Sunday-schools where
it was practicable. He said he had done both " with
happy success at Martineau's Hall." Here I opened
my eyes very wide, and Mr. Martineau bent his
head in confirmation. Miss Emma slily pinched
her sister, who returned the compliment with her
fingers, while her lips smiled a polite approval of
these pious proceedings. Meanwhile, Mr. Buckly
had gone on to say that he had also been permitted to preach to the slaves on the estate of Madam
Felix, and was not without hopes of establishing
a Sunday-school in that vicinity, under her direct
patronage.

"I was under the impression that Madam Felix
was a strict Roman Catholic," observed Mrs. Davis.

"So she is, at present, madam, but God has en-
dowed her with a feeling heart, and, I trust, under
His grace, she may yet be a brand snatched from
the burning."

At these words I intercepted a curious glance simultaneously directed to the immovable face of Mr. Martineau from both Mr. Holgrave and my master; but as my duties in the breakfast-parlor ended in serving the missionary with coffee and a sandwich, I was forced to withdraw my inquisitive ears and eyes.

Most of the missionaries were at first looked down upon by the gentry, who did not approve of their holding forth to the negro population, or teaching them any other doctrine than unlimited obedience to their *masters*. They were regarded as needy hypocrites, who came "to act the shark with the *quashies*, and live out of their calabashes." A later and more intimate experience has cured me of this false and uncharitable judgment, but at that time I naturally believed with the white gentry, whose positions enabled them to form more exact opinions of each other than a poor black boy could be expected to attain.

Through the thin vail of their politeness I could see that my master and his family had no respect for Mr. Buckly, though he bore an excellent character among the negroes and people of color. He was, however, very severe in his denunciations, and had a great deal to say about hell-fire, which he described in such red-hot colors that Mr. Martineau used to say the words issued from his mouth in a blaze of fire, and had burned his very whiskers and eyebrows. These were red by nature, and rather thin and straggling. His eyes were also red, and ever in motion, and this Mr. Martineau attributed likewise to the brimstone within him, and the consuming fire which nothing quenches. The preacher was devout with me, however. I was ordered to attend him to his room when he retired, and before he would let me off he made a long prayer for my conversion, beside favoring me with a general lecture on my lost and depraved condition. I had to kneel with him, but saved my faith whole by repeating to myself with great zeal and rapidity all the verses of the Koran I could heap together, without stopping to consider their sense or connection.

Before he dismissed me, the reverend gentleman dropped some remarks about Mr. Martineau and Madam Felix, which had a quicker and more enlightening effect on my mental darkness than all his preaching. He suspected Mr. Martineau of being a pretender to the affections of the rich quadroon, and I half suspected his reverence of a

similar proclivity. I rather liked the interest of
such a game, and, at all events, was not backward
to hint my belief that the rich, amiable, and handsome widow would not give her heart to a face like
Mr. Martineau's.

The planter had represented the missionary as a
spiritual Maroon, and I was inclined to believe him.
The missionary broadly hinted that the planter was
a godless reprobate, and I believed him too. As I
passed my master's door to put out the parlor lights,
I heard him say, confidentially, to my mistress, that
the island could not produce such another brace of
disagreeables as the pair of them, and, like a dutiful
servant, I implicitly accepted his opinion.

CHAPTER X.

THE PLANTER.

WHATEVER of good or ill the white gentlemen might think of each other, the poor black boy did not find the way any the clearer to the haven of his hopes.

When my day and evening duties were over, I prostrated myself in prayer in a corner of the garden, and I fervently besought Alla to help me to liberty; but I was no Christian, and did not ask God for the grace to accept my lot in humble faith. I invoked the spirit of my mother, and of Hadji Ali, whom I now counted among the blessed, to come and guide me. Arising from the ground, I wandered round to the far side of the wing, in which Mr. Holgrave and his friend Martineau had their sleeping-rooms, in the faint hope of seeing lights, and finding them still up. The light was not out, and I peeped through Mr. Holgrave's lattice to see whether he was reading, as was his custom when he could not sleep—as too often happened for the good of his health. He was in bed, with the light, transparent musquito-curtains disposed around it for the night; but Mr. Martineau stood by the table, lighting his cigar, and even as I put my eyes to the slats to look in, he approached to throw the window open. He then seated himself on the ledge, with his face inclined outward, that the smoke of his cigar might be wafted abroad, and not trouble his friend, who, I may 'as well remark here, never used tobacco in any form.

"You are too fastidious, Holgrave. You are childishly scrupulous, I tell you," said Mr. Martineau, as he settled himself in the window-seat, and I subsided behind the rose-bushes nearly under it. I had no time to get away, or do any thing but drop down in this ready ambush. Mr. Martineau was evidently pursuing a conversation broken by his lighting a cigar, and had fixed himself in a place to enjoy both. I did not catch Mr. Holgrave's answer, but he did, for he replied pettishly, "Sheer nonsense! She is rich enough to give you half a dozen boys like this Mahmadee, and never feel it. Besides that, Davis is behaving like a prince—as he always does—and names a price below what he gave for him, half his value, in short."

9

"Once for all, Martineau, I am too poor to accept such presents, and I will not," said Mr. Holgrave, distinctly.   I was afraid they would hear my heart beat; its throbs sounded to me louder than the low, clear voices of the gentlemen.

"You are cursed ungenerous, beside being an idiot," was Martineau's next speech. "Our poor friend has her heart set upon it. She has taken it in her head that this charcoal prince worships you, and that, next to herself, he would be the best nurse in creation in your sick-turns."

"I am sorry to oppose her wishes, for she is one of the best of women," said Mr. Holgrave, gently.

"There is not a better woman—no, nor a more perfect lady in Jamaica," was Mr. Martineau's answer, as he knocked the ashes off his cigar. I did not consider his face so very ugly, after all, as he leaned a trifle toward my hiding-place, in his earnestness. It is true it was rather in the shade from his attitude, and only presented in profile.

"She certainly deserves a better fate than to marry that bigoted zealot Buckly," remarked Mr. Holgrave, slightly moving in his bed.

"Marry the devil!" said the planter, scornfully. "She never threw away the tenth part of a thought on the vulgar, canting hypocrite. We insult her in supposing it."

"Possibly; but I suspect he is thinking very seriously of her," was Mr. Holgrave's bland reply.

If Mr. Holgrave brought up the preacher to divert the' planter from pressing me as a gift upon him, he hit the nail on the head. Mr. Martineau tossed away the remnant of his cigar, and, without reverting again to poor me, retired to his own apartment. I crept out of my hiding-place, and, after hesitating a minute or two, concluded not to intrude upon Mr. Holgrave that night.

I had thus accidentally learned that it would be useless to trouble my mistress about selling, or not selling me, and I resolved not to speak on the subject, even to Mr. Holgrave; but from that night an intense longing for personal freedom began to possess me. How or when it was to happen I could not discern, but that it must and would happen, and that I should some day belong to myself, settled firmly into my mind. It was as sure as death. Death and freedom might come very nearly together, but liberty would come first. I .should die as I was born, free.

Yet I was very unhappy at losing the hope of living with Mr. Holgrave. I loved him almost with the passionate tenderness I had felt for the lost darling, and at the same time with the dutiful—I may even dare to say the filial—devotion due to a kind, and wise, and inexpressibly venerated parent.

Mr. Buckly had obtained the consent of my master and mistress to preach and baptize among the slaves, who greatly preferred his vehement ministrations to those of the Episcopal curate. The house-servants—and I generally among them—attended family service, which was regularly read in the Great House every Sunday, either by my mistress or one of the young ladies, one or the other of whom remained at home for the purpose, even when all the rest went to church. There was the most perfect toleration at Orange Grove, only that all the field-hands were advised and expected to go and hear Mr. Wodenlone or attend the Wesleyan Chapel—if they did not like the regular Church service—at least every other Sabbath. The family service and its catechism-class were held more exclusively for the servants attached to the house and grounds. The maids, waiters, cooks, stablemen, gardeners, and so on, made a congregation of about twenty blacks. The Sunday after Mr. Buckly's first appearance on our stage, he held forth to a most respectful and believing audience of field-negroes, in what was called " the old trash-house," which the overseer had caused to be cleaned and fitted up as a kind of free chapel. The negroes may not have understood all he expounded to them, but it was devoutly received; and the melody of their hymns, as it floated over to us at the Great House, touched me more than any thing I had yet heard or seen of the Christian religion since I was brought a manacled slave within the sphere of its teachings.

The young ladies and their father had gone in the carriage to the Episcopal church, and Mrs. Davis read the service to those of the servants who had not begged permission to attend Mr. Buckly's. Mr. Holgrave was a prisoner in his room, and I in attendance on him, under one of his periodical attacks. His complaint had baffled the best physicians, so he had taken his case entirely into his own hands. "Diet and care are the only doctors I require," he used to say; and, during the six months in which I was constantly near him, I had learned to prepare his ptisans and the various little messes which he liked, and agreed best with him, more to his taste than either the cook or Ned.

"I shall be sorry to part with you, Mahmadee," he said to me that Sunday, as I was arranging his room. "I like your neat and handy ways, to say nothing of your being able to read to me when it is not prudent to read myself, and yet am not sick enough to dispense with my books altogether; but it is impossible to make any arrangements about you until I return from England. If I live to return at all," he added, with a half sigh.

"Return from England, sir?" I exclaimed, in consternation, for it was the first hint I had heard of such an intention.

"Yes, I have about decided to go there in the spring. I have business there which will detain me several months, and I may be absent a year or more."

"Oh, take me with you, sir. Do take me with you, dear, dear master," and I sank on my knees before him, in an outburst of tears and supplication.

"So I would, Mahmadee, if I felt able to buy you, but I am not. I do not mind telling you—for I know you are a discreet boy—that I am in debt, and that every pound I spend is so much added to it. My only object in taking this voyage is to collect the remnants of my father's property, that I may clear off those galling incumbrances, and, if possible, settle myself on a small coffee-estate."

"But, if you will only take me with you, I will return with you, and Mr. Davis will not lose his slave."

"Will you swear to that, Mahmadee?"

"Yes, by the sacred stone of Mecca, by the soul of my father, by Allah and his Prophet, I will swear to come back freely, if my master will let me go with you."

How I did plead for the privilege of riveting my own fetters! and I did it in deep sincerity, for the idea of losing Mr. Holgrave drove, for the time, out of my heart, all my dreams and resolutions about becoming a free man.

Mr. Holgrave was evidently moved, but he only said, after reflecting a moment, "Go, now, and send in Ned." I did so, and in less than half an hour, Ned came to me, and, with a sour look, said gruffly, "Mr. Holgrave wants you." I flew to him. He lay with his face to the wall, and he did not turn toward me, as he said quietly :—

"Ned has an old promise from me, to be taken to England, and have his freedom whenever I should go, and he will not consent to wait for his freedom until my return."

"Ned will not wait until his master returns?" I repeated, in amazement at his master's condescension. "Ned dare to say that?"

"It was promised to him, and is, therefore, his right. Tell him to bring in my ptisan, and I will try to sleep."

I found Ned in the center of a gaping circle of the out-door servants, setting forth his brilliant prospects of freedom, and a residence in England.

"What will you do with Ettee and the children, if you settle in England?" asked Pompey, coming into the ring of excited auditors.

"I'll send for the old woman when I'se settled down *home*," Ned answered, with a grand air.

"You'll have to buy her freedom first, I s'pose?" said Pompey, scoffingly.

"In course I will, ef I don't marry some rich buckra widow out dere," said Ned, candidly.

"You had better carry your master his ptisan," I put in, impatiently. "If you attend to him in this way, he may not live to take you *home*."

This talk of going *home*, as everybody in Jamaica, black and white, styles the mother country, chafed my bruised spirit beyond bounds. It did not tend to soothe me, to' hear from Rachel that evening, that my master had offered to keep Ned in my place, and that she heard him also say to my mistress, that he was ready to accommodate Mr. Holgrave in any way whatever about me, for there was not another boy in the county of Cornwall that would suit him so well, but that Mr. Holgrave felt bound to take Ned and decline me.

Soon after this, Mr. Holgrave returned to Savannah-la-Mar, Mr. Buckly went to make a round of missionary visits, and I took up my arithmetic, under my old mulatto teacher, in his evening school. Rachel, too, was smitten with a desire to learn to read, and her mistress consented to her going to the evening school with me, part of the week, though, truth to say, she tired of it very soon, and threw up school and spelling-book together. Still, the fit lasted long enough to help console me in the dull and lonely first weeks that followed the departure of Mr. Holgrave to his own house.

Rachel and Tatee were my comforters in every difficulty—one by her arch, unfailing cheerfulness,

9*

and the other by sound advice and warm sympathy. Tatee had a fixed belief that I was to acquire my freedom by dint of learning; *how* she did not exactly see, any more than I did myself, but it seemed to her contrary to nature that a man should remain a slave who could read and write, and "*preach buckra*," as she, and the other slaves who had heard me declaim, called my "Robin Hood" and other recitations in verse.

"You are but a boy yet, Mahmadee, and you must have patience," she said to me, one Saturday afternoon, while she was helping me to weed the flowers I had planted around darling Henry's little grave. "You must wait till you are a man, to be free. It won't come till then; for what would a boy do with his freedom? But when it does come to you, you must help me buy my freedom, too."

"I certainly will, if ever I am able, Tatee—and Brad's, too," I said, half in jest, but half in earnest as well, for I had again begun to dream dreams of belonging to myself.

"Brad does not expect you to give him free papers; he wants to take care of your horses, the same as he takes care of buckra master's," said Tatee, with perfect seriousness. This was too magnificcnt. It brought me back to my real situation; and I laid my head on the little mound beside me, not to pour out unavailing tears, as I had done so often, but to talk to Tatee about the probabilities of Mr. Holgrave buying me on his return from England, and eventually giving me freedom, as he was about doing by Ned. That seemed my happiest hope, and Tatee was as sanguine that nothing else could happen, as if the facts were visibly before her. She started up.

"There is a horse coming. It must be the master. Run, Mahmadee, and open the other gate for him, and I will see to this one. There was a mere bridle-path, but little used, that passed by the graveyard. This "cross-cut" lane had two outlets, one to the sugar-works, which Tatee went to open, the other by a separate gate, close to the corner of the burying-ground, and this opened by a picket gate directly into the lawn. I stood ready to wait upon it, but it was a stranger, a rather handsome, well-dressed, well-mounted man; but even while I took off my hat and held open the gate, with the humility becoming my position, there was that in his face and mien which secretly enraged me. He checked his horse midway in the gate, and, turning in the saddle, measured me with a supercilious stare, and asked if there was not a "straight-haired nigger on this estate named Prince."

"There is a man named Prince on the estate, but he has not straight hair," I compelled myself to say, in perfectly respectful tones, and in as correct English as he used himself.

"Ah, I recollect now, he is a prince himself, and his name is Mammy Dear," drawling out the name affectedly. "I have something for him from Martineau Hall," drawing a package from his pocket.

I curbed my rising temper, and said: "I presume it is intended for me, sir; my name is Mahmadee." He mimicked my expression.

"I presume your sable highness is right. There it is, Mammy Dear," and throwing at, rather than handing to me, the little parcel, he spurred on, and left the gateway free to be secured again. The package was from Mr. Martineau, and contained seven bulbs of a fine white lily, for Master Henry's grave, with directions about the planting and time of bearing. If planted at once, and carefully tended, they would give a succession of flowers from Christmas to Easter. Mr. Martineau had noticed the rose-bushes at little Henry's grave, and observed that a close row—like a miniature hedge —of white lilies would be the most appropriate ornament for the grave of a young child. I was surprised to hear any thing about flowers come out of a head like his; and how much greater was my surprise at his having had the kindness to send them to me! I planted and watered the precious bulbs before I left the place, and then I walked to the house in such a state of gratitude to Mr. Martineau, that I was ready to forgive and forget the tyrannical airs of his messenger. I say tyrannical, for what else is it, when a white man abuses the advantages of his complexion to insult one who has given no provocation, who has even been circumspectly exact in his deference, and only because his victim cannot resist or resent?

When I attended the supper-table, the visitor was not there, though the family had a great deal to say about a Mr. McGregor, a master-mechanic, who had made very handsome work of rebuilding the sugar-works at Martineau Hall, and of repairing the Hall itself, and, still more, of his undertaking a large still-house, on an improved plan of construction, at Orange Grove.

"Martineau writes me that he is a superior

workman, and has made good use of his seven years in Scotland," said my master to his lady, while I was waiting on the supper-table. "He has given high satisfaction at Martineau Hall."

"Did he pass for white there?" put in Miss Emma.

"My daughter!" said her mother, in a tone of grave warning.

"Oh, I only asked out of innocent curiosity," said the young lady, carelessly. "I am sure I hope he will come and build up all you want, papa, in no time, and then we may get the billiard-room you promised Lucy and me if we would speak French together for a year."

"Which you do, at the rate of twenty words in a week," replied her father. "Your billiard-room will be a long time in building, if it keeps time with your French."

"The girls do better than you give them credit for," interposed their indulgent mother. "But I shall insist upon a more steady practice of French, for I intend to hold their papa to the new billiard-room. It will be a great resource in a rainy day, especially when we have friends staying with us."

"The billiard-room is, I see, a settled thing. There is no escape for me, it appears, and I will step over to the overseer's house and talk to McGregor about that, with the rest of the plans."

So this insulting stranger was a master-builder, who was coming to do plenty of work here, and he "*passes*" for white. That expression puzzled me, and I was still pondering over it, when my master went by me into the parlor, with a quick step, and said, in a hurried, anxious tone, "Holgrave is very sick, McGregor tells me—so sick, that Martineau has gone down to stay with him."

"It is singular that he has not sent to inform us, if he is seriously ill," observed my mistress.

"He is so delicate about giving trouble to his friends!" said Miss Lucy, who seemed to read his heart better than any one. "How I wish he were here, or had Mahmadee with him! Could you not send Mahmadee to him, papa?"

Mr. Davis looked at his wife, as if to consult her wishes.

"I think we may spare him," she replied to his looks.

"Then he may go to-morrow morning," said my master, instantly, "and as early as he can get off."

"I could start before daylight, if master pleases," I said, as composedly as I could manage to utter it, for I wanted to borrow wings and fly to him that instant.

"So you had better, Mahmadee. Go tell the cook to put you up something for the road, while I write your pass and a note to Mr. Holgrave."

The pass was written, the preparations made, and all my directions received, including many kind messages from the young ladies and my mistress— for the family loved Mr. Holgrave more like a brother than a cousin—before ten, and I was at liberty to start as early in the morning as I liked. I went to Pompey, to ask him to answer the bell for me, if, by any chance, my master should ring for me in the night, and then set off on my long walk to Savannah-la-Mar. It is called twelve good miles from Orange Grove to Savannah-la-Mar, and I was at Mr. Holgrave's door before one in the morning. All was still in the house, and, judging from this silent calm that the master was sleeping, I threw myself on the floor of the piazza, to wait for daylight, without disturbing anybody. I awoke at about the dawning, a little chilled and stiff, but happy to find myself so near Mr. Holgrave.

At fair daybreak I marched into the kitchen, and startled up the cook, who was, however, very glad

to see me, for, beside being a favorite with her, I
told her I had come to cure her master. She informed me that he was a little better now; that
Mr. Martineau had staid with him three days, but
went home yesterday; that her master had no appetite, and was still too weak to sit up. "Hi! dere
him bell now, and Ned done jes gone wid him
horses. Him mighty soon (early) dis ere mornin'."

"Never mind, Mrs. Bates, you know I can do
as well as Ned for Mr. Holgrave." And I bounded
to the door of his bed-room. I opened it gently,
and stepped inside.

"Bring me something to drink," was all Mr.
Holgrave said, as he lay with his back rather toward
me, his thin white hand still resting on the bell-rope,
as if it was too much of an effort to remove it.

I went softly to a covered pitcher, poured out
some of the contents in a glass, laid the letter from
my master beside it on the waiter, and carried it
to the side of the bed. Mr. Holgrave extended his
hand to take the glass, and, raising his eyes at the
same moment, they met mine, suffused with heart-
felt emotion.

"My dear, good boy," said he, grasping my
hand.

Those words, and that gentle pressure, would have repaid me for ten thousand hours of bondage.

My master's note Mr. Holgrave told me to read. It was only this :—

"MY DEAR HOLGRAVE—I send you Mahmadee, with my deep regrets for your illness. Keep him as long as you please. My wife and the girls desire me to say that they *forbid* the boy's return to Orange Grove while you are on the island, unless *you* will come with him for a long visit, which, we all pray, may be very soon.

"Ever faithfully, yours,

"WM. L. DAVIS."

"My master writes a beautiful letter," I exclaimed, in unbounded satisfaction. It seemed to me almost like a deed of manumission.

"Pithily, and to the purpose, for us, Mahmadee," replied Mr. Holgrave; and that was all he ever said about it to me, but he had a fuller conversation with Mr. Martineau, when he joined us, a few days afterward, one that finally settled my fate, though not immediately.

Mr. Holgrave gradually recovered his usual health, and I settled down in my old way, attending

to my duties, studying my lessons regularly, keeping my journal, and reading poetry and novels—
when I could get them—at every spare interval.

Mr. Martineau made us two or three visits, to
the immense annoyance of the cook, who was firmly
persuaded that he was a cruel monster, a sort of
ogre, who had an unquenchable thirst for human
blood, and she averred to me, in the most solemn
manner, though, of course, under the strictest
pledge of secrecy—which I trust that every one
who has it from me will respect as religiously as I
have done—that she *knew* he often buried his slaves
alive. After one of Mr. Martineau's visits, I ventured
to hint to Mr. Holgrave that very cruel things were
reported about that gentleman among the blacks,
and especially that he was much given to burying
people alive. Mr. Holgrave then gave me his own
brief version of a very singular story, which I afterward had confirmed by other parties, and which
is so odd, even for " that eccentric wit Martineau,"
that it is worth recording.

CHAPTER XI.

A SINGULAR ADJUSTMENT.

MR. MARTINEAU was such a remarkable man, and made such a figure in the *scan. mag.* of Jamaica, that he shall have a chapter all to himself. As he is now beyond the reach of friend or foe, and has left no one behind him that will be pained in the slightest by the recital, I shall tell the story, as I had it from those who knew the facts, point by point. He was an only child, and inherited a handsome fortune, but he gave himself up to riotous living until he run out, one after the other, three valuable sugar- estates. At thirty-eight, he had no other income than the commissions he received *on his own late property*, as "managing attorney," as we call, in Jamaica, those very expensive agents who control the incomes and estates of rich absentees! These he had secured in a way not less peculiar than his general mode of life and his striking personal appearance.

After becoming so involved as to be unable to

pay even the interest on his mortgages, from the
diminished proceeds of the estates, he submitted
quietly to the *usurpation*, as he called it, of his
creditor. The creditor successively possessed himself of all the three properties, which Mr. Martineau
yielded, almost without any opposition, upon a
promise of being allowed still to be attorney for
them, and to draw his commissions—six per cent.—
on the proceeds. The commissions were considerable; and, though a portion of them was appropri-
ated to the payment of the other debts, he still retained nearly as good an income as the nominal proprietor was able to derive from his investment—
some said a better one. The new proprietor, not
finding the returns at all satisfactory, put these estates up for sale in England, and Mr. Martineau contrived to have them bid in for him at the auction,
by means of paying down five per cent. upon the
price for which they sold. The purchases were
never completed; notwithstanding which, Mr. Martineau re-entered as proprietor. Being on the spot
and in actual occupation, as attorney, this was no
difficult matter. Having already lamented his folly
in once resigning them, he was determined to keep
what he could, and to try whether force and in-

trigue together would not secure him against a second abdication. His accounts became more and more confused; his management was not improved; and the rest of the purchase-money remaining unpaid, the British capitalist, still holding a mortgage from Mr. Martineau, as a second time proprietor, sued him again in chancery, for restitution of the estates and arrears. In course of time he got an order, and proceeded again to sale. Here was confusion on confusion. Mr. Martineau was summoned to give up possession; judgment after judgment was obtained against him, and the deputy-marshal became a frequent visitor in the neighborhood. Some few of the negroes were levied on, but, in spite of the law officers, he contrived to keep possession for several years, until the mortgagee died, and his rights devolved, by inheritance, to a young man born in the island, but who had then just finished his education, and been called to the bar in England.

This young gentleman, being of a somewhat romantic turn of mind, determined on personally ejecting Mr. Martineau, and forthwith transported himself to the island for the purpose. He arrived, and finding the island-marshal actually fearful of enforcing his judgment, he had himself made a deputy-marshal for the sake of serving his writ in person. He came, with a couple of negro-servants, to the abode of Mr. Martineau, stating, however, his real name and his desire to see the property.

Mr. Martineau knew, therefore, whom he was called upon to entertain; and very courteously did he entertain him. Mr. Martineau was ever hospitable and disposed to good-fellowship. He received his guest as became him, feasted him, plied him, though not unreasonably, with wine, and amused him with his conversation. In short, he did the honors of the house so well, that the stranger's heart was touched, and he almost felt reluctant to produce his writ and complete the important business in which he had embarked himself. After a long pause in their conversation, by which Mr. Martineau had begun to suspect what was coming, the young man essayed to open his budget.

"I am afraid," said he—but he could proceed no further, for the other caught him up in a moment, by exclaiming that he should fear nothing.

"Fear nothing!" repeated Mr. Martineau, "I have no fears."

"No fears?" rejoined the young gentleman. "I

am not a coward, but there are some things which deserve to be respected, if not feared. I am afraid of infringing the laws of hospitality."

"Not a whit," said Mr. Martineau; "you cannot do it here. This is Liberty Hall, my dear sir."

The stranger thanked him, and again attempted a movement toward his exculpation.

"You know my situation; my uncle's will; I am his heir-at-law. I have come out with full powers."

Mr. Martineau smiled, and helped him to a glass of wine. "Powers!" said he, "powers! full powers —full bumpers—ah, sir, my service to you; we do not care here for the powers above; we have a great contempt for all powers. This is Liberty Hall, sir; therefore, say and do what you like. Believe me, I shall set you the example of so doing, if you are backward."

"Why, then," replied the stranger, "here is a writ I have against you; and, to insure its being served according to law, I am myself a deputy-marshal, and you are my prisoner. As heir-at-law to my uncle, and, with this order from the court of chancery, I take possession of this house and estate."

So saying, he took the key of the door out of the

lock, put it into his pocket, walked across the room, replaced it, and sat down again, in no little confusion. Mr. M. only smiled, and begged the gentleman to realize that he was entirely at home.

" I am *your* guest instead of you being *mine*. Very well. You see this *is* Liberty Hall. We shall now understand each other. But will you not drink to your guest ? Boy (to a negro within hearing), bring more wine."

Another bottle of Madeira is placed upon the table, and Mr. Martineau having—in a parenthesis, as it were—sent for the head-driver, wittily entertains the heir-at-law, and tries his utmost to restore the equanimity which the youth had lost, talking of any other subject than the one in question, to beguile the time. It was growing dusk when the driver arrived, a sturdy sambo, with a neck like that of Hercules, whose name he bore. He had his long whip coiled two or three times across his breast, from shoulder to hip, and, having made obeisance, asked his master's orders.

" Open the door, Hercules, and call the waiting-men. He whispered in his butler's ear, making, however, an apology to his guest—or his host—and told another waiting-man to go and fetch a spade.

10

"I shall give you possession," said he to the stranger, "in due form—a handful of the soil."

The young lawyer was a little puzzled at the conduct of Mr. Martineau, not knowing whether he was serious, not serious enough, or too serious. "A spade," thought he, "cannot be necessary."

"Have you arms?" said Mr. Martineau.

The youth had not, but Hercules was directed to search his coat-pockets for pistols.

"We must have nothing with our wine but your powers," said Mr. Martineau, always smiling. "Nothing but your powers—nothing."

Hercules was a little confounded, though he executed his master's orders faithfully and civilly, laughing, however, as if he thought it a kind of practical joke. The gentleman was not refractory, and the waiting-man returned with the spade by the time the search was completed.

"The negroes are there," said he.

"Then come in, and shut the door," replied Mr. Martineau. "Now, Hercules, pull up this plank in the floor, and that, and the next to it."

The lawyer began to imagine that perhaps there might be some treasure concealed below, which the proprietor wished to take away with him, and looked on, a patient spectator, while Hercules, with the assistance of Simon, the butler, and by means of the spade, tore up the planks designated by their late master. There was an interval of a foot beneath, between the earth and the floor timbers, which last were wide enough to allow a man to pass through them, and to dig the soil up.

Mr. Martineau bid Hercules descend and dig; the negro obeyed, and turned a spadeful on the floor, which the young aspirant handled, either for possession's sake, or to see the nature of the soil. Mr. M. made signs to Hercules for more. "Dig," said he, "dig heartily, dig a hole—in short, dig me a grave."

The lawyer shuddered as he laughed. Could it be that his discomfited host was about to make away with himself in despair, or rather, that he would affect to do so, by way of trying some experiment on the feelings of the young man? He had been confounded at the search for arms, and all this was a new perplexity.

Hercules dug, and Simon looked on. The sun had just set when the work began, and a ruddy twilight gleamed into the room through the open *jealousie*. The lawyer sat with his back to

the window, and contemplated in silence, for some
time, the effect of the fading light upon the features of Mr. Martineau, as well as the bewildered
expression upon those of Simon.   Mr. Martineau
looked grim and melancholy, sighed now and then
profoundly, and the countenance of Simon sad-
dened, perhaps by sympathy; at least the lawyer
thought so, especially as, during the labor of Massa
Hercules, the light so died away that these expressions ceased to be any longer visible.   But in
the dark the young man's fancy illuminated them
afresh, and gave to them a still more gloomy character.   There was no treasure, no box of parch-
ments, no title-deeds, to account for the operation;
and Mr. Martineau, becoming still more melancholy,
almost groaned as well as sighed.

" What will you do ?" said the lawyer.   " What
is this pit for ?"

Hercules had by this time almost buried himself; the grave was five feet deep, and the interval
between the earth and the floor timbers had sunk
him out of sight.   Still he toiled on until his master bade him stop.   Hercules desisted, and ascended
in a foam of perspiration.   Mr. Martineau poured
him out a tumbler of wine, and bade him rest him-

self, and recover his strength. He then walked to the window, and closed the jealousie.

"We will have no noise," said he, taking off his neckcloth, "I would choose to die with decency; would not you, young bailiff?"

The lawyer's heart sank within him. His imagination had conceived, no doubt, the idea of such a purpose; but he had combated it.

"Die!" echoed he—"die! you are jesting, Mr. Martineau."

The host groaned again—the lawyer moved toward the door.

"Stir not," said the host; "this grave is made for you or me, or both. You, Simon, guard the door—you, Hercules, are either my slave or this man's; if he buries me, swear both of you to obey him, and never to betray him; never to own how I came by my death. Swear, swear in your own fashion."

He made them swear upon a prayer-book, and imprecate all sorts of curses in case of perjury.

"Now, if I bury this young marshalman, you must be just as true to me."

They swore again.

"Lawyer," said he, "heir-at-law, deputy-marshal, man of powers—here is my handkerchief; I give it to Hercules. There are some dollars in it; guess if they are odd or even. If you guess right, I swear that you shall bury me—if wrong, you shall descend into the grave. But you must make no noise. We will not use violence. This is no murder; this is as fair as any other duel. Fortune shall decide for us. You have, it is true, deceived me, taken unfair advantages—you came as a spy and a traitor, and have broken the sacred laws of hospitality. You came with powers to seize me, and imprison me, and to confiscate the possessions of my ancestors; but let that pass. You are in my power; I can inter you alive or dead : but I will take no unfair advantage. You have entered the lion's den to exterminate the lion; and the lion takes up his own line of battle. Are you agreed to the terms of this arrangement ?"

"No, no," exclaimed the barrister, "I am not content. I will not abide by any such agreement. I will *not* bury you, if I guess right; nor will I consent to be buried myself, if I guess wrong. In short, I will not guess at all."

"If you decline the chance," said Mr. Martineau, "there is nothing left but to dispose of you at once, or to guess for you. Simon shall take your guess for you. Cry, Simon, odd or even."

" No, no," again rejoined the lawyer.

" Silence !" retorted the host, "there is no other alternative; guess, or die."

He moved toward him, ordering Hercules also to advance.

" One word, and you are dead; our business admits of no other compromise, my brave bailiff. I must be ruined, or you be buried. If the turn of this trial of fate decides my ruin, I would rather die than live."

So saying, he and Hercules closed up on each side of the lawyer, and Simon, shaking the money, cried, "*Even*."

" It is odd," said Hercules, opening the handkerchief. "Here are five pieces."

" Why did you speak for me ?" demanded the agitated young man. " Let me try my own chance; but, for God's sake, Mr. Martineau, spare my life! Let us do no murder. I forego my advantage; let me depart as I came, and let the writ be served by a regular officer."

" No, no," Mr. Martineau replied, "this is too late; you have staked all upon a die; you must abide the throw; your hour is come; death is, after all, no great matter; we must all die; dust to dust. This is a vile world, not worth the living in. By leaving it at once you will avoid the miseries that I . have suffered."

Here the young man made a spring, as if he would escape from the window, but Mr. Martineau caught him by the arm, and said, with set teeth, fiercely, " Be quiet, sir! If you repeat that, we'll strangle you at once." Then he added, more pacifically, " You shall have steel or poison, opium or brandy, to give you courage—or insensibility, which is another word for it—but you must die."

He continued to hold his victim gently, yet firmly, by the arm, while Hercules assisted him on the other side. The lawyer choked with the intolerable thirst of fear, and gasped for breath and life before any sort of force was used—" Mr. Martineau, Mr. Martineau, for Heaven's sake, don't murder me! *Murder!*" Hercules stopped his mouth with his hand; he could proceed no further.

" If you cry murder again," said Mr. Martineau, "all is over. Dare not even attempt to call out. See where you are! But you shall have your chance. Take you the handkerchief, put in it what you please, and I will guess, and stand to my lot. He took out and pocketed his own five pieces in the dark. While he was doing this the lawyer, in a subdued tone of voice, entreated Mr. Martineau to swear that he would abide by the decision, and at least allow him life and liberty, if he guessed wrong.

"No, don't hope it. You must bury me, or I must bury you; I and you must swear to it," said the host.

"I cannot, I will not swear!" gasped the almost frantic lawyer.

"You must, you must—no trifling—swear, or get into the grave!"

"O Heaven!" exclaimed the youth, "was ever man so mad? O Liberty Hall!"

The host grasped him: "Swear!"

"I swear, then."

The lawyer wrapped up a handful of pistoles in the neckcloth, not knowing if they were odd or even. He gave them to the negro.

"Count them into his hand," said Mr. Martineau. "I say they are odd—for every thing is odd in this world, and in this house."

Hercules began: "One, two, three." The law-
10*

yer knew that there were many more. He shuddered still in the grasp of his opponent, who never
flinched a whit—" Four, five, six"—the " seventh "
fell down on the floor, and rolled to Simon's feet;
it was recovered.

" Keep it, Simon," said the lawyer, " and save me."

Hercules went on : " Eight, nine, and ten." The
negro stopped. The tale might be no more—"Eleven,
twelve."

" How many are there ?" sighed Mr. Martineau,
" twelve ?"

" This is thirteen, and this is all," said Hercules,
having forgotten whether his master had cried odd
or even.

" Your money shall lie with you," whispered
Mr. Martineau ; " what do you wish to do ?"

" Oh, let me commend my soul to God !" They
lifted him up, and placed him in the grave, where
he fell down flat in despair, with his face downward, waiting for the earth to be heaped on him.
" Yet, hold a. moment," he cried again. " I may
still save my life, and give up all ; hold, Mr. Martineau." The negro threw in a spadeful of earth.
" Keep the estates ; let me go back to England ; I
renounce all."

"For what?" said Mr. Martineau.

"For my life."

"For your forfeited, lost life?"

"Yes, yes, for my forfeited, lost life!" repeated the young deputy-sheriff.

"What security have I that you will keep your promise?"

"My word of honor. My oath."

"That will not do, sir."

"My bond, then. A discharge in full of all demands."

"Such an act would require witnesses."

"I will write a legal satisfaction, a receipt in full on the back of the writ," urged the lawyer, anxiously.

"Ah, do you swear to that?"

"I will—I do; so help me Heaven—so help me God!"

Mr. Martineau sent Simon for a light, and led the lawyer into the piazza. A book-keeper was ordered up from the overseer's house, and witnessed the payment of thirteen pistoles to the deputy-marshal, in full of all demands, from John Sylvester S——, against the estates of Alexander Martineau. No question was asked, no unneces-

sary word spoken; the signature was witnessed,
and the book-keeper dismissed, while Hercules and
Simon returned into Liberty Hall, and filled up
the grave again.   Mr. Martineau followed them,
leading in his guest, and, with his own hands, assisted to complete the job by sweeping in the remnants of the dust with a clothes-brush that lay on
the sofa.   He even jested upon the whole transaction; but his guest had no appetite left for jesting.
Although it was night, he chose to decamp with
his two negroes—who had been locked up in the
hospital during this affair—rather than accept a
bed upon the premises to which he had now resigned all claim.

The lawyer considered himself bound by his
agreement, notwithstanding the circumstances which
had forced him to enter into it; but Mr. Martineau
had compassion enough to forego it, and pay his
debts.   He held the estates in trust, and paid a
certain portion of the annual proceeds to his friend,
the deputy-marshal, who retired to the mother
country, and professes to be satisfied with the con-
signments of produce he received.

By the judicious sale of his claims—such as they
were—on his other properties, he cleared his best

estate, Martineau Hall, of all incumbrances; and, as I have already stated, he consigned the produce of his estate, for several years, to his British creditor, until all was settled. Neither of them was ever heard to complain of the peculiar mode of the grand adjustment. The young lawyer had, as report went, a decided aversion to the discussion of the subject, and so Jamaica society did not choose to take up the story too closely on the eccentric planter.

Mr. Martineau settled down on his estate, and devoted his time to the business of making sugar and rum. He never sold a slave, and would never buy any; but those he had, throve and multiplied under his personal supervision. He lived handsomely and hospitably, as is the custom of the Jamaica planters, but he mingled as little as he well could in the society of the fair sex. He owned nearly a hundred slaves, which was not far from the number at Orange Grove; but it was believed that although he was, like Mr. Davis, a humane master, he drew a larger revenue from his property than my master.

It was believed by Madame Felix's servants that Mr. Martineau was in love with their mistress "for good and true," but that Mr. Buckly was " courtin'

her for lub of de Lord and to save her blessed soul,"
and they were nearly unanimous in the wish that
she would marry the preacher—"if she must give
we a master," they would say, in proviso, for she
had not a slave on the property who did not think
that she and they were best off as they were.

Madam Felix played them off against each other,
or rather, she used to beat off the attentions of
the reverend suitor by communicating some rather
alarming particulars about Mr. Martineau. The
preacher could see that he was a man to be dreaded.
He would almost lose his ruddy color when the
planter bent upon him those fearful eyes of his,
with their fixed, unwinking stare. The sound of
his slow, measured step, as he walked up and down
the room, turning upon him at every wheel one of
those unearthly looks, was always sufficient, at any
time, to drive Mr. Buckly out of the house in five
minutes. The approaching sound of the ungodly
planter's voice or step was a spell upon the carriage and demeanor of the holy man. His own
voice and gait became constrained, and he never
failed to instantly retire from the field. How far
he knew the real truth of the burying-alive tale I
cannot vouch, but the facts were as I have stated

them. I had a version of it from Hercules, a portion of it from Mr. Holgrave, and I heard Mr. Martineau relate some parts of the drama himself, to that gentleman. When asked if he would have really buried the lawyer, but for his capitulation, he evaded an answer. Probably he had counted on the young man's fears, and calculated on the actual result. Both chances had turned in his favor, and when I knew him he was in possession of the fruits of his audacity.

Until I knew both their characters more intimately, I wondered much how a man of Mr. Holgrave's mild disposition and delicate tastes could be attached—as he certainly was—to such a law-despising creature as Mr. Martineau. But it was still more singular to me to see and hear the planter in Mr. Holgrave's sick-room. He was as quiet, pleasant, and attentive as any woman could be, and his conversation was always witty and acceptable. When Mr. Holgrave was comparatively well, the planter would often nearly petrify me by his savage way of looking at me, and with many a short declaration that the patient "ought to be hanged," or shot, for not doing this or that for himself; but the climax of all was a threat, one day, that he would

bury me alive if I neglected certain directions he
was giving me. I thought *that* was too serious for
him to jest about. I got used to his ways, and, to
my own intense surprise, grew attached to him.
He received graciously my thanks for the lily-bulbs
—which Mr. Holgrave was informed, in a note
from Miss Lucy, were all doing well—and promised
me plenty more when Mr. Holgrave returned, and
we should be settled on a place which *he* said—
though Mr. Holgrave did not confirm it—we were
next year to live upon in the Mountains of St. Eliz-
abeth. It was a place, he declared, so very healthy,
that when the inhabitants tired of life, they were
obliged to commit suicide, or go somewhere else
to find death.

Madam Felix, who happened to be present,
asked him why he did not, at once, seek the benefit
of those mountains for himself.

"Because I am sacrificing myself to save *you*
from the fangs of the missionary Maroon," he answered, not with the smile of a gentleman uttering
a jest or a compliment, but with the same immovable face with which he would threaten to bury me
alive, or tell Mr. Holgrave he would shoot him.

At last the time arrived for the breaking up of

the attached circle. In May, Mr. Holgrave sailed
for England, Mr. Martineau retired to his plantation, and I went back to my master at Orange
Grove.

Mr. Martineau had been recalled to his plantation about ten days before Mr. Holgrave's departure, and only returned, to say farewell, the day
before he embarked.   During that time, Madam
Felix, and her maid Victorine, were in Savannah-
la-Mar almost every day, to attend to various little
matters.   The gay, rattling Mademoiselle Amée
would come with them to see "Mahmadee, our Mahometan," because, as she constantly declared, she
wanted to make him a Christian. She was naturally very tender-hearted, and she had associated,
somehow, such dreadful ideas of deceit and cruelty
with my particular faith, that it became almost a
passion with the child to have me renounce it.   She
had, before that, teased her godmother, Madam
Felix, into buying me a handsome prayer-book; and
now, after gravely instructing me in the Apostles'
Creed, she exacted a parting promise that I would
say the Lord's Prayer every day.   It was a singular
request for such a lively, romping little girl to make;
but it was made, and I kept the promise.

CHAPTER XII.

MY FIRST LOVE.

I CARRIED back a heavy heart to Orange Grove. Nothing looked bright and hopeful about the place. The cloud on my own spirits seemed to dim the very sunshine. Yet there was, at first, but little real change. Brad was still head-groom, and my morning duty at the stables was little more than a pleasant chat with him. My light work was mere pastime, for I love horses, and am not a lazy fellow. Tatee had a little boy, which she wished to have baptized by my name, Sidi Mahmadee, but Mr. Buckly objected. He had become the prophet and high-priest of about fifty slave families belonging to Orange Grove and the adjoining plantation. Among his most zealous converts were, Dickie Smith, Tatee's husband, and my old shipmate Bryan. How that fellow would sing the "praises of the Lamb" on Sunday, and how he would rave and tear at his brother-Christians the rest of the week! Yet

Bryan was not a bad man at heart, and far from being a cruel driver—for he was now a driver over the African gang of field-hands—only he had a savage manner and a hasty temper. Mr. Buckly's unction of grace never went deep enough to cure that, as one person, at least, learned to his cost—but that was at a later day. Dickie Smith, the cooper, was an affectionate mate to my good friend Tatee, and she naturally adopted his ideas on religion. Having passed her "probation," she was to be married and baptized on the same day. Other couples were to share in the same rites in company with her and her husband. Dickie and his fellow-slaves had been in the habit of taking their wives as Adam had taken Eve, but the pious missionary would receive none to the Lord's Supper, in full membership, who lived together in this primitive disregard to forms. The overseer and book-keepers sneered at this strictness, and affected to believe that "Brudder Buckeye" was only looking to the little presents which the very poorest and most thriftless of the slaves will contrive to scrape up and offer their pastor on these occasions. But truth is truth. I never liked Mr. Buckly, from first to last. I had my own reasons for *not* respecting him; but, in all his inconsistent wanderings, he was never any thing but true and untiring in his labors with and for the slaves. When Quashie brought his mate with him, to ask the marriage-blessing, or Quasheba brought her picaninny to receive its name and place in Christian life, Mr. Buckly was always ready with an encouraging word, and he has officiated more than once when it would have been far more to his personal comfort, and just as agreeable to the whites about him, to have omitted the occasion.

There was always a great feasting among the slaves when the sugar-season closed. They had a week allowed them to work in their ground, feast, frolic, or have prayer-meetings, at their own choice and pleasure. Several slave couples used the occasion to be married, and others had their children baptized. My friend Tatee did both, and was herself baptized and married on the same Sunday. To marry five couples, baptize eleven children and three adults, preach two sermons, and review the singing-class in the evening, was not a light day's work for the missionary, but Mr. Buckly was equal to the emergency. He would not christen Tatee's baby by the unchristian name of Sidi, but he so far humored the wishes of the mother as to give it the name of

Sidney, which she accepted as a fair English substi-
tute. The child grew up to answer to the name of
Sid, which was exactly what my playmates in Kashna generally called me, so that we were namesakes,
after all. Tatee herself was baptized Kitty, and
both her own Houssa name and the Beauty, written down for her on the slave-book of the estate,
were rubbed out by the new Christian appellation.
A general feast—to provide which, all the parties
assisted with "bread-stuff," as they call yams,
cocos, potatoes, and cassava, from their own gardens, and the master contributed rum and sugar for
the punch—wound up the holiday. I had but little
share in any part of it. The house was full of company, and I was kept so busy early and late, that it
was only by stealing an hour or two from the time
needed for sleep, that I could gratify Tatee—I beg
her pardon, Mrs. Kitty Smith—by attending her
wedding-supper.

Directly after this holiday, the alterations and
repairs about the buildings were pressed with vigor
—rigor would be the better word, for never, while I
knew the place, were all the slaves kept so unremit-
tingly to work. The usual amount of labor was carried on in the field, the service in the house was

even increased, for there was an unusual influx of visitors, and yet every week there were one hundred days of extra work called for—and *done* too—on the buildings. To meet this increased demand for labor, only three men—mechanics from an adjoining estate —were hired. To perform all this additional work, boys and women had tasks almost beyond their strength imposed upon them. All this was the work of Mr. McGregor, the Scotchman, as he called himself, though we blacks were not slow to learn that he was born on the island, and only sent young to Scotland for his education. He gave it as his opinion, that the estate-force was quite sufficient for all purposes—with proper management—and that piqued the overseer into undertaking to have it done. He drove up the drivers, and they drove the poor slaves nearly to death. The field and the building work went on well and rapidly, however; and that, with his visiting and visitors to occupy him, was about all my master had time to inquire into. Brad worked hard in the stables, for Pompey and I had no chance to give him a helping hand.

At the close of the summer, Rachel had to go to the overseer's house to take the place of a stout woman, who was drafted for some heavier duty elsewhere. One new maid-servant, a free French quadroon from St. Domingo, who could not speak English—that being, in fact, her principal merit—was the only increase of help to meet the increased house duties, and she did not half, no, nor quarter, make up for the absence of Rachel. I had to rise at dawn to have the hall, sideboard, and coffee-table ready for the early hour at which it is usual to take the morning-cup in Jamaica. Then there was breakfast, luncheon, dinner, and supper. There were rides, and dances, and tableaux, and finally, a series of parlor dramas, to be arranged and waited upon; and, one night with another, I seldom tasted repose until midnight or past.

It was a singular time, for a boy of fifteen, to select for falling in love—or fancying he was in love—which is just as bad. When I now look back at my absurd sufferings, I smile with a sort of incredulous contempt at their imagined bitterness, but my heart was sore enough then. When I first came back to Orange Grove after Mr. Holgrave had sailed for England, Rachel laid herself out to drive away my low spirits. I had shot up into a tall youth, nearly or quite as tall, indeed, as I ever became, used better language, and had more correct manners—thanks

to Mr. Holgrave's training—than any black, slave or
free, I had ever seen, or she either; and, above all, I
had self-conceit enough to stock the whole plantation. In one word, I thought myself entitled to
make love to any damsel of my own condition, that
came in my way. Rachel was older than I by,
perhaps, two years, but that was no objection to a
lover of fifteen, and she, at first, did not seem to regard the difference in our ages as an obstacle to our
love-making. It is true she was of a much lighter
shade than I, for, though Pompey, her father, and
Myrtilla, her mother, were both of them fully as
dark as I am, Rachel, their only child, was, by one
of those unaccountable freaks of Nature which occasionally occur on plantations, a clear mulatto; but
she was not scornful because she was of a more favored complexion. I declared my love and admiration in every form and at all seasons, that I could
command, and, if she did not exactly profess to love
me in return, she certainly allowed me—and all the
rest of the servants as well—to understand that I
stood foremost in her good graces. She permitted
me to speak to Pompey, and ask him to obtain the
consent of my master to our marriage at a suitable
time. The old man made no objection, except that

we were too young; but we expected to wait awhile,
and he · was ˙ satisfied. Myrtilla proposed that I
should make myself a Christian, and be baptized—
for my stubborn Mahometanism was a standing
theme of surprise and disapprobation in the household—but when I anxiously submitted this delicate
point to Rachel, she replied, with the easy liberality
of perfect indifference, that "such . Christians as
Massa Buckly makes are plenty as rats on this estate, and I wants none of 'em."

Thus accepted and sustained, what more could
be desired ? For a few weeks I was in the seventh
heaven of contentment, only in place of the innumer-
able houris, which await the true believer there, I
had but one lively, ready-witted, dark-skinned damsel to comfort me here below. She suited me, however, much better than the distant beauties of paradise. The unusual number of visitors pressed somewhat hardly on both of us, but I contrived to relieve
Rachel of some hours' labor by sitting up later at ⸱
night. The silver, of which there was a good deal
in daily use when the family was large, had been
thrown upon us to clean and account for, and it was
happiness for me to coax her to take an hour's rest
on the wide hall-lounge, while I attended to the

11

plate, and when the last spoon and dish-cover had received its polishing touch, to wake her with a light kiss and tell her our work was all finished, and she could go to her night's rest without care for the table duties of the morning. Then she would say so kindly: "You are too good, Mahmadee, to do all my work, as well as your own, but I was *so* tired!"

Part of the company went away, and then, the overseer having Mr. McGregor at his table and Mr. McGregor's room to be taken care of, Rachel had to go over there to wait on the table and do the chamberwork. It was impossible for me to relieve her there, for I was incessantly occupied at the Great House through the day; but she had to be at hand every evening, for Rosa, the new French girl, was raw then, and useless to my mistress, who did not speak any language but English. But Rachel was no longer the same to me, after she began to wait at the overseer's house. She became cold and distant; and when I entreated her to let me know in what I had offended her, she cut me off with short answers that bruised my very heart. She refused my assistance, when, in the hope of softening her sudden hardness to me, I would hang about and watch the chance to offer it. I grew wildly jealous at last, and accused her of deceit, and of breaking her engagement. She laughed scornfully, and denied the engagement. I must be crazy, she said, to suppose she had ever thought of a boy like me. I think she did set me half crazy, but she never would have had that power over me if she had not, in the first place, flattered and fooled me with a very winning show of affection.

I had not the sense and resolution to take my dismissal like a man, for I was, alas, but a fond and foolish boy. I could not give up Rachel. I would have bought her with my heart's blood. I would have turned Christian for her sake, and was ready to be married to her in church. I went so far as to tell my mistress so, but she, who was once so bent on my Christian salvation, only laughed at me.

I appealed to Mr. Buckly, but he told me I must learn my catechism, and look out for some other girl.

I went to the overseer, who told me to call again, in two years' time, and he would give me an answer. I applied to the parson of the parish, who called me a sensual beast, and said he would not baptize me under such circumstances.

No one had a word of comfort for me. Pompey told me I was a fool, and so did his wife; but none among them all put me on the right track, until Tatee—that is, Kitty Smith—sent for me, and said, without much preamble:—

"That white-faced master-builder is a-going to stay at Orange Grove, and he picks out Rachel to be his housekeeper. That's the whole story, my poor Mahmadee, and there is no use in your fighting against it. Rachel sets herself up for a grand lady, now, and will never look at a black boy again, if he is a king's son."

It was as clear as the sunshine, but it was too much for my strength. The fatigue, excitement, and unseasonable hours, joined to the worry of my pursuit of Rachel, and the bitter shock of the final disappointment, overcame me. I was taken sick, and ordered into the infirmary by the estate doctor. I was not kept to my bed more than three days, but it was a fortnight before I was able to return to my duties, and it was nearly two months before the doctor would allow me to take hold of any kind of heavy work.

This Dr. Marsh was the same gentleman who passed us on the road the night we ran away, and

whom Bryan was wild enough to propose to rob
and kill. I had opposed the motion, and Brad, in
particular, had sided with me, when I declared it
should not be done, and that I would call out and
warn the doctor if Bryan attempted to approach
him. I had almost forgotten the circumstance, and
in no case whatever would have dreamed of reveal-
ing it; but, to my surprise, Dr. Marsh mentioned
it to me himself, and asked how such a mere child
as I was at that time had dared to oppose myself
to a powerful savage like Bryan. I attempted to
evade the question, by saying I could not see how
any one could get up such a story about poor Bryan.

"Bryan himself is my authority for the story,"
said the doctor; "and I only want to hear from
you what induced you to oppose him so stoutly."

"I believe it was from my horror of the crime
of murder," I answered.

"It was not, then, from a calculation of the
consequences?" pursued the doctor.

"I was too young for much calculation; but I
hope that old affair won't bring Bryan into trouble
now," I said, anxiously, for there was no mercy in
those days for the negro who had threatened the
life of a white man.

" Be at ease about that," the doctor said. " The
confession tumbled out head foremost when he was
sick, and I would have then asked you about your
own part in it, if you had not been absent attending
my friend Mr. Holgrave. I like your courage."

I did not see any courage in it, to speak of, but
I was pleased to receive the approbation of the doc-
tor, for he was quite a personage at the Great
House.

Dr. Marsh was always esteemed by the family,
and about that time had become a frequent visitor.
He also began to take notice of me, and finally fell
into the habit of hearing me read and recite poetry.
He was a tall, thin man, and had been very sickly
in England, and in Jamaica, too, for some time.
But he had been brought up a doctor—for his father
was one before him—and knew how to manage his
complaint, which was an affection of the lungs. He
was a rather silent and reserved person, but with a
great fund of knowledge in his long head. He was
a very fine musician, too, and a poet. He wrote
verses, and painted landscapes in water-colors, for
the mistress. He used to accompany the young
ladies when they played the piano, and he gave
them lessons in drawing. This gentleman gave me

a Latin grammar and a Corderius, though rather against the consent of my master, who did not approve of my education being extended to the dead languages, perhaps because he had very little recollection of them himself. However, I begged hard to be allowed to learn, and he consented, though with a sort of growl.

" So our prince wants to be a black bishop, as he can't be a king. Well, in for a penny, in for the pound."

My memory is of the strongest stuff. It holds any and every thing. But of all things I ever piled into it, the contents of that Latin grammar were the least relishing. Yet I as regularly dosed myself with a page or two of it, while I was cleaning the plate, as I counted the spoons. It helped me to forget my foolish passion for Rachel.

My mistress had not been altogether pleased with her transfer to the overseer's house, and her face was almost as rarely seen at the Great House as mine in the region of the " works "—which was never. The overseer and book-keepers were a distinct circle from the family society. It was a step in the direction of the laboring herd, but only a step, for the distance between any white man and a being stained with the African tint, even though but in the fourth or fifth degree, was inconceivable, immeasurable. Dr. Marsh used to style our three classes on the plantation—lords, commons, and people. Mr. Davis was the sovereign—and a pretty absolute one, too—of the whole community.

During my illness my old mulatto teacher came to see me, and had a great deal to say about my gifts and my learning, and of my duty to behave like·the son of a king, and of being looked up to accordingly. These visits were paid to me while I was confined to the estate hospital—for negro visitors are not much tolerated to the servants of the Great House—and did not then much attract my notice, but after-circumstances raised them to an alarming significance. I had ceased to be his pupil, when I had learned of him considerably more of arithmetic than he knew himself; but I had assisted him pretty regularly with his singing-class on Sunday evenings, until Mr. Buckly made his appearance. It was only when the missionary joined forces with the schoolmaster, in the pious determination to bring me into the Christian fold by the hair of my head, that I beat a retreat.

In the busiest time, with more visitors and fewer

servants than usual, my indulgent mistress, and the kind, considerate Miss Lucy, would grant me permission to attend the singing-class; but Rachel's coquetries, and the mortification and illness that followed the loss of her fickle heart, had kept me away for many weeks. The mulatto teacher now urged me to come to the singing-school, if not to sing, at least to see my old friends. Mr. Buckly had collected such a number of "sacrament members and probationers" (I use his own phrase, and hope it is correct), that the Sunday evening was not sufficient, and had to appoint a singing-practice for the "ladies and gentlemen of that standing on Thursday." Again I use his own words, and therefore I again venture to hope I am quite correct. On attending the Thursday night singing-practice, I generally met, beside our own people, a large collection of slaves from the plantations on each side of Orange Grove, who had permission to come and sing hymns with their neighbors. They were not all, nor even a majority of them, of Mr. Buckly's special congregation; but the Baptists, Wesleyans, and Moravians have many sacred songs in common, and it was not a subject of surprise that members of the different faiths should meet to sing them together. So, for

11*

a time, I found a soothing relief in being present at these exercises, in which I was, to the last, a welcome and petted leader, although known to be, all the while, an obstinate Mahometan.

My master and the ladies encouraged my regular attendance at these meetings for "singing-practice," and Dr. Marsh was uniformly kind and instructive in his notice of me, but I was not at ease.

Mr. Holgrave spent a week at Orange Grove, prior to his departure for England; and after he sailed, Mr. Martineau often passed a day with the family. Pompey told me that he overheard him make an agreement with my master for my permanent transfer to Mr. Holgrave, on that gentleman's return to Jamaica, but no hint to that effect reached me from any other source. I had something to occupy me in teaching the other slaves their Sunday-school hymns, and in learning the first elements of the healing art under Dr. Marsh, who was kindness itself.

The family were much absent in the fall; and when they were away I was placed, at his own particular request, under the exclusive charge of Dr. Marsh. He asked for me, nominally, to assist him in making up medicines, but, in reality, to enable

me to pursue my studies under his directions. I
soon learned to feel a pulse, judge of the tongue,
and, in slight cases, attend the out-door patients;
and from that practice I acquired a love for the
profession which has lasted through life.

The other whites on the plantation hated me for
the distinction of an education already superior to
their own, which they considered a sort of treason
to the lordly dignity of their race.

It was then almost a crime for a black to aspire
to an education, and scarcely less criminal in a white
to assist him to attain one.

The overseer, who had some slight idea of what
I was doing with the slaves, treated me with cold
contempt. The book-keepers—I presume so called
on Jamaica estates because they usually have nothing to do with books—were bountiful of derision.
They called me *Mammy Dear*, Dr. Nigga, the charcoal Euclid, the darky poet, and the Black Prince—
though that last expression was used very freely—
and not in unkindness—by the doctor and his visiting friends. The book-keepers would scream out a
hundred yards off for me to come and solve what
they called equations. As, for instance: Suppose a
goat lost one of his horns, how far would that make

it from his tail to Christmas, and again from Christmas to Capricornus in the Zodiac. This choice wit was chiefly coined in the brain of my *bête noir* McGregor; and, silly as it may seem to one above the reach of such petty shafts, they stung me to the quick in those days, for I felt, in my burning spirit, that Rachel often heard and admired the malicious sallies launched at the helpless head of her discarded lover.

It all helped to burn deeper into my heart of hearts the desire—*the determination*—to become a freeman. With Rachel I might have sunk lower, and settled down in the mire of slavery in stupid content. Scorned of her, and in the desperate need of something to fill the craving void, I began to hoard up, penny by penny, a little " white music," as work-house Ben had advised me, in the Medinet pouch of his gift, with a steadfast aim to future freedom.

CHAPTER XIII.

THE CONSPIRACY.

IT was while my master and mistress were on a short visit to Savannah-la-Mar, that I was very particularly invited to attend the singing-practice on Saturday evening, instead of Thursday, as usual. I went in company with my old shipmates Brad and Bryan, who were both very devout believers in Mr. Buckly and his ministrations, and had a common passion for hymn-singing. There was something unusual in the respectful attention accorded to me, a boy as yet short of sixteen, by the assembly. I noticed, at the time, that there were many of the ablest men, and but few women, from the neighboring estates, but I did not dwell upon it. I had a seat beside my old mulatto schoolmaster, who then and always seemed to take much pride in parading me as a sign-board of his teaching capabilities, and was very politely requested by him to open the meeting with a speech on my experience at Savannah-la-Mar. I had no experience to relate, and said so, but I contrived to entertain them with an account of some missionary meetings I had attended while living with Mr. Holgrave.

The schoolmaster followed this up by a glowing account of various meetings all over the country, and concluded by asking me if I had not read in books that there were two black church-members in Jamaica for every white one. I had read some report to that effect, and stated my belief in its accuracy, whereupon a man arose, and said, "The *brothers of the good cause* were much obliged and very thankful to Prince Mahmadee."

I have here italicized "the *brothers of the good cause*," though, at the time they were uttered, I only noticed that they were pronounced in good English instead of the negro lingo, but so were many of Mr. Buckly's pet phrases, by dint of admiring repetition. We had three or four of these meetings before my suspicions were fully aroused, and even then they were not directed to the true point of danger.

I was invited to assist in teaching Bryan and Belton to read. They had secretly learned the alphabet, and each of them had a small printed sheet, the size of a page in a common Testament, containing the alphabet in large capitals, and a few words, such as RAT, CAT, BAT, printed in small letters at the bottom. On the back of the sheet were two columns of such words, with small cuts of the animals opposite the names. It was an attractive way of teaching young children—or our ignorant blacks, who were but young children in their mental development—how to form letters into words and connect them with a meaning.

My master had exacted from me a promise, which I kept faithfully, not to instruct any other slave without his express permission; and Mr. Holgrave, with all his liberality, enforced on me the necessity of keeping this obligation sacred. Hitherto there was not much occasion for it. I had until then never found a brother-negro anxious for real instruction, or, at least, ready to encounter the difficulties of acquiring knowledge. I did not think, therefore, I was depriving my old friends of any very important benefit, when I declined teaching them to read. I was, however, often amused—but did not mention the fact to any white person—to see Dickie Smith sitting up at night, and laboring by the hour, with Brad and Bryan over their C-A-T, *cat*, and R–A–T, *rat*, and thought it almost too late to arrest the progress of their education.

This was in 1810. The United States had suppressed the slave-trade, and England had kept step in this great beginning in the march of civilization. It was rumored among the slaves that the king of England had "promised God to make *free Christians* of all the negroes in the world." Our white masters were careful not to discuss these matters in the hearing of the slaves—or thought they were—but the dark, broken hints of discontent with the general aspect of affairs, and the uneasy distrust of the planters as to the future policy of the Government at home, would escape them while over their wine, or in family conversations, and they trickled down to the lower levels, and were there shaped and circulated as a pledge of early emancipation. The frequent, and often violent, dissensions between the governor—who was appointed by the king—and the island Parliament, which was elected by the planters, greatly confused the minds of men at once eager for the great boon of emancipation, and ignorant of any possible road to it, except by the direct act of an absolute king—or, by the extermination of the whites.

A belief that the king willed their emancipation,
and that his governors had orders to set them free,
but that the House of Assembly prevented it, was
gaining ground among the blacks in town and country. Only a crafty, able, unscrupulous leader was
wanting to light the match, and desolate the island
with blood and flame. The planters felt insecure;
property depreciated; those who could, mortgaged
their estates to British capitalists, as the most direct
way of raising large sums of money wherewith to
take their families out of the island. These omens
of change escaped me then, but in looking back I
now see, by the light of experience, that it was not
the abolition of slavery so much as the blind dread
of its effects, and the still more blind neglect to prepare for it, which, for half a century, kept the finest
British colony in those seas on the verge of utter
ruin.

My master had returned, and was sitting with
Dr. Marsh and a neighboring planter on the piazza,
enjoying the fresh evening and a bowl of punch,
when I returned from the singing-practice, for the
first time fully awake to the fact that a great mischief was brewing. The meeting was that night almost wholly composed of men, and various frag-

ments of hymns had been sung, which, as they were given out in mutilated parts, had in them much more of war than religion. I had gone from the meeting to Dickie Smith's in company with Bryan, and had drawn from them a general admission that there was something great on hand. Bryan hinted at a speedy revenge on one of the book-keepers, and promised me the same on McGregor. It was taken for granted that I must and would seize the opportunity to pay back the smarts I had suffered, and that from my free birth and buckra education I would be proud of the leadership they were ready to offer me, as they said, "when the cane was cut and the sugar a-boiling."

I gathered all I could of the plan, which was not much, for they were not trusted entirely with the hights and depths of the plot, and, after many and earnest injunctions from me to be silent and on their guard, I left them to seek out Brad. He was not in his place—he had gone to the schoolmaster's. It was already late for my night duties, and I hastened to the Great House, where I found the three gentlemen discussing punch and politics on the piazza. The doctor rose almost immediately, and, bidding me come with him to the dispensary for some medicines, led off toward the estate-hospital. As soon as we were inside, he forgot the medicines, and began to cross-examine me about the singing-meetings. I was not disposed to betray my fellow-slaves, but I was anxious beyond measure to check the rash insurrection, for I knew it could only end, as all previous ones had ended, in the defeat and cruel chastisement of the blacks. I affected, therefore, to understand him only in the sense he had always treated these meetings, as a harmless imitation of the sectarian congregations of the whites. The doctor made the same feint to deceive me, but, of the two, I was the most successful hypocrite.

"This Buckly is getting up a great congregation. Our regular parson must look sharp, or he will not have a black soul left in his care," said the doctor, with an affectation of carelessness. "How many, think you, has he baptized, and married, and fleeced, among our slaves?"

"Thirty or so, I should say, but he has more members on the estates round Orange Grove," I answered, as sure of the next question as if it were already uttered.

"And how many people have you usually at the singing-schools you attend, Mahmadee?"

"Just as it happens," I replied, now perfectly on my guard. "When the evening is clear and pleasant, so as to bring out the young girls to show their fine buckra dresses, there will be a gathering of forty or fifty singers from the different estates."

I did not say I had seen nearly twice as many robust, excited *men* together that very night.

"It will be well to stop this business of running about to different estates, and collecting in such numbers."

The doctor said this in a quick, anxious way, as if the words slipped out unawares, but I chose to consider it a remark addressed to myself.

"Yes, sir, the congregations are too large for comfort, and beside that, there is danger of their getting into fights. Such ignorant people are always ready to run themselves into scrapes."

The doctor looked so very keenly at me, that I felt my cheeks burn, but blushes don't show through a black skin. I have, more than once, found that a decided convenience.

"Mahmadee, I think you appreciate what has been done for you and are grateful for it," said the doctor, after a pause that began to make me uncomfortable.

"I do appreciate it, sir, with all my heart and soul," I said, with sincere warmth. "If I had the power to prove it, even with my life, you and my master, and Mr. Holgrave, and the ladies, too, would be convinced that a grateful heart can beat under a black skin."

"Well, let us suppose a case. If, for example, you had lived in Trelawney when the blacks had a rising there, you would have put your master on his guard against the conspirators, and defended him and his family to the death. Would you not?"

"Undoubtedly I would defend my master against such murderers and house-burners, while I had a drop of blood left in my body, but, excuse me for saying, that if there had not been white fools as well as black ones, in Trelawney, all those lives might have been saved."

"In what way, Mahmadee? I don't understand you."

"The plan of insurrection was suspected some time before it broke out, and I think there ought to have been men found competent to dive into the plots of the ringleaders, and frustrate them."

"Yes, I see. Work into their confidence and expose them, before they could bring their hellish

plots into execution. Excellent! excellent! if it can
be managed," said the doctor, warmly, quite forgetting that we were not talking of any thing of present
concern, but only of far away and suppositious cases.
I was more wary, and stuck to the Trelawney text
in answering his suggestion.

"If there had been any faith or good sense among
those Trelawney negroes, some of them would have
had influence enough upon the poor, ignorant rebels,
to persuade them out of their mad schemes, and so
saved their own lives and their masters' property.
It seems to me the white gentlemen were to blame,
in not setting their better-instructed servants to
search into the bottom of the affair as soon as they
suspected it. They might have cured the folly by
discouraging it, instead of 'burning up the house
to kill the rats,' as we say in Africa."

He remained silent for some time, and then, with
a kind of sigh, he locked up the medicine-case, and,
putting the key in his pocket, walked out of the
door. I followed him with my eyes until he had
entered the house, and then I went back to the
cooper's cabin, at the risk of being wanted and
missed at the Great House.

I had decided on my part while talking with the

doctor. It was precisely what I told him the Trelawney masters ought to have done: dive into the plans of the ringleaders, and frustrate their mad plot without betraying the conspirators. Affairs went on as if my master and the doctor read the inmost thoughts of my mind, for whatever I asked was instantly granted, and that without a look of suspicion or a word of question. Either would have disconcerted me. I went from man to man, and from meeting to meeting, and by always talking of what I would like to do to McGregor—but only at the proper time—by holding out promises of universal freedom pretty soon—but not exactly fixing the time when—and dilating upon the bright days when we and the buckras should own estates together, and a thousand other things too silly to repeat, but which did what I was aiming at, I soon created a party disposed to be wary and patient, rather than rash and violent. All—even those who were opposed to my extremely cautious policy of waiting until the governor himself should call us out—trusted me with their own ideas, and let me into the inner heart of the plot. It was organized at Kingston, and I soon found it had a fearfully-wide, though wretchedly-organized, range Those little alphabet sheets, with their few words of reading, were to be used as passports by the messengers of uprising and desolation. A very simple, yet most cunningly-devised, combination of those few short words had volumes of bloody teachings. I need not dwell upon it. *Rat* meant the negro who, at the appointed hour, would *eat up* the life and stores of the whites. The *bat* was the white man fancying himself a winged bird, but in reality living only in the dark. *Cat* was the military force, which were to be foiled by the cunning rats.

Suffice it to say, that having learned that the Kingston blacks were to find arms and second the uprising of the country negroes, I and my party resolved to keep quiet until the Kingston negroes had actually risen and obtained arms for us, and this sensible idea of waiting for arms was spread as far as our means of communication reached. When I had made sure of my ground, I told the doctor and my master this much, and no more, for it was all the case required. I assured them that our slaves had been somewhat moved by the idea that the king of England had or was about to have them all made free, and that they believed the governor was ready to act upon it, but was not permitted to do so. I also told them that the negroes of Kingston were, in their own fashion, planning to rise upon the whites, to obtain, as they thought, their own liberty and that of the governor, and that it was quite likely there were those about Orange Grove who might be wrought upon to follow such a lead, but that I felt confident I could manage to keep them out of the fire.

The doctor set off for Kingston to avert the storm, if possible, and arrived at that city just in time to find it under martial law. The conspiracy had been discovered, and the desperate plot broken up. There had been one or two rash attempts at rising—and not far from us either—but they were speedily and severely crushed. Those of our slaves who had been saved from these horrors, by taking my advice, were so thankful to me, that I had as much trouble to keep them from betraying themselves in that way, as I had gone through to prevent them from throwing themselves headlong into a bloody and fruitless uprising.

My master never said much to me on the subject, but he was so deeply impressed with the insecurity of life and property in Jamaica, that he

12

determined to sell or dispose of the estate in some way, and remove with his family to England.

Mr. Holgrave had now been absent ten months, and in his last letters named from four to six months as the earliest period of his return. I felt heart-sick at this long delay, but I had also the comfort of being kindly remembered by him in every letter. By this last vessel he had sent me six volumes of history, ancient and modern, with several maps. He also sent sheets of music, and volumes of poetry to the young ladies, and a microscope, with some other articles, to Dr. Marsh. His affairs in England went well, he wrote, but that the British winters were too severe for him, and that nothing there could make up to him the loss of the delicious climate and perpetual verdure of the coffee mountains of Jamaica.

Mr. Holgrave was informed, in reply, of the uneasy state of the island, and of the "faithful courage and superior intelligence displayed by Mahmadee, in keeping the slaves of Orange Grove and the adjoining plantations in perfect quiet. In justice to his services," my master went on to say, "I would instantly set him free, but he will be so much better off under your instructions, that I make him

over to you until such time as we can provide a
suitable line of livelihood for him." My master
read me this part of his letter, but recommended
me to keep silent about it while I remained on the
plantation.

Mr. Buckly, however, came in for the chief
credit of suppressing the conspiracy, with the other
planters; and even my master took his word for
it that his admonitions had done wonders in restraining the slaves under his teachings from outbreak and violence. He said he had broken down
his riding-horse, hurrying from point to point to
-enjoin peace and obedience to their masters. To
atone for this loss in their service, our fine pacing-
pony Easy was presented to him, and he ambled
off on it in high content, leaving his miserable old
hack to be nursed up for sale by his zealous pro-
bationer, Brad. I well knew the exact value—or
rather no value—of his peace-keeping services among
the slaves, but I said nothing, for to prate much
would be to let out what I labored and prayed
to have buried in oblivion. I wished to keep secret
forever the daring extent of the conspiracy, for I
knew that if it were once completely understood,
there would be an end of comfort for master or

slave on that plantation; and I was glad to see the family prepare to leave for England without pressing the inquiry too closely.

I remained at the plantation until Mr. Holgrave arrived to assume the entire charge of me. Dr. Marsh was the only person who had the right, meanwhile, to give me orders; and after Mr. Davis left, the book-keepers, and more particularly Mr. McGregor, was made to understand that I no longer counted for an ordinary plantation slave. I was kept steadily to my work and my books, however, and had glowing visions of how much my dear Mr. Holgrave would be pleased with my improvement.

Mr. Martineau came to see the family before the final removal from Orange Grove, and took the precaution to have papers made out, to the effect that I was to have my freedom, without conditions, January, 1812, but that, in the mean time, my personal services were to remain at the exclusive command of Philip Holgrave, Esq.

CHAPTER XIV.

MIRAFLOR.

NEARLY a month sooner than I had dared hope for Mr. Holgrave's return, my old friend Hercules rode in with the joyful tidings that my dear master had landed at Kingston, and was well on the road to his own house in Savannah-la-Mar. Mr. Martineau had gone to meet him, and meanwhile had sent his own man, Hercules, to bring me to my future home. Dr. Marsh had been kind to me, far beyond my merits, but my heart never melted and bowed down before him as it did in the mild warmth of Mr. Holgrave's presence. I was grateful to him, and still more to my late master, Mr. Davis; but it was a cold feeling compared to the devout, admiring love I cherished for my new and ever-gentle owner.

I parted with Kitty Smith (we no longer called her Tatee) with sincere regret, but she promised to take care of the flowers around little Henry's

grave; and, that arranged, I shook hands with Brad
and the rest, and set out eagerly for my long-prayed-
for home with Mr. Holgrave.

The first winter of his return Mr. Holgrave enjoyed unusually good health; and Mr. Martineau,
who was more than half his time with him, grew
in grace and good looks every day. Madam Felix
would drive in once or twice a week, for a couple
of hours in the afternoon, and there was always a
store of delicacies in the carriage for her "spoiled
children." On other days, I drove out the two
gentlemen for an evening at her house. It was
the occasion of some sneering criticisms, that two
white gentlemen should maintain such an open and
respectful intimacy with a quadroon. Had the intimacy been equally open, and *not* respectful, it
would have passed without an ill-natured comment.
It was the evident respectability of the transaction
which gave edge and point to the scandal. The
friends kept each other in countenance and their
critics at bay, by always going together. A smooth,
sedate gentleman—I think he was the rector of the
parish—called one morning, and, as if half in jest,
asked them what they found so attractive in that
person of color, that they bestowed upon her the

attentions generally reserved, by gentlemen of their standing in society, for ladies of their own condition.

"Madam Felix is a most estimable and intelligent woman, and has been to me the kindest of friends and nurses," said Mr. Holgrave.

"No doubt—no doubt, my dear sir, but she is, nevertheless, a person of color, and out of question as—as—as an associate."

"My health—and my inclination, sir," replied Mr. Holgrave, with a freezing bow, "must regulate my habits and associates."

I was charmed to hear gentle Mr. Holgrave take such a firm tone. The reverend gentleman was a little disconcerted, but he had the nerve to look into Mr. Martineau's cast-iron face, and say that he presumed he too found a tender nurse in Madam Felix.

"Inestimable, sir, inestimable; and in order to secure the treasure to myself, I am soliciting her hand in marriage."

"*In-deed*, sir?" dragged out the venerable visitor, taking up his hat and bowing himself out, perfectly overwhelmed by the cool audacity of word and look with which the planter spoke and stared

him down. It was altogether indescribable, but
never to be forgotten. .

Mr. Holgrave courteously attended the gentleman to the door, and then, throwing himself on the
lounge, he laughed as I had never heard him laugh
before. Mr. Martineau never moved a muscle of
that stony face, though I had to nearly bite my
tongue through to maintain the decorous non-ob-
serving so becoming my position.

"Here, you Prince of Darkness, what are you
waiting for?. If you don't hurry out with those
glasses, I'll flay you alive!"

This was to me, of course, and with the same
look, though with a milder voice than he had vouch-
safed to the clerical visitor. I retreated in silence;
and I imagined that I heard his. sharp, dry "Ha!
ha!" mingling with Mr. Holgrave's uncommon fit of
merriment, but it may have been but an imagining. ·

They went out that evening on purpose, I really
believe, to relate to Madam Felix the formal declaration of his views on her hand and heart, which Mr.
Martineau had made to the clergyman. As I was
flirting with Victorine, on the piazza—by way of
antidote to the bitter memories of my Rachel-mania
—I heard Mr. Holgrave presenting a version of the

affaii well calculated to raise the planter in her esteem. While they were all on the subject, Mr.
Buckly ambled up on my old pet, Easy, but seeing
me—which meant that certain gentlemen were not
far off—he declined alighting. He said he had only
called to inform the house-servants there would be
service and singing-practice the next Sabbath evening. As all the house-servants were Catholics, like
their mistress, they never attended his preaching,
and, speaking next to no English, they could not
understand him if they had ; but it was an available
excuse for a visit to the rich and captivating quadroon, and the zealous missionary made the most
of it.

"Evil communications corrupt good manners,"
was one of the copies set for my writing-lessons,
and I pin much faith on that maxim. It must have
been Mr. Martineau's wicked example—unless it was
a deferential setting forth in practice of my sense
of the truth of Mr. Buckly's assurances, that I was
by nature a bottomless abyss of depravity—that in-
stigated me to vex the spirit of this saintly suitor.
I managed, while patting Easy and receiving his
message, to mention the fact—confidentially, and
with a respectful petition that he would not allow

12*

my name to get out—that I heard Mr. Martineau speak to the clergyman about his intended marriage to Madam Felix. This sudden announcement brought matters to a crisis. The holy man had abandoned the hope of making me a Christian, so he made me his confidant. I intimated an opinion that the planter had made himself a little too sure of the lady, touched upon how much every slave on the property, even to the house-servants, would prefer him for a master to such a stern man as Mr. Martineau—which was true enough, for they all stood in mortal awe of the man who was suspected of the irregular practice of burying his slaves alive—and closed with a sigh of regret that I, a poor slave, had no power to influence the amiable lady to be careful of her happiness.

"But you have influence, my boy," he whispered, eagerly. "You have uncommon influence, both with Madam Felix and Mr. Holgrave. You can drop a word here and there, that will sprout, and grow, and take root, like kernels of wheat in good ground."

I heaved up another sigh by main force, and declared my readiness to go through fire and water to serve such a kind, excellent lady, if I but knew how. The pious man thought the way plain enough. It was to aid her union with him. To serve this interest was to secure her happiness in this world and the next.

"This is not clear to you now, Mahmadee" (it certainly was not), "but when your heart is opened to gospel light, you will understand that it would be like linking her precious soul to eternal perdition to join in wedlock with a godless mate."

With this bit of spiritual unction, a fervent pressure of the hand, a whispered hint that my freedom would be secured in the "rescue of that lamb from the spoiler," and a louder charge to lay his admonitions to heart—the good man went his ways.

On second thoughts, I was not quite so much delighted with myself as I had felt while playing my game with Mr. Buckly. I rather feared he had won it. I had prated of things said and done before me—a fault I had been schooled to avoid, and one Mr. Holgrave—to say nothing of Mr. Martineau and his stern, staring eye—would not look upon with indulgence, if it came back to him in an unfavorable shape, which might happen any day. I had pretended to lend myself as a spy and informer to the missionary, and I had undoubtedly put him

on a scent which he was sure to follow up hotly,
and—like the bungler he was—equally sure to betray
himself, and whoever else was fool enough to mix
up in his business.   I half resolved to tell Mr. Holgrave all about it; but, beside the doubt how he
would take it, I felt some compunction about betraying the preacher's confidence, after inviting it
by a hypocritical show of devotion to his interests:
so, upon the whole, I concluded to keep my own
counsel for the present, and be more cautious in
future.

In all this time—I mean while the winter and
spring were slipping away, and Mr. Holgrave was
settling up his affairs, to remove to some healthy,
bracing situation in the mountain—my own future
destiny remained undecided, or, at least, undeclared.
Mr. Holgrave had, in every respect, assumed the
entire control of me, and never used any other language than that of admitted ownership.   He told
Mr. Buckly, one day, that he should not part with
me while he lived, but that, on his death, he would
make a bequest of me to his sect, if they would engage to make me as good a missionary as himself,
and send me out to Africa to convert my countrymen, and cure them of slave-trading.   The preacher

caught at that, and hinted that it would be a wholesome thing for his own soul, as well as mine, if I
were handed, at once, over to his instructions; but
Mr. Holgrave said that I must remain yet a while,
to attend to his bodily ailments.

With the early spring rains, a visible change for
the worse came over Mr. Holgrave, and Madam
Felix invited him to go up to Miraflor, a coffee-estate
she owned in St. Ann's, and be nursed through the
rainy months. Mr. Martineau promised to be of
the party, and after some hesitation he consented
to the plan. Arrangements were made accordingly,
and by the end of May we were comfortably established in the most charming place I had then ever
seen. Madam Felix had preceded us a fortnight, to
have the house in readiness, and had taken with her
the whole staff of French servants.

An incident of the trip to the mountains nearly
deprived me of the best of masters. In crossing a
mountain-stream, which the late rains had swelled
to a torrent, the horse rode by Mr. Holgrave missed
his footing, and threw his rider into the water. I
had my eye on hiss—as I always had in rough
places, on account of his feeble health—and I managed to swing myself below him in the current, and

secured him, I never could really understand how,
on my left arm and shoulder, and so bore him up,
and landed him safely on the other side. I had to
let go of my horse, and was nearly carried away
myself, while I was helping Mr. Holgrave up the
bank. Mr. Martineau, who rode a fine, powerful
horse, was in time to seize me by the collar, and
steady me up to firm standing-ground, while his
man Hercules saved our floating horses. Luckily,
we were almost at the end of our journey, and had
the enjoyment of dry clothes and a hot dinner, at
Miraflor, before we had time to get chilled. I was
almost ashamed to hear Mr. Holgrave say he owed
his life to my courage and presence of mind, when
I knew there was no presence of mind about it. I
saw his horse plunge him into the water, and in my
fright—not my courage—I plunged in to catch him.
How I managed to do it I had so little idea, that
my first thought and first word was of thanks to
Allah, for *His* mercy in saving my master. If gratitude was due anywhere among us, it was to Mr.
Martineau, in forcing his horse into the foaming
eddy, and risking his life to save me, a poor slave-
boy, from being carried under. But when I ven-

tured to say as much, he ordered me to keep my
silly tongue inside of my black numskull.

We were all on the wide piazza, Mr. Martineau
walking up and down its length, Mr. Holgrave reclining on the lounge, from which he could look far
away, over hill and dale, to the sea, shining like a
silver floor, under a starry roof. I had been serving
him with his light supper of arrow-root when this
conversation took place. Madam Felix was tuning
her guitar, to favor the planter with a particular
chanson, at his request, and she now begged him to
sit down, as I had a message to deliver him. He
obeyed, and she beckoned to me. I approached her
with the little silver waiter on which I had handed
Mr. Holgrave his cup of arrow-root. She drew a
diamond ring from her finger, and said, in French,
" Mahmadee begs to offer this ring to his brave
preserver, in the name of all who may have a drop
of African blood in their veins." I knelt as I presented the salver for the ring, and she again repeated the words as she laid it down. I crossed the
room, and repeated them with great exactness, as,
again bending the keee, I held forward the ring.
Mr. Martineau rose, took it up, and, turning toward
Madam Felix, bowed with grace, and kissed it, say-

ing that none but a Bayard, *sans peur et sans reproche*, was worthy of the precious gift, but that he could at least appreciate it. There was a degree of grace and emotion in that act of Mr. Martineau that made me wonder why I once thought him so very ugly. I had taken my cue in this little scene from others, half serious, half playful, which were often got up in that circle. They all retired soon after, and Mr. Holgrave remarked, that he had not passed so pleasant an evening in the last three weeks.

Mr. Martineau's room was separated from Mr. Holgrave's by a narrow passage, or ante-room, in which a pallet was laid at night for me, and he had literally to step over me when he came to Mr. Holgrave's door, later in the evening, and said, laughing—actually laughing—"The missionary has been here before us, Holgrave. That is something to keep us alive—eh?" as he stepped back over my body. I was inclined to think this odd genius had buried himself in Westmoreland, and another spirit had borrowed and improved his body for this social gathering in the mountains. It was a delightful visit in a delightful region.

The hills of Jamaica are celebrated for their health-restoring properties, and Miraflor is one of the coolest and most invigorating situations on the island. It is somewhat difficult for an invalid to reach, for there is no carriage-road to it, and the steep mountain bridle-paths are very fatiguing; but when you are fairly up on the spreading table-lands, you are in a lovely paradise. The prospect from Miraflor is magnificent. No pen can depict the brilliant charms of nature in these enchanted regions. No pencil can paint the bright and endless variety of colors that deck the fruits and flowers of these gardens of nature. The air, too, was fragrant with the invigorating odors of the pimento (all-spice) groves, and this peculiar balm acted like a tonic on Mr. Holgrave. Miraflor was, indeed, a residence to charm him. Beside the grand mountain scenery to the right and left, it commanded a view over the sea, and a great many estates below us. There was a fine garden, and a pretty grotto, which, like one or two others I know of, contained a range of curious caverns under it, of unknown extent.

CHAPTER XV.

THE GROTTO.

THE grand open arch of the grotto at Miraflor extended at least fifty feet back into the rocky heart of the hill.   At the extreme rear a long shelf had been niched into the living rock by dint of human labor, and on it was ranged a row of skulls.

Like some other grottoes in St. Ann's, this had been used by the Indians as a temple, and it is stated, in the early history of the island, that the old Red Race used to resort to these rock temples at certain seasons of the year, to celebrate, with songs and dances, the exploits of their high chiefs, of whom, tradition says, these skulls were the honored relics.

These remains of a persecuted and almost extinguished race were not offensively displayed.   They were ranged along a ledge or cornice hewed out of the rear wall of the grotto, and only the top fronts of the skulls could be discerned in the obscurity of that part of the arched vault.   It was only by stepping upon a large, flat rock, which rose in front of this cornice, like a natural altar, that one could see that the glimmering row of something lighter than the gray walls of the grotto they leaned against, were relics of human beings. We had been several days at Miraflor before Mr. Martineau made the discovery. The front of this grotto opened toward the sea in a wide and regular arch thirty feet high, and faced, on each side, by walls of rock as true and perpendicular as mortal architect could have made them. Within, the sides, the floor, and the vaulted roof were more like a grand old cathedral than the work of Nature. In this noble archway, Mr. Holgrave loved to sit and muse or read, or, more frequently still, have me read to him. A large arm-chair, well stuffed and cushioned; was brought there for his accommodation; and, when he was too languid for reading, Mr. Martineau would take his cigar and walk up and down the grass-plot before the grotto, while dreamily contemplating the clouds and sunshine, as they chased each other in fantastic frolics over the lower plains and valleys that unrolled between those mountain-thrones and the sea. Sometimes, while Miraflor was in serenest sunshine, we would observe a sudden muster of clouds form and cover the sea from sight. They would rise, spread, and burst in a storm of rain, then roll off to the northward with all the flashing pomp and thunder of heaven's own artillery, and later, like an army withdrawn, leave the field silent and clear—and all within the space of an hour. Mr. Holgrave loved to witness these conflicts of Nature from this .rock-temple of her own rearing, and he improved—not as rapidly as we all wished, but steadily—under those influences. Madam Felix would bring her work or her guitar, and sit with him here, as ever, a most attentive friend and nurse in his sickness. They used to dine in the cave, until Mr. Martineau objected to the company of the skulls, which Madam Felix—who had a reverence for these remains of Indian glory—would not allow to be displaced, and all three adjourned to the house for their meals. But we had not been long here, before our preaching-friend arrived. Mr. Buckly was enamored of the grotto, and affected to gaze on the skulls with enthusiasm—while he did not fail to honor Madam Felix with all his vacant hours. Notwithstanding that the pursuit of a quadroon wife would, in those times, have been considered somewhat equivocal, and might have affected his own social standing, he took no sort of shame to himself for his frequenting her house. He boldly displayed himself to all the country round, preaching whenever occasion offered; and he even talked openly of uniting himself with her by marriage.

Meanwhile we were all happy together. Mr. Holgrave was particularly obliging and considerate to me. I saw that he had really a regard for me, and I strove to do every thing in my power to serve him to his heart's content. Madam. Felix declared that the estate was his; she had such confidence in him, that I believe she would have given him her heart and soul, if they could have been transferred, and would have been of service to him. Mr. Martineau unbent himself day by day, until even Victorine owned to me, that we had been too severe on the poor gentleman.

Little Aimée had been sent for to her boarding-school somewhere on the coast, and joined us, with her *governess*, a purely white Frenchwoman, who had been imported by Madam Felix, with her last invoice of finery and French wine, for the special business of waiting upon this lively little quadroon. If the fastidious gentry of Savannah-la-Mar were so intensely shocked at our gentlemen visiting a quad-

roon of fortune, intelligence, and character, what
would they say to a white governess—so accomplished, and recommended—and paid as not many
of them could afford for their own daughters, for the
exclusive service of a little quadroon, that was nobody's daughter apparently, and whose whole fortune was her share in the affectionate heart of this
woman of color? It was a tough social problem, and
I noted it down in my journal, with the wonderful
equations propounded to me by the sage book-
keepers at Orange Grove.

Aimée, to the amazement of everybody, fell in
love with Mr. Martineau the first day she came
home, at least she declared she had; and the second
day, equally to the general amazement, she made
war on the missionary. Mr. Holgrave said it only
proved that children of a certain age loved fairy
tales better than their catechism. But then to think
of the curt and crusty planter condescending to tell
fairy stories to a romping child! He did that and
more, for, at her request, he arranged tableaux and
little parlor dramas of one act, in which she was a
wonderfully important heroine. We had a curious
version of Othello, in which I performed the jealous
Moor, and had nearly all the speech-making to my-

self, and in which a young niece of Othello's—very improperly omitted in the ordinary versions of Shakespeare—appears at the proper moment with " the handkerchief," and turns the smothering scene into a graceful tableau of reconciliation. The missionary was shocked at the display of these profane amusements; but Madam Felix would amuse her guests, and Mr. Martineau, in his new *rôle* of Monseur Aimable, was a capital king of the revels. Beside this improved edition of Othello, in which Aimée personated the Moor's young niece, which we were to repeat at the house of Mr. St. John, we had some Scriptural tableaux, in which I recollect that Madam Felix represented Miriam and Dora with such exquisite grace, that, taken in the sense of an illustration of sacred history, they might not be objectionable. There were these tableaux or singing and recitations every evening, for they amused Mr. Holgrave, without fatiguing him to pay more attention to any of these things than he pleased. The preacher felt it necessary, for consistency's sake, to put in a mild protest against our dances, but he did not, for all that, renounce our company nor his aims on the widow's hand and fortune. Mr. Martineau would send me to bring

in three or four brown girls belonging to the property, as there was in the house a rather superior
barrel-organ, which he would grind away to them
by the hour together. I was permitted sometimes
to have a dance with them and some of the younger
black damsels, and we had occasional visitors who
did not disdain to dance reels and country dances
with our quadroon chamber-maids. I cannot take
upon me to say that this system of living was altogether compatible with the professions of Mr.
Preacher; nor was it strictly in accordance with
the outward exhibition of social proprieties in
Jamaica.

In the morning the gentlemen rode out; and if
I remained at home, Madam Felix or the governess
would give me a lesson in French. Still it troubled
me to note that when I had attended the gentlemen to dinner at the neighboring estates, the white
ladies, if any, were often somewhat satirical upon
them for their mode of life. Mr. Martineau was as
indifferent to their sarcasms as a brazen statue
would have been; but Mr. Holgrave was fully sensible that he was not exactly in the most popular
situation which he could have chosen. He gave
out that he had come to see about buying and

settling among the coffee-mountains for his health, and Mr. Buckly whispered that he attended him to cure his soul, and wean him from all carnal affections. Beside that, he meant to make a martyr of himself, and set an example of Christian humility, in holding at naught the prejudices of caste and color. Another missionary, whom he met at the Sabbath service on a neighboring estate, put the question plumply, whether he entertained the idea of marrying the rich French quadroon. He replied that as a man of God, the servant of Him who was no respecter of persons, it did not become him to be governed by such vain, carnal distinctions. They were but snares for unwary souls. Someway the missionary always found excellent reasons and the best Scripture warrant for taking his own way.

I learned, through the servants and other by-ways, that Mr. Buckly had obtained a very accurate account of the quadroon's property, but there was a trifling point he did not know. This very estate had been transferred to Mr. Holgrave, in return for certain investments in England. She had wanted him to accept it at a very low price, half its value, perhaps, and Mr. Martineau had urged him to take the bargain, but he was firm to his old answer, " I

13

am too poor to accept favors, and unable to confer them." His English investment was a tolerably fair equivalent for the coffee-property without the slaves. The transfer of this property was then in the hands of the lawyers, and Mr. Martineau contrived a plan to represent the quadroon as having in reality a very moderate fortune, and that entirely dependent on her remaining single.

He wrote to a friend what to do and say, in case Mr. Buckly gave him an opportunity to go into a statement of her affairs. Then, taking a wicked advantage of Madam Felix being absent on a visit to Mr. St. John's place, he assailed the preacher for " trifling with the lady's feelings." He appealed to Mr. Holgrave to say whether his attentions had not been of that pointed character which no gentleman —much less an ordained minister of the Gospel— ought ever to pay any woman, unless with a view to marriage. Mr. Holgrave confirmed the opinion to the last letter, and added, on his own account, that though it was a delicate subject for him to touch upon, between two such friends, he would venture to observe that he considered it but justice in Mr. Buckly to reflect, whether, after having superseded the honorable intentions of another gentle-

man of character and fortune, he ought not immediately to secure the happiness of Madam Felix, or
retire from the field altogether. To be gravely reproached for not doing that which he was all but
frantic to accomplish, mystified the preacher to such
an extent, that what little he had of mother wit and
worldly experience went to sea at once, without
pilot or compass. He declared that the only reason
why he had not formally proposed to Madam Felix
months ago, was that she was so modest and backward, and her knowledge of English so very limited,
that he had, out of "pure regard and prudence,"
refrained from pressing her, but that now he would
be "entirely guided by the advice of their mutual
friends."

How those "mutual friends" kept their coun-
tenances so completely, passes my understanding.
I could hardly restrain myself sufficiently to wait
upon them with propriety. This conversation was
held at luncheon, when—Madam being absent—I
alone attended in the breakfast-parlor. Mr. Holgrave said, in reply to Mr. Buckly's appeal for
advice, that his own sympathies were too strongly
enlisted (he did not specify in what way) for a fair
opinion, and he must be excused the responsibility

of any further discussion of the subject; and leaving the other two gentlemen to come to their own conclusions, he retreated to his favorite seat in the deep archway of the Temple Grotto.

The last I knew of the affair—for the time, that is—Mr. Buckly was talking of going to Spanish Town to make the necessary arrangements, sipping, as he went on, a strong glass of brandy-and-water; while Mr. Martineau was writing a line or two, in pencil, to the address of Madam Felix's trustee, who happened also to be his own solicitor, and the friend of Mr. Holgrave. Before I could get through with my house duties and join Mr. Holgrave at the grotto, Mr. Martineau was there, as usual, walking up and down, and smoking his cigar.

It seems Mr. Holgrave felt a little compunction, but this "mutual friend" swore that it was time "to extinguish the canting hypocrite;" and if there was no other way, he would throw him into the caverns under the grotto, and keep him there until he turned Mussulman.

"You had better sort together your Koran fragments, Mahmadee, for I shall shut you up with Mr. Preacher until you have converted him, or he you."

I only bowed a respectful acquiescence, and

craved permission to go down with Hercules and select a convenient site for my future labors.

I began to pique myself on my correct English in those days, and the pages of my journal, in which these incidents are recorded, contain more long words than I ever saw crowded together in one company outside of a dictionary. If I were not ashamed of its grandeur, I would here transcribe my account of the subterranean wonders of this grotto, but I am not quite stoical enough to laugh at myself in public, although I have had many a smile in private at my youthful flights of composition.

But to the grotto caverns. Between what was considered and called the Indian altar and the wall behind it, gaped a deep, well-like fissure, by means of which an active, sure-footed person could be let down into another vault somewhat like the grotto, but on a smaller and rougher scale. The grotto itself opened from the level of the outside ground into the side of the hill; but this cavern was deeper under the hill, and branched off into low, broken, winding passages, through which a man could creep with difficulty. These led in different directions, and with an endless perplexity of branchings, to unknown depths. Hercules and I had been twice down with lights, and marked, as far as we went, with arrows pointing back to the entrance; but we were that day to have a grand exploration, under the direction of the head man of the estate. Every thing was prepared for a long stay below, but none of us were prepared for Mr. Martineau's resolution to join us. Extra lights were ordered, and, when we had reached the lower vault, Mr. Martineau, with Hercules, took one passage, while the head man and I followed another. We had toiled for some time through the intricacies of these narrow fissures and dark chambers, when we were suddenly startled by a wild, unearthly sound, that echoed and re-echoed on every side of us, but whether near or distant we were unable to judge. We were in a small dome-shaped chamber, rough on the floor and sides, with sharp ledges of rock, but the coved roof was beautifully regular and richly decked with white and lustrous pendants, that glittered in our upraised lights, like carvings of alabaster set with diamonds. Before we came to this chamber, we had seen but few and dull specimens of stalactites, and we were gazing at this display in a transport of admiration, when we were startled—I may say enveloped—by this frightful chaos of sounds. They died away, and

we were finding the composure to question each
other as to their meaning, when a voice, above the
line of our heads, exclaimed, in the welcome tones
of Hercules, " Hi, master! here are the oder black
devils for sure."

We climbed up to the ledge on which he lay, like
a giant spread out on a shelf to dry, and then crept
along this shelf into a room of dazzling splendor.
Fancy an immense saloon hung with massive folds
of white tapestry, its lofty roof fretted with jewels,
furnished with tables and sofas of purest marble,
supported by stately columns with sculptured forms
reclining at their bases, all of the same rich material,
and all seen in the uncertain gleams—but not the less
charming in effect—of three or four quivering lights.
Such caverns are not rare in Jamaica. St. Ann
abounds in them; but it was the first I had ever seen,
and I was enchanted with its magical splendors. Mr.
Martineau had explored other wonderful caverns,
but he maintained to Mr. Holgrave, that this grand
hall was the noblest and the most perfectly beautiful
he had ever seen.

To our surprise it was dark night when we returned to the upper world. We had been seven
hours under ground. The head man had never

before seen nor heard of this fine hall in the cavern, and could not tell for his life what Mr. Martineau meant by it when he said he went down expressly to look it up, as he had "promised it to Mr. Buckly and Mahmadee for a *mosque.*" It is now called, however, the "Hall of Echoes," on account of the singular manner in which it echoes and multiplies sounds.

While we were exploring the caverns, Mr. Holgrave had received a visit from Mr. St. John, of Rose Hill, and he had promised to spend the coming week with that gentleman. Mr. Martineau had previously engaged to devote that time to two young officers, lately out from England, whom he had met at one of the houses he had visited. There was a bet of fifty guineas in question. In speaking of a remarkable succession of rapids and cataracts on the White River, which, in describing, he called the Magic Cascades, Mr. Martineau asserted that "in the parish of St. Ann alone there was a more numereus collection of natural curiosities—which were at once eminently curious and attractively beautiful—than could be found in any part of the known world within the compass of a territory equal to the whole island of Jamaica." The officers, who had made the tour of Europe, deemed this impossible, and, like true Englishmen, clinched their opinion with a bet. Mr. Martineau accepted it, made a note of the point to be decided—which I copied in my journal—and agreed to leave it to their own word of honor at the end of one week's excursion. While Mr. Martineau and Hercules were away to bring this bet to a conclusion—which I may here say he won triumphantly—Mr. Holgrave and I were to see for ourselves whether Mr. St. John lived in the style of " oriental luxury and laxity " spoken of by the gentlemen at whose house the bet I have mentioned was made. Unfortunately, our visit had to be postponed for several days. Mr. Holgrave had a relapse, and was at one time on the point of not going to Rose Hill at all; but as he rallied he returned to the original purpose.

Madam Felix went over there in advance, to have every thing in readiness to accommodate Mr. Holgrave's invalid habits, and I marvelled much how it was that any quadroon, even though rich and a lady bred—as she certainly was—could enjoy such easy liberty in the house of an aristocratic white planter like Mr. St. John.

18*

CHAPTER XVI.

ROSE HILL.

AT last Mr. Holgrave felt able to make the long promised visit to Rose Hill.

Mr. Martineau, whose curiosity had been piqued by the contradictory stories about the style and habits of that elegant mansion, wished, of all earthly things, to go there too; but Mr. St. John had, at that period, such a prejudice against him, that he would neither ask him nor receive him beyond his hall. Food and lodging he denied to no man, but the interior of his dwelling was reserved for his peculiar friends, or for those persons whose manners attracted him. He had a horror of Mr. Martineau, without, however, knowing much of his burying the deputy-marshal.

. There was no other gentleman at Rose Hill when Mr. Holgrave arrived, which I was not sorry to learn, as it gave him a little repose. His health was still very delicate, and he had never been there previously, though frequently invited. We arrived about three o'clock in the afternoon, and were received by Madam Felix, who shed tears at the sight of his pale face, and at the signs of his debility. She was accompanied to the hall by four beautiful quadroons, all vieing with one another in expressions of sympathy and good will. They led him directly to his apartment, to rest a while before he went into the bath, and, as I would not be needed immediately, I amused myself by looking about the house and grounds.

I had never seen any thing like the one or the other in my life. All other places which I had seen inhabited by white men were evidently built merely to live in. Their grounds are laid out for profit—rum, sugar, coffee, guinea-grass, corn, pimento—in some or all of the exportable or eatable productions of the tropics; but Mr. St. John had built his house and laid out his grounds for enjoying life.

The house was placed upon an elevated platform, in the center of a garden full of flowers of all hues, and fruits of every description that I ever saw in Africa or Jamaica. Around the garden were the woods, with long glades cut through them, in every direction, and these green glades were kept mowed as smooth and rolled as level as the floor. Beyond these glades might be seen distant mountains in one direction, extensive plains in another, the sea in a third. Nothing could be more beautiful to my eyes, and I have heard all Englishmen who knew the place, declare it was a gem of beauty, a perfect paradise.

The house was built in a square, two stories high, with a court in the centre, and in the court a fountain, where the marble statue of a woman with long hair seemed melting into water, which trickled all over her. The fountain was surrounded with orange-trees, and the rest of the court was full of flowers of the brightest colors, mixed with rose-trees and geraniums. There was likewise an aviary along one side of the building, with a great many birds in it with which I was unacquainted. I had seen parrots and macaws in the walks and about the garden ; and peacocks, both white and in their natural colors, were now and then visible in the glades, and on the trees in the woods. In these last, too, were an infinity of doves of various descriptions. The woods themselves were beautiful : oranges, shaddocks, and all sorts of fruit-trees, were mixed among the lofty palms, cedars, and other trees. All the woods in Jamaica are very beautiful, but here a great deal of pains had been taken to improve their appearance, and make them subservient to the taste and inclinations of their master.

The inside of the house was no less delightful than the exterior. The hall was paved with marble, and furnished with paintings of white people, especially women, all of them handsome and happy looking, and mostly dressed in light, flowing robes. I soon learned from Mr. Holgrave that these lovely pictures were taken from the ancient mythology, and I was delighted with the study which explained to me the faith, as well as the history of the grand old Romans, although with their millions of white slaves, and slaves of all colors, it must be admitted that they were terribly hard masters. But this learning came to me by degrees. Mr. St. John's hall I ran through more rapidly on that first day. Two pictures particularly fascinated me ; Diana, with her bow and quiver, and Europa—I know their names now—riding upon a bull, as my countrywomen do in Africa. The bull was a pretty beast, covered all over with roses and hyacinths, though swimming through the sea.

Beside the pictures, there were statues of marble, some of black women, smooth and shining; but they were not like negresses, for the sculptor had given them long, black hair, flowing loose over their shoulders, in two or three instances; in others, tied up fancifully in plaits round their heads. These statues represented women standing in rather free and easy postures, as in my utter inexperience of the fine arts I then thought. One or two of them were lying down, and one was crouching as if she was ashamed; but they were all very beautiful, and even the black ones had features like those of the whites. I noticed that not one had negro noses or lips.

In the middle of the hall was a marble basin, about six feet in diameter, in which water bubbled up from the bottom, and found its way out again through the mouth of a fish, which seemed to be swimming with its mouth open, as if to devour a figure chained to a rock. There were sofas around this hall, between the statues, and it was illuminated by a skylight above. But to prevent the glare of the sun from being too powerful, as it would of course be for some hours in the day, there was a linen curtain drawn across the skylight, which cast rather a melancholy shade upon every thing to one coming from the open air; but in a few minutes this was forgotten. There were four doors opening into the hall, and two of them were set open at the time. These would allow a current of air to pass through from every quarter, in case of the heat becoming oppressive. I entered one of the apartments into which the open doors led, and saw it was a room for dining or breakfasting. It looked toward the sea, through two immense avenues in the woods. The floor of this room, like that of the last, was of stone. There were two large pictures in it: one representing a ship sinking in a storm; the other was a calm, with the sun rising, and sailors in boats, towing a fleet out of a harbor into the sea. There was a fine sideboard with plate and glasses arranged upon it, and two sofas, covered with purple, besides the chairs and tables. In front of this room was a piazza.

From the dining-room I glanced through a side-door into a large, handsome bedroom, where the musquito net was of pink muslin; there was a bath at one end, and water running into it from a lion's mouth fixed in the wall. The lion's head, for there was no more than that, was of brass, and above it was a silver plate with four lines engraved in letters which I could not read. I know the English of

them, now, and to what they refer. Mr. Holgrave
translated them : "Ask of the swarthy African, son
of Europa, the fair and long-haired, why he pours
water from a lion's mouth rather than from that of
any other animal."

Mr. St. John himself explained to me that it was
copied from an old Greek palace, and was an allu-
sion to the rise of the Nile in the sign of Leo. This
room, I thought, could only belong to the master or
mistress of this splendid residence. I noticed two
looking-glasses here : one in the wall, the other in
a frame, both five or six feet high, and a drawing
of a quadroon (Jamaica), dressed in white, with a
garland of wild coffee-flowers on her head. This
was in a gilded frame, with a glass over it. The
floor of the room was of hard wood, polished with
wax. The next room was filled with books of all
sizes, arranged along the walls with great neatness
and regularity. There were two globes, and a very
large telescope on a stand ; lamps and inkstands
upon a black table, and various articles of furniture,
for which I could find no name or use. There was
a square piano-forte in the middle of the room, and
a set of glass vases in a sort of frame. These were
of different sizes, diminishing regularly, from the

largest to the smallest, and were made for music. There were, beside, models of houses and ships, and maps of every country in the world, I believe, and many, to me strange, implements and instruments.

The furniture of this apartment was no less elegant than that of the others, being all mahogany, very strong and elegantly finished. I could have lingered here an hour, but I dared not, being apprehensive it might give offense. "Sidi Mahmadee," thought I, "these whites are indeed our masters." I passed on still, without meeting any one, through another bedroom fitted up no less elegantly than the last, and entered a sort of saloon, furnished with several looking-glasses and the kind of sofas called ottomans. There was a fountain also, level with the floor, and there were essences and perfumes on a marble table, which was opposite an immense mirror. The walls of this saloon were painted all over with scenes from other climates, of which I had read; for there were mountains of ice, and valleys, and plains, white with snow, represented on them; trees without a single leaf, and men and women skating or driving in sledges. There was an antiroom adjoining this, covered with a rich paper, with porcelain vases standing, some on gilded brackets, which projected from the wall, some on tripods of brass, and filled with flowers. In this room was another large piano-forte, and a harp stood beside it. A white handkerchief lay on a stool of blue silk, rose-scented so strongly, that it could only belong to a lady. There were here also figures and vases, cut in alabaster, and upon the latter were devices which I did not comprehend. The ceiling of this apartment was painted with a sun in the middle, and a parcel of figures signifying the stars and constellations, as I afterward understood, men and women, and the many figures of the zodiac.

A long passage, or enclosed piazza, led from this second saloon or vestibule to a light, airy room intended for servants. There was a statue in the middle representing a negro, bearing a globe on his head. I suppose it meant that we (the negroes) are doomed by God to be slaves, and to bear burdens for the white men. There was a bath also here, with running water, and in large letters on the wall I read, " Wash, and be clean," which words made me think this gentleman must be of my religion. From the bath, another passage led me back to the hall where we had first entered, and here I observed the

staircase to the upper rooms. I had never before
seen so elegant a staircase in my life, and as no one
interfered with me—as, in short, I saw and heard no
one—I took the liberty of walking up.

The steps were of mahogany, highly polished,
and the bannisters of ebony. A bronze lamp hung
down from the roof, ornamented with faces of women. Birds of all sorts were painted on the walls,
some in the water, others in the air, and many more
in trees and on the ground. The trees bore fruits
as well; some of which I had seen, while others, I
suppose, belonged to different countries. The windows which gave light upon the staircase were not
obscured by *jalousies*, but covered with cloths,
which had not long before been wetted. On the
landing-place above there was a large space, hardly
to be called a room, as there were outlets in three or
four directions. It was, however, furnished with
sofas covered with some kind of flowered stuff.
The wood-work was of ebony, and gilded here and
there. I ought not, properly, to have proceeded
farther; indeed, my curiosity hitherto was hardly
excusable, considering that I was in a strange gentleman's house, and that, in all probability, my master would soon have taken his bath, and asked for

me; but I found all so still, so beautiful, and so enticing, that I went on.

An open door invited me into a small bedroom, which led me to a second. They were both furnished with window-curtains of blue muslin, spangled with silver stars. The musquito-nets were of the same material, and the bedsteads of yellow sanders-wood. There was a coronet of silver over the first, to which the musquito net was attached, and the other was crowned with a garland of flowers. There were three chests of drawers in this apartment, of cedar-wood and yellow sanders intermixed; and on the top of each was a slab of beautiful white marble. The chairs were of the same wood as the bedsteads, covered with sky-blue silk, and there were cushions on the floor to put the feet upon. A marble table stood before a window, with a china basin and water-jug upon it. On another table there was a little army of boxes, bottles, napkins, and what not, all in the finest order, and as clean as if a score of slaves were employed to keep them so. The walls were alternate pictures and looking-glasses, and the floor was almost as bright as a mirror. I did not know the meaning of the pictures, but I remember they were full of little boys,

Cupids, with wings, flying about in all directions, floating in the air, like humming-birds sucking honey from flowers of the sea-side jessamine.

As I turned from this hasty survey back into the landing-place at the head of the stairs, I heard voices below me in the bath-room, as I supposed. They were sounds of mirth, of girls laughing, and I could distinguish the voice of Mr. Holgrave speaking French to Madam Felix. I listened a moment, but as all was quiet, I presumed that he had only just come out of the bath, and had still to dress for dinner. He asked for me, but I could hear the women say that they would shave him and dress his hair. I hastened to him and attended him to his own room. He had slept an hour and felt much refreshed, but he begged to be excused from the regular dinner-table, and Madam Felix replied that he should be served in his own way, that Mr. St. John had ordered the servants to attend to his wishes in every thing, and would be much grieved if Mr. Holgrave did not make himself as completely at home at Rose Hill as he could be at Miraflor or Savannah-la-Mar. I wondered how it happened that this polite Mr. St. John did not appear in person to receive his guest, and why Madam Felix, herself but a visitor, should be performing those acts of attentive hospitality which in every other house that Mr. Holgrave could be prevailed on to enter— and they were not many—I had always seen the master and all his family so forward to proffer. But it was not for me to notice, even by a look, my secret discontent.

Two black girls laid out a small table in the music-room—the one containing the harp and piano —and they waited upon my master and Madam Felix, who sat down with him to his weak tea and toast and arrow-root custard. The three servants— including myself—had nothing to do, and the kind- est could do no more for this poor invalid. He rigorously forbade himself high living, but he en- joyed this light supper, and when it was over he requested Madam Felix to take her guitar and favor him with a *chanson*. The two black girls cleared the table. In that house all the work was arranged in pairs and trios; I never saw one girl at work by herself, even in arranging the chambers; and after Mr. Holgrave's supper was out of the way they took me with them to share their own.

When I returned to the music-room, Madam Felix was looking at the pictures of the gods and god-

desses in a work on mythology, which Mr. Holgrave
was explaining to her. "You are to go through
this book as your next study, Mahmadee," said Mr.
Holgrave, handing it to me. "You shall read me
to sleep with the first chapter to-night by way of
beginning;" and so I did.

Before I slept myself, however, Victorine astonished me with the news that Orange Grove was
actually sold, and on the point of delivery, to a rich
Jew merchant of Kingston, and that the present
owner not requiring such a large force, many of the
slaves were to be sold off and scattered among new
masters.

Even while I devoutly thanked the All-Merciful
Allah that my own destiny had placed me in the
hands of the indulgent Mr. Holgrave, I thought,·
with a heavy heart, of the possible fate of my kind
Tatee and the good-natured Brad. I touched upon
these anxieties to Mr. Holgrave in the morning, but
he only said, "Be at ease, Mahmadee; your old
Houssa friends are prime hands, and good servants
are pretty sure to find good masters."

CHAPTER XVII.

MR. ST. JOHN.

I HEARD a slight stir in the house, and the tink-
ling of a bell in the direction of the library about
midnight. Thereabouts was the master's own bed-
room, as the two black damsels who had favored
me with their company and a nice supper the evening before had, among other things, explained to
me, and I judged, therefore, that these movements
announced the return of Mr. St. John. These girls
were twins, as they informed me, and were named
Belle and Bessie. They waited on the table and
the kitchen—bringing in and taking out the dishes—
and cleaned the windows and furniture in all the
lower rooms. Two other black girls did the same
for the upper rooms. There were the parlor maids
to do the nice work, dusting, arranging, and bringing fresh flowers and fruits into the drawing and
dining-rooms, which Mr. St. John had done every
day of the year, they said. The four black girls

were called the hall and chamber maids; the others
—that is, the parlor-maids—had nothing to do with
the kitchen or rough house-cleaning; but, beside
sewing and other fine work, they waited at the side-
tables in the dining-room, and had plenty to do in
attending to their own business. Mr. St. John
would not endure the least speck of dust, and any
thing like rude noises or disorder was carefully
avoided as the price of his favor. Those who neglected these rules were sent out of the house, and
that Belle and Bessie regarded as the heaviest misfortune that could befall them. I fell asleep very
much of their opinion respecting this charming
residence. I longed to see the noble master of this
noble mansion; and when I heard his bell I wished
for the dawn to hurry on, that I might the sooner
have an opportunity to survey him in the midst of
all these beautiful surroundings.

I slept in a small dressing-room, with one large
window, facing a long avenue of roses and pome-
granates. It had a fanciful affair at the far end of it
they called the *kiosk*, but it afterwards caught the
title of Mahmadee's Mosque. I was up, and had
been for some time admiring this clean, beautiful
walk, with its border of blooming roses glittering

14

in the dew, and hesitating about venturing to stop out of the window on an exploring expedition, when Mr. Holgrave awoke. His cup of cocoa and a biscuit were brought to the door by Madam Felix's maid Victorine, just as she had done at Miraflor, as soon as the bell was touched for it. If it had been her sole and entire business to watch for it, the silver tray and its belongings could not have answered the call more speedily, and in better order. It was the same all the rest of the time we spent at Rose Hill. Madam Felix made it her chief study to nurse and console my invalid master.

After his morning cup, I read to Mr. Holgrave the selections he made from the mythology, relating to the pictures in the hall. The story of Europa he told me might be a fable, invented to convey the idea that the fair races of the North had, in the most ancient days, obtained their domestic cattle from Africa, and with them the most essential comforts of civilized life. Although in such delicate health, these lessons, half reading, half conversation, never seemed to fatigue Mr. Holgrave. He would recline on his sofa for hours together, directing me to take down this book or that, and read to him the captions of the chapters, until I came to the subject

he wanted, and then he would say: "Begin that
chapter, and read it to me. Read it in a proper
tone, as if you relished its meaning." When it was
finished, or I had reached the point he wished to explain, he would take up the thread, and make what
had seemed the dullest of themes perfectly clear and
interesting, by his happy comments. After our
morning lesson I attended him to the bathing-room,
where he said he should allow himself but ten minutes, during which time I might study the pictures
in the hall, and prepare my mind for another dose
of heathen mythology for the next morning. I now
gazed with enlightened eyes, not only on the pictures, which had most forcibly attracted my attention on my first entrance into this spacious apartment, but on their companions, Venus in her chariot,
and Minerva conferring the Palladium, which were
now equally beautiful to me. These four pictures
were all of one size, framed to match, in rich gild-
ing, and were placed two on each of the longest
sides of the hall. A wide door opened between
each pair of pictures into the two next largest rooms
in the house. In each corner were statues and
groups, on pedestals of variegated marble. Under
each of those pictures was a sofa, with a kind of

small moveable frame of dark wood at the end, which might serve for a little stand for reading and drawing, or to hold refreshments. My first impression had been of a confused mixture of statues, and pictures, and furniture, and water, but the moment I re-entered it, I saw that luxury was combined with order and convenience. I have seen, in later years, the halls of the rich and noble in Europe, but I have never yet beheld the match, in charming effect and finished taste, of this one planned and built in the mountains of Jamaica.

I met a gentleman coming out of his room just as I was summoned to dress Mr. Holgrave for breakfast—the luxurious eleven o'clock breakfast of a Jamaica planter of the olden time—and I knew it must be Mr. St. John. I could not refrain from expressing to Mr. Holgrave my delight in the novelties around, and he agreed that the whole establishment seemed admirable. Our conversation was interrupted by Bessie, who came to say, from Madam Felix, that I must wait at table, and bid me go into the bath and wash myself. The black girls were astonished, and could not account for this exception to the rules of the house. I obeyed the order, and was shewn into the bath I had previously seen, where they brought me a pair of linen trowsers, a clean shirt, and a frock of blue stuff, with a belt of red morocco, and a neat buckle to fasten it round my waist. They gave me likewise soap and brushes, and perfumed my frock, and left me a pair of red morocco shoes with woolen soles, to wait in.

I was troubled, though pleased, at all this, for I hoped I might be able to win the good opinion of Mr. St. John; and yet all this washing seemed to imply an affectation on their part, as if I were an unclean beast. However, as his house was full of baths and fountains, I conjectured he felt the need of them himself, and moreover, as a Mahometan, washing was all right and proper.

After all these ablutions, and arrangings, and perfumings were duly accomplished, I went into the breakfast-parlor, where the four black girls awaited me. We ranged ourselves before the sideboard, myself in the center, and two of the negresses on either side of me. Mr. St. John quickly made his appearance, and the breakfast was served. I should state that he came into the room first and alone, but was soon followed by Mr. Holgrave, who was led in by Madam Felix. Poor gentleman! he

scarcely seemed refreshed by his bath, and leaned
for support on his quadroon friend.

I had now an opportunity of observing Mr. St.
John more closely. He was rather tall, and about
thirty-five years of age, with a high forehead and
curly brown hair, a little gray about the temples.
He had a straight nose, rather large lips for a
white man, and blue eyes. He was dressed much
in the Jamaica fashion, with a white waistcoat and
trowsers, and a blue coat, lined with silk. He had
a ring on one of his fingers, and a blue ribbon,
with two or three seals, hung from his watch.
There were only two covers laid, one for each of
the gentlemen. Madam Felix sat upon a stool beside Mr. Holgrave, and helped him to the plain
broiled partridge, and any thing else he asked for.
I stood sentinel at the sideboard, and poured out
the coffee—and wine, or other liquors, when demanded—and the girls handed them on silver
waiters. There was nothing remarkable in the
breakfast, except that all the dishes, of which there
were a good many, were very small, and were
served one at a time. It consisted of the ordinary
productions of the island: fish and poultry, kid or
lamb, eggs and omelet, with such vegetables as are

to be seen at every gentleman's table in Jamaica.
A pot of incense was set on fire while they were
eating, and a musical machine played of itself some
very sweet tunes during the repast. Mr. St. John
smiled at me when he first came in, and Madam
Felix would have won my heart, if she had not
possessed it before, by a glance replete with good
humor and kindly encouragement. The black girls
went out, in turn, for the various dishes, and changed
the plates for the gentlemen.

The center of the table was occupied by a large
stand, representing a cluster of myrtle shrubs, whose
twisted stalks supported China baskets filled with
the finest and freshest fruits of the season. These
were more for ornament than use, for they were not
touched at all, but the same kinds of fruit were
ready on a side-table to offer round. Vases filled
with flowers, chiefly roses and jessamine, stood on
each side of this beautiful center ornament; and,
taken together with the silver bread-baskets, the
butter and salt-holders, and other such shining matters, the table was abundantly and beautifully set
out, without putting upon it the dishes with food.

When they were first seated at the table, Mr. St.
John remarked, as if in continuation of a previous

conversation, that he hoped the affair which had
called him out so unexpectedly at the moment when
he would have been so much more agreeably employed in receiving Mr. Holgrave, would not disturb
the guest of Rose Hill while he was an inmate.

"I should only think of it so far as it caused
annoyance to you and others," replied Mr. Holgrave.
"I have known him for some time; he was a pas-
senger in the same ship when I came from England
last May, and if he is not altogether insane, he is
as near it as I ever saw any man out of a mad-
house."

"I suspected as much myself," said Mr. St. John.
"And now that you have confirmed me in this
opinion, I shall be prepared to act accordingly."

The conversation turned off at that point, but it
run in my head all day.

"Who could this crazy *him* be, that both gentlemen seemed to agree might become very trouble-
some. Could trouble enter this enchanted hall?"

Presently Mr. Martineau's name was brought
forward, and it was plain that Mr. St. John had
heard shocking stories about his wild acts of cruelty
to man and beast, and he seemed much surprised
when Mr. Holgrave seriously assured him the

planter was one of the most "considerate and consistently humane masters he had ever known. Somewhat given to rough practical jokes, and too ready, perhaps, with a sharp, sarcastic tongue, for the world in general, but with a warm and faithful heart for his friends."

"If he is your friend, my dear sir, I am quite ready to believe that public report has been over severe on Mr. Martineau," said Mr. St. John, politely.

"You may depend upon my word, it is in this case, Mr. St. John. Public report is rarely acccurate. You know the ancients represented Madam Rumor with many wings and feet, and monstrous ears, but with only one pair of half-shut eyes," answered Mr. Holgrave.

"I trust we shall have the pleasure of a visit from your friend while you are here," observed Mr. St. John, but not until after he had heard an account of the bet with the cavalry officers respecting the natural marvels of St. Ann.

"I would not like to be one in the chase among woods and hills for the cascades, and in the dark labyrinths under the ground, to explore caverns to which Hercules and his master will lead them.

14*

These explorations are not my element," said Mr. Holgrave, as he closed.

" You may be surprised to hear that I have a passion for them. I fancy Madam Felix will never forget one she made last year, in which she and I, and six of our servants, remained under ground twenty hours," replied Mr. St. John.

" Twenty hours ?" exclaimed Mr. Holgrave.

" Yes, twenty, and when we reached sunshine again, we had not only entered upon another day but on another domain."

" How the people were frightened when we rushed upon them, like so many returned Indian spirits !" said Madam Felix, laughing gaily at the recollection.

" This is all new to me," said Mr. Holgrave.

It was new to me, also. Madam Felix had never mentioned it in my hearing, nor, for that matter, had she often mentioned Mr. St. John himself.

" It is all quite true, however. The cavern has one entrance in a ravine near the limits of my estate, another outlet in an Indian temple or grotto, half a mile distant, but most of the connecting links are extremely narrow and intricate."

"We had plenty of lights, and wine and biscuits with us, and we enjoyed our refreshments in magnificent saloons—saloons composed of nothing but precious stones. It was not at all a bad affair. On the contrary, it was far more amusing than tiresome. Still, I had enough of caverns," observed the fair quadroon.

"Should your friend Martineau favor us with a visit of some days—as I hope you will persuade him to do, Mr. Holgrave—I shall propose a visit to our cavern," said Mr. St. John, returning to the planter, in a manner that proved his strong prejudices had been materially softened by Mr. Holgrave's candid and friendly explanations.

Mr. Buckly was then discussed, and, in his case, Miss Public Report had been as falsely partial in painting his imaginary virtues as she had been lavish of her darkest colors in shading the portrait of Mr. Martineau. Mr. St. John had never seen him, he said, but he knew the lady at Kingston to whom he was paying his addresses.

"Ah, the missionary has then a susceptible heart?" said Madam Felix, with an arch smile. "Pray describe the fair captivator. I have a curiosity to learn by what charms a spirit so wholly given up to God was brought down to this wicked world of ours."

"She is a rich widow, not handsome, but amiable I am told, and devoted to the missionary. She is, beside, a convert of his, for she was a Jewess until lately," said Mr. St. John.

"A Jewess!" exclaimed Madam Felix, in surprise.

"Yes, a Jewess. At least she is the reputed daughter of a Jew, and certainly the widow of a well-known Israelite."

"I cannot trace Jewish features in her brother McGregor," said Mr. Holgrave, carelessly, "though our friend Davis, who had him employed at Orange Grove, insisted that his hair has to be kept particularly short, to keep its kinking tendencies out of sight. But McGregor has a very fair complexion."

"So had his mother; but there was more of the chalk mixture than of the white rose in it. When I first came to the Island," continued Mr. St. John, "I was sadly puzzled to reconcile her unusually fair skin with the undeniable wooliness of the octoroon lodging-housekeeper's head." Surprise upon surprise was this to me.

This arrogant mechanic, who never looked at or

spoke to me without casting an insult on the color
of my skin—which he who gave it knew was so far
from being my own choice or fault—this man, whom
I had often heard say that the law should prohibit
the education of negroes, had the taint of the de-
spised race in his own veins, and my master and Mr.
Holgrave's friend, the doctor, had known it all the
time. I now understood why Miss Lucy had alluded
to "his passing for white," and why the family at
the Great House had always kept him at arm's
length.

Again the conversation wandered from this—the
point nearest my heart—to the extensive merits of
Mr. Buckly; to his zeal in teaching hymns and good
morals to the blacks, and especially to his prudence
and industry in restraining them to their duties—
that is, their duties to their masters, which is the
sum total of slave morality—and of his uncommon
success and usefulness in general. It then gleamed
upon me, for the first time, that the parson had sold
his missionary efforts and influence to the slave-
owners—not exactly betrayed the slaves for a price
but had sold or hired himself out to do for wages
what I had done for love. *I believed it then—I
know it now ;* and if there are those in Jamaica, or

elsewhere, who will take offence at this or other jot-
tings of those days, I can only say, What is written
is written.

But then I was a slave in waiting on my masters
at Rose Hill, presumed to have ears, limbs, and
speech, only to hear and obey; and though hunger-
ing for a larger supply, I was still thankful for these
crumbs of information.

It was to be a day of surprising, but always imperfect intelligence. When Mr. Holgrave retired to
his room, I managed by a roundabout path to hint
at the reserve of Madam Felix in speaking of Mr.
St. John, and yet making such long and intimate
visits at his house, and even going into cave excur-
sions with him.

" The poor woman is afraid of being thought to
boast of her relationship with Mr. St. John, and
yet she is too much attached to him to refuse the
kindness he really entertains for her," said Mr. Holgrave, settling himself on the pillow for his regular
noontide slumber.

"Relationship to Mr. St. John?" I repeated,
with a surprise amounting to dismay, for I recalled
some sneering inuendoes over the bottle in the
house, where St. John and his establishment had

been so keenly criticised. "Boasting of her relationship with Mr. St. John," I repeated, the second
time, almost unconsciously.

"Yes, she is his sister. His father, when a wid-
ower, went to Port-au-Prince, and made his fortune.
The mother of Claire—that is, Madam Felix—was a
young, handsome, intelligent, and independent quadroon. She gave herself and fortune to the Mr. St.
John of those days, without precisely insisting on a
wedding-ring. She died while Claire was a child,
and he formed other ties; but every penny of her
own fortune, with a neat addition from his own, was
firmly settled on Claire. This St. John, of Rose
Hill, has become her trustee by the death of the
former St. John's solicitor, and, much as he dislikes
business, he is, I believe, strictly attentive to her
interests."

"I had always supposed that you, sir, was her
trustee."

"So I am—that is, Mr. Martineau and I, jointly—
for her property on this island, but the principal part
of her fortune is in England, in charge of Mr. St.
John's solicitor," said Mr. Holgrave, resettling himself to his pillows, which he had disturbed in talking
to me.

"Then the Missionary Maroon, as Mr. Martineau calls him, will, in fact, capture no property—nothing but the lady's own person." I was repeating the planter's own words to Mr. Holgrave as I heard them fall from his lips in the Temple Grotto, after that interesting luncheon, in which he had urged the preacher to wind up the chase.

There was no answer, and I stepped softly out of the room. Mr. St. John had also retired to his room to his *siesta*, and I knew that Madam Felix and Victorine were always invisible for a couple of hours at this time of day. There was no call for my services, therefore, and I went in search of the waiter-girls and something to eat, for I could not be spared from Mr. Holgrave until he had betaken himself to his noontide repose.

Bella and Bessie had provided for me, and we had a long chat about the house and their duties in it.

It appears that the most promising girls are selected from the children of the field negroes, and trained with great care for the general service of the house. First in the kitchen and laundry, as inferior assistants, and after a certain probation, to test their conduct and fitness for the house, they are brought in, two at a time, to serve and learn under two older ones, who have already been instructed. As soon as they are promoted to the house-service they may, if they choose, begin learning to read. There was a regular schoolroom and a black schoolmaster (a better teacher than the brown genius who taught my young ideas how to shoot), whose evening work was to teach the privileged servants to read and write. They learned, or not, as they chose; and after they had learned, they read what they pleased —the Bible and sermons, or novels and poetry. A price was set on them, and they might earn their own freedom, if they could, and they were promised, after four years' service, that they might go and seek other service, if they liked, so they paid twenty pounds a year. They cleaned the house, and kept every thing, as I have described it. Their master never flogged any body.

"Indeed?" said I.

"Nobody about the house, and very seldom allowed any punishment upon his estate."

They, in turn, asked me about myself. In what part of Africa I was born, when brought over, and whether my master was kind, and the like. They said Victorine had told them my father was a king, and that I was to have my freedom some day, and be made a preacher. I gravely told them the last was impossible, as I was a Mahometan, and would never give up my own faith to become a Christian. Much did I know then of the difference! But I have seen very pious zealots who were almost as ignorant of the divinest part of their religion as I was at that time.

These girls did not afflict their mind with points of faith, good or bad. Their ideas run more on love and matrimony.

" Had I a wife ?"

" No, I was not seventeen years old, and had no need of a wife yet;" upon which they all began to laugh, and said I was a silly fool, a stupid Congo, and I know not what beside. They bid me look at them, and say, if I dared, that they—any one of them—were not fit for me. They insisted that I should signify at once which I preferred of them, and what I would do to merit their good graces. I suppose four servant girls, in any other country, who had caught one raw boy among them, would have made game of him, as they did of me.

They were taken at twelve or thirteen, according to their appearance, into the house, and it was only on condition of their living like vestals for the time of their servitude that they were entitled to the advantages I have enumerated. If they were guilty of the least dishonesty or impropriety, expulsion from the house followed, of course. They were free to do as they pleased, but by remaining single, and conforming to certain conditions, they obtained certain privileges. In any case, they could but return to the field from whence they came.

The hall clock striking one broke up our confab. They had their tables to arrange, and I started for an hour's survey of the premises.

CHAPTER XVIII.

THE FAIR STRANGER.

THE house had subsided into the perfect stillness of a tropical siesta. Even the parlor-maids had disappeared, and I seemed to be the only being awake in that spacious mansion. The hall-doors were open for the circulation of air, but the *jalousies* were turned to exclude the sun, and a soft, fragrant dreaminess pervaded the whole place. I alone was restless. It was too warm and sunny for the rounds of the park, so I read a page or too in the Mythology, and strayed through the music-room, library, and drawing-room, and then back to the hall, scanning, admiring, and wondering at this flood of riches in which St. John disported, like a happy bather in a crystal and brimming river. I came out again at the foot of the wide and polished staircase. I looked up, and recollecting that Madam Felix had said no one of the family ever used the upper rooms, which were always kept in perfect readiness for chosen vis-

itors, it occurred to me that a discreet tour of inspec-
tion in that exclusive region would be interesting.
I went up, half hesitating, for I was conscious that
it was a bold freedom, if not an inexcusable impertinence, to penetrate in this manner into the most private chambers of a strange house, even though they
were unoccupied. But still I went on. The landing-place, I now observed, opened on the left into a
gallery overlooking the fountain in the hall. There
were pillars, with curtains between them, which could
be let down, but only the space between the two
farthest pillars was, at the moment, closed in this
way; the others were drawn up nearly to the ceiling in regular festoons. On the right were the
rooms I had looked into the day before, but the
outside door, then open, was now closed. Turning
from that, and walking along the gallery, I came to
a half-open door at the end of it, where the curtain
on one side was opposite the recess of a large window, with a curtain corresponding to that between
the pillars, and thus formed a sort of vestibule of its
own for the door in front of me. As I put my
hand to the door to push it wider, my attention was
arrested by the fragrant odor of burning incense.
It was not exactly like that burned in the breakfast-

parlor; it was more powerful. My first impression was that the maids were burning pimento to perfume the house, as their master was so addicted to perfuming every thing and everybody, but a moment's observation corrected that opinion. This was more delicate, though equally penetrating. I entered the room and discovered, on a marble table, a blue vapor gently curling from something which I had never seen before, and thought must be a foreign preparation. It consisted of several sticks, set upright in a silver crucible, with holes in the cover, through which they protruded. This was the most beautiful apartment I had yet seen. It was hung with rose-colored silk, and all the ornaments were of cut glass; the handles of the doors, the points of the bedsteads and sofas; the toilet equipage, jugs and basins for washing; vases for flowers; rosettes for the long, flowing window-curtains, which were of thin figured muslin. The room fairly sparkled with crystals, although the light was subdued. The floor was inlaid—as may be seen in a few of the best Jamaica houses—with the richest island woods of different colors. But the pictures along the walls quickly attracted my attention. One side of the room was almost entirely taken up by a painting of

the sea, with figures of mermaids, or some such beings, swimming round a chariot drawn by horses
with fishes' tails. There was a lady in the chariot,
and a man beside it, half in the water, half above
the waves. She was white, but he was brown, and
there was another brown man, with one eye in the
middle of his forehead, throwing stones at them
from a mountain. The ceiling represented a dance
of Cupids, like those I have before mentioned.
They were dancing in a ring, and in the centre of
the ceiling was a lady, a goddess, kissing another
Cupid. There was another picture of a black, stern
man, with a lovely white woman, in a chariot drawn
by black horses. The lady was very averse, it
seemed, to be carried off, and not without reason, I
think, for the chariot was going down under ground
through the mouth of a cavern. The negro had a
fork in his hand, such as the sailors put into the
hands of him whom they dress up for Neptune,
when they cross the line. Of course, there was a
meaning to all this, but I did not then understand it.
It was all beautiful, nevertheless; especially the children. I never saw any living thing like them, for
grace and loveliness.

The *jalousies* of this room were not closed, as

the windows looked to the east, and the sea-breeze was still blowing fresh. I had been so occupied with looking at the floor, the pictures, and the ceiling, that I had not noticed the bed; nor should I, perhaps, have thought of doing so at present, but for a sound, like a gentle sigh, which startled me, it was so unexpected in those unused chambers. I turned toward the bed, and was bewildered with surprise to see a beautiful young lady lying upon it fast asleep. She was evidently a lady of pure white race. She had a very clear complexion, and her glossy hair was light, almost yellow in color. It was bound with a blue sash, so that it might not fall over her face. She was very handsome, more beautiful even than the Cupids, and had the sweetest air of repose. I meant to quit the room the instant I beheld her, and had taken a step or two on tiptoe for the purpose, when a murmur, as if people were bathing and talking in the room below, arrested my attention again, and chained me, for a moment, to the spot. My thoughts were occupied with the noise, but my eyes were fixed on the beauty, whose cheeks were flushed with sleeping, and the color of her lips appeared to me as red as coral. Her eyebrows were dark brown, and her

THE FAIR STRANGER. 331

eyelashes seemed black, as they lay upon her white skin. My head turned, I was dizzy with a troop of sudden emotions.

"Oh, Allah! Mahomet! is this one of thy houris?"

I would I could have cast my skin, and appeared before her eyes, when she should open them, as a handsome cavalier of her own color. I prayed, fool that I was, that such a marvel might occur to me. I invoked the Spirit and his Prophet for—I know not what. I kneeled, and bowed my head down to the floor. Some of her garments lay beside her, within side the musquito net through which I gazed on her; at least, a scarf or shawl of black lace lay there. She had rings, too, on the fourth finger of her left hand, one a gold hoop, a wedding-ring, and the other a black mourning-ring.

It was an absurd, momentary infatuation, but I could not help kneeling to her, or for her; but I did not move any nearer the bed, and it was but for an instant. Yet, while thus fixed, like the statue of an admiring idiot, in the middle of the room, the lady suddenly opened her eyes. She started in surprise, and sat upright in her bed. I really believe I could not have been more alarmed, if our Azrael, the angel

15

of death, had summoned me away from this world
to the next; or, if a jealous tyrant, detecting me in
the chamber of this beauty, had drawn his sword to
transfix me.   I scarcely knew what I did—I murmured something about, " Mistress, forgive me ;"
and, clasping my hands together in a supplicating
posture, I hid my face with them.

She looked at me a while in perplexity, as I
saw through my fingers, and her features became
clouded, as I thought, with anger.   She was not
undressed, having only taken off her black lace
shawl and scarf, and I could see that her person
was no less perfect than her face.   Notwithstanding
I had been for half an hour contemplating statues
and pictures, this young houri seemed more lovely
than all the works of art.   She was, however, more
surprised than angry, as it seemed, from the tone in
which she asked me whom I wanted.

" Nobody, mistress," I replied.

" What brought you here ?"

" Me no know, mistress ; me walk about the
house to see the pictures and the figures," I stammered, in slave lingo.

" Can't you talk any thing but negro," she
replied, " and why are you on your knees ?   Did

your master tell you to come here and kneel to
me ?"

"I knelt, mistress," said I, stammering. "I
knelt—" I did not know what to say; I was
ashamed to even attempt to explain myself. I did
not know but that I might be ordered to be flogged
for being found here, and I was sure of being
laughed at, if not flogged, for telling what had sent
me down on my knees; but the lady was inquisitive,
and would be satisfied. She saw that I was in some
blunder, and began to pity me. She smiled, and
repeated her question; and when she smiled, her
white teeth, which looked so even and so white,
and the kind expression which enlivened her face,
upset my understanding completely. I said some
nonsense, which was not all untruth, about believing
she was a goddess, and prayed—then I broke down.

"Prayed for what ?"

I looked, I suppose, as I felt, like the greatest
fool upon the earth. She laughed outright.

"You did not come to 'tief, beau ?"

"No, mistress—never, never; I would die first,
my lady."

The suspicion stung me to my heart, though it
was quite natural.

"So you can speak English," she replied. "You are an African." She knew this by my face and my marks. "Go through that door," pointing to one covered with silk, "and call for Angela."

I opened the door, which let me into a small chamber, about twelve feet square, which was painted all over, to represent a bower of roses. There was a lounge in it, and upon this Angela, notwithstanding all the conversation I had had with her mistress, was fast asleep.

At the first glance the girl's beauty appeared scarce inferior to that of her mistress; but she was a beauty of a different description, and not the fairest of quadroons. I had not time, however, to make many remarks. I called to Angela—her mistress also called; but Angela slept like a negro. I was obliged to lay my hand on her to wake her. She started at my touch, and almost turned white at the sight of me. She was so astonished that she could not find a word to say, until I moved again toward the larger apartment. Then she called out to me, and, springing off the lounge, caught hold of me by the arm.

"You are a saucy fellow," said she. "Where are you going? That is my mistress's room. How did you come here?" looking suspiciously at the window of her own.

"Not by the window, Miss Angela," I answered. "Your mistress wants you," I added.

The girl stared at me, and said she had dreamed about me, as, at the summons of the lady, she finally permitted me to re-enter the other chamber. But I was no sooner in the room than they both began to question me about my intrusion, and join in a laugh at me. The waiting-maid disowned me as *her* visitor, notwithstanding what she had said of her dream, and the lady was cruel enough to enjoy my confusion. I would have hastily retired, but the lady prevented me. She had left the couch while I went in to call her maid, and Angela arranged her beautiful curls while they were maliciously tormenting me. I sometimes affected the negro jargon with strange gentlefolks; for in those days many of the whites, especially those of inferior education, regarded the use of correct language by a negro as something very like impertinence; and in my first instinct of self-abasement I began my excuses in it, but the lady's demand, whether I could speak nothing but negro, put me upon my best English. She was evidently at a loss what to make of me—

the more so as I became more distinct in my answers. I had already explained that I was the servant of Mr. Holgrave, then visiting at the house, and
that I had strayed into that room under the belief
that the upper story was altogether unoccupied, but
they affected not to believe me.

"What is your name?"

"Mahmadee."

"That is a Mahometan name," said the lady.

"It is, mistress; and I am a Mahometan in
faith."

"What! a Turk! a horrid cannibal Turk!" exclaimed Angela. "The mistress must let me cut off
his head."

"You should know better than to intrude in the
female apartments, Mr. Moslem," said the lady, with
pretended severity. "We must call on Mr. St.
John to impale you."

"Perhaps he came to rob and kill us," said Angela. "I must search you, Mr. Mahmadee."

It was in vain I talked of Mr. Holgrave. She
would, and did search me, much as I protested my
innocence; while her mistress arranged her hair,
and tied a black sash round it, instead of the blue
one, in which she had been sleeping. She sighed

two or three times while she was doing this, and I thought she had a sad, anxious look. Angela found nothing on my person to make me appear still more ridiculous—for that was all the business of her search. So she only pulled my hair and slapped my face, for looking in her mistress's chamber, and then she turned me out of the room, and shut the door upon me. Notwithstanding her raillery and roguery, I turned from the door with a deep sigh, and felt half disposed to exclaim against the injustice of Heaven for making me a negro and a slave. What with the pictures, the perfumes, and the fine lady, I was drunk, intoxicated, and withal so melancholy, I could have sat down and cried for an hour.

I had no sooner reached the landing-place, than I was accosted by Mr. St. John himself, who came up-stairs, and seeing me in confusion, asked me what was the matter. I made a bow, and begged his pardon; said, Mr. Holgrave being asleep, I had walked about the house out of curiosity, looking at the pictures and other pretty things, and I hoped the master was not angry.

"Angry, beau?" repeated he. "Oh no. Are you pleased with what you saw? We should not want you in the house, only that your master wishes it. Have you been to the bath ?"

I answered all these questions as became me, and he showed me another staircase, by which I descended to the offices below—a suite of rooms, all nicely arranged, in the last of which were all the four black girls, dressed in white frocks, with sprigs of myrtle and orange twigs twisted together, and made fast as chaplets in their hair. They had been seated, but rose at my approach, and asked me where I had been. They were surprised at the account I gave of myself, and said they had wondered why and where I had hid myself, for they were very anxious to see me.

"Anxious to see me! why?" said I.

"To laugh with, for there were no men in the house."

"No men in the house!"

"None but your master, Mr. St. John, and his guests. The grooms and stablemen never come into this house, except when they are ordered in; but Mr. Holgrave has petitioned for you."

"And are there no waiting-men?" I asked.

"We are the waiting-men—we have no others. The men go home at night; we sleep in the house and live in the house, and we shall try to make you happy while you stay with us."

"And who is that pretty lady—the—white lady?" I had forgotten myself. The words had no sooner escaped my lips than I recollected I had done better not to have mentioned a word of the matter. They stared at me, and asked me, in tones of surprise, where I had seen her, as I might have expected they would. What could I answer? I was confused and abashed, and they won from me some slight account of my imprudence before I obtained any satisfaction from their. They were much interested with even my limited revelation. They only knew that the lady and her waiting-maid had come to the house the day before, and only an hour or two in advance of Mr. Holgrave. They had an idea that the visit was altogether unexpected by their master, though he had received her with great respect. The lady had desired to be served with her supper and breakfast in her own room, and was, of course, obeyed. They also said that Mr. St. John had mounted his horse and rode away in a great hurry, directly after he had received the lady, not even taking a servant with him, and had returned very late at night. They had scarcely seen the lady,

15*

but she would be down to dinner, they thought; for
the parlor-maid, as well as themselves, were ordered
to be in "company dress," which these damsels certainly were. "They also knew the strange lady
was to be addressed as Mistress Marriot," and there
their knowledge ended.

I then inquired about the four quadroon girls.

"Oh, they are pretty much free women. Have
their own table, and feel plenty above such right
black servants as we or you, I can tell you that for
your comfort, Mr. Mahmadee," said Miss Bella, with
a shade of asperity.

"They do nothing but wait on the table and
fuss about. Oh, to be sure, they are our master's
wives," chimed in Miss Bessie. The other two girls
only laughed.

"Mr. St. John's wives! Four wives!" I exclaimed, in astonishment.

The girls laughed merrily at my simplicity, and
and soon after went out together to attend to their
dinner arrangements.

When left to my meditations, I—Mahometan and
negro though I am—was astounded at such daring
immorality. It never occurred to me that the black
damsels were slightly tinged with malice, or might

be playing on my credulity. I accepted the facts
as they stated them, and they were hard to digest.

"What! four beautiful young girls! quadroons,
almost as fair as the white lady!" Nothing could
exceed my bewilderment. "Four wives!" repeated
I; "four wives! Is he a Musselman? How can a
Christian have four wives? And a beautiful houri,
too, with golden hair and blue eyes—all for St.
John! He cannot be a Christian. He is a Turk,
and it is enough to make me renounce my faith.
It is disgusting, abominable! Gracious heaven! is
this the privilege of a white skin? and I, a slave,
robbed even of my poor Rachel, my one pet lamb!"
But I must own I had overcome my disappointment
respecting Rachel, and the beauty of this Mistress
Marriot had driven the last trace of her out of my
heart, as if by magic.

I waited with impatience for the hour which
would call me to the service of the drawing-room,
that I might see her in company and hear her con-
verse with the white gentleman. Dinner came on,
and was served in much the same order as the
breakfast. I was ranged with two of the four black
girls at the sideboard; the other two brought in the
soup and the dishes that followed it. Mr. St. John

led in Mrs. Marriot, and Mr. Holgrave followed, having, as it appeared, been introduced to her before they entered the room. The music-box rung out its melody, the vapor of the incense, mingled with the perfume of flowers, floating in from the garden through the now open *jalousies*. The music-box went out with the soup tureen, but it was almost instantly replaced by the sound of a guitar, and the better music of soft female voices. It was two of the quadroon waiting-girls, stationed in the next apartment. They had been taught to sing and play a portion of the dinner-hour, even when Mr. St. John dined alone. It was one of his peculiar luxuries. There was very little conversation during our dinner. The music occupied the attention of Mr. Holgrave, who was passionately fond of it, and Mrs. Marriot talked only about the house, the statues, the pictures, and the flowers in the garden. Her conversation was addressed almost entirely to Mr. St. John, except that once or twice she looked toward me, and asked some questions about Africa. She inquired, too, if I could sing or dance in my country fashion, and if I knew any thing of music.

Mr. Holgrave replied, "That I was, for my opportunities, no contemptible performer on the guitar,

but that my passion was poetry and the drama.
If Mahmadee had not neglected to bring his dress
with him, he should give you Robin Hood in character, but he has his white tunic for Othello, and he
will, if you like, declaim the part of the jealous
Moor for you this evening."

Mrs. Marriot declared she would be delighted to
hear it. And, as soon as the quadroon girls came in
to serve desert, as is their duty and custom, I retired
to put on the dress, and with it, quite an absurd
share of the tumultuous emotions and sentiments
belonging to the part. When I returned to the
ante-room, I heard the sweet voice of Mrs. Marriot
singing in a foreign language. She accompanied
herself on a guitar; it was nothing to me that I
understood not the words; the voice and the music
were the sweetest I had ever heard. When she had
done, the quadroon beauties performed a kind of
flower-dance, while the music-box was set again in
motion. As I stood by the door, I could see all
their motions, and I perceived, of course, that they
saw me. Mr. St. John likewise saw me, but made
no remark. Mrs. Marriot seemed pleased with him.
They were engaged together in conversation, and
she smiled at almost every thing he said. Indeed,

he had a very engaging manner, and I made no
doubt but that the lady would soon be, if she were
not already, deeply in love with him. ·

But I had not much time for many reflections
before the music ceased, and the dance ended. The
black girls returned to the dining-room with fresh
napkins and crystal basins, having each a few leaves
of citron floating on the water within them. They
placed them on the table, while one of the quadroons
poured out, from a long-necked bottle, to the lady
and the two gentlemen, each a large glass of some
sparkling wine. The lady only tasted hers, and set
it down again, but seeing me following the black
girls, she beckoned to me, and made me a present
of the rest of it.

"Drink, Mahmadee," said she, "the Prophet will
forgive you."

I took the glass in my right hand, placed the
other on my bosom, and made my obeisance to her,
and then to Mr. St. John, and, finally, to Mr. Holgrave. Had it been fire, I should have swallowed
it—aye, if the Prophet himself had stood before
me; yet, I secretly prayed to him to forgive me. It
was delicious wine, and doubly intoxicating to me;
but, while I wondered at this condescension, she had

washed her hands, and the gentlemen rose to attend her to the saloon. The black girls led the way, then Mrs. Marriot, between the gentlemen. The quadroons followed, and I brought up the rear, carrying in my hands the silver incense-burner.

In this order we marched into the saloon, which was cool and fresh with the fountain; not by the route which I had taken before, but by an ante-room I had not yet seen. It was made, as I understood afterward, to represent the inside of a tomb. The roof was arched, and supported by a row of pillars on either side, the capitals of which were black marble, upon shafts as white as alabaster. There were no windows or openings except the two doors, opposite each other, through which we marched like a funeral procession. This solemn-looking place—so different from the light cheerfulness of the rest of the house—was dimly lighted by a single lamp, in the form of an hour-glass, suspended from the center of the dome. The light burned in the upper half of the hour-glass, and I thought I could descry, in the sand that partly filled the lower division, a little white image, like a shrouded figure, kneeling on a coffin. Yet I took in all the chief features of the place as we passed through it, in almost a single

glance. There were niches in the walls between the
pillars, and in one of them an urn; on the other side
there was a recumbent statue, representing a woman
asleep or dead—I could not determine which; it
was of white marble, and the person seemed young,
and even beautiful. There was also a figure of an
old man with a scythe, at one end of this vault-like
place, and a more ghastly figure of a skeleton, with
a javelin in his right hand, at the other. I did not
like this latter gentleman, nor did the white lady;
she put her handkerchief to her face, and held down
her head, but Mr. Holgrave stopped to look around
him.

"This vault seems strong enough to stand an
earthquake," he said.

"It is the strongest part of the fabric," replied
his host. "The walls are four feet thick, of mason-
work."

The lady rather hurried him on; and he, remark-
ing her dislike to the tomb, obeyed the motion, and
led her immediately away. I heard him reason
with her as they entered the saloon, and say there
was nothing that should alarm us in death—our
youth soon passes away, our pleasures are fleeting,
our means of enjoyment must cease, and death is

inevitable. Who but must think of this—in this
island, too, where human life is so precarious?

"I have tried, Mrs. Marriot, to prepare my mind
for all things; I look to the tomb as a quiet abode
for the body. If I have a soul, it looks farther than
this vault, and I pass through it daily, without apprehension."

Madam Felix now entered to see the lamps
lighted, and fresh preparations made for dancing.
Madam Felix went to the great piano-forte in the
next room, and Victorine and I and the quadroons
danced a sort of minuet. Mr. St. John and Mrs.
Marriot sang, at the same time, some words which
I did not comprehend. The quadroons sang again,
after they had been seated, a hunting duet and
chorus in English; it was something about the sun
rising over the dewy woods, but I have no recollection of it.

After a while Bessie and Bella (for it was their
week of duty) brought in porcelain cups, filled with
tea and coffee, and the company all partook of them.

There was plenty of conversation in the midst of
all this dancing. Madam Felix remained by Mr.
Holgrave, who reclined upon an ottoman. They
commented upon the singers, the dancers, and talked

of the white lady and her misfortunes. I could not understand the whole story, but they both spoke of her with respect and sympathy.

It appeared that her father was a planter of Jamaica, but that, while spending two or three years in England, his daughter became engaged to a young naval officer. When the planter returned to the island, her promised husband followed soon after, being either lieutenant or captain, I could not tell which, of a brig-of-war; but in the passage out he had a battle with a French ship, and received a wound in his head, which very much unsettled his reason. She married him, however, at the entreaty of her friends, although she entertained no particular love for him, and only kept her engagement from a sense of duty.

The young couple had spent but a week together on shore, when he was compelled to sail. He died of a fever on board his ship, and was buried at sea. He was of a good family, and had bequeathed to her a sufficient income, with a small estate he had purchased in the parish of St. Mary, adjoining that of her father.

Mr. St. John and the lady joined them, and the subject was freely continued. The lady spoke seriously of all this, but not sorrowfully; and I should have inferred that, notwithstanding her having plighted her faith to the sailor-officer, she had not doated on him when living, nor too deeply regretted him when dead. Mr. St. John said she had done her duty hitherto, and was now, at any rate, her own mistress. She replied to this, that she must still live to please the world, and not forget that her father was living, and had fixed his heart on a new choice for her, though she was a widow but of eight months, and by no means ready to follow her father's caprices in blind obedience.

During the latter part of the evening I heard Mr. Holgrave say to Madam Felix—who attended him constantly—that, next to Mr. Martineau, Mr. St. John was the worst understood man in Jamaica. So far from being a mere selfish sensualist, he was a man of heart and mind, and almost the only wealthy and educated gentleman that he knew of in the island who enjoyed himself, or valued properly the means of enjoyment which the country afforded. His house, his pictures, his grounds, and every thing about them, would do honor to the taste of of any man of any times.

Here Mrs. Marriot called for Othello, and I

stepped before her, and, after bending the knee and head until my lips touched the outflowing hem of her garment, I rose like one inspired, and went through my part. My soul was in it, and I was not surprised when they all united to praise the force and nature I had thrown into my voice and gestures throughout the whole performance.

At ten the whole family prepared to separate. Victorine found a chance to propose a walk, after her mistress was in bed and Mr. Holgrave had dismissed me for the night. The day had been one round of excitement, and I wished above all things to return to myself, as it were, in a night of rest and solitude, but I could not meet kindness with coldness; so I went to seek her, as she had directed me, in the garden-walks, screened by tall shrubs and flowers. It was a fine, bright moonlight, and we sauntered from the garden into one of the glades of the park, and seated ourselves in a bower beside the stream, which supplied the baths and. fountains in Mr. St. John's house.

CHAPTER XIX.

THE NIGHT-RIDER.

Victorine had a touch of the diplomat in her roguish little head, but she scorned to waste her fine arts on me. She came at once to the pith of the matter.

"Mahmadee, you know Mr. Buckly has gone on a fool's errand to Spanish Town. He wants to find out what my mistress is worth, and to bring back a marriage-license."

"Do you call that foolish work, Victorine?"

"There, there, don't talk like a fool yourself. Pray don't, Mahmadee, or I shall have to box your ears. You know all this is a trick of Mr. Martineau's."

"What has Mr. Martineau to do with Mr. Buckly's marrying your mistress?" I asked, for I was inclined to play the innocent, and learn by whom and to what extent Miss Victorine had been trusted. She saved me the trouble.

"My mistress never thought of marrying him, and never will, but she wouldn't consent to give him pain. Mr. Martineau means to drive him away altogether, but it must be done in such a manner as not to compromise Madam. Whatever trick may be put upon the missionary, we must take care to keep the plan out of her knowledge, and, above all, never allow her to know our share in it."

"But, Miss Victorine, I thought you were in the preacher's interest, and not at all in favor of Mr. Martineau."

"The preacher is such a mean creature, he is a dreadful miser," said Victorine; "yet I would not help to play pranks upon him, did we not see that it is my mistress's fortune, and not my mistress herself, that he is so warm to marry. So we must be ready for whatever offers, when he shows himself again. I wanted to tell you all this, and to bespeak your help if it is needed."

"And what," said I, "does Mr. Martineau give *you* for your assistance and silence?"

"He gives me nothing," replied the girl, laughing. "He flatters me, and tells me I am handsome."

"Negroes," said I, interrupting her, "do nothing

for white men without being paid for it. , What do
you expect for your pains ?"

"Indeed, I expect nothing," she persisted. "Mr.
Martineau may give me a new dress or a pair of ear-
rings, if the missionary is driven fairly off the road,
but I have no promise of any thing."

I asked the girl what recompense I was to have
for my assistance, and she had the assurance to tell
me that I should be overpaid with her thanks.

"No," said I, "that would not do. Victorine
must repay me with her help and good word."

I stopped here, for fear of betraying myself, my
mind still harping upon Mrs. Marriot ; and, just at
this moment, while I was still at a loss to finish my
speech, a horseman came galloping down the glade
in which we sat. We saw by the moonlight that
it was a large man, muffled up in a cloak, and
mounted upon a white horse, which snorted as he
approached the water, and started as he passed the
bower. The rider, however, was no way disconcerted; he continued his course till he came into
the garden, and he then rode gently forward at a
foot's pace.

We had left the bower as soon as he had passed
us, expecting that he would return by the same road

again, and we had fled through the thicket toward
the very path to the garden which he had now
chosen. My white tunic, which I had not put off,
betrayed me. He halted as he saw me, and would
have accosted me, but the horse refused to proceed,
alarmed at my presence, or troubled at the perfumes
about my dress. The strange rider muttered something in a croaking voice, about man or devil, and
reined back his animal to a stand still for a minute,
then muffled himself up afresh, and galloped back toward the glade which contained the bower. We
returned again to look on him, and watched him gallop down the glade, as far as we could see.

"A lover," thought I, stung anew with an insane
jealousy—I thought aloud, for Victorine took up
my words, imagining them directed to herself.

"A lover, indeed? No lover of mine; he may
be come to see some of these pretty girls here,
which is not unlikely. Such a beauty as our white
lady does not want admirers. There should be a
watchman here, but I suppose he is gone down to
the works at the next estate, where they have been
dancing as gaily as the quadroons in Massa St.
John's saloon."

I heard the goombay now; I listened to it, and,

as I could not get rid of Victorine, who did not seem disposed to quit me, I proposed that we should walk down and see the merriment below. We followed the avenue taken by the muffled gentleman, and, in about half an hour, reached the end of the glade from whence we descended by a very abrupt path to a row of negro houses. It was a scene of festivities no less precious to the performers than those which I had left, and quite as rational, though not altogether, perhaps, as refined. The nights in Jamaica are more beautiful than the days in England. I state this for the benefit of those who do not know the climate. It will account for the negroes dancing and singing, sometimes almost all night long. Their music, upon this occasion, sounded very barbarous to my ears, after the delicate strains I had listened to all the evening. The music and songs of Rose Hill had so bewildered my imagination, that the drumming of the goombay inspired me with horror rather than delight. But the case was different with Victorine; she must needs dance, and wanted me to stand up with her. One of the head people, seeing we were strangers, and that I was rather fancifully dressed, paid his compliments to us, and bade us welcome. They had a fiddler among them, and

16

were performing Scotch reels; but the violin
squeaked, and the fiddler made the most abominable grimaces. I could not think of dancing, so I
sat down on a bench beside an old·man, with a head
as white as flour, and left the lively quadroon, who
I thought disgraced herself thereby, to dance away
with the head-driver and a stout creole girl, who
flung about her calicos like the sails of a wind-mill.

The old man made room for me on the bench
very courteously, and, seeing my peculiarity of costume, and no doubt smelling the odors which had
been sprinkled on my linen, asked me, very civilly,
if I did not belong to Mr. St. John's "own self," that
is to say, his valet or body-servant, as we say in Jamaica. I stated the truth, on which he began to
speak in a very favorable manner of that gentleman;
said he was very clever, a conjuror, and a *great magician*, that he could read the stars, and had fore-
told the abolition of the slave-trade. I inquired if it
was true that he had four wives—(the old man
stared)—and I also asked, if that was not against
the Christian religion. He knew nothing about
these particulars, observing only, that in these matters the grand buckras did as they liked, he believed,
as I must have seen since I had been in the island.

He said that no one knew much about Mr. St. John's household. He had people from Kingston and Spanish Town, and people had come to him from St. Domingo. He had done much for his negroes. They were well fed, happy, and contented; and there were so many of them, that their work was very light. Their numbers increased every year, and it was a considerable expense, he was sure, to furnish them with so many things from England. The old man thought Massa St. John might make all that come right, if he would take in more cane-field, and make, as he ought to do, double the sugar he now did; but nothing, said the old man, could induce Mr. St. John to plant an extra acre of canes. He said he would rather have negroes than hogsheads; he had enough. "He has three or four estates," added the old man. As to his wives, and the management of his house, scarcely anybody knew for certain how he conducted himself. Servants from other estates were very seldom there, and his own did not tell much about the matter, for it seemed they were not admitted into his secrets. He had never heard of any children, and, as to the four wives, he could not say; he had never heard about them one way or the other.

Here a woman, who had sat down by us, in a violent heat with dancing, said that Mr. St. John was a *Shadow Catcher;* that is, a sort of obeah-man. She declared, that everybody knew that his house was full of buckra women, and *nigger* girls, all turned into *rock-a-tone* (rockstone, i. e. marble), by Obiah and magic; that he had got some shadows of people, whom he had caught, stuck to the walls on cloth and *osnabriggs.* She also assured her hearers, that all his fountains were to prevent the spirits he employed from getting the mastery over him, and that he could charm anybody by throwing some of the water in his face, and saying, " Wel-come." Nobody who had been in that water was ever able to tell any thing about him.

" Didn't he put you in a bath ?" said this fat mumma to me, " and after that, what do you know about him ? He bewitches everybody; the very niggers fall in love with the women there, and that is the reason he won't let any niggers come into the house; nor any people, any white men, but what are sober and religious (?) and particular. He hates fools, and especially old fools, such as old Massa L——, and Jack F——, and (she named one or two more) who are always fancying themselves young

as ever, and making love when they should be at
their prayers, and talking of getting married, when
they are not fit for any thing but the John-crows."
Here she recollected herself. "I tell you, massa
nigger—(and I wish to state, once for all, that in
this and many other instances, I use the language
that most clearly expresses the *meaning*, without
much regarding the exact words of the speakers)—
"I tell you that you *dare not*, and you know that
your tongue *cannot* speak of what you see at Mr. St.
John's. You know you dare not; he would turn
you into a rock-a-tone, and 'tan you (make you
stand) upon one leg there in his hall, for a thousand years, or catch your shadow on the wall as
you passed, and fasten it there in an image, while
his spirits took your soul into hell-fire."

"Hell-fire! why, what has Mr. St. John to do
with that place?" said I.

The woman turned up the whites of her eyes,
elevating her eyebrows and forehead at the same
time.

"I have heard that said of him by them who can
preach out of the Bible; but if you keep his secrets,
he can do you no harm. His house is full of all
kinds of pleasure, but he is a shadow-catcher, a sor-

cerer. His people are all happy and love him, but he deals with spirits; he is wise and clever, for true, but he is a debbil (devil), and no Christian."

So saying, plump Rosalind got up and offered me a glass of negro beer, which had been handed to her; but I could not touch it. The recollection of Mrs. Marriot's glass of wine made me think this a cup of abominations, and I declined it, though not without offending her, and she sprinkled my face with some of it, as she said, to unbewitch me.

There was some sort of excuse for what the mumma had detailed respecting Mr. St. John, however absurd had been her story, and I concluded that some one had been preaching to her and others about this gentleman; probably a negro, from the ideas she entertained of the statues and pictures.

Rosalind was no sooner gone than the old man with the white head took up her argument, and urged deliberately the fact of shadow-catching, and told me of an obeah-man, who had been hanged three or four years before, for having charmed at least a dozen negroes to death. He used a box made of *yacca* wood, in the form of a coffin, which he carried in his pocket; and when, for any purpose of revenge, or gain, or cruelty, or curiosity, he had

a mind to entrap some negro's shadow, he contrived
to get his object between himself and the sun. He
then slipped the box from under his frock, and
when the shadow fell upon it, snapped it like a rat-
trap, saying, at the same time, "Me· hab you deady,
now—your flesh to the worms—your soul to wait on
me." His victim was sure to die; and so afraid, at
last, were the negroes of him, that no one dared
approach him, except against the sun, and many entered into a compromise with him, and paid so much
to be unmolested. Others paid him still more to
catch any one against whom they had a grudge.
He was hanged for this, and asserted his power even
at the gallows, refusing all communion with a parson
who would have baptized him. This old man with
the white head, on finding I was an African, insisted
that this sorcery came from my country, but I denied it; at least I had never heard of it there. I
told him, beside, that I was brought up a true believer, not in Him of Nazareth, but in Mahomet, the
only prophet of God. He shrunk from me at this
confession, but he returned again, and held his hand
to me.

"I have known many such," said he; "but they
did not remain Mahometans long. They nearly all

turned out good Christians, or good for nothing, at last. You will turn Christian, I hope."

I might have answered him that I had already volunteered to do so, if that could have won me Rachel, and been refused, but I was not in the humor for such a frank confession of folly. I was rather in the humor to listen than to talk, and was just about to inquire about the gentleman whom we had seen on the white horse, when the same apparition dashed by, muffled up as before, in a long black cloak. There was an immediate alarm among the negroes, most of whom ran into the houses directly, or into the bushes. The old man got up in such a hurry to save himself that he stumbled and fell down, and before he could recover himself, the figure had rode away. His face was uncovered, and by the light of the moon, which shone full upon it, I saw a pale, stern, stony countenance, that chilled me. He had a black cap upon his head, and an immensity of cloak wrapped around him, all black. His horse was quite white, with a long mane and tail, and carried him at a canter over the ground where the crowd had been dancing. The tramp of his horse's feet in passing made a severe impression on my gray-headed neighbor. He groaned deeply as

it went by, and was convulsed as if he had spasms,
until the sound had died away. It was not until
the figure was totally out of sight that he ventured
to get up, or that his comrades peeped out of their
homes, like rats peeping out of their holes. The
horseman stared at me again, as he did near the
garden-gate, but he did not speak, nor did I shrink
from him.

In a few minutes the people all re-assembled, and
began to talk about the ghost. The grayhead resumed his seat, and all the voices made such a med-
ley of noises that it was impossible to hear any one
distinctly, or to comprehend what was the general
feeling about this midnight cavalier. One said it
was the *nightmare;* another, that it was old Mc-
Murdoch's ghost, who was strangled in bed by a
᾽mulatto girl; a third, that it was Captain Martin,
who shot a soldier-officer in the maroon-war, after
the officer had once saved Martin's life. Others said
it was old Massa Gowdie's maroon overseer, who
murdered his master. There were fifty opinions: it
was three-fingered Jack; he was white, he was
black, he was gray—with fiery eyes, with no eyes,
with saucer eyes—with blue flames smoking out of
his teeth. But what had become of him? Had he
16*

gone into the sea, toward which he had ridden, and
would not he come back again? My old friend
with the white head said it was Sir Henry Morgan,
the buccaneer. He had looked him steadily in the
face, and he was sure of him! I did not think it
necessary to contradict the old man, but I asked
him and them, why it must be a ghost at all.
" Could it not be a man riding about for his amusement, or on business ?"

There was Victorine with a crowd around her,
giving an account of our first rencontre with him,
and of his riding into Mr. St. John's garden. But
even she had come to the conclusion that it was no
living man or horse. This settled the opinion that
it was a spirit, indeed. Then it was Helim, or Heli-
ma, the obeah-man, the shadow-catcher, of whom I
had just heard. It seemed he had been seen the
night before, by one or two negroes only, and that
he had ridden down to the sea, as they said, and
leaped—horse and man—into the water.

" Then he must be the buccaneer," said the grayhead.

" Do you remember the year—de year of our
Lord Hannah Dormity, 'bout tirty, forty year ago,
Lord Rodney fight wid the French king's fleet, and

take him so? You may 'bleeve me, massa nigger, when me tell you he take 'em all, like so many crawfish 'toxicate wi' lime. Berry well, 'bout dat year in de fall, dere cum a hurricane, mash every ting in dis here island of Jamaica, 'poil all de crop. Buckra no make no sugar dat year, and nigger man 'tarve; him no hab plantain, no cocoa; nutting at all for nyam, no mo (only) fish and duck and teal, dat come wi' de norts off de salt water every day at sundown.

"Now dere was a 'Panish ship full of dollar and doubloon, coming from America, and de men all tire in de gale, all sick and wet, and no lie down, no sleep for two, tree day and night, and de ship run right upon de rocks between Runaway Bay and de Salt Ponds. Massa Kilmore lib den on a plantation by de sea-side, and him walk out at sundown to shoot de duck and teal, as 'em come to feed 'bout de Salt Ponds. Massa Kilmore hear de 'Paniards fire him guns; he see de big ship bilge, and de mast go overboard; he run down to de sea, when de men came ashore in tree boat, all fill wi' chests of money. He take de men home to him great house, and say nutting to nobody, and no one eber see dese 'Paniards agin, *nebba, nebba.* 'Fore dat, Massa Kilmore a poor man, in debt to him mer-

chant, and bery much afraid of de marshal-man.
Well, he grow rich in a hurry now, and you may
b'leeve me, massa nigger, nobody nebba see de
'Paniard sailor no mo. Massa Kilmore tell de other
buckra how dem all go off again in dem boat; but
nobody nebba see 'em go, nor hear 'em, nor 'peak to
'em; an' so, ater some time, buckra begin to
whisper about de 'Paniard ship, an' nigger (him
always hab too much mout) he 'gin to talk out,
and say somebody see Massa Kilmore at moonlight in de Salt Pond bury him cask unner de
sand. So Massa Kilmore, de buccaneer, keep all
de dollar for himself one, an' nobody trouble him.
No so hisself, for now he 'gin to be afear wi'out
reason; 'foretime he no hab no fear but for de
debbity marshal. Him house shut up always, him
nebba see nobody, nor 'peak when he meet 'em, but
him walk about in a night time, an' him groan an'
talk to hisself 'bout deady, an' ghost, an' funerals.
Sometime him ride dat gray mare, an' come gallop,
gallop to pieces all night lang, into de sea, ober de
racks, an' among de canes, and den he sit from cock-
crow till dawn, on him mare, an' fix him yeye 'pon
de rack where him see de 'Panish ship go down.
At lass, him lose him head, an go raving, ramping

mad, an' put up a gallows where de grabe dig, an' call him nigger to hang him up fa murder de 'Paniard. So him hab a 'trait waiscoat, an' die, an' long, long arter, him ghost walk, walk, ebery night. Nobody lib in a great house, too much noise da; no rest; eben do rat run out, so frighten wi' de noise, an' de debbil dat lash him soul ebery night."

Here the old man ceased, and his hearers remained half petrified with horror and wonder. "No doubt it was the ghost which they had seen," and every eye was turned anxiously round for another glimpse of this mysterious personage. I was, in some measure, infected myself with the general apprehension, and Victorine was afraid to return again to Mr. St. John's, though the night was so brilliant, and she resolved to await the daylight.

The negroes, after a time, resumed their dancing, though not with genuine hilarity, although a good allowance of rum and water was handed about on all sides. I sat upon the grass beside Victorine, who had had enough of exercise, and seemed contented now with the company of her fellow-servant. As we leaned our tired heads against the trunk of a fallen cocoa-nut-tree, for rest, sleep overtook us both. Side by side we slumbered, in spite of the fiddle and

the goombay, until the old head man roused us.
The eastern sky had begun to brighten, and the
moon looked cold and pale. We got up and took
leave of Massa Whitehead. The driver, too, Miss
Victorine's partner, saluted her at parting, and the
negroes kindly bade us farewell.

We had a toilsome march up the broken ground
till we reached the end of the glade upon the table-
land, which conducted us to the house. The birds
were already on the wing in the avenue, the peacocks screamed, the parrots· chattered, and the
whole feathered tribe were in full stir. It was a
Sunday morning, so there was no shell-blow, and
no negroes in the grounds to note our return; but
on our arrival in the garden I found all the doors
and windows closed and fastened. We tried in
vain, for some time, to get into the house, and
began to gaze at each other in some confusion, when
a window opened above us, and Mrs. Marriot's look
of contemptuous surprise met my hasty, upward
glance. We were admitted and reproved, like the
culprits we felt ourselves. Victorine had more difficulty than I experienced in explaining the night's
adventures. Mr. Holgrave believed and pardoned
me, but no one else in the house had any charity for

either of us. The consequence of all this was, that I had to explain, protest, defend, and even resent for Victorine, until the truth was finally vindicated; and by that time she and everybody else set me down as her exclusive property, which, certainly, was no part of my plan.

Yet that affair brought to me some unexpected good. At the dance I noticed a young girl, about the age of Aimée, who sat cowering against the wall of one of the negro houses, too ill to share in the amusements going on around her. I felt her pulse, looked at her tongue, and asked a few questions. She had the measles, and so had a child that was fretting unheeded at her side. In my zealous love of the study of medicine I had learned the uses of many simple herbs, beside what Dr. Marsh in his kindness had taught me, and I prescribed with confidence for these sudden patients. It proved to be a success, and from that time I was often called upon by the negroes about us, under the imposing title of *Doctor Mahmadee.*

CHAPTER XX.

MAD FROLICS.

IN my journal of the memorable month I am about to review, I closed the last note of the occurrences with these words : " We all caught craziness from each other." I suppose as children take measles, by coming in contact with the fever and contagious humors of those already infected. For this chapter, then, I shall follow pretty closely the notes as they were then written. Were they not before me, I should be inclined to distrust their accuracy, there is about them such an air of extravagance and exaggeration. I can only say they are really true.

July 1st.—Two young gentlemen arrived to-day from Kingston. They are strangers in the island, and have brought out a letter for Mr. St. John from friends in England. They are what the servants call "Johnny Newcomes."

July 2d.—These Newcomes think our "Jamaica manners excessively odd." Stella and Lina,

the quadroon parlor-maids, say, "The manners of
these 'Newcome' buckras are 'more excessively
odder.'" They asked these girls, when they came
to their rooms with flowers and fresh napkins,
whether it was not also their duty to wait upon
visitors to the baths. Stella, who is a great rogue,
answered with a courtesy, "Certainly, sir," and they
all went down into the shower-bath room together.
Stella cast off the cords, instead of showing the
"Newcomes" how to manage them, and ran away.
The water came down in a rush, and there was a
terrible splashing and calling out; but when the girls
were brought to an account, they demurely excused
their conduct by saying, that they went to show the
gentlemen where the baths were situated—as is their
duty, there being no men-waiters, except those belonging to visitors—but that just as they laid hold
of the "pulls," the gentlemen began to take off their
coats, which so startled them both that they gave
the "pulls" a jerk and left the place. Mr. St. John
chose to accept the excuse. These four quadroon·
parlor-maids have a spice of the black demon in
them. One of them, named Hyacinth, is the most
beautiful creature—next to Mrs. Marriot—I ever
beheld. I thought them all dazzling beauties the

day they came into the hall with wreaths of flowers
on their heads, and silk sashes round their pretty
white dresses, but now I find, on noticing them
more closely, that they are only good-looking—not
so handsome, in fact, as Victorine—only that they
are fairer in complexion. Hyacinth is only an octoroon—but one-eighth African, she says—and is being educated for a music-teacher. She sings well,
and plays sweetly on the guitar.

July 7th.—The "Johnny Newcomes" have been
established in the Garden House. This is a pretty
building at the corner of the garden. It is built
against the side of a steep hill, and in the lower
part the gardener lives with his family, with his side
faceing the vegetable garden. The upper story has
its own front-door, and looks toward the House. It
has three neat rooms for single gentlemen, and is
used when the House overflows with visitors—or,
perhaps, when single "Newcomes" cannot suit their
own behavior to "the excessively odd habits of Jamaica."

July 11th.—Last evening was very gay. The
gentlemen wanted a play acted by negro children.
A burlesque they called it, in which there was not
much talking, but plenty of ridiculous acting, and

some not bad dancing. Madam Felix has been teaching them all the week, and the maids have dressed them in very showy costumes. All the actors were girls of ten or twelve years, but the four tallest were dressed to represent hunchbacked gentlemen of some foreign country. Three more represented young ladies—all of them were dressed in the brightest colors—red, blue, and orange, with plenty of spangles and gold lace.

The play was called "The Four My-Lords." In the first act there was a hunchback lord asleep in his castle. He was awaked by a knocking, and swore a little, and said that he had sent away his porter because he was a drunken traitor; then he opened the castle-door, and in came three hunchbacks, like himself in size and shape, dancing and singing, with guitars. They saluted the lord of the castle now and then, by hunching up their shoulders as they drew toward him, and hailing him, "Brother, my lord," at which he was very indignant, and, in his rage, he flies round in a Congo hornpipe. Suddenly his three nieces, young ladies of fortune, came into a gallery, and looked down into the hall, where their uncle was stamping and scolding. He called them down, and gave them a glass of wine, and then wished them good-by. He shut the door upon them, and said he never hoped to see them again, and yet, in five minutes, he went out to look after them, and see whither they were gone.

As soon as he was gone himself, the three young ladies came back, having made signals to the "my lords," and let them in again, for they had been hidden in the bushes about the castle. .Then they all fell to singing and dancing; and, last of all, they prepare for a feast, the nieces bringing in a cold turkey and other things, and lay a cloth.   In the midst of these arrangements, the lord of the castle returns, and knocks for admittance; for, though he has the key, they have barricaded the door.   Of course there was considerable scuffling to hide away the table and the good things, and the ladies, not knowing what to do with the hunchbacks, hid them also in three barrels, which my lord happened to have in his hall.   Then they let him in, and he began to scold and skip about, till they all ran up stairs.

It seems the old gentleman had listened at the door, for he suspects some roguery; and, hearing a sneeze in one of the barrels, he takes it up and flings it out of the window into a river outside his castle-walls. He serves the other two barrels in the same way, and so the young hunchbacks are disposed of. But they have their waiting-men outside the castle, and these, seeing the barrels pitched into the river, jump in and pull them ashore, as it appears afterward.

In the second act comes a trumpeter, and demands the three young ladies in marriage for three barons, to whom he declares the king has promised their hands and fortunes. As the hunchback lord dare not refuse to produce them, they came down and made a courtesy to the trumpeter. The baron of the castle is obliged to say the other barons will be welcome. The trumpeter gives him their credentials, and ends by telling him that the young noblemen are in his nieces' chambers. Then the ladies shriek, and the baron storms, and the trumpeter goes on to state that they had come disguised as singing-men and dancers, and that they had been seen to enter the castle. The ladies whisper, and agree to tell their uncle how they had bestowed the young hunchbacks, saying, at the same time, that although they could be amused with seeing such fellows dance, they would never hear of such a thing as marrying them. The three little ones shake their woolly heads, and scream, "What! three young beauties like us wed hunchbacks? No, no, no." The uncle vowed his lovely nieces were young and rich enough to expect young men without humps. However, the trumpeter flies into a passion because his three "my lords" are not produced, and goes away calling the uncle a murderer, and the young women coquettes, and threatening to inform King George.

In the third act, the uncle comes in, saying, that a nobleman like him must protect his dignity and his interest, and, therefore, he must go and fish up his lost barrels. The trumpeter interrupts him by returning with the three "my lords," but who are no longer humpbacked. He knows their faces, and asks with interest after their humps. They tell him how they lost these by being thrown out of the window into the river, and the baron, who is in love with all the three nieces, and wishes to marry them all, that he may have their fortunes (for it seems the castle is theirs), is persuaded to try the same remedy for his bump, and is flung out of the window, and I suppose drowned, for he appears no more. Then the three young lords marry the young ladies, and the cold turkey is brought in again, and they make a feast, and dance and sing, and praise each other's beauty immoderately, all the while twisting their African features into the drollest contortions. The young imps could not have helped that if they had wanted to; but the whole wit of the play is in this high talk of love and lordships by little, woolly-headed negroes.

The music was very sweet, and what made the rest of it seem more ridiculous was, that the white gentle-folks were the musicians, while the six little negroes (the three my lords and their young ladies) were dancing and making love at the close of the third act.

July 12*th.*—The gentlemen go down to the sea for a bath every morning, and Mr. Holgrave is now so much better, that he is able to go with them to the beach. They ride down to the sea on horseback, and after bathing comes breakfast; then they adjourn to the library, where, amid books and pictures, a great portion of the morning is consumed. Mr. St. John is a painter, and so is one of the new-comers. The other is very curious in flowers, and walks about with a great tin box, in which he brings home loads of weeds, which he and Mr. St. John register in a great book. Hyacinth and Stella, two of the quadroons, are collecting and pressing ferns for them.

July 17*th.*—We have an addition of five to our family. Two more gentlemen have arrived from Spanish Town, one a Mr. Lewis, a short, stout man, who is always at the piano-forte making songs; the other a lawyer, going somewhere to plead at quarter-sessions. The lawyer has brought his three daughters to pass a week here with Mrs. Marriot. These young ladies are so pretty they are called the "Three Graces." Neither of them can compare with Mrs. Marriot. The "Three Graces" have just returned from England, where they were sent to be educated. They are related to Mr. St. John, and were school-fellows with Mrs. Marriot, so there is to be no end of feasting and gaiety.

July 24*th.*—There was a grand dinner-party day before yesterday. Six more gentlemen were added to the company, and they were waited upon exclusively by the girls, my business being only at the side-board. It was the duty of the black girls to bring the dishes from the servants' room to the dining-room door; so I heard all their conversation, both at dinner and after. They talked a little freely after dinner, and toasted the healths of all the girls in succession. Mr. Lewis left early to go and enjoy the piano, where he played and sang. Mr. St. John . joined him, while his guests drank his madeira and claret like fishes. As for the "Graces," they never tasted any thing but water; all the luxuries were wasted upon them. Coffee was served in the saloon by the four quadroons, dressed in their white frocks, with blue sashes and borders of the same color around the neck, short sleeves and hems, all to correspond. This is the uniform of the parlor-maids for service in the saloon, only that, as Hyacinth is required for the guitar, Victorine wears the dress also, to make up the four waiters at the wine, dessert, and coffee. Madam Felix watches over every thing without seeming to interfere. The ladies all treat her with perfect politeness, almost as if she were white like themselves. It may be because they know she is Mr. St. John's sister, and almost as rich as he is himself.

After they had taken coffee, they all danced country-dances, except Mrs. Marriot and Mr. St. John, who sat on a sofa almost the whole evening, engaged in conversation, every sound of which cut Sidi Mahmadee to the heart. I must except, also, Mr. Holgrave, who sat near them, and called occasionally

17

one of the girls to fan him. The intervals in the
dancing were filled up with songs, duets, trios, and
choruses in English, and, I believe, in Italian.   I
handed, meanwhile, all sorts of liquid refreshments
—soda-water, lemonade, champagne, and liqueurs.
The negro children were brought in again, and sang
some of their songs in the play.   The "Graces" indulged the company with a figure-dance, which they
had learned in England.   I thought some of the gentlemen began to be a little excited with the champagne.   They laughed and talked louder, and were
a little disposed to romp with the young ladies,
when, who should arrive at the house-door, but Mr.
Buckly.   One of the black girls came, and told me
that a buckra man wished to see me.   I found it
was the missionary, and ran back to the saloon to
tell Mr. St. John who it was—I told Madam Felix
also, who was thunderstruck, and called him an infatuated donkey.

The missionary had given me to understand that
his visit was principally to Madam Felix, and I said
as much to her and to Mr. Holgrave also, who was
somewhat annoyed; but Mr. St. John desired that
he might be admitted, and sent all the negro children who had been dancing to receive and usher

him into the saloon. I went with them, and delivered Mr. St. John's invitation, while a stableman
took the parson's horse. He was surprised at the
courtesy of the children, and somewhat abashed at
the sight of the Graces, who received him in the
saloon. He was hot and tired with riding, and
damp with dusty perspiration. I doubt if such a
man, in such a pickle, had ever made his appearance
in that saloon before. Mr. St. John rose to receive
him, as did Mrs. Marriot. The rest of the company
were forming to dance. There were flowers, music,
motion, perfumes, lamps, and wax candles blazing,
and such an air of revelry, luxury, and pleasure,
occupied the room and reigned around, that Mr.
Buckly looked and seemed to feel like a ghost—and
a most earth-soiled ghost at that—in the happy circle. He was confused beyond expression, turning
his eyes right and left, encountering smiles from
every face,—and courtesies, as well as smiles, from the
ladies. He was quite bewildered. One made room
for him on a sofa, another gave him a perfumed
handkerchief to wipe the perspiration from his face,
a third offered him a fan sparkling with diamonds,
and Hyacinth brought him sangaree and wine.
Mr. St. John assured him he was welcome, the gen-

tleman all bowed to him, and Mrs. Marriot allowed him to shake hands with her. Madam Felix, only, took no notice of him; she could not imagine what affair had brought him to this abode of worldly pursuit and pleasures. He sat in silence, engaged for some time in cooling himself, and ruminating, no doubt, upon his reception. Hyacinth waited upon him with a fresh handkerchief, to dry the abundant moisture which oozed from his pores, after the draught of sangaree which he had taken. She also hastened to bring him a fan, and smiled so kindly and good-humoredly on him, that a more sensible person could not have been indifferent to her attentions or her charms. He was a little out of countenance when his eyes met those of Madam Felix, as she retired with the white ladies. They seeing, perhaps, that the gentlemen were becoming a little too vivacious, arose, and withdrew in a body. Mr. Holgrave excused himself, also, on the plea of his delicate health, and after attending the ladies, with Mr. St. John and Mr. Lewis, to the foot of the stairs, he went to his room, while the other two gentlemen returned to the saloon. I followed Mr. Holgrave to his apartment to see if he wished any thing, but he directed me to go back and wait upon the gentle-

men, who, he said, were in for a frolic. I found one
of the Johnny Newcomes had already taken my
place at the sideboard, and was opening and pour-
ing out champagne as if he had never done any
thing else in his life—and I think he had done a
good deal in that way, first and last. His companion was directing—or trying to direct—the four
quadroons in some variations in a figure, which he
wished to improve into a German waltz, and he
ended by seizing Hyacinth, and flying round the
room with her. Lewis dashed off the music, and
the other Newcome—the gentleman who thought
Jamaica manners "so excessively odd"—caught Victorine by the waist, and sailed round as if in chase
of the first couple. I—who had drank no wine, and
had never before seen waltzing—thought the world
was coming to an end, when I saw two English gentlemen sail off with a pair of quadroons, in that
style, in Mr. St. John's drawing-room, and in Mr.
St. John's presence. Mr. Buckly stared, and drank
a large goblet of wine; then stared again, and took
another brimmer, and by that time his own eyes
were dancing waltzes.

When he first sat down, and was relishing the
sangaree, he might have considered that this com-

pany was not precisely suited to his profession, or
to his character as a man of God. He might think,
too, that Madam Felix was rather ashamed of him,
under these circumstances, or ashamed of being seen
by himself in a society apparently devoted to pleasure. Hyacinth came to him when the waltz was
over, and gave him no time for reflection. She asked
him question upon question, in a manner so arch
and so amiable, that she had half intoxicated him
with administering to his vanity and his thirst, before he was aware that such a thing was possible.
Meanwhile the dancing continued, with plenty of
music, and some singing.

In one of the intervals, Mr. Buckly told Hyacinth
that dancing was invented by the Evil One to deceive mankind, and, by inflaming the fancy, to lead
young men and women into sin, to the certain and
utter destruction of their immortal souls.

Hyacinth fixed her large black eyes on him, and
they seemed filled with tears. It was his turn to
comfort her. He blushed, bid her be of good cheer,
and said he would not preach at present; but this
was not enough, the girl still wept, and every eye
was quickly turned on her. She appeared to sob,
and every one came to comfort her. Mr. Lewis,

among others, seated himself by her, and whispered something in her ear. She put her handkerchief to her eyes again, so as to cover her face as well, and there was a movement which *might* be a suppressed sobbing, but then I thought again that it might be a stifled laugh, as Mr. Lewis walked slowly away, leaving the preacher, for a minute, quite dismayed at the effect of the few words he had uttered, and out of countenance at the manners of the gentlemen. But this confusion was of short duration.

The gentlemen having declared they would "make a night of it," corresponding orders had been sent to the kitchen, and now the signal came for supper. All the company marched into the dining-room (not through the tomb), and Hyacinth, with dry eyes, again devoted her attentions to Mr. Buckly. He was hungry, and ate heartily, the waiting-girls supplying him with cold chicken and ham, and tempting him with sweetmeats and confectionery. I poured out hock, which they handed to him. He was as thirsty as he was hungry, and devoured as much as four of the other gentlemen. They plied him with wine, and invited him to drink, until I could perceive that his eyes were apparently enlarged, and his speech was not altogether so fluent as heretofore; but, though less fluent, it was more free. He stuttered pretty speeches to waiting-girls, talked to Hyacinth of her black eyes, and her sweet breath, told her her teeth were pearls, and her lip the bow of Cupid. He heard the other gentlemen talking nonsense, and he followed their fashions to the end, and a bow-shot beyond it. Mr. Lewis sang drinking-choruses and tipsy love-ditties, and cried bravo, over and over, at the end of his own songs.

Before the company returned to the saloon Mr. Buckly was drunk, and totally off his guard. He laughed, and even sang, and finally danced about the room with Hyacinth. He professed himself her adorer, said she was an angel of beauty and simplicity; that he could worship her, and lay his life and fortune, if he had one, at her feet. The whole party was convulsed with laughter. The quadroons joined freely in the mirth, for the ordinary decorums of rank and condition had been turned out of doors two hours before that. The very black girls in the ante-rooms tittered audibly at the vagaries of the besotted parson.

He attempted a reel with Hyacinth and Victorine, for they both kept dancing around him, and they would step out and in the figure so quick and

dexterously, that a man less far gone than Mr.
Buckly might be as puzzled as he was, when he was
uncertain whether he saw double, or " Hy-hy-cin-the
had added herself into two."

Once or twice I attempted to pass off on him
water in place of champagne, and even seized an
unobserved moment to pray him to retire, but he
replied with texts of Scripture, and even loudly
denounced the only person that felt for him, as the
evil spirit. " Get thee behind me, Satan," said he;
" I shall dance, like holy David, before the ark, or,
like Jephthah's daughter, before that judge of Israel.
The daughter of Saul despiseth me not. Noah
drank of the fruit of the vine, and Solomon, in all
his glory, had seven hundred wives." He made
other Scriptural allusions, which I forbear to mention, and drank and talked till he became nearly unintelligible. In this state he was carried to a bed on
the ground floor, in the room adjoining the dining-
apartment, where the lion's mouth was fixed in the
wall. I undressed and put him in bed, and left a
lamp burning on a table in the middle of the room.
Then I lay down on a mat- in the now deserted
dining-room, that I might be near him in case of
need, and soon dropped asleep.

17*

CHAPTER XXI.

AN ALARM.

IT was not much past midnight when the preacher was put to rest, as I hoped; and I probably had not slept an hour when I was aroused by the plashing of water and the noisy muttering Mr. Buckly was making in his room. I did not move at first, being unwilling to disturb him or myself, for I was very sleepy, and hoped he would get into bed again; but I lay awake and listened to his soliloquies, which ran on like one of his sermons. He made speeches to the mirrors, and to his own image reflected in them, calling it a bewitched brute, an evil monster, and a drunken beast. Then he addressed the picture of "Jamaica," crowned with coffee-flowers, whom he took to be Hyacinth, and extolled her beauty. Then he broke out and abused her. "A Dalilah," said he, "for whom Samson was shorn of his strength, of his hair, of his wits! No Dalilah had half these charms. What have I done and said to Dame Felix?"

He groaned, staggered about a little, and began to preach again. When he is sober he declares he was born for a preacher—called from his early youth to bear the Word to the uttermost parts of the earth—and it seems that even when he has drank his reason out of doors he keeps up sermonizing, though on strange texts.

"She's an enticing devil — a lovely limb of Satan. Why are women angels, but to make us devils? That portrait has been placed here to undo me. Satan has graven the original on my heart. But what is this?" He had the lamp in his hand, and moved toward the bath again. "This head of bronze, with the heathen characters about it, and this vile scrawl of Greek or Hebrew; but the water is deliciously cool."

He seemed to be talking to his sober self. He talked nonsense, but I could hear that his speech was less thick, and that his words marched off in some order, whereas when he went into the room they all tumbled out together in senseless confusion. I had now taken post just without the communicating door, and opposite the large window opening into the garden. He was balancing himself pretty well on his feet. His back toward me, and bowing,

as it were, to the lion's head, which he had set running, and so splashed himself that the water was
dripping from him to the floor.   Another groan.

" What an ungodly sinner this St. John must
be!   Satan will surely get the debauched, unbelieving wretch.   Revelling in ungodly wealth and luxuries : baths, wine, women, statues, pictures !   He
has the flowery path to heaven—to hell, I mean—
aye, to hell.   There will be no calling for champagne there, no dancing."

Here he walked again toward the portrait, but,
in his progress, he stumbled over something or
other, and dropped his lamp.   I heard the glass
shade smash, and I heard him also exclaim against
his own awkwardness.

" Ominous," said he ; " my light is quenched, my
sole light flickers, expires before this Magdalen with
the wreath—ah !"

He heaved a terribly long sigh, which ended,
however, in a hiccup; and, being afraid of the
broken glass, as I supposed, he walked toward the
window.   The glass of the window was open, as I
had left it, but the jalousies were shut, and he
fumbled at these for some minutes before he got
them apart.

"What a night is here!" continued he; "more lovely than the finest day! Would I had never seen that Hyacinth. How cool, how refreshing is the air!"

As he went out of the window, I slipped into the room and stopped off the running water, and then followed him to watch his next proceedings. He was standing about three yards off, talking away. "Another statue. Who gives all these things to the ungodly reprobate? Who, but the father of lies? Who else has statues like these? That black horseman is like life. The tail of the horse almost waves. Ah, my poor eyes! How my head aches! I don't like statues. The man is black, the steed is white. My God, it must be Death on the pale horse! It is awful to make such statues. An abomination before the Lord."

I shuddered at these words, for I knew there was no such statue in the garden. Before he was through I, too, had discovered the object of fear. At the far end of the walk sat the same black horseman, the "Night-mare" who had so alarmed the people at the negro dance. It stood so motionless and ghostlike that I would scarce have had the courage to approach it. But Mr. Buckly, with the

reckless and restless state of nerves of a wine-soaked
man, walked toward it as he speechified. It was
about fifty yards from the house, the head of the
horse fronting us, and the head of the man turned
upward toward Mrs. Marriot's windows. They
were both motionless, and their effect might well
impose upon Mr. Buckly, who. had seen statues,
black and white, about the house. I did not like
to follow directly behind him, lest he should be
alarmed, so I ran out by the hall, and the great
entrance, which, like that of most Jamaica houses,
was wide open. I got into the garden, and, by the
shelter of a hedge of hibiscus, was within ten yards
of the night-rider, just as Mr. Buckly had arrived
opposite to it from his window. He walked pretty
straight toward the figure, muttering all the way
something about a libertine destroyed; but as he
came closer to it, he apostrophised the rider as
Death. "Death," said he, "on the pale-colored
horse! Do you come for my cup-bearer, my Hebe?"
He spoke in a deep, sepulchral, bass tone, which
made me feel almost uncomfortable. The words
appeared to be dragged from the bottomless pit.
"Or have you come for the lost, undone, ungodly
St. John?"

Here the white horse snorted.

" My God !" exclaimed the preacher, " it's alive. What art thou, in the name of —?" He recoiled as if he had trod on a yellow snake, and it had hissed at him. He stood so fixed in his place that I could have almost fancied him turned statue himself. " In the name of the living God, who art thou, and what is thy business? Answer me, in the name of Him who died for the sins of all believers. Art thou a man, a spirit, or a demon? What! no answer? Am I then forsaken of heaven, and for this one sin ?"

The ghost kept a most provoking silence, fixing only his eyes, which were not empty sockets, on Mr. Buckly's face. It was all so still, not a breath stirring, that truly the preacher might begin again to think he had been deceived. He held his hand toward the horse, while he made a retrograde movement in the direction of the house.

But here the scene changed. The night-rider raised his hand and spoke vehemently, while the preacher was checked into a statue.

" Miserable, heartless seducer, how dare you appeal to heaven? I have come to demand if you mean to marry my daughter? Wretch, you shall marry my daughter."

"Your daughter!" stammered the parson. "Who is she?"

The figure fixed his eyes in fury on the preacher. I could see them, by the moonlight, swell from their sockets.

"My daughter!" it continued, "coward and seducer that you are, did I not hear you talking of her? Swear to marry my daughter. Swear it."

"Your daughter! your daughter!" again exclaimed the preacher, in a hurry. "Can it be Madam? I have offended her forever."

"Yes, you have offended her and me. Swear."

"Who is she? Is it Hyacinth?"

"Villain, do you mock me?" cried the figure, in a rage, and suddenly presenting a frightfully long horse-pistol. Mr. Buckly flounced down upon his face, calling out for mercy.

"I'll swear," said he; "I'll swear to marry the devil, so you spare my life. Oh Lord! oh Lord! I took you for a statue—this is some trick—this is Mr. Martineau's work. I'll marry her, nevertheless."

"Arise, then; I will follow you to the house," rejoined the figure.

I had been very much afraid that the night-rider might shoot the preacher; and, stealing back again by the hibiscus hedge, I called to Mr. Buckly from the corner of the house, as well to encourage him,. as to let the stranger know there was some relief at hand for the poor parson. Mr. Buckly got up, on hearing my voice, and ran toward me, but the cavalier pursued him, and chased us round the house into the court-yard. He was upon our flanks as we passed the gate, brandishing still the pistol, and we could not prevent his following us into the hall itself. What a clatter he made. I thought the steps might have stopped him, but the horse sprang up these, as if possessed of supernatural power, and entered the hall.

On reaching the top, the rider, grasping hold of Mr. Buckly, hurled him—or dragged him, uninten-tionally, perhaps—to the ground. The lamp was burning in the hall, and the light was sufficient to exhibit our ghostly visitor to perfection, and it is not likely we should long want spectators to wonder at, if not to enjoy the scene. The Johnny New-comes came first, drawn from their rooms by the clatter on the stone steps, and staring as if they had lost their wits; and Mr. Lewis followed, in no less

amazement. I believe they thought it was an insurrection of the negroes, for one of them appealed to
me: "Dear Mahmadee, spare our lives." Mr. St.
John came last. He entered the hall with a sword
in his hand, and having a cloak wrapped round him
over his night-clothes. He seemed very little disconcerted, though he was somewhat astonished at
the figure, whose horse was more alarmed than even
Mr. Buckly.

"You have mistaken me," said this last, beginning, but half sober as he was, to comprehend for
whom the ghost intended his visit. "I am a stranger here. This is Mr. St. John."

The figure stared at Mr. St. John, and again presented his pistol, but as quickly replaced it in a
holster, saying: "This, then, is the seducer, the
epicure, the selfish traitor, which that drunken fool
was trying to personate."

"Not at all," said the preacher. "I took you
for a statue."

"Peace, idiot!" rejoined the figure.

"You, sir," to Mr. St. John, "must account with
me. An injured, wretched father demands repara-
tion for the ruin of his daughter. What can ex-

ceed your baseness? Reprobate, where is my daughter?"

"Name her," said Mr. St. John, with surprising calmness.

"What," rejoined he, "has he so many victims here that I must name my child ere I recover her from the herd with which she is confounded? Monster, give me back my daughter before her soul is sealed to everlasting perdition."

"Need there be any question about losing souls here?" said Mr. St. John, still preserving a cold, steady manner, and keeping his eyes fixed on the stranger, who thus abused him like one in frenzy, and whose looks were even wilder than his words. "Call your daughter by name," continued Mr. St. John. "Call her, sir, and if she be here she will obey your call."

"Look at me," replied the figure; "I am a white man; my wife was also a white lady."

"Egad," said Mr. Lewis, aside, "he is as ugly as the devil. He can't be Mrs. Marriot's father, and whom else can he be after?"

"You are many," continued the wild man. "You are in your own castle; I demand my daughter—give her to me. I could have laid you dead at my feet, but I only want to have back my child in safety. Ah! I hear her voice."

He wheeled his horse toward the three gentle-men-visitors, who were all huddled together, in some alarm and more amazement. They receded before him, as he showed signs of riding them down. I was thankful that Mr. Holgrave was not there to be agitated and annoyed.

"Stand off, inquiring fools! let me have room for my sorrows, and no witness."

He waved to the gentlemen to leave him alone, a summons which was seconded with effect by Mr. St. John. Some of the girls had joined the throng, and, as the ghostly gentleman had intimated, he really had heard her voice. Mrs. Marriot made her ap-pearance at the foot of the stairs, followed by An-gela.

"Mrs. Marriot," said Mr. St. John, closing the door upon the other guests, "is this your father?"

She was dressed in a white wrapper, and her hair was tied up with the blue ribbons, as I had seen her in her sleep. She answered "*yes*" to Mr. St. John's question, and approached the horseman timidly, but without any air of guilt.

The father fixed his eyes upon her as she drew

near. " Would that you had been in your grave,"
said he, " so that I had never known this hour,
degenerate, abandoned girl."

" You are unjust, father," replied the daughter,
weeping; " quit your horse a moment, and hear me,
for Heaven's sake! Why should you come at this
dead hour to alarm the house and its inhabitants,
rather than ask for me at noon-day? It is you who
will destroy my character, and furnish matter of
scandal and ridicule to the whole island."

I thought the ghost looked somewhat ashamed,
and, taking courage myself, I offered to hold his
horse, but he put me back a moment.

" Mary," continued he, " are you so debased as
to minister to this monster's pleasures? You must
instantly come with me. Better be dead, and in
your tomb, than here."

" If there is any violence intended," said the
lady, suspecting from his manner, perhaps, that he
thought of putting her to death, " I am fixed here.
It is true I am your daughter, but I disclaim your
right to keep me in constant terror and unhap-
piness."

" Ah! miserable girl, you wish to remain here
and live in sinful delight," said the stranger.

"There you are deceived," rejoined the daughter, spiritedly, "abused beyond measure; but if you talk of reason, get off your horse, and let the household be quieted. Mr. St. John, beg of him to listen to me."

Mr. St. John, at this request, bade me assist the gentleman to dismount, and said, though I thought rather coolly, that if the gentleman would honor him with his attention, he would engage to impress him with different views. I again took hold of the horse's bridle, and the gentleman's off stirrup. His daughter came up to him, took his hand and kissed it, and, partly by entreaty, partly by a little force, prevailed on him to dismount. Mrs. Marriot held out her arms to him as he touched the floor, and burst into tears. How beautiful she looked! Her father took her in his arms, and hung upon her neck. It was an affecting sight; I could scarce avoid shedding tears myself.

I led away the horse, but was much troubled to get him down the steps, which he had mounted so easily; having succeeded, and shut him in the stable, I returned to the house. There was no one in the hall, except one or two of the quadroons, who were anxious to learn what they could from me about the matter. The gentlemen had all retired again to their rooms. Mrs. Marriot led her father into the dining-apartment, where Mr. St. John was making a speech to him. To be sure, how Mr. St. John did preach, and how meekly the man took it!

"I tell you, sir," said he, "that you neither prove your authority nor your discretion by such insane conduct. You watched your daughter's window with a telescope, you say, to see what might take place in her room. Very well, sir, you have seen nothing. You reproach me with base offenses against her? What are your own? You made your daughter marry a madman; but now she is a widow, and surely her own mistress. You have all your life, sir, been a slave to your pride, to your cupidity. You would sacrifice your innocent daughter to your evil spirit. Were she guilty of all with which you wrongfully reproach her and me, she would still be spotless by your side. You have threatened and tormented her out of her own house. Had I not interrupted her, as she was passing here, in her flight, she would, by this time, have been in some foreign land; she would have taken the first ship that would carry her away. You came near driving a helpless lamb among strangers, perhaps into a herd of wolves. I have received her like an honored sister. At my urgent invitation, three young ladies of good family have joined her here. They are those in this island whom your ill-used daughter loves best, and they have come expressly to spend a few weeks with her at Rose Hill. This is all my crime, sir, and, by heaven! I will persist in it. Mrs. Marriot shall *not* go back to your sole company, to be made the victim of your cruel caprices, while there is one gentleman left alive in Jamaica. I tell you, sir, that we *know you to be a madman*," and, as Mr. St. John said this in a key more loud and stern, the man quaked, " and, if you attempt to molest your daughter again, we will put you in a strait waistcoat, and chain you to the floor."

The stranger seemed actually to be scared, not only into good behavior, but into good sense. He rather argued for his daughter's return than demanded it. He implied pretty plainly, though, that he considered Mr. St. John a dangerous companion.

"You mistake the whole case, sir," was Mr. St. John's reply. " I respect innocence, and I will defend it. You, sir, have probably caused more tears and planted more thorns, than I have ever done, or than I would be willing to take on my conscience. You came here to disturb my house, perhaps to asssail my life. You were liberal in your insults. You publicly defamed your daughter, and violently denounced me. You reproached me before my friends, my guests, my servants. I hope I bore it with sufficient temper. I shall now leave you to your daughter. If you are inclined to repose yourself, she will show you an apartment, and if you have any farther *arguments* to urge, to-morrow morning I shall be at your disposal."

So saying, he rose, and walked out of the room. How Mr. Ghost looked I cannot guess. He never spoke until Mr. St. John had taken his leave, and what he said then, I know not exactly, for I heard Mr. St. John calling for me, and ran to meet him. He was scarcely at all agitated, and I fancied there was even a smile upon his face. He gave me the sword, and a small pistol, and bid me wait within hearing, in case Mrs. Marriot's father should be unreasonable. I was to fire the pistol as a signal— that is, if he should appear disposed to offer violence to his daughter, and to protect her with the sword at all hazards, until farther assistance arrived.

Mr. St. John was scarcely gone before Mr. Buckly returned into the hall, wishing to pass

18

through to his room, which was within the dining-room. He was still stupid, his red eyes staring wide open, his gait very unsteady, and his mind full of horrible fancies. He came toward me moaning.

"Dead," said he, "dying, nearly killed, shot. How my head beats, beats; all for my sins, Mahmadee. I have committed a thousand follies, but all this was predestined. I verily believed that madman a statue on horseback. Had I not been confused with all this music and dancing, and my spirit beside itself with the sight of all these follies, I had not been so mistaken. I would have known him for a horse-grenadier, or some such thing, and shunned him—amen! Now let us go to bed again."

"Master parson," said I, "you called me a brazen idiot for not bringing you more wine."

"Alas! it was in my potations; but thou art a heathen, nevertheless, a follower of that accursed imposter, Mahomet. My soul yearns to save your precious soul from endless perdition,.Mahmadee. I tell you, my dearly beloved brother, that hell yawns for you. Upon my soul it yawns for you." (Here he yawned himself.) "What are you laughing at, you poor blinded heathen? Oh, my head, my poor head! I am undone, sick, very sick!"

He felt his pulse, and began to sing a psalm. I thought I had never seen so complete a fool. He was afraid to pass through the dining-room when I told him that the horse-ghost was there; so I took him round ·by the saloon into the library, and put ·him on a sofa.

When I returned to the hall, I found the girls going into the dining-room with some sheets for Mr. Ghost. He was walking backward and forward, in a little perturbation; but he was civil now, and even condescended to take a draught of sangaree; he was very taciturn, however, and looked very sullen. He would not go to bed when he heard that Mr. Buckly had been sleeping there, but wrapped himself up in his dark blue cloak, and lay on one of the sofas for an hour or two, but he slept very little. I heard him roll and toss about, and breathe very deep, sighing repeatedly.

He arose at the first break of daylight, and decamped. I brought his horse at his request, and saw him off. He took the road down the avenue, where I had first encountered him, and, as before, he hurried along the glade at a good gallop, never once casting a look behind him. There were other eyes that looked on him beside mine, for the whole house having been alarmed, scarce an individual had composed himself thoroughly to rest again. The jalousies were all open, and several heads peeped out at him in the early light. Among others, Victorine looked out from her window, and muttered a parting blessing : " You want to carry off the little lady did you ? You don't wait for the sun, for fear Mr. St. John catch your shadow, and stand you in the garden."

When I turned back to the house, I was surprised to find Mr. St. John and my master up, and only waiting for their horses to go to the beach for an early sea-bath. I was ordered to take my mule and attend them. They were discussing the "mad frolics," as they called them, of the parson and the maniac. They both spoke of Mrs. Marriot with extreme pity and respect, and were in every way severe on her father. They imputed his madness to habitual intemperance.

Among other things, Mr. St. John said : "I love to hear music and see happy faces, but it does not follow that I would destroy them at once and forever. If I have some very beautiful flowers in my garden, I should scarcely pluck them up by the roots to enhance their hue and fragrance."

Something Mr. Holgrave said of me (for I caught my name) amused Mr. St. John prodigiously. He half turned his horse toward me and said, still laughing, " So the servants have made me a present of four wives? Well, I am not of your faith, Mahmadee, and I promise you—that is, Mr. Holgrave and I have agreed—that you may have for a wife any one of them you can win—after their time is out, mind you, though. While they are in service, I cannot have too many fools on hand at once."

I had long before that arrived at the conviction that the black girls were quizzing me, and had flattered myself that the gentlemen would never hear of it. I perceived Victorine's busy tongue in it, and was as much provoked with her as I was ashamed of myself, but I had just then no leisure to think of reprisals, for we were now at the edge of the surf.

The gentlemen bathed just as the sun rose, and I rode outside of them to keep away the sharks, while they swam. I was so sleepy all the time, that I believe I actually did fall asleep, for I tumbled off the mule into the sea, and wetted my clothes, so that I was obliged to take them off, and spread them on the sand to dry. I was quite happy when we got back again to the Great House, for I lay down on my bed and slept undisturbed till two o'clock in the afternoon.

Madam Felix sent for me to her room before dinner, and questioned me very closely about Mr. Martineau instigating Mr. Buckly to go to Spanish Town to get a marriage license. "That is Miss Victorine, again," thought I to myself. For my own part, I professed the purest ignorance of every thing and everybody's business. The slave must make a rule of it, unless he has a taste for being the scapegrace of everybody's sins. I knew she would be sure to apply to Mr. Holgrave at last, and felt that Mr. Martineau was tolerably safe in his friendly hands to win a pardon.

She had already accepted his mediation for the parson, all of whose "little follies" of the night before had been smoothed over, and himself graciously dismissed. He was already gone when I arose from my pallet. Mrs. Marriot had not appeared at breakfast, but the usual circle met at dinner, and the evening passed off in music and conversation, as bright and calm as if nobody in the world ever drank to excess, or was ever so wild as to disturb any one else with their mad frolics.

CHAPTER XXII.

PARLOR DRAMAS.

MR. MARTIN, the father of the Three Graces, was at the time absent on his professional' engagements—having a great lawsuit on hand at Spanish Town—but was to return for his daughters in about two weeks, and our "Johnny Newcomes"—Mr. Haldiman and Mr. Hopeton—were to be of their party home. Mrs. Marriot, on whose account, chiefly, this visit had been made, had decided to leave at the same time for Plessis Fount, her own place in St. Mary's. Her maid Angela described it as a dull, secluded place, with rather limited house accommodations for company, though, not too small for the proper convenience of its mistress and her crazy father. That gentleman, not content with living upon his daughter's means, was so dreadfully ill-tempered and unreasonable, that Mrs. Marriot scarcely dared invite a friend to pass a day with her, so sure was she that her father would manage to insult him out of the house. Mr. Holgrave strongly advised her to take up her residence in Kingston—and I believe that Mr. St. John privately added his influence to the suggestion—but I gathered from her replies, that her fortune would hardly justify such an establishment as her father would force her to maintain; and worse than that, his "eccentricities", would be more painfully conspicuous, if not more violent, in the social stir of the city than in the quiet of a country house. Poor lady! young, beautiful, independent, innocent, and beloved, she was the victim of more anxious and unhappy hours than any slave-girl in the house. Mr. St. John, too, looked somewhat restless and unhappy when I noticed him pacing the oleander-walk, which leads from the piazza back of his own room to the stables. It was planted so as to insure to the master a direct, shaded, and private way to his horses, and all that pertained to them, unseen by the guests and servants. The saddle-room door was the only part of that range of buildings that gave a glimpse into this walk, and if I had not had occasion to be in that room a few minutes, one morning, I should never have dreamed that any thing could so ruffle the placid lord of Rose Hill. But there was no mistaking the downcast eye, the set teeth, and the contracted brow, as he walked up and down that graveled aisle. In the house he was always the same polite, smiling, attentive gentleman, and, as before, never long absent from the side of Mrs. Marriot.

There were four gentlemen to four ladies, and just enough to dance a quadrille to Hyacinth's music, as they occasionally did; for Mr. Holgrave was now able to go through one figure without fatigue. After that we have dances for four or six, with music, singing, and conversation, until our parlor-dramas became the absorbing theme. If the visit of Mrs. Marriot's father—whom the negroes were not far wrong in calling the "Nightmare"—had thrown a secret chill on the pleasures of Rose Hill, there was no outward show of change. Mr. Buckly had made a lodgment with the manager of a neighboring estate—a genial, hospitable Scotchman, who, without being exactly a religious man himself, respected the cloth; and, believing the missionary a safer pastor for the slaves than some others he knew, he made him welcome at his own house and table, and gave his evangelical labors the amplest encouragement.

In that day, the liberal hospitality, which Jamaica still practices, was carried to excess; but a man like

Mr. Buckly would not have been welcome at Mr. St.
John's breakfast-table, under ordinary circumstances.
It was his supposed services in disconcerting the late
negro conspiracies, that gilded over his natural
coarseness so far as to secure his polite toleration at
Rose Hill. He had sense enough not to come too
often, nor stay too long. As the drunken antics of
Mrs. Marriot's half-crazy father were tenderly handled as "eccentricities," so Mr. Buckly's ridiculous
conduct was only spoken of as "the parson's little
slip," and, I think, was never even alluded to in his
presence. This toleration put him at ease, and he
even strove to set up again the airs and pretensions
of a saintly missionary.

The painter and the botanist amused themselves
and the young ladies by drawing him out. The
latter was something of an astronomer, and gave
the young ladies some lectures on the subject.
The painter set them at sketching some of the adjoining scenery. Mr. St. John was clever at all
these things, and for the short time they remained,
Rose Hill was apparently turned, every morning,
into an academy of arts and sciences.

The preacher came about every other morning,
and joined the circle in the library, as if he too was

a learned gentleman and a lady-killer. Indeed, so little notice had been taken of Mr. Buckly's mishap, and he had apparently so little recollection of the absurdities which he had committed, that he ventured again upon the mystical part of his profession, and held forth whenever he could squeeze in a word upon faith, hope, and grace. He talked of the prophecies, and a beast* upon seven hills, and the bottomless pit, and mixed up, very promiscuously, Bonaparte, Armageddon, and the restoration of the Jews. Mr. St. John showed a disposition to smile, and sometimes argued with him a little; but he never thwarted him, nor denied him a free course to run over by himself. Neither Mr. Holgrave nor Mr. St. John ever made a butt of him, as the painter and botanist continually did; but they now and then put him some sly questions about Scripture history and the patriarchal customs that puzzled him badly.

Yet in the midst of all this sanctified talk, Mr. Buckly had his mind still fixed on possessing. Hyacinth. I say, without fear of being contradicted, that he begged and prayed of me, offered me bribes, and promised to take care of my soul, if I would prevail upon that girl to listen to him. He had courted Madam Felix, who was also a really

beautiful creature, more for her money than for her
person; but when he knew she had assigned her
property, he gave her up and became downright
foolishly in love with Hyacinth. His passion was
as absurd as my own worship of Mrs. Marriot. I
know he even offered to marry her, for he was not
rich enough to buy her, nor to make her any pecu-
niary settlement, and that he condescended to en-
treat for her of Mr. St. John, to whom she referred
him. *He* referred him back to the girl.

"She would obey her master," she told him one
morning, when, without regarding my presence, he
offered to marry her if she desired it. She did not
desire it, however. She did not love him, and preferred freedom without him. Mr. St. John had now
but a limited claim on her. Hyacinth, and her sister Zephyr, having served their four years with faithfulness and propriety, would, in the course of a
month or two, be free to hire their own time at the
wages of common servants. As fine seamstresses,
marchands, or ladies' maids, they could earn double
the money, and, after paying the wages to their
master, enough would remain for them to gradually
pay for their freedom. Several of Mr. St. John's
slaves had done, or were doing, this, and it was an

object of ambition with numbers of his best people
to be put in the list.

There was one curious exception to this, which
I will now mention, for that exceptional individual
was afterward somewhat mixed up in my own destiny. It was a shrewd old black fellow, named Andrew, who acted as doctor's man, and was so much
of a practitioner himself among the free blacks
around, that he had acquired over a thousand pounds
of his own; yet he would never use his money to
buy himself. He hired his own time of his master,
Mr. St. John, at twenty pounds a year, and then
hired himself out again for forty, as a sort of deputy-
doctor to the regular physician of Rose Hill and
Laurel Pen, Mr. St. John's two estates. Dr. O'Donnell, the regular physician, was enabled by means of
this assistant to take the medical charge of two additional estates. The negroes had immense respect
for the black doctor's abilities, and he really had remarkable success in curing the numerous cases in-
trusted to him. He was a keen, smooth-tongued
fellow, and Mr. St. John, after giving this sketch of
his character and condition to the ladies, sent for
him to the library, under pretence of inquiring how
his vaccine patients were progressing. The intro-

duction of the saving process of vaccination was not
then so general in Jamaica as might be wished, but
it was carefully attended to on the four estates under the charge of Dr. O'Donnell, and the whole of
that part of his business was now left to Andrew.
When the vaccine questions were asked and answered, Mr. St. John told him that, as he was now
worth upward of one thousand pounds, it was time
to decide upon how much of it he would give for his
freedom.

"I doesn't want my freedom, master. I'm better off as I am, with a good master such as I have
got," the black doctor replied, with an insinuating
bow to Mr. St. John. "What I wants is to settle
myself, if you please to consent to it, sir."

"Settle yourself, beau? In what way?"

"I wants to get married, and have my wife on a
place of our own."

"Want a wife, Andrew?" exclaimed his master.
"Why, Dr. O'Donnell informs me, that you have two
wives now, and, what makes bad worse, that sometimes you beat them. Look out that the *busha*
(overseer) don't have you up and flogged for your
cruelty and immorality."

"Yes, master, it am a fact that I had to c'rect

Lucy for going to dances on the sly and getting drunk; but there's Sally whips me—or, tries to—and all that is a disgrace to the place, master, so I wants to get married in church, and settle down 'spectably," said Andrew, in the coolest and most business-like of tones.

"Have you made choice of a bride yet?" asked Mr. St. John.

"Yes, master, but—but," and, for the first time, Andrew showed some embarrassment.

"Well, who is it? Some one belonging to me?" said his master, who appeared to enjoy his embarrassment. "If it is so, speak out, beau. You know I leave hearts free on my estates."

"If you please, master," and he broke down again; then, rallying as well as he could, he begged to be excused for that day.

He was excused, and so he left without informing the company of the sable beauty who was to supersede both the reigning wives.

While the party in the library were amusing themselves with the black doctor, who was so partial to bondage that he wanted to add the fetters of matrimony to the yoke of slavery, Mr. Buckly was in the parlor urging Hyacinth to join him in soliciting her master's consent to their marriage, and with it some arrangement for her immediate freedom; but the quadroon had other views. She wished to get to Kingston, and, by teaching music, and singing for pay at parties in private houses, she hoped to earn money for her freedom and enjoy life in her own way at the same time. Zephyr could assist her, and take in fine embroidery, at which she was an adept, and not even the rare and envied distinction of having a white preacher in lawful wedlock, tempted her to resign her plan. She was, however, a coquette to the heart's core, and contrived to encourage the infatuated man to persevere in his addresses, and to write to her any number of silly love-letters. She could read and write, but, under pretence of being unable to decipher them, she brought them to me "to make out what the missionary meant to say," as she would demurely remark. Those letters had considerable private circulation. But these interesting proceedings between the preacher and quadroon extended beyond the limits of Mrs. Marriot's stay at Rose Hill, and I return to that.

I have spoken of our parlor-drama of Othello, which, from a single declamation by me at Savannah-la-Mar and Orange Grove, had been gradually modified into a play of three acts, in which, besides the Othello, Desdemona, Emilia, Cassio, and Iago, in common use, there was an additional character introduced. This was done partly to find place for Aimée, Madam Felix's little ward, and also to give more variety and effect to the closing tableau, and partly to help the change which ends the play in a reconciliation, instead of the murder of Desdemona.

The story of Othello haunted me. I could never forget that a black man had been recognized as a brave and honored soldier, and that he had won by his gallant deeds the love of the fair and gentle Desdemona. What dangers would I not have braved, what sufferings endured, to be praised by the living Desdemona whom I served every day at table, were it but in the same calm and sweet measure in which she so often praised white men of note! It was a blind and frantic worship. I knew it then nearly as well as I know it now, but it was a pure, ennobling blaze, that lifted me upward, far, far upward in my soul, and in all my views. It burnt out of me many debasing tendencies, which, but for her high influence, might have kept me in low and miry paths forever. I was eager to repeat our version of Othello in her presence, and, when it was in preparation, I was

on the alert to stimulate Hyacinth and Zephyr, the
Desdemona and Emilia of the play, into a warm appreciation of their parts.

I had written out the whole drama as it had been
modified and arranged by Mr. Martineau, with dupli-
cate parts for the others to study. At Miraflor the
governess had condescended to take Desdemona, for
there was but little to be said by the other actors,
and Victorine did the little that was required of
Iago; but here we had a force sufficient to bring it
out to the full extent of Mr. Martineau's arrangement. Victorine kept her own part, and Laura, the
tallest of the quadroons, accepted and learned the
part of Cassio, while to Hyacinth was assigned that
of Desdemona. Madam Felix went over to Miraflor
and brought back Aimée to take her part, and Saturday evening was appointed for the performance. Mr.
Martineau was expected by then, and Dr. O'Donnell
and his wife, with three or four other gentlemen and
ladies from the neighboring estates, were invited to
be present at the play and the supper which was to
follow it.

Leaving Othello at this point, I go back to I
know not exactly what date, but certainly as far
back as the first recitation at Miraflor. In making

the suppressions and adaptations necessary to reduce
Othello to the limited capabilities of our performers,
I had more than once ventured to suggest short and
simple phrases in substitution of those long and
eloquent sentences, which *our* performers would find
it difficult to master, and Mr. Martineau generally accepted them. From that I had gone a step farther,
and prepared a kind of ballet, borrowed from Robin
Hood. A number of short and easy songs, and little
bits of dialogue, were strung into a kind of festive
plot, which I called "The Maroon's Bride," and
which I and the brown girls at Miraflor had sang
and danced through for the entertainment of Mr.
Holgrave and some gentlemen visitors.

In getting up the burlesque of the "Four My
Lords," I had assisted in pruning it down somewhat,
and I was now called upon to operate on Othello,
because, as Mr. Holgrave and Madam Felix asserted,
I had such a decided turn for dramatic arrangements.
I produced the prepared manuscript of Othello, and
even Mr. St. John complimented me strongly on my
clear and handsome writing. Mrs. Marriot took it
in her hand, and read several pages without speaking. My heart swelled to painfulness, as I watched
her earnest, attentive look, and saw her white

hand turn over leaf after leaf, without raising her eyes.

"Gentlemen," said she, handing back the manuscript to my master, and addressing him and Mr. St. John together, "gentlemen, the young man of seventeen who can write like that, ought not to remain a slave. Let us see if we cannot find something better for him to do than groom our horses and wait behind our chairs." I could have died in grateful joy at her feet.

"Your wishes shall be our law," said Mr. St. John, with a bow, offering his arm to lead her to dinner, and Mr. Holgrave said something to the same effect.

From that hour I never was a slave. The mind cast off its shackled habits, and, though many days of servitude were still before me, all my thoughts, desires, and resolutions, were fixed, not merely upon ceasing to be a slave, but on rising morally and mentally to the rank of a freeman.

Mrs. Marriot and the young ladies now resolved to have the "Maroon's Bride" acted immediately, and assigned the part of bride to Zephyr, and of the bride's mistress to Hyacinth. The plot is simply this. The Maroon-chief loves a slave-girl, and finally wins her for his bride, in recompense for the daring services he has rendered to the betrothed of the lady, her mistress. This is recited partly in song, partly in dialogue. The dancing and the choruses are the celebration of the bride's emancipation. The best songs were by Mr. Martineau; the others, and all the dialogue, were mine. They would never have been produced at Rose Hill if Mrs. Marriot had not recalled what Madam Felix had said about the "Maroon's Bride," and asked to see it. The painter, Mr. Haldiman, called on me to read it aloud, and when it was done, asked if that was all I had ever written. It was a searching question; for from the night—the night of the first day I ever saw her—on which I had recited Othello, I had been writing out on paper snatches of the extravagant dream-drama which was seething in my heart and brain. I hesitated at the question. It was pressed home, and I finally confessed that I had attempted something like a little drama for the Miraflor company, but it was scarcely finished. Mr. Haldiman desired me to bring it over to his room, and I did so immediately. No one, not even Mr. Holgrave, had an idea of its existence, although it was written in his own dressing-room, and often in his own presence. If he saw me writing, he supposed I was busy with my journal.

This wild production of an excited spirit was called " The Black Prince." The admiral of a Spanish war-galley intercepts a pilgrim ship, on the coast of Morocco, and presents to the lady of his love a young prince—whom she causes to be educated as a Christian. Her favorite attendant falls in love with him (I dared not, even in a play, imitate the soaring ambition of Othello)—but his heart is fixed on a fellow-captive, the fair daughter of a Moor of rank, who is held a strict prisoner by King Ferdinand. The Black Prince vows to effect the release of her father, in recompense for the gentle Zulema's preference for himself. He communicates with the prisoner by a song, chanted in their own Arabic, under his prison walls, and again with Zulema, whose jealous mistress has imprisoned her, under an unfounded suspicion that her lord, the admiral, has cast an eye of favor upon her. The captive Moor effects his escape through the exertions of the Black Prince, and sends to ransom both his daughter and her deliverer, and unites them in marriage.

Mr. Haldiman pruned and corrected my little drama, but he also praised it, and particularly that part of it in which I poured out the fiercest impatience of bondage. He praised also the fervid pictures of love, and the sorrowful sympathy for the captive Zulema, expressed in the simple chants of the Black Prince. It was agreed that it should be represented as directly after we had gone through with Othello as the parts could be learned, and that, until after the verdict of Mr. St. John and his other guests had been obtained on it, the extent of my share in its production should not be dwelt upon in public.

The "Maroon's Bride" was the first of the series, and no one beyond the usual circle was present, except the estate overseer and doctor. The little negro dancers made up much of the show, but what Hyacinth and Zephyr had to do was done with grace and spirit. Hyacinth electrified them with her power of acting. We were all elated with our success. Dr. O'Donnell said "The Maroon's Bride" would be a standing resource whenever a large company happened to assemble at either of the neighboring estates, and Mr. St. John assured him, that so far as he was himself concerned, he would like to see a collection of similar ballets arranged for the improvement and amusement of all his slaves.

I had so much to do in getting up these things that I was excused from all other duties, except the one labor of love—attending to Mr. Holgrave; but even that had become a mere trifle, for never since I had known him had his health been so steadily on the gain.

"The Maroon's Bride" was given on Thursday, and the next day but one—Saturday—we had Othello, and it too was a success. Othello, after winning his bride, was treated to a dance of negro children, a feature which the ordinary editions of Shakspeare do not contain—more's the pity—any more than they do the niece of Othello. I can only say, those lamentable deficiencies do not exist in the Rose Hill copy.

The supper followed so closely upon the play that I had no time to change, and took my place at the sideboard in the costume of the jealous Moor. Desdemona had barely time to subside from the high estate of a patrician's daughter into the white and blue of Mr. St. John's table-waiters, where she was required to hand plates and serve cake and coffee; but no one regarded these slight changes of character.

Mr. Martineau had been specially invited, but

he did not come, and Mr. Buckly, who was not invited, did come, and was, if possible, more in love than ever on seeing Hyacinth in Desdemona. He wrote her a letter about the sinfulness of such performances, and his desire to save her from evil, as he would a lamb from slaughter. But the beautiful quadroon was too deeply enlisted in this pleasant sinfulness to turn from it at the warning of such a shepherd.

On the succeeding Thursday we had "The Black Prince" before nearly the same audience that heard Othello. I had almost nothing to do, compared to the Othello; but the love-scenes, and the singing, and the wailing chant of the captive, were freely applauded. Zephyr, when she avows her love with tears of regret that the fate which had brought their hearts together had, at the same time, bound them in an iron slavery—fettered apart—her voice faltered and real tears rose to her eyes. She was applauded, and so was Hyacinth, but not so much; for though the latter was the best actress, her sister had by far the most effective part.

At the close, Mr. Haldiman informed the party that the Black Prince was himself the author of the little drama just performed. Some very kind and

19

encouraging remarks were made by the gentleman; but the one sweet and touching compliment of Mrs. Marriot was worth them all. That made me rich indeed.

"You have surpassed our best expectations, Mahmadee," she paused to say, as Mr. St. John was conducting her to the supper-room. "You will do credit to your friends and freedom."

Yes, lovely and honored lady, I will strive, while life lasts, to justify your generous prediction.

Mr. Martin arrived the day previous to the performance of "The Black Prince," and he was so much pleased with it that he seriously advised Mr. St. John to let the whole party go down to Kingston and give it and our Rose Hill edition of Othello alternately, for fifteen or twenty nights. Hyacinth and Zephyr would have been delighted with the arrangement, but Mr. St. John would not hear of it. Madam Felix had been over to Miraflor and back several times, while we were occupied with our parlor-dramas; and now that the last was said and done, she began to be pressing for Mr. Holgrave to name a time on which he would meet Mr. Martineau at her own house, for she wished to have both these together.

Mr. St. John hated to part with Mr. Holgrave, and made them agree to bring Mr. Martineau to Rose Hill for a week, and then promised to escort both the gentlemen safely to Miraflor and pass a day or two there himself.

The dreaded morning arrived in which Mrs. Marriot and the Three Graces took their departure. I did not know until the evening before that I was to attend the sweet lady to her home at Plessis Fount. She had left her own place with a desperate resolution to fly the country, in order to escape the persecutions of her half-mad father, and only had with her, besides Angela, a stupid old Congo, in charge of the sumpter mule. She had stopped for an hour's rest for herself and animals at Dr. O'Donnell's, and he had managed, with the aid of Madam Felix, to persuade her to accept the safe refuge of Rose Hill for a few days.

The gallant master of Rose Hill had promptly sent messengers to Spanish Town, and in reply to his appeal, Mr. Martin had brought his daughters to bear her company until some measures could be taken to protect her from her father's violence.

No earthly measures were necessary for her further protection, for when we reached Plessis

Fount the old man was dying. We met the messenger, who had been dispatched to inform his daughter, scarce two miles from the house. It was a painful, trying time, but the gentle lady bore it like an angel. I remained, at her orders, until it was over, and then hastened back to Rose Hill with the startling intelligence that Mrs. Marriot was indeed alone in the world.

The first person I saw belonging to the estate was the black doctor, Andrew. He was on a visit to a patient at the farther side of the estate, and it was but a chance; but Dr. Andrew considered it a special providence. The wife he wanted was no other than Mrs. Marriot's ward, Angela, to whom he had promised her liberty and a wedding-ring for accepting him. He wanted me to obtain Mr. Holgrave's mediation, and offered me five pounds toward my own freedom if it could be brought about.

CHAPTER XXIII.

GREAT CHANGES.

As I rode up to the side-gate, on my return to Rose Hill, a very well-dressed black man opened it to me, with a salutation in Arabic.

"Welcome, son of my king," he said, with a low inclination. "In the name of the prophet, a hundred times welcome to my eyes."

"There is but one God, and Mahomet is his prophet," I replied, in surprise, throwing myself from my horse and returning his salute, after the fashion of my faith and country.

"Go to your master now," said the stranger, "and when your work is over for the evening we can meet there," pointing to the kiosk or summerhouse, at the end of the pomegranate walk.

I hastily promised, and turned to the Great House to find, and report to, Mr. Holgrave. He went with my tidings to Mr. St. John, and they remained together in the library till a late hour.

I was told to get my supper and come to Mr. Holgrave in the morning. The evening was left'at my disposal, and it may be believed that I devoted it to the stranger who had met me at the gate.

On leaving Mr. Holgrave I was met by Stella and Hyacinth, who, besides doing me the grace of inviting me to take supper with them, gave me, in exchange for my news from Plessis Fount, a world of grateful intelligence. Mr. Martineau had bought for Mr. St. John six of the slaves lately sold at Orange Grove, and his man Hercules was hourly expected with them at Rose Hill. This was known through Victorine, who had heard her mistress read a letter to Mr. Holgrave, stating that the cooper, Dickie Smith, and his wife Kitty—my dear, kind Tatee—and the stableman, Bradwell, with his wife, a Houssa girl, had, with two other prime hands, been bought in one lot, at an excellent bargain. The girls said that it was the first time since their recollection their master had bought more servants, and that in only one instance had they ever known him to sell a slave, and that was in a case of gross misconduct.

"And who is this stranger I saw at the gate? It is the first time I have ever been addressed in

Arabic since I landed on the island, but I had no time to speak with him then."

"Oh, he is a Mahometan, like yourself, Mahmadee, and a famous scholar, too. It is a wonder you never heard of him, for he keeps his master's books and buys and sells mahogany and other fine woods."

"Then he, too, is a slave?"

"Yes, indeed, but he is not to be a slave always, any more than yourself. He is from your own country, he says, and was taken away from Kashna the night your father, King Abdallah, was killed."

"Then he may know my dear Hadji Ali!" I exclaimed, starting up from the table.

"To be sure he did. His own father was a priest in the same mosque in Kashna."

I waited for no more, but flew to the kiosk to meet and embrace my almost brother. There a singular scene awaited me. It was just sunset, and a faint glow fell on the white dress and earnest face of Aimée, as she bent over a book from which she was reading. The book lay on the little table of the kiosk, and the child stood by it reading in rather low, but clear and serious tones an account of the conversion of St. Paul. She did not stop on my approach, nor did the strange negro, who sat on the

ground behind her, raise his head till she had fiu-
ished the chapter.   Then she closed the book and
warmly welcomed me back, for she had ever been
sweet and kindly to me.

"Did Mr. Holgrave tell you, Dr. Mahmadee, that
you were to be my tutor, when we go back to dear
old Miraflor?" she asked, with a pleasant smile.

"Your tutor, Miss Aimée?" I said, in surprise.
"It is not possible that Madam Felix could select
me for such an honor.   What would Mr. Holgrave
say?"

"I selected you myself, and Mr. Holgrave says I
am quite right," said the charming girl, with all her
natural vivacity.   "My lady governess went off
without an hour's warning.   She found out that it
was a dreadful disgrace for a white lady to teach a
colored girl, and at the same time she found another
white lady, who desired her services.   So she went,
and my poor godmother said she did not know what
to do for a teacher for wild little me, and I promised
to be a pattern girl, and learn my lessons better than
ever, if you would assist me.   That's all about it."

"And Madam Felix?"   I asked, in breathless
anxiety, for it seemed to open to my vision an enchanted kingdom of delights.

"Oh," she said, "it might answer for the time, if Mr. Holgrave approved, and Mr. Holgrave did approve. So, if you please, Doctor Mahmadee is now my tutor." And leaving me to recover from my happy astonishment, she tripped off to the house.

"It is a wonderful little lady. A chosen one of the Prophet," said the stranger, looking after her admiringly.

This recalled me to him and his history. The occasion of his visit to Rose Hill just then was the purchase of some fine timber of Mr. St. John, and then, for the first time, he had learned of my existence. The other servants had told him of me, of my faith, of my country, and even of the report that some day I was to have my freedom. The same hope had been held out to Ali by his master, and on that he had built a steadfast plan of returning to his own country, a missionary of civilization. It was a singular meeting. We were, perhaps, the only two educated Mahometan slaves in the island, who had retained the faith and the sacred language of the Koran, and who had also won the good-will, and—to a certain degree—the learning of their masters. Ali entreated me by the *Caaba* of Mecca never

19*

to depart from the precepts of the Prophet, and promised, when he returned to Kashna, to bear witness to my faithfulness among our countrymen.

"Let us go back together, Sidi Mahmadee," he urged, in his enthusiasm. "Let us go back together to Kashna, and fill the places of our fathers."

A new thought, a new ambition flashed into my soul. It sent a hot thrill of faith and hope to the inmost depths of my being. We, who had scarcely two hours before met for the first time, clasped hands on the pledge that we would mutually hold fast to our religion and to this aim of returning to our land. Slaves both of us, and with the certainty of years of servitude before us! Ali had the promise of freedom in nine years, and perhaps earlier, if his master prospered in certain undertakings. And here I may state that he did prosper splendidly, and very much through Ali's untiring zeal and capacity in selecting fine woods and bringing them to market; but it did not gain the faithful slave his liberty much the sooner. For my own part, I avowed my determination never to leave Mr. Holgrave while he lived, for his frail health needed such care as only a constant and devoted attendant could supply. Yet we neither of us had the slightest misgivings as to our final return to Kashna. So sanguine is youth and inexperience!

It was late when we separated for the night, but to my alarm—for it boded no good to his health—I found Mr. Holgrave had not yet retired, and was more disposed to talk than to sleep. He asked me various questions about Ali, with whom he had already had some conversation, and drew from me much of our mutual, though far-off plan for returning to our own country, as teachers of civilization.

"What do you propose to do in Kashna—in case you succeed in getting back there?" asked Mr. Holgrave, turning on the sofa so as to look me in the eye. "Do you accept Aimée's missionary plan?"

"Miss Aimée can hardly expect to make a good missionary out of a Mahometan," I replied, somewhat in the dark as to Mr. Holgrave's own views for me.

"Aimée is, on the contrary, perfectly convinced that you and Ali are wonderfully adapted to the vocation—predestined to it, in fact. She has rather mixed ideas on religious subjects, it is true, but she is deeply in earnest for a child of her age and her gay, impulsive temperament."

"I have thought of studying medicine, sir," I

ventured to say, in the hope it might bring out a word of approval, which, with Mr. Holgrave, would certainly lead to aid and direction.

"I have thought of that, too, and so has Mr. Martineau. He writes me that Dr. Marsh will send you some books and anatomical drawings that will aid you greatly."

"God bless Mr. Martineau!" burst involuntarily from my lips.

"Aimée has taken Ali in hand quite seriously," said Mr. Holgrave, a few minutes afterward, as he was preparing for bed. "She repeats to him the Arabic verses she has learned of you, and in return makes him recite the creed and Lord's prayer in English, just as she did by you a year ago. She begged me to select a chapter of the Testament to read to him this evening."

I could only observe, that "I' had understood from Mr. Buckly, that Catholics, like Madam Felix and Miss Aimée, did not read the Testament in that way."

"Neither do they, as a rule, learn verses from the Koran, and recite the Mahometan confession of faith; but, as I said before, Aimée's religious ideas are of a rather mixed order. But she sincerely desires to do right." He paused and added, "You will find her a bright and docile pupil, Mahmadee."

So it was really and truly settled that I was to become the teacher of this interesting child, who, on her part, had resolved to have me a missionary. I was kept awake half the night planning what Ali and I would do when we should return to Kashna; he to preside in the mosque, and I to shine as a great physician.

The next night—and the next after that—Ali and I had long consultations in the kiosk on our future plans, and on both nights did Aimée come attended by Victorine, to read to us a chapter or two from the Scriptures, and make us repeat a prayer and the Apostles' creed. Madam Felix did not oppose her since Mr. Holgrave seemed to approve of the child's self-imposed task.

What seems more singular to me in looking over the record of those days, is the sincere and unconscious faith we both bestowed on every word of those Christian teachings. The Mahometans acknowledge Jesus, the son of Mary, as a divinely-inspired prophet, but we leaned less on that dim, undefined point of faith than on the pure and simple sincerity of the innocent young creature, who, to our half-developed minds, seemed inspired to lead us aright. It was to that we yielded such implicit confidence. Years after, when. we had in very fact touched the soil of Africa, with hearts and faces turned to Kashna, Ali—still believing himself a strict Mahometan—constantly taught to others the texts of Scripture he had learned of Aimée.

The third day after my return from Plessis Fount, Ali shared with me the pleasure of seeing the arrival of my old Houssa friends, Tatee and Brad, among the slaves bought from the Orange Grove sale. They were much later from their country than Ali, and we spent nearly the whole night talking of our native land. Many, many happy Sundays did I spend with my recovered friends in the two years I passed in the still dearly-remembered hills of St. Ann. There Dickie Smith and his wife, and honest Brad and his wife lived on, under the mild sway of Mr. St. John, until the general act of emancipation made them and theirs freemen and landholders.

A day or two after my Houssa friends were settled at Rose Hill, I attended Madam Felix to Miraflor, and began a regular course of studies with Aimée, under the general direction of Mr. Holgrave. Mr. Martineau had preceded us by two days, and

Mr. St. John came in company with Mr. Holgrave, and spent a week at Miraflor.

During the whole winter the gentlemen exchanged many visits, and were much together, but Madam Felix, Aimée, and I scarcely left Miraflor for two years. It was a time of serene happiness —those last studious, contented years in Jamaica. The first incident that broke the even current of our lives was the return of Mrs. Marriot—now Mrs. St. John—as a bride to Rose Hill.

A year after this event came the rather sudden determination of Mr. Holgrave to pass a year or two in the south of France and Italy. The death of a maiden aunt had added something handsome to his income, and he was taken with a desire to revisit the scenes of his youthful travels. Mr. Martineau resolved to accompany him, and a general breaking up followed. Madam Felix had long entertained the idea of settling for life in some part of Europe, where her almost imperceptible taint of African blood would not form the iron wall of social exclusion which she was made to feel so severely in Jamaica. Yet all this had been settled upon so quietly that Aimée fairly took me by surprise when she danced one morning into the piazza, where I was serving Mr. Holgrave with his early cup of chocolate, exclaiming, in great glee, "We are all to sail for England in June, Dr. Mahmadee!" She had been pleased to give me the title of Doctor, and make all the blacks about us address me in that way, until the whole family had fallen into the use of the word also.

"Now you will be made a real learned *Médécin*, and can go to Kashna and convert all your people, and stop slave-stealing." I looked at Mr. Holgrave for a glance of confirmation.

"Yes, Doctor, I have decided to visit Europe again, and while there you shall have an opportunity to pursue your medical studies," said Mr. Holgrave, kindly.

I was dizzy with conflicting emotions. My fondest dreams seemed on the point of realization—and yet would they all be worth weighing against the loss of my kind friends—the separation from my bright and amiable pupil, Aimée? There was a black drop of dread and discontent in the heart of my budding ambition.

It was like walking in a dream, when I went to make a farewell visit to Brad, and Kitty Smith, and the rest of my old friends at Rose Hill I dared not trust my voice when the lovely lady of Rose Hill gave me, with many kind wishes, a neat gold cravat-pin as a parting present. I still retain this precious memorial of the fair and noble lady, whose generous words of encouragement had lifted the spirit of the poor black slave so many degrees above its old level.

Mr. St. John made many judicious, as well as liberal additions to my wardrobe, and almost every servant about the place had for me some kind token of good-will. How poor and unable I felt to manifest the grateful love that overflowed my heart. I had my own freedom and future so well assured, that I gave all the "white music" which I had hoarded in my Medinet purse to Tatee—to help out a plan—cherished by her husband, Dickie Smith, even more than herself—of buying the freedom of my namesake, Sid.

At last we were all gathered on board the brig Caroline, and under weigh for England. I walked the deck a free man, and ranking not as the servant, but the secretary of Mr. Holgrave. How changed my lot, since seven years before I had been brought a kidnapped boy into that harbor, in a crowded slave-ship!

"Do you not thank God for all these mercies, Dr. Mahmadee," said Aimée, in a softened tone, and as if in answer to my thronging recollections, when she came to my side and looked with me at the receding houses of Kingston. Most devoutly did I thank Him.

Hercules had been promised his liberty, but, at the last moment, he begged to be taken along. He had made a match with Victorine, and as she went with her mistress, Hercules, like a dutiful servant and husband, wished to go too.

We had a pleasant passage to England, and, after a brief stay, to enable Mr. Holgrave to make a short visit to Mr. Davis and the family, the whole party proceeded to Paris for the winter. I was immediately entered for a course of medical lectures; but my mornings and evenings were devoted, as usual, to my labors of love about Mr. Holgrave.

Miss Aimée was placed in a convent for two years, to finish her education, but not before she and I had witnessed the private marriage of Mr. Martineau. Madam Felix was never known for a day, in France, as other than the wife of Mr. Martineau, and she entered at once into a social sphere equal in wealth, refinement, and distinction, to the best of those aristocratic families of Jamaica, within whose charmed ring nothing tinged with African blood could penetrate. At Paris—as afterwards at Marseilles—no one asked, or cared for the lineage of Madam Martineau, who was always callèd "the charming American," and whose agreeable reception-evenings were constantly adorned by the presence of the learned and titled lions of French society.

Mr. Holgrave had apartments in the same hotel at first, but soon after Christmas he began to complain of the climate, and made arrangements with Dr. Dumont, of Marseilles, with whom he became acquainted at Paris, to return with him and have lodgings at his house. Dr. Dumont was a *savan* and a bachelor, like Mr. Holgrave, and, besides accommodating us with rooms in his house, he accepted me as a pupil. He was a round, florid, smiling little man; a bit of a gourmand, and slightly self-indulgent, but genial and tolerant to all the world. He had been a great traveler, had been on a mission to the Emperor of Morocco, and had a pet theory about the distinct origin of the black, red, and white races of men, which he proved—to his own intense satisfaction—from the Bible. He was also a warm Freemason, as well as Mr. Holgrave and Mr. Mar-

tineau; and these high members of that ancient
order caused me to be accepted and initiated in
their own lodge, at Marseilles, directly after I had
finished my first medical course.

Four leagues from Marseilles there was for sale
a fine old estate, with a commodious chateau, which
had belonged to Madam's grandfather, and Dr. Dumont's brother had charge of the affair. I think it
was in the course of the purchase of this property
by Mr. Martineau that we all came to know and
esteem Dr. Dumont so well; but, be that as it may,
the whole party were assembled at the chateau for a
month of domestic recreation, early in the summer.
Martineau Hall had been taken, just as it stood, for
a term of years, by my old friend Dr. Marsh, and all
the rest of their property—except Miraflor, on which
Mr. Holgrave had a lien—was sold by the Martineau's, and invested in this French estate.

The chateau was to be their permanent home,
but the next winter they thought to pass in Italy
with Mr. Holgrave, leaving me behind to pursue my
studies in France. When winter came, however,
Mr. Holgrave was disinclined to travel, and so he
passed his second year in Europe between his comfortable apartments in Dr. Dumont's spacious house

in Marseilles, and the chateau. He became more and more interested in me as I advanced in my studies, and the good Dr. Dumont was loud in his commendations of my steady assiduity. He had entered with enthusiasm into my project of returning to Africa, and even wrote to the master of my friend Ali, offering to take charge of the outfit and education of the poor slave, if his freedom could be granted within a certain time. For two years these letters remained unanswered, and, just as we had given up all hopes of a favorable response, there came, in reply to a still later one from Mr. Holgrave, a brief note, to the effect that Ali was worth three ordinary slaves, but that in four years from that date he should have his liberty, or before that, on the payment of a moderate sum.

Our second summer at Marseilles was drawing to a close when Dr. Dumont announced to us the birth of a fine boy at the chateau, who was already named Philip Holgrave. Aimée, whose school-term was nearly over, wrote for permission to come home to the christening, and it was granted.

I entered the saloon of the chateau the first time Madam Martineau descended to it to receive company, after her recovery, with some trepidation.

She was attended by a tall, elegant girl, whom my beating heart at once recognized as the gentle and beloved Aimée, whom I had not seen for more than two years. She looked dark—very dark—amid that long array of white ladies, and I saw Mr. Holgrave's eyes follow her with a sort of mournful compassion, as she mingled with them in the dance. I too felt for myself a profound and painful sense of the distinctions of race, which, even in the stolid abasement of slavery, had never pierced me so keenly before.

Yet, neither then, nor for weeks and months afterward, when my heart was devoured by sentiments I could not banish and dared not express, did I even allude to the subject. A terrible crisis brought forth the words of fate.

I had taken the prize of the year, and was exulting over the approaching close of my final studies, when I was hastily summoned to the chateau. Mr. Holgrave lay on his couch, his lips wearing a smile of heavenly repose, but his eyes were closed forever on this world of sin and suffering. He had left one half of his property in England to me, the other half to Mr. Martineau, in trust for Aimée. Once only in his life, and that in the last hour, had he used to this child the sacred, the explaining word, *daughter.*

The last rites had been paid, and all my measures taken for my final return to Africa, and still I presumed not to speak the thoughts that were burning in my heart, when, one happy morning, Aimée said to me : "I think it was a sacred inspiration that urged me to insist so constantly on your missionary vocation. God's seal has stamped you African, that you may serve Africa."

"And I am too conscious, dear Aimée, of the iron distinctions of race. It is a weakness, but I wish to escape from them into a working realm of utility."

"Yes," she replied, with a half-sigh, "we have here in France a generous, social tolerance ; but even here it is not social equality."

"That does not apply to you, Aimée. You, the petted ornament of this charming social circle, could find nowhere else so many sources of happiness." .

"I would be more happy if I lived in a sphere of useful effort. I envy even your privations, Mahmadee, for they carry with them a sense of security that you are living where no one can despise you for your color, and that you live to some purpose."

Something in the sweet, tremulous tones darted a sudden life to my heart. I eagerly searched her eye; it fell before my ardent gaze. I presumed to raise her hand to my lips; it trembled in my agitated grasp, but it was not withdrawn. I led her to Madam Martineau, and, kneeling at the feet of my early and ever-indulgent protectress, I begged her to pardon the presumption of my suit, and favor me with her precious approval.

THE END.